The bellhop escorted Tullio and Magdalena to their room. Champagne waited in a silver bucket of ice, and everywhere they looked there were roses. Magdalena walked to the window as Tullio filled two glasses.

"Come see, Tullio," she said. "It's beautiful."

Together, they gazed down at Central Park. It was covered with snow, and the frozen lake was filled with ice skaters. As Tullio's eyes strayed from the view, Magdalena detected that he missed Italy.

"Tullio," she murmured, "we don't have to stay in America. I'll go anywhere you want to."

They were getting into a dangerous area. He was not going to discuss his reasons for sending her away, for keeping her in seclusion on Long Island. Instead he put his fingers gently to her lips.

"Enough talk, Magdalena," he whispered and he kissed her hungrily on the lips. In his fantasies during their two years of separation he had dreamed of taking her gently, tenderly, but now he surprised himself with his own eagerness. She responded in kind, and they were both undressed and on the bed in seconds. He seemed to want every inch of her at once as his hands and tongue explored her body. She matched him caress for caress, stroke for stroke, kiss for kiss. She was a new Magdalena, a hungry, almost insatiable woman—utterly abandoned to the act of love.

BY AGATHA DELLA ANASTASI

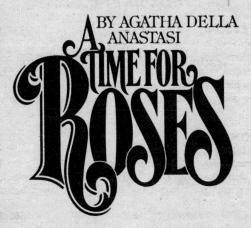

A TIME FOR ROSES

ZEBRA BOOKS
KENSINGTON PUBLISHING CORP.

ZEBRA BOOKS

are published by

KENSINGTON PUBLISHING CORP.
475 Park Avenue South
New York, N.Y. 10016

Printed in the United States of America

'Tis all a Chequer-board of Nights and Days
Where Destiny with Men for Pieces plays:
Hither and thither moves, and mates, and slays.
And one by one back in the Closet lays.

—Omar Khayyam

Magdalena Barragatto stood alone on the first class deck of the *Asheley Queen* and stared down at the dark swirling sea. They had sailed from Genoa at dawn and it was now almost midnight. The blue-black ocean below her was as dark as the starless sky above. Sometimes sounds of laughter or the music of the ship's orchestra drifted out from the ballroom where other passengers were dancing. She did not feel like dancing. She was a married woman, after all, and she was travelling to a strange land without her husband.

Tullio, Tullio, she thought, I've tried to be a good wife. In my fine clothes and my fine manners, who would know I was a gypsy girl? You would be proud of me Tullio.

But Tullio, her husband, was not there, and for all she knew, by the time she docked in New York she might be a widow.

She stared down at the dark swirling waters and it seemed as if every face from her past stared back. Her first husband, handsome blond Tomaso Disanti. Poor boy! They hardly knew each other before he was carried off to the Great War. And Mikel, her gypsy father, leader of the Mostra clan. But all the Mostras were dead now. And there was her dark and handsome Tullio, and her baby, Stefano.

7

Don't cry, little Stefano. They told me you were dead, but I don't believe it. No, the gypsy promised, we will be reunited.

She shivered for a moment and silently cursed the face of Tea, the half-Moor gypsy woman who'd seduced her beloved Tullio while his first loyalty was still to the Church. But she could forgive Tea even that, because it had brought Tullio to her own arms. It also brought his dark-skinned daughter, who slept even now in Magdalena's cabin.

Suddenly her reverie was broken as she felt a light touch on her arm. She turned around and faced one of the ship's younger officers. Since leaving Genoa she had visited the radio room many times, always asking about a telegram, so that they were all familiar with the signora.

"Buona sera, signora," the young officer said as he handed her a small blue envelope. "I would have waited until morning, but you seemed so anxious. Someone was lost?"

She tore open the envelope and her eyes quickly scanned the message:

TULLIO SAFE IN GUIDONIA. ALL IS WELL. ALEKSEY KOSTE-
NOV WILL MEET YOU IN NEW YORK.
                    CIAO, ERNESTO CRISPINO

She looked up at the young man and smiled for the first time since boarding the ship.

"Yes," she answered. "Someone was lost. But now he's found."

The Old Country

Chapter One

"I saw you standing outside these barracks all day long," the guard told him. "Why'd you wait so long to come in? I can't let you see the major now. Come back tomorrow."

Ernesto Crispino gave the soldier a large ruby. "No. I have to speak to him tonight."

"Why?"

"It's none of your business," he replied; and, after parting with a second ruby, was told to wait in the major's office. After an hour the major himself appeared: a thin, nervous man in a uniform too large for him.

"My name is Ernesto Crispino."

"This is a ridiculous hour," the major snapped. "Your business had better be urgent."

"It is, major. It concerns the life of my cousin. He's being held at Voltri. He'll face a firing squad in two days, and you can prevent it."

"Why should I? What's your cousin's name? Why is he being executed?"

"His name is Tullio Barragatto."

"I don't know him."

"Yes, I know."

11

"Why should I help somebody I don't even know? Also, you haven't answered my other question. Why is he being executed?"

"Because he's a deserter." He took a pouch from his pocket.

The officer scowled and slapped his hand down hard on the desk. "You have the nerve to walk into this office and ask *me* to help a deserter? To whom do you think you're talking? Who do you think you are?"

Ernesto emptied his pouch on the major's desk. Twelve large white diamonds spilled out. "I know who I'm talking to, and I've already told you who I am."

The officer stared at the gems and then at Ernesto.

"All you have to do is hear what I have to say, major."

"Get out, or I'll have you thrown out!"

"These stones are flawless. All you have to do is listen to me, and six of them are yours to keep . . . or to give to your beautiful wife in Rome. I'm sure she would love them." He paused, then continued: "You don't have to do a thing but listen. There isn't anything illegal in listening, is there?"

The man watched Ernesto return the six largest gems to the pouch, pull its drawstring tightly and lay it on the desk. After a moment's silence, he placed the six remaining diamonds in his own pocket and said, "All right, I'm listening."

"My cousin was here over a year ago. He'd been arrested on some stupid charge of insubordination. He spoke back to a general . . . or, something like that. Later, the charge became arson. To escape the arson sentence, he volunteered for duty at the Front, figuring that anything would be better than spending fifteen years in a stockade."

The major raised an eyebrow. "He's not only a deserter, but an arsonist, as well?"

"Yes," Ernesto replied. "He meant to burn down a latrine; but, by accident, part of the barracks caught fire, too. So, you see, he's not some crazy maniac who goes around setting fires. The one small one he'd set was for a good reason. You know what these army latrines smell like, don't you? The fire just got a little out of hand, that's all. I know you hadn't taken command of this rathole yet; so, if you want to check it out, you'll find the story in his records."

The major buzzed for his aide and asked for Tullio Barragatto's file. After reading it, he said to Ernesto, "Now, I've listened. And, what you've said agrees with what's been recorded. What else?"

Ernesto played with the pouch, then pushed it carelessly toward the major. "If Tullio hadn't volunteered, then, he'd never have been at the Front. He'd still be here, serving a sentence for arson. And, all they'd be holding in Voltri was someone who'd escaped from the stockade, not a deserter. If that file were to be changed, he'd be returned to this stockade. He wouldn't be executed."

"I told you I'd listen to your story. That's all I promised. I never said I'd change an official record. It would be too risky. Even if you were to give me the rest of those stones, it wouldn't be worth the risk."

"Army records could be changed very easily, major. No one would be the wiser. Nobody would ever suspect. They'd simply return your prisoner to you."

"No."

"Anyway, the larger diamonds weren't for you. They're a present from my father to your wife. The other one. The one who's living in Turin."

The major didn't reply.

"Army records get changed . . . and lost . . . every single day. Especially now . . . during this stupid war . . . with all the confusion . . . nobody would care."

Still, the major was silent.

Ernesto continued, "I'm sure you must realize that it wasn't really necessary for us to part with these stones. They're worth a small fortune. However, my father has always taught us to be fair. Nothing for nothing. Remember that, when my cousin's your prisoner."

"Blackmail is a serious crime."

Ernesto shrugged. "So is bigamy."

The major stood. "It's too late to send a telegram. The office is closed, and I don't know where the telegrapher is."

"Send it the first thing in the morning. It will arrive in Voltri either late tomorrow night or the following day. The execution is set for Wednesday at sundown." When leaving the major's office, Ernesto added, "My father congratulates you for your stamina and wishes you many years of continued happiness."

"I didn't say I'd do this."

Ernesto didn't answer. He'd been instructed to wait for a different response.

The major sat again and, not facing Ernesto, asked, "What if I did send the message and it arrived too late? It wouldn't be my fault if it were to arrive too late."

Now, Ernesto could reply: "In that case, major, everybody would lose."

The young man left, breathed deeply, and thought: God, make it reach Voltri in time!

"Tullio, listen to me," Federico Crispino pleaded. "Look at me."

"I am."

"We don't have much time left."

"I'm listening, Zio. I'm listening."

Crispino stared at his nephew; he didn't believe he'd ever see him again. Still, he must try. "Certain arrangements are being made. The only reason I'm telling you about them is that you have to know how to act and what to say in each case . . . otherwise, I wouldn't be telling you anything at all."

He understood: "There's no way out of here, Zio. *Believe me.*"

"I know. We're not thinking of an escape. If we're successful, the Army, itself, is going to get you out of here."

He repeated: "There's no way out of here, Zio. Forget it. You'll only get yourself in trouble if you try anything crazy."

"No! There is a way out . . . but . . . ."

14

He interrupted his uncle. "When is the execution? Have you found out? They don't tell us anything down here. Please, I want to know. It's important that I know. It's driving me crazy not knowing."

"The execution is set for Wednesday night . . . but, you won't be here . . . because, you'll have left for Guidonia early Wednesday morning."

"Guidonia! Guidonia?"

"Listen to me, Tullio! Listen! On Wednesday, there'll be an official request from Guidonia to have you returned to them. The request will say you escaped the stockade. You'll be sent back to serve out a sentence for arson and jailbreak. No one will know you were ever at the Front. The desertion charge will be erased."

Tullio's expression changed. "Arson and jailbreak . . . that's about twenty years, Zio. I can't spend twenty years in that stockade, Zio. I'd rather be dead. You don't have any idea of what that place is like. No . . . call it off . . . I can't go back there. I can't go back to Guidonia. . . . I'd go crazy . . . twenty years . . . Guidonia . . . it's worse than the trenches."

The elder clutched his nephew's shirt. "Do you think we'd forget you're in there? You do as I say! If, on Wednesday morning, they tell you they're returning you to Guidonia, you don't say a thing! You go! You hear me? You go! Wednesday, you leave for that stockade!"

He watched the old man leave. *You don't know what it's like in there, Zio. . . . I can't go back.*

But, on that fateful Wednesday morning, Tullio Barragatto returned to Guidonia Prison. He remained there, within its rotting walls, for the next two years before his cousins could buy his release; and, often, he cursed himself for not having chosen the firing squad in Voltri.

There was a stench in Guidonia. It wasn't one so much of filth or sickness or even of foul body odor. It was a stench, nevertheless; and, it took him almost a half a year to realize

15

what it was. "What it was," he tried to explain to his cousin, "was the smell of what men were thinking."

"How can you smell thoughts?" Ernesto had laughed about this.

"You can. Believe it or not: you can. A human being can get to be as sensitive about smells as a dog is. How do you think a dog senses when you're afraid of him . . . or friendly . . . or about to throw a rock at him? He can smell your intentions. Sometimes, he knows what you're going to do even before you, yourself, do."

He stopped then; he realized that Ernesto was not the one to be telling things like this to. If he'd been speaking with one of Ernesto's older brothers—Salvatore or Benedetto—it would be different. He could say to either of them: It got so that I knew what men were thinking just by the smell of them. I knew when a man was thinking about a woman; a few seconds after the smell would come to me, I'd look around at him . . . and, sure enough, it would be visible even before he spoke. I even knew when someone was sick inside his soul; I'd turn around, and there he'd be . . . staring at the ceiling and crying without making a single solitary sound. I swear, it got uncanny. I knew when a man was going to kill himself once. That's when it scared the hell out of me, because that's when I finally realized I'd become a dog. No, he could never tell these things to Ernesto.

There were many, many things he couldn't talk about. One was the way in which his memory had saved his sanity. During the hot, rainy days and nights, when Guidonia was at its worst—this was when most of the suicides took place: when it rained—pictures and sounds from his past would present themselves. The situations could have taken place ten or fifteen years before; but they would be recalled exactly whenever his mind needed to ignore what now was.

He is in Milan studying for the priesthood. He'd just been in a street fight, defending the Fascists. The Counsellor has called

16

him to his office. He is ashamed of Tullio; tells him so. He suggests he leave Milan and go to work the farm of a needy widow in Lombardy.

"It will do your soul good, Tullio," he says. "Remember, you are studying to be a good priest, not a politician on a soapbox."

"I mean no disrespect, sir, but my concern for others is part, I believe, of being a good priest. Am I being sent away because of my concern for others?"

"No, believe me . . . I know how good your intentions are, but you can't see that you're being misled. I can. I've seen much more than your young years have permitted, and I know what's best for you. . . ."

Tullio interrupts: ". . . and you feel that it's best that I remain silent? And you feel that I should study and pray while all else around me is falling apart? Are these the actions of a good priest?—to close his eyes to the sufferings of others?—to hold his hands up, cupping his ears, lest he should hear the crying all around him! The disobedience of eating an apple might have been Man's original sin, but apathy, by far, is his most grievous. Is our Holy Mother, the Church, guilty of this most grievous sin?"

"Don't blaspheme!"

"Will her Confessor grant absolution for this *most* grievous sin?"

"Tullio! You're forgetting yourself! Silence!" He points to a chair and the student sits down. He continues: "Tullio, picture the Church as a great army. That army has one chief, scores of generals, hundreds of officers, and several thousand foot soldiers. Now, because he is an expert in his profession, the chief recognizes a situation that might imperil his charges. Does he rush out, slashing at the enemy, not caring how many casualties the action might cause? No! Does he turn and run in the opposite direction? No! Well, you tell me. What does he do?"

Tullio is about to reply, but the elder says, "I'll tell you what he does. He sends out his scouts to assess the enemy. He directs his lieutenants to gather information. He summons his generals and listens to their suggestions. Only after all of this has been done, does the wise chief plan his strategy. Sometimes, it's a waiting game, lulling the enemy into a false sense of security. Sometimes, he sends spies into the enemy's ranks. All the while, the chief isn't wasting any time; instead, he's gathering allies; he's securing financial support; he's sabotaging the enemy's plans; he's weakening the enemy's position in every way possible.

"Mind you, now, that this particular chief has so many followers that he can neither lose his job nor have to bend to any political pressures. No head of state can spur him into hasty action. The chief has all the time he needs.

"The enemy, on the other hand, is not so fortunate, for he must act swiftly if he's to gain ground. Not a complete dummy, he realizes that he's surrounded by the chief's allies. He starts to give some concessions. He begins to modify some of his earlier demands.

"All the while, fully aware that some of his charges are being killed by enemy snipers, the chief continues to accept platitudes from the enemy. The good chief even becomes suspected of cowardice; but, he doesn't care about his reputation—ultimate victory is his main concern.

"And, you know what, Tullio? Eventually, the chief wins, managing to do so with the least harm to his own people."

Tullio is fidgeting. "Sir," he responds, "I don't know what this has to do with me or with the questions I asked you."

"It's very much the same situation, Tullio. Suppose some of the chief's foot soldiers had become impatient, not obeyed orders, just burst out and started shooting their cannons while the enemy was still partially camouflaged. Would they have been very effective? They might have won lots of little battles on the way, but, surely, they would lose the war. No?"

"Yes," the student answers. "They would lose the war."

The counsellor continues, "Then, you agree that to wage a

18

victorious war, not only must you have a good leader, but you must have soldiers who are completely obedient?"

"Of course, sir. But, we are not waging war."

"We are waging war, Tullio. A war against evil. And Fascism is evil!"

"Fascism is neither evil nor our enemy, sir. On the contrary, it's likely to prove God-sent."

"Tullio, let your chief decide that," the teacher replies. "The Pope is the chief, Vicar of Christ; the cardinals are Christ's generals; I am one of His lower ranking officers; you are studying to be one of His foot soldiers. As a soldier in the army of Christ, you must never question the wisdom of His chief, never accuse nor suspect him of cowardice, much less, apathy. If the Holy Father permitted dissension in his ranks, where would the Church be? The Pope has decided and announced that Fascism is evil, but his strategy to overcome it will never be shared with you or me. The only thing he asks of his army is complete submission, absolute obedience."

He looks at his counsellor. He answers: "Benito would do nothing wrong. You just don't understand him. He wants only what we want. Nothing else. He'll destroy the communists and *i malandrini*. He'll build schools. He'll irrigate the South. Our whole country could be united and mighty under him. I intend to support him until he's right at the head of our government, where he belongs."

The counsellor warns him: "If you persist in this train of thought, I'll have no choice but to expel you from this seminary."

"No!"

"Tullio, it's no dishonor not to be a priest. There are some people who should not be priests, no matter how true they think their vocations are."

"I've never had any other thought to be anything else. Look, I'll do whatever you want. Just don't expel me." He is very nervous now. He's frightened. This man doesn't make idle threats.

19

"Some day, you might forsake these foolish Fascist ideas of yours and become a good businessman, like your father, a credit to his nation and his family; but, to be a mediocre, disobedient priest could be disastrous to your soul. The Church would survive, but you might not."

His words are barely audible now: "Just let me continue at the seminary. I'll do whatever you say. Okay?"

The elder thinks for a while. He makes the student wait in silence and worry. Eventually, he answers: "Very well, I'll give you this one chance. You go to Lombardy as I've suggested. Spend the summer months there and think about what I've said. Examine your conscience. Remain there until after the harvest, away from Milan and all its confusion and politics. Decide, for yourself, if you have enough obedience in you to be one of Christ's soldiers. Whatever you do, though, decide honestly. Be fair to yourself."

He's never pleaded for anything before. He knows the Counsellor has already guessed this, and he feels humiliated. Nevertheless, he says, *"Grazie,"* and waits to be dismissed.

There is a gentle spring shower. A prisoner called Fallanca has murdered a guard. He hears the sirens; he watches the man run across the yard; sees him slip in the mud; and then, climb over the wall. He wonders how far Fallanca will get. He lies down on his cot again and remembers another spring shower. He is travelling from Milan to Lombardy, and is stopping in to see his former tutor and confidant, Aleksey Kostenov. They eat and they drink more than either of them is accustomed to, and Aleksey tells him of his life before he became his tutor.

Born in Russia, Aleksey Kostenov was the son of the head gamekeeper on one of the czar's cousin's estates. He could remember how his father used to brush the hunting dogs' coats to the high lustre of sable. As a reward for excellent service, the czar provided the servant's son with an education he could never have received, and Aleksey became a professor of philosophy.

One of his youngest students, Anna Petrov, allowed him to court her.

"I was at least twice her age. She was the sweetest, most gentle, most beautiful girl who ever lived," he says. "She was slender, with flame-red hair and her skin was as fragile as white blossoms."

"What happened to her?" Tullio asks.

"We were married."

Tullio hesitates. "Is she dead?"

With a half smile, Kostenov says: "Some of the working men of the world united."

"But, you and Anna weren't the oppressors."

"Men think only in solitude. A mob has no mind."

"You don't have to go on, sir."

"Why not? It's history. You can't change history. You can only make it." Aleksey continues, his tongue loosened by the wine he'd drunk forbidding silence. "There were lots of little revolutions in those days, all quickly crushed—as if there is really such a thing as a *little* revolution."

On a rainy night, he sees the farm in Lombardy. It is near one of the tributaries of the Po River. It's an extensive farm, about two hundred acres; but, the farmhouse is tiny. The widow who owns the place is very young, perhaps in her mid-teens, but she already has an infant son.

"I'm Tullio Barragatto, signora."

"The seminarian from Milan? My new laborer?"

"Yes."

"But, I didn't expect you to be so grand!"

During another downpour, he's in the trenches. There is a lull in the bombardment and the chaplain says, "Tell me a little more about yourself. When did you decide not to enter the priesthood?"

"When I decided I'd rather get married."

"And, did you?"

"Yes."

"Any children yet?"

"Not yet."

"What's your wife's name?"

"Her name is Magdalena."

"Well, when the war is over, it will be good that you'll have someone to go back to."

He wonders: When it's over? Can I wait that long?

It rains so often in Guidonia.

Chapter Two

While he'd still expected to be executed for desertion—Tullio Barragatto had arranged for his wife to be sent to America, there, to live under the protective roof of his former tutor, Aleksey Kostenoy. The ship was to sail on the day before the scheduled execution.

It had been difficult for his secretary to convince Magdalena to board the ship, but once on board he'd explained the plan to her and had added: "Signora, if the execution does take place, there's nothing you or any of us can do about it. They certainly won't let you witness it! . . . And, if the Guidonia plan should work out, then, marvelous . . . but, you wouldn't be able to visit him there. Nobody gets visitors in Guidonia."

"How would I know about tomorrow? How could I sail, not knowing if he'll be dead, tomorrow, or in Guidonia? You expect me to leave, not knowing if my Tullio is dead or alive?" She'd clutched the silver cup her husband had once given her, and had cried, "Oh, God, I don't know what to do."

"Do what your husband said to do. Stay on this ship. Don't get off, no matter what."

"I've heard so much about those stockades. Tullio won't go back. He won't let them send him back."

"You'd be surprised what men would do to live," he answered. "They'd do anything. Anything. He might *think* he'd rather die than be in that stockade for so long . . . but, when the time comes. . . ."

"You could have made up this whole story! . . . just to keep me from getting off this ship!"

"I didn't. I assure you, signora, I didn't. Have faith."

"But, what if the telegram doesn't reach Voltri in time?"

"Signora, we're wasting time. I have to leave, now. That's the signal for all visitors to get off the ship."

"No!"

"Be kind to your husband, signora! Sail, as he wanted! Do this one last favor for him! Let him have one less worry on his mind! That's the least you can do for him, isn't it?"

She'd watched the stateroom door close behind the man. She'd sat on the floor, staring at the door, long after the ship had begun moving.

The Great War had started decades before being recognized or officially named. During the middle and late 1800s, tiny principalities were destroying one another. The actions were called boundary disputes and little revolutions, and even family feuds; yet, entire nationalities disappeared, their languages died as villagers ran from country to country, mixing with others who'd fled from similar distant ruins. Thousands of families were completely dispersed, their names dying with them; but, survivors clung to each other, forming caravans of frightened wanderers who, through subsequent generations, would fuse so often with other fleeing emigrants that they couldn't ever remember not being gypsies.

During those chaotic years, a band of Serbians followed the great Po River's tributaries westward. They'd already been chased from boundary to boundary and were loyal to no flag. Shortly before the dawn of the Great War, they'd received permission to camp on the unplowed fields of Tomaso Disanti. Their leader was called Mikel Mostra.

Mikel Mostra had many wives and many children, but his favorite child was Magdalena. For the first few years, the child was cared for, mainly, by whoever his current wife was.

By the summer of 1914 she had become a beauty. Her red hair shone in the Lombardy sun. Like her hair, her light green eyes and her pale cream complexion were unusual for a Serbian gypsy, but no one dared to comment on this. Her father, Mikel Mostra, was, after all, a king.

It was her lovely color—and her ripening figure—that caught the eye of Tomaso Disanti.

After some very serious consideration, the gypsy king decided that he'd marry her off to his gracious landlord, the Lombardian farmer. She was fourteen years old, time for a gypsy girl to be married.

By now, though, the war had a name; and, with it, came conscription. A few months after they'd been wed, Magdalena watched her husband being marched away, knowing she'd never see him again. Two months later, her son, Stefano, was born. The day after she delivered, news reached her that Tomaso was dead. It was not news to Magdalena, however, for Mikel had told her that she would never see her husband again.

It was in this way that the daughter of Mikel, leader of the Mostra clan, had become mistress of some of the Po Valley's most valuable land. Now, her name was Magadalena Mostra Disanti.

One morning, Magdalena had journeyed to the rectory. Her only purpose for going was to seek a laborer to plow her land; but, the priest talked her into baptizing her son.

"You see, Donna Magdalena," the priest said, "this one volume contains the histories of many families. A section of it is devoted to the Disanti family. In it, is recorded the births and names of each of the Disanti children. Now, that Stefano is baptized, his name will join the others. It serves as a permanent record for everyone to know that your Stefano is the legal heir to his father's lands. It even outlines the boundaries of his lands. Through it, you can trace the Disanti family all the way back over a hundred years or more. All the wives' names are here, and even the names of the wives' families, too."

"Mine, too?" she asked.

"No. I'm sorry to say that your name isn't written in it, because you weren't married in church. But, at least, nobody will ever question the rights of Stefano. Now, that he's been baptized, he'll always be protected."

She watched the old pastor write her son's name in the ledger and she swelled with pride. Then, she left, because it was such a long journey back to the farm. She'd return again, she'd said, to be baptized, herself.

The road was a beige velvet ribbon, narrow and winding, and she squinted because its scattered pebbles sparkled like gems. Her clothing clung to her damp skin, and she wished the summer were over, not just beginning. She skipped parts of the way, and twirled the infant in her arms very often because she liked the way it made him laugh. Under a large shade tree, she ate the small lunch the priest's cook had packed for her. After nursing Stefano, she sang to him as the happy, squealing baby tugged at her necklaces.

"Stefano, your name is in a big book. And someday, when you grow up and go away with Mikel, you can come back and live in the same house because the book says that the house belongs to you." She kissed him. "When I get baptized, my name will also be in the book. All the wives' names are in it, and their families, too. That means Mikel will be in it, and . . ."

Magdalena stopped, her hand to her mouth, and said: "Stefano, I don't know my mother's name! I have to remember to ask Mikel, so her name can be in the book, just like the other wives' mothers."

She tried to remember ever having heard anything at all about her mother; but, no . . . nobody had ever talked of her. Had the woman shamed the clan? Was her memory taboo?

"Stefano, I don't know what to do. If her memory is taboo, then it's not safe to ask about her. But, how will I know if I don't ask? It must be taboo, or Mikel would have mentioned her. No? But, maybe it's not taboo."

She jumped three times and clapped her hands twice, because this was how to summon the gods.

"Listen, all great and beautiful gods!" the girl shouted. "Listen to me! I won't break the taboo! I promise! I just want to find out if there is one!"

Even when she spoke seriously, the baby would laugh aloud, so Magdalena kept talking until he fell asleep.

Hours later, she entered the dark front room of her little farmhouse and, exhausted by her long, arduous day, went directly to bed.

And then, Magdalena had turned fifteen, and Tullio had come along—an act of charity: a young widow needed help with her farm. And he'd lived there. And while there, he'd taught her to read and write; and which fork to use; and that she wasn't a child any longer; and that she should be making plans for herself and her son's future.

The student's coming to her farm made her unhappy, though; because, for the first time, she realized that she was poor. She was the poor daughter of a poor gypsy, and she'd married a poor farmer.

One afternoon, she'd visited the Mostra camp at the riverbank. She'd found Mikel fishing, and told him of her new feelings.

"Magdalena," he queried, "aren't you proud of your Mikel anymore?" He tried to sound frivolous, but the girl knew he meant the question, and didn't take it lightly. "Don't you want Stefano to be like me, and be king when I die?"

"Mikel," she hesitated, "I want him to grow up just like you, but . . ."

"But, he should be one of them? Not of the wagons? He shouldn't be free to move on when the snows come? He shouldn't be free to do whatever he wants? He should have to talk a special way and say only what others say is all right? He

27

should have to wear what others say? Do like they want? Sleep where they tell him to? Eat certain foods? Obey stupid laws? Pay taxes? Fight wars? Is that what Stefano's mother wants for him? That he should never have the time to just sit here and look at the sky and the trees and the water? Magdalena, look at how the brook moves. It's alive. Look. You see how, in some places, it looks like silver ribbons? You see how it plays with the sun? You see how it shines? No farmer could see that, but we can. And, Stefano can, if he follows the wagons."

"But, Mikel!"

"Magdalena! That's what's important—the real things . . . like the brook . . . things that are beautiful because they are that way . . . and not because it would be nice to have them, because no one could ever have them. Nobody could have the silver ribbons that hide at night and come back the next morning. And, nobody could have its fishes that are more shiny than gold. As soon as you touch it, the ribbons disappear; and as soon as you grab its fish, they die. Anybody can have lots of boots like that new laborer of yours! Little One, what's happened to you? Do you want more skirts? I'll give them to you. The women have a lot of skirts. I'll give them all to you."

"But, it's not the same, Mikel. They'd be other women's skirts, not mine. Anyway, it's not just for myself that I want things. It's for Stefano. That's why I have to have a plan . . . so I can get enough money to buy them."

"Magdalena," he pleaded, removing a final fish from his rod, "have I ever done the wrong thing for you? Have I ever told you the wrong things or lied to you, or tried to confuse you? I'll tell you when you have to start making plans. Haven't I always told you everything you had to know?"

"Well, there are some things. . . ."

"Like what?" he asked.

"You never told me about my mother."

The man was shocked. He'd never expected such a retort.

"Is her memory taboo? If it is, just tell me so, and I won't ask any more questions," Magdalena told him.

28

"Magdalena, we were talking about you and me and how we used to discuss everything before making plans."

"Please, Mikel, is her memory taboo? I have to know, Mikel . . . and, if it is, I won't ask, not ever again. If it's taboo, then, I can understand that you can't talk about her. But, if it isn't taboo, then I have a right to know about her, don't I?" She was speaking rapidly, nervously, because she'd finally broached the subject.

"Why?"

"Because I'm learning how to read. And then, soon, I'll be baptized. And, when I'm baptized, my mother's name will be in the book in the rectory. And, your name will be there, too. Remember? I told you about the book."

"Yes, I remember."

"Well, is her memory taboo?"

"It's taboo." He held his head down, pondering. Shortly, he took a small emerald brooch from his trousers. "Here, Little One. This was hers. It matched her eyes as it does yours. Pin it inside your skirt pocket where nobody can see it and steal it from you. I've been meaning, for a long time, now, to give it to you.

"It's as fine as anything of that laborer of yours."

"Oh, how pretty! I'll pin it on my blouse."

"No!" he ordered. "Do as I say and wear it inside your skirt."

"I promise, Mikel. But, it's so pretty. I really want to wear it where it will show. But, I won't. I promise."

"Do as I say or I won't let you have it."

"Yes, Mikel. I promise."

"It's almost as beautiful as you are." Smiling, he handed the brooch to Magdalena, and watched her fasten it to the inner top part of her skirt.

They walked back to camp, not speaking for a long time. Mikel was too taken back by Magdalena's question about her mother to have any further conversation right now. Had his Little One taken the advantage by catching him off-guard, hoping to exact the truth? And why now, after all these years? Did she really care about a name's being in a book? Was it that important to her?

But, why not tell her? he asked himself. They'd loved and trusted one another for so long; surely, Magdalena couldn't love him less because of an accident of birth! Hadn't he always treated her better than any of the other children? Had he ever shared secrets with the others? No! Had he ever gone fishing with the others? No! Had he ever taken days' journeys away from the wagons with any of the others? No! Only with Magdalena!

Neither a lie nor a doubt lives alone, though; and, if he'd admit he'd lied about her mother, would the girl suspect him in other matters? Already, she seemed to doubt his wisdom—this conferring with a village priest and a laborer about plans and books, and even about Stefano, his beautiful grandson, without having asked him, Mikel, first—what further proof could he ask? And, what of Stefano? If the girl were to find that her son had no Mostra blood in him, could he, Mikel, possibly hope the child would someday join him? Especially now, when Magdalena was starting to think like one of the others? . . . about useless, fancy clothes? . . . about making plans? . . . and about putting names in books? . . . and of reading? How long had she wanted these luxuries? Had she always secretly yearned for them?

There were so many seeds that Tullio Barragatto had planted within her that summer.

"Did you know that there are carts that go without horses?" she asked Mikel one afternoon.

"Who told you such a thing?"

"Tullio Barragatto. He said 'that, in Milan, people ride in carts that don't need a horse."

"You don't believe that, do you?" Mikel laughed.

"I don't know. But, why would he make up such a story?"

"Well, I don't know. But, it doesn't make any sense. How can a cart go ahead without something pulling it?"

"I don't know, but he said there are such things. You know what else he said? He said there are things called electric somethings that light up without fire."

"Little One! How can you believe such things?"

"It's true, maybe. He said that the electric things make a room brighter than candles."

"Ha!"

"You know what else he said? He said that there are things called telephones, and that people talk into them, and their voices go far away, to somebody else who has a telephone."

"And?"

"And then, the people—the ones who are far away—talk back into their own telephones, and their voices go all the way back to the first person who was talking."

"Ha! Ha! Ha! That's the silliest thing I've ever heard in my life! And, you believed him!"

"You mean he was lying? Tullio was lying?"

"No, Magdalena. He was just making a joke with you. He made it all up. For a joke! Ha, ha, ha!"

Magdalena was insulted to think that Tullio would have made up all those stories and that, perhaps, he was laughing at her. "Mikel, are you sure he was joking?"

"Of course! But, don't be angry with him. I like Tullio. He's a good boy. He likes to make jokes. That's all. He just likes to make jokes."

"He was just joking all the time?"

"Yes! Of course!"

Noticing his daughter's cross look, Mikel playfully pinched her nose. "Hey, Magdalena, what's the matter with you? Can't you take a joke no more? Come on, smile, or I'll pull your nose off."

Because he was hurting her, Magdalena smiled reluctantly and said, "I thought there really were such things. I believed him."

"That's okay, Little One. But remember: Believe nothing you hear and only half of what you see. Okay?"

31

"Okay, Mikel," she answered, but her disappointment was evident, and Mikel was sorry he'd spoiled the myth.

It was that same evening that her beloved Mikel was in a drunken brawl and injured so seriously that he never recovered. She wept, almost uncontrollably, in Tullio's arms; and he—who'd not until then realized he'd fallen in love with the young widow—consoled her. While doing so, he understood what his counsellor had already perceived: that he wasn't meant for the priesthood.

She stared at the stateroom door and wondered: Why am I thinking of these things now? All that really matters, now, is tomorrow. Tullio might be dead by tomorrow. God, don't let that happen! And, she didn't know if she'd said this aloud or if she'd merely thought it.

"Will you marry me, Magdalena?"
"Okay, Tullio, I'll marry you."
There, it was said. He looked at her stupidly. He'd asked and she'd accepted. It was done.
"I'll take you back to Orvietto with me."
"Orvietto? But, what about my farm? Stefano's farm?"
"It will always be there."

But, what else is there to do but think? Should I unpack? No, later. God, make him live tomorrow!

She looked around at the grandeur of her stateroom. It was almost as huge as their bedroom in Orvietto; but, then, everything in Orvietto was overwhelming, if only to her.

There is a high wall that stretches the width of a little summer palace. It is almost completely covered by vines that climb to its top with lavender blossoms. Tullio stops the wagon in front of its huge bronze gate and she smiles. She thinks he's about to pick some of the flowers. He likes her to wear flowers in her hair.

"We're here."

"Where?" she asks him.

"This is my father's house. We're home."

She hated Orvietto. She hated the big house and its large rooms and its long, narrow corridors that never ended. She hated its frescoed ceilings and its shadows and the way it creaked very late at night. She hated to wear high-buttoned dresses and pointed shoes that pinched her feet. She hated her hair pulled back tightly in a bun, and her waist cinched until she could barely breathe. She hated the French lessons, and the catechism lessons, and the diction lessons, and the deportment lessons. She hated the dance instructor and the piano teacher. And, above all, she hated the *respectable courtship period*, for she must live it with his aunts.

He visits her once weekly now—this is all that's permitted—and he sits at the far side of the parlor from her and his aunts. When he leaves, she envies his freedom. She wants to run from Orvietto, but how? She has no money . . . she has no wagon . . . she's so far away from Lombardy . . . how would she get there?

"But, when can we be married? We've been here so long now!"

"Soon," the aunts tell her. "Very soon, now."

But, she's heard this before, and so has he; so, they can hardly believe their ears when the date is set for the first Sunday after Easter. He sends her a present that evening—the chalice he would have used as a priest. She's very pleased with the silver cup. It's a very expensive gift. He told her about other chalices that were encrusted with jewels, and so soon, she will solder her mother's emerald onto the cup.

But these are foolish things. These are yesterday. Only tomorrow is important. Dear God, make him live! Please?

33

Chapter Three

During his first day in Guidonia, Tullio's head was shaved. He'd not expected this; it hadn't been done the last time he was here. He was lying on his cot, unconsciously skimming his fingers over where the hair had been, when his new cellmate said, "You never suspect how many in's and out's you have on your head until you're bald. Right?"

He replied with a question: "How come some are shaved and some aren't?"

"Only the long-termers are shaved. When their hair starts to grow back, they're shaved again. That's how the guards know who to watch out for. They go easy on the ones with hair, because they know they'll be getting out soon and might get even with them in an alley some night."

He muttered, "Something new."

Their room had been a monk's cell, never meant for two. Their cots were bunked on one wall, but the remaining floor space was still so narrow that they couldn't both stand at the same time. Noticing Tullio's frustration over the cramped quarters, the cellmate said: "I know what you're thinking, but, whatever you do, don't complain to any of the guards about it. We'll be in here only a few days, anyway, or a week at the most."

34

It takes them that long to sew your name on your uniform. Then, we'll be transferred to the bigger block across the yard."

"You just came here," Tullio said. "How come you already know so much about the place?"

He told him that he'd escaped and that they'd just caught him. This was his first day back.

A guard looked through the small bar opening. "Oh, if it isn't our old friend, Giulio Fallanca. They told me you were back. Well, we're going to have a lot of fun this time around, aren't we, Fallanca?"

The man laughed then, and left; and Giulio Fallanca said: "I'm going to kill that one some day, even if it's the last thing I do."

A few days later, they were transferred to separate blocks, and the two seldom saw one another again. Tullio was assigned a bed at the far end of his block. A window was above his bed and he smirked and shook his head because he'd, again, been placed alongside a latrine, one which smelled almost as bad as that which he'd burned down years before.

During the long voyage to New York, Magdalena Barragatto dreamed often of Tullio. Sometimes she dreamed of the carefree moments they had shared while still living on the farm by the Po. She remembered the first time she saw him. He sat high atop his dark brown horse, a ruffled shirt showing through his gray suede jacket, his wide brimmed gray hat tilted rakishly over one eye. He didn't look like any laborer she'd ever seen, and he certainly didn't look like a future priest. He looked like a prince. She still laughed at the thought of his endless supply of silk shirts and his four pairs of boots. She who'd owned one skirt and who'd never even worn shoes until he brought her to Orvietto.

But these memories were not always enough and sometimes as she lay alone in her stateroom she would remember how it was the first time they made love by the banks of the river. She would pretend Tullio was there in bed beside her; she could almost feel the warmth of him as he became aware of her presence. He would begin to caress her, his lips on hers, his elegant hands exploring every secret place. He would take her in his arms, his well-muscled body hardened and darkened by long hours in the Lombardy fields, and it was as if there had never been any other for either of them.

At other times, the dreams were frightening. They relived her months of waiting and of wondering if he were still alive at the Front; and of how used and worn he'd looked when he'd returned. These dreams would waken her because the man who'd come back to Orvietto was so different than the one who'd left.

The third kind of dream was a bagful of mixed memories. One was of a visit she'd made to a gypsy in Orvietto. The woman had travelled with the Mostra clan until a year after Magdalena had been born. Now, she was living alone; and, because Mikel was dead and she no longer needed to fear him, she told Magdalena of the mystery of her birth. It had shocked Magdalena, and, in her dream, she could remember her own astonished, unhappy words: ". . . but, I will always consider Mikel my real father . . . he was very good to me . . . it's funny, but I used to think my mother's memory was taboo. . . ."

Although her nights drifted to the past, her days were different. She would never dwell on yesterdays during her waking moments. Instead, she would worry about how her husband was faring in Guidonia; or if she would miss Aleksey Kostenov at the dock and get lost; or if her house in America might be larger than the one in Orvietto.

The Atlantic was choppy, and Magdalena wasn't a good sailor. She was very grateful when the journey was over.

On the morning when the S/S *Asheley Queen* docked, Aleksey Kostenov reread the letter his former pupil had written to him from Guidonia. He'd almost cried the first time he'd read it, because he loved Tullio like a son. Now, the whole affair eemed like a nightmare that was about to end. Yet, he couldn't throw the letter away, and he knew its words by heart. It said:

Dear Aleksey,

Aleksey, this cell is remarkable. There are only a cot, a candle, and a table to write on. There's no window and no chair. I don't know if it's day or night. You have to pull the table to the cot in order to sit and write. There are stacks of thousands of sheets of paper in the corner and dozens of pens all filled with ink. I've never seen so much paper. I suspect everybody who sits here must write and write and write. We must all be the same. Our generals might not know us very well, but our jailers do. It's beyond me. Maybe you can figure that out. I can't. I've learned that mail from these cells isn't subject to censor. It might be that they know it's easier to write all the things that you won't let yourself say in confession. I don't know. They ask you if you want a priest, but they don't ask you if you want the paper.

There's a lot that's happened since I've last seen you, none of which I've ever written to you about. I won't waste my time or yours by trying to recount any of those events. The things that we do aren't as important as why we let them happen. Aleksey, now I know that nothing takes place unless we permit it. Not a single thing. Nothing just happens. You must have told me that a thousand times, but I never heard you. You told me about trees that were cut down, and about slaves who built temples, and about what you called little revolutions. You even showed me the true holy men who help bandits, and farmers who have to sell their children. I didn't know what you were saying. I know now. I'm very grateful to you.

Regarding Carmine Pace, whom I'm sure you've met by now: Advise Salvatore that he must outsmart Pace's people at all costs. You can't, but he might be able to. He knows how they think. It's time for a change. I've learned that it's never

37

too late. When you don't want war, you don't sit behind closed doors and discuss terms; the only way to end a war is to stop fighting. Likewise, if a tradition is wrong, you simply break it; you change it.

I would like you to be the executor of my estate.

1. Devise a profit-making fund for the Fascist cause. It's my country's only salvation. If Italy's soul is to survive Fascism is the only answer. If Fascism is defeated, the Bolsheviks and the Pace's of the world will eventually take over.

2. Magdalena, my wife, and you will be equal legal guardians over Rebecca.

3. My entire estate belongs to Magdalena. My family may remain living on the land in the style to which they're accustomed. However, tell Salvatore to make it clear to my family that if anything happens to Magdalena, everything becomes the property of Benito Mussolini.

My secretary will probably be here this afternoon. I'll have him draw up a legal will in case this letter doesn't reach you.

Aleksey, I am sending Magdalena to America. She's so innocent that she'd have no idea how wealthy she'll be, so please guide her as much as possible. I can die without any concern at all if you'll take her under your roof. She needs your protection, and despite what anyone might later tell you, she's the one joy of my life.

I can hear the guards bringing lunch around. I didn't think it was that late. They collect all the mail at lunchtime, so I'll end this letter now to get it in today's post.

I don't think there's anything else to say, Aleksey, except that I'm surprised how calm I feel, because I would like very much to live. I think I could grow very good grapes again. Thank you for all your years of loyalty.

Tullio

He was about to knock, but the cabin door was already open

One of the porters was stacking trunks in front of the bed. "Is this Signora Barragatto's stateroom?" he asked the young man.

"Yes," a woman replied. She was wearing a well-cut dark green travelling suit and although her red hair was covered by a fashionable cloche hat he recognized her instantly. Tullio had not underestimated his wife's beauty.

He bowed slightly. "I am Aleksey Kostenov. And you are Magdalena Barragatto?"

"Yes." She smiled at him and extended her hand. He was exactly as Tullio had described: a tall, very thin man with thick white hair that spilled in his eyes as soon as he removed his hat. His china-blue eyes stared at her thoughtfully.

"I beg your pardon, signora," he said as he kissed her hand. "Have we met before?"

Magdalena shook her head. "Is something wrong?" she asked. The old man seemed pale.

"No," he assured her. "Perhaps your husband has told me so much about you that you are no longer a stranger." Yes, he told himself. That was why the girl seemed so familiar.

A uniformed woman who looked like a nurse entered the stateroom with a very dark little girl who looked to be about four years old.

"Ah, Rebecca," Magdalena smiled. "This is Signor Kostenov." The little girl extended her hand shyly, and the old man kissed it, then turned back to Magdalena.

"Come, Magdalena . . . may I call you Magdalena?"

"Yes, please do," she said.

"Come. My driver will take care of the luggage. I'll take you home now."

She followed the old man off the ship and didn't even try to hide her fascination with the city as they drove through its crowded, bustling streets. When they left the city and hit the parkway, the little girl and her nurse were fast asleep.

"You didn't seem surprised about Rebecca," Magdalena said.

Aleksey shook his head. "Tullio wrote me about her." He handed her a letter. "His latest arrived today. You may read it if you'd like."

She did, and asked: "Who is this Pace person he mentioned?"

"Nobody for you to be concerned about," Kostenov replied. "Just some businessman who wants to buy North American Distributors. Remarkable, isn't it? Even in jail, Tullio is concerned about the business. He's certainly become his father's son, hasn't he? Can you imagine anybody else writing about business at a time like this?"

"No," she answered.

Kostenov took a few minutes to phrase his delicate question. "Little Rebecca—she's rather dark isn't she?"

She explained: "In Lombardy, there was a woman who had married one of the men in my clan. Then, the man had died, but she stayed with our wagons. She was half Moor . . . and she was very . . . experienced . . . you see, she was much older than Tullio . . . and, that was the summer when he was fresh out of the seminary . . . and he used to go to her before we . . ."

"It's all right," Kostenov said. "I understand. And, what were you doing all this time while he was going to see her? Weren't you jealous?"

"No. You see, we didn't even know that we loved each other. To me, he was just a laborer who was there for the summer. When fall came, I'd expected him to go back to the seminary. Of course, knowing about him and the Moor, I realized that he might make a very ridiculous priest . . . but, after all, it was none of my business, was it? He was still just a summer laborer to me."

Aleksey laughed, then asked, "Will it bother you to have Rebecca here?"

"No."

"Are you certain you could raise her as your own? Another woman's child?"

"Yes. Rebecca is Tullio's daughter. How could I not want her?"

He already knew that he liked the young woman immensely. He smiled at her again, and looked at her as pensively as before. "Sit back and enjoy the ride, Magdalena. The traffic is heavy today and it will take a little while before we get home."

"Where is home?"

"On Long Island, on the North Shore."

The Gold Coast

Chapter One

Jutting into the Atlantic Ocean, directly east of New York City, there is a narrow stretch of land called Long Island; and, along its north-western tip, beginning at the Queens-Nassau borderline, lies the bittersweet remnants of a once magnificent, but short-lived, phenomenon called the Gold Coast.

The Gold Coast was the only real-life fairyland that has ever existed. Undoubtedly, nothing even remotely resembling it shall ever reappear. It received its name because of its inhabitants, for they had the most social prestige, the most economic strength and the greatest political power in the country; and, also, because everything they did, everything they had, everything they bought, and everything they even proposed was more flamboyant, more extravagant, and most important of all—for this is what led to their downfall—more widely-publicized than anything in recorded history.

The Gold Coast wasn't a large area. On the contrary, it was a tiny corridor, barely twenty miles long, its width ranging from less than one mile at each end to under ten miles in its middle, a mere 110 square miles which comprised only about ten percent of the entire island. Yet an invisible line segregated it from the rest of the world. Its people were unique unto themselves.

They associated only with one another and formed a private nation, if not legally, then certainly, psychologically, adopting a strict code of behavior, specialized mannerisms and speech patterns, and an inner-circle hierarchy which only they could understand or appreciate.

The original North Shore natives had chosen the locale because of its proximity to New York. They were the diplomats, the politicians, the publishers, the stockbrokers and the businessmen who had to be close to one another, as well as within easy access of the nation's pulse, in order to survive. So, from the beginning, the common tie among the inhabitants was their interdependence; and, the immense wealth their professions afforded them only served to strengthen their unity. They lived together, worked side by side, shared the same interests, and intermarried. Their circle was secure; and, whether they liked one another or not, they *loved* one another because every one of them was an extension of the other.

The Gold Coast people wouldn't even vacation separately. For this reason, *seasons* were established, and entire families, just like great swarms of migrating birds, moved *en masse* to the same other localities at certain times of the year. They managed, this way, to preserve their strong self-identity, and in doing so, their social structure became even more unified. Most of them maintained a summer residence in Bar Harbor, Maine, or in Newport, Rhode Island; and they had a New York apartment, of course, for winter use. It was during the spring and fall that Long Island was in season, and only a brave non-conformist would spend a weekend "at home" when home was off-season.

There were lots of names by which these original Gold Coast people were called. They were referred to as the *American aristocracy* or the *Upper-class* or the *Upper-upper-class* or the *Elite;* or, some simply labeled them *Society.* However they were called, they regarded themselves as occupying the uppermost level of the social strata. They could not sin.

Yet, to safeguard that special state of grace which they called "social position," Society paid dearly, the price being the most ostentatious display of wealth ever seen in America. Neither their winter apartments nor their summer retreats were large enough to afford the proper ostentation—so, they focused most of their wealth upon their North Shore homes.

On the North Shore, home was an estate.

Within the first two decades of this century there were about six hundred estates in the area. They existed in a virtually unbroken sequence, located one right after the other. Because of the decreasing availability of land over the years, the earlier an estate had been established, the larger it was; and also, the higher on the social scale were its owners. There were, however, certain characteristics common to all estates, whether as small as twenty acres or as large as two thousand acres—and, not one of the original Six Hundred (later to be called the Old Estates) deviated from these rules.

The first consideration for an estate concerned the placement of its one large, main residence. If the estate were inland, the main residence would be in the direct center of the property. If the estate were close to the shore, the main residence fronted on the water. In either case, the family's living quarters extended as far back as possible from the roadway. There were two reasons for this: one was to keep all contact with outsiders at a minimum; the other was that a long impressive driveway could be built from the estate's entrance to the main residence. There were times when a driveway—for instance, one on an estate of five hundred acres—would easily extend for more than a mile.

The second consideration regarded the placement of the outbuildings. Included within those facilities were servants' houses, guest cottages, greenhouses, garages and (set aside from other employees' quarters) chauffeurs' apartments. Farther away from these buildings would be the stables and dog runs. All of these particular facilities were the necessities, the basics for estate life—not to be confused with those *extras*, which were determined by individual preference and the geo-

47

graphical location of the estate site.

An *extra* might be an eighteen-hole golf course. Other estates would boast elaborate formal gardens and orchards. Others had tennis courts or hunting preserves or race tracks. It was extremely rare when one estate had all of these extra facilities—but every estate contained at least one of them, and several estates a few of them. Because of this, the overall number of employees varied widely, the smallest of properties utilizing a minimum of a dozen servants and the larger, older ones employing upwards of fifty or a hundred persons.

Everything the Gold Coast dwellers demanded for their pursuits for happiness abounded within the area. Lovers of the sea settled near the shore, for the Long Island Sound had countless coves and inlets that were a yachtsman's delight. And, if you were part of those called the "horsey set," an inland estate was ideal, because of the island's central hills. For the hunters, there were thousands of acres of wooded fields; and, for the gentleman-farmer, little plateaus of fertile topsoil lay begging to be plowed.

But even fairylands, if they are to become famous ones, have to be helped along. Despite everything they had, the Elite, encumbered by the same insecurities as crowned heads, were frightened—for that elusive brass ring called "social position" must constantly be polished. It demanded publicity.

The necessities of estate life, coupled with the natural bounties the land provided and the "extras" the builder included within his property, were all put to use. Before long, widely publicized events began to take place. They ranged from small charity affairs to international tournaments sponsored entirely by individual estate owners. Special trophies and cups inscribed with the estate name were awarded for excellence in particular sports, and gala affairs preceding and ending each fete—many, more grandiose than kings' coronations—received notoriety in most of the world's newspapers.

There was never a lack of publicity, for so many of the estate owners were also publishers, or cousins of publishers, or daughters of publishers, the intermarrying of their ancestors reaping this reward. And, there was no limit to the extremes to which the estate dweller would go to see his home or family name in print. Daily accounts in newspapers and feature spreads in magazines spoke of great homes being built, many larger and more costly than hotels.

One tabloid, describing a society matron's dilemma because her property had no hill upon which to build her mansion, later praised her inventiveness, saying that "the lady has simply constructed her own hill . . . much higher than any in the neighboring estates . . . and now, she can look down from her bedroom window upon everyone else's low-lying little homestead."

Another columnist reported: ". . . and, to make sure his guest of honor, the sheik, would feel comfortable, the host converted a good portion of his estate (only temporarily, he assures us) into a desert, importing the sand, of course, from his guest's own country."

Many of the hills, still there, gracing the North Shore, are man-made. So are some unexpected little forests. Babbling brooks. And sand basins.

Detailed descriptions of extravagant parties were widely published explaining the wearing apparel of each guest, what they ate, how many personal servants each brought with her, and who was not with his proper mate.

Even the birthdays of the youngest children's pets received mention, for there was almost nothing the Gold Coast people did that wasn't considered newsworthy.

The nation was awestruck. She turned to this little corridor, this playground for the immensely wealthy, and was excited by it. She began to observe the Gold Coast people, devoured everything that was written about them, and started to recognize their surnames, just as though they belonged to intimate friends or relatives. Her poor cursed them. Her middle-class laughed at them. Her intelligentsia tried to analyze them. And, her newest breed, the *nouveaux riches*, suddenly began to think very seriously about them. For they—the Estates People—represented the closest America would ever come to her own royal family.

And then, catastrophe—the original owner-builders of the magnificent estates began to die.

The extra-wealthy had families as large as those of the extremely poor; so when a patriarch died, his heirs split his property into as many subdivisions. Not having inherited that unique neuroticism that is required for estate-owning, many of these heirs lacked the desire to keep the places and all the responsibilities attached to them. An estate was a dream-house. An heir didn't want to live within somebody else's dreams. He wanted to build his own. In his own style. On his own hill. And, not necessarily on the island. Some heirs (those with a social conscience) donated their land to institutions like universities and religious organizations which would bear their family name. Others, unwilling to disassociate themselves from their childhood friends and surroundings, turned their properties into country clubs. But, a majority of the heirs—to the chagrin of those who chose to remain on their subdivided estates—began to seek out the highest bidders for their land; and this group sold to the newly rich.

Thus, began the demise of the Gold Coast.

By the early 1920s, estate building had virtually ceased, the great properties' lifespans having run parallel to the lives of their original owner-builders. The area was now inhabited by a small vestige of old wealth families and some of the newly rich. The cliques seldom mixed.

There was a third group that was starting to frequent Long Island: deposed European royalty and statesmen, the millionaire gypsies. They lived in the guest cottages of both old and new money because they couldn't tell the difference. Dependent upon the length of stay and upon the Old World rank of those she was supporting, a Gold Coast matron's name was dropped either casually or completely, so the cottages had become as important as the country clubs in which one

50

was enrolled.

Many of the European visitors were not really millionaires. Most were, in fact, penniless, having fled their homelands with only their clothing and jewelry. They were mindful, however, of the strange American awe of royalty; and, they understood society's need for publicity. Moving from one estate to another, they began living, totally at their hosts' expense, more grandly than they'd ever dreamed.

Numerous townships and villages, named after the estates they'd replaced, began dotting the North Shore. They had their own churches and schools; hospitals and country clubs; tennis courts and golf courses—all private, all restricted to their own groups, and all resembling one another.

The new estates weren't dissimilar, either. Every main residence was far off from the road, carefully hidden by shrubbery behind iron gates, brick or stone walls, and rough-hewn wooden fences; and, were it not for an occasional mailbox along the roadside, a passing motorist would never suspect there were other humans nearby.

One of the townships was called Jericho; and, in Jericho, as throughout the rest of the North Shore, every house had a name, not an address, for that was the fashion. Jericho's largest was *Swansgarten*. It was owned by Louise and Earl Asheley.

The Asheleys had entered the business world through the unlikely portals of an illegal still, jumping from that venture to a legitimate, but modest brewery. Timing and circumstances had favored them and, soon, Earl had widened his horizons, amassing a fortune through the acquisition of an established shipping line. But the Asheley fortune had come too quickly to command respect from New York's old money.

As with others in her situation, the fiftyish Louise Asheley had been attracted to the Gold Coast because of its publicity. Imitating the old estates people, she'd made her large fortune as evident as possible, succeeding, very often, in being more ostentatious than the original owners of the original estates;

and, while her extreme wealth had gained her entry to the area, her position within its hierarchy had never been a secure one. Certainly, she had the requisite money, but she lacked certain traditional characteristics of the elite. She had neither the formal education, nor the cultured manner, nor the family background—and these were considered a weakness in her very character.

Mr. Asheley spent his days in his Manhattan office, and, in business, he was the equal of anyone he encountered. He couldn't care less about the perplexing need for what his wife called "social standing," and the most unhappy note of his life, second only to the loss of their only child, was watching Louise's determination to be accepted by society dominate her every waking moment.

During the years, Mrs. Asheley had managed to gain a seat on numerous committees that protected the ecological balance of the surrounding areas, a noteworthy achievement for someone whose ancestors hadn't lived there. She was known for her luxurious parties and her philanthropical works. She was invited to most of the charity fund-raisers—but still, never to society's houses, and never to its daughters' weddings; and, for this ostracism, she'd payed a heavy emotional toll, tottering often on the brink of alcoholism and a nervous breakdown.

Earl Carter Asheley rested forlornly in his rocking chair, remembering how excited Louise had been when she'd bought it for him. It had been the first piece of furniture they'd purchased as newlyweds. Even though the other rooms at *Swansgarten* reflected opulence and wealth, this one corner sunroom was "Earl's place," and represented a simpler time in their lives. There was the heavy oak coffee table; there, the antique cuspidor which she'd found during one of their Pennsylvania trips; there, in the corner, was the old trophy case that she'd filled with his model ships. The window bench had cracked while being delivered; but, he'd convinced Louise that it added to its rustic quality. There was the great Oriental

52

rug that she'd been so proud of; the cast iron gas lamps; the specially-made bay window. There were two entrances to his study, one from the upper foyer, and one from their bedroom. Now, with bated breath, he stared at the bedroom door until the physician emerged.

The doctor shook his head, smiled benevolently, and said, "I'm sorry, Earl. To a point, I could help her if it were only a medical problem, but it's not. At the risk of sounding very unprofessional, my opinion is that Louise's ailment stems from her not being able to face facts. Look, we both know the hell she's gone through all these years with these snobs. And, of course, when your son and his wife died . . . well . . ."

"Yes," Earl answered. "That hasn't helped the situation at all, has it?"

"No. Naturally, if you want a second opinion, I would be happy to give another physician her complete medical history."

"No. That won't be necessary. You know us better than we know ourselves. I won't need another opinion. I think that I knew the problem all along, but just needed to have it confirmed."

"Well," the physician replied, "she'll be better again in a day or two. You'll see; she'll come out of this again. In the meantime, just keep humoring her. There isn't much else that can be done."

"Thank you. I appreciate you coming all the way out here to see her again."

The two men shook hands and the doctor left Earl alone with his thoughts. "My poor Louise," he said, knowing that, during these times, she couldn't understand much of anything, "my poor Louise. How hard you try. Not one of those spoiled, worthless women is as fine as you."

The woman smiled innocently at her husband and refilled her snifter with brandy.

Earl returned to his newspapers, then to his business papers, which he'd grown accustomed to bringing home with him from the office.

It had been a long, busy week of meetings with lawyers, salesmen, accountants, bookkeepers, printers; and, as he stared at the batch of correspondence on his desk, he grew disgusted with the seemingly unending details awaiting his attention. "Who needs it?" he asked himself, looking at the reports. "Who needs it?" He pushed the papers aside and napped.

The sad state of Louise Asheley's mental well-being was the subject of many discussions between her concerned husband and his business manager and close friend, Aleksey Kostenov. Aleksey owned the adjacent estate. It was known as *The Walls of Jericho;* many people called it *The Walls.*

The selection and purchase of the sprawling, inland property had been negotiated by Louise Asheley even before Aleksey Kostenov had reached this country. He would have preferred a small apartment close to his office in Manhattan; but, wishing not to offend the well-meaning woman, who'd obviously gone to a great deal of trouble, he'd pretended to be enchanted by the place. Money, he'd reasoned, was of no consequence; his new position paid him more than he could ever spend. Also, the long commutation between the estate and Manhattan—(he and Earl would ride in together on the railroad)—gave the two businessmen some uninterrupted time to read their daily mail from Sr. Barragatto.

Shortly after North American Distributors had been established, though, Sr. Barragatto had died. Upon the elder's death, Aleksey's former pupil, the young Tullio, assumed leadership. Almost all directives originated from Tullio Barragatto from his office in Milan.

Like his father before him, Tullio Barragatto held Aleksey Kostenov and Earl Asheley in high esteem. Nevertheless, there were certain matters which he could not trust to them. Not only were they from a different generation, but, more important, they were of a different ethnic background; he couldn't expect them to understand his methods or reasoning. So, to guard the Barragatto interests in the United States even further, he sent his cousin, Salvatore Crispino, to join them. This decision proved fruitful: with Aleksey Kostenov, the patient coordinator; Earl Asheley, the experienced American; and Salvatore Crispino, the young, legal mind, North American Distributors, under Tullio Barragatto's visionary guidance, had soon emerged as a small empire, spanning the Atlantic. It imported the *Barragatto* wines, but it also established vineyards in New York State and called its domestic version *Piccolo Villaggio*. It expanded its breweries, opening warehouses in several states; and it refurbished its steamships until they were considered the most luxurious afloat. Then, diversifying further, it became one of the pioneers in the tourism industry; and, further still, it entered the publishing business. It was the best combination of old and new world; and it was mighty because its principals were bound by mutual respect and bloodlines, and not by written contracts.

Tullio Barragatto and Earl Asheley each owned forty percent of North American Distributors. The remainder was divided between Aleksey Kostenov and Salvatore Crispino. Each man was satisfied with the arrangement, and, had he not been, it would most certainly have been changed.

Then, back to back, came World War I and Prohibition. With the first, international shipping and tourism virtually ceased. With the second, the breweries and stateside vineyards were closed. To Asheley and Kostenov, it appeared that heaven, itself, was testing them. Only their publishing house wasn't affected; and, on this one facet of their operation, they'd focused most of their attention.

When the war ended, the ships and tourists again began moving. The elders were content: they were willing to settle for half a pie.

This wasn't true, though, for Tullio and Salvatore; for they had a problem they couldn't share with their associates. For them, a different kind of war was just beginning. And this was the real reason why Tullio, when finally released from Guidonia, could not permit his wife and children to return to Orvietto.

Chapter Two

The Walls was far grander than Tullio's ancestral home in Orvietto. For one thing it was surrounded by 500 acres. True, the Barragattos owned more land than in Orvietto, but it was all covered with vineyards. This land seemed to have no other purpose but to be beautiful and to amuse Magdalena. She had come in late September, in time to see the many shades of green change abruptly to wonderful tints of gold and flame and red.

The only shadow on her happiness was knowing that her beloved little Stefano was growing up with someone else. She prayed that she would have the strength to continue this charade.

The huge Georgian mansion was grander than the finest palace in Venice. She and Aleksey were met at the door by a tall man in black. Aleksey explained that he was Marcello, her butler. Lined up behind him were several dark haired young women, all in uniform and white lace caps. They lowered their eyes shyly as Aleksey introduced each one: Angela, Sophia, Claudia and Monica. They would be her housemaids. Finally, a stout gray haired woman of about fifty emerged. She smiled at Magdalena broadly as Aleksey introduced her: Lena, the cook.

Magdalena said a few words to each of her new employees, then Aleksey nodded to Marcello who dismissed them, then excused himself. Aleksey explained that she would relay all her orders to Marcello, who would supervise the others.

"They all speak Italian," Magdalena said suddenly.

"Of course," Aleksey smiled. "As does their mistress."

It was kind and thoughtful of him to engage an Italian-speaking staff, but she must learn English as quickly as possible. Who knew how long she might be here?

"I've arranged for a tutor who will be brought to the house daily. He arrives tomorrow at ten. Is that all right?"

"Oh, Aleksey, you think of everything!" she said and kissed him on the cheek.

The old man colored slightly. "I'm glad to do anything to make you comfortable," he said. "Of course, your teacher isn't American. I imported him from London. It's impossible to learn English from an American, you know."

"Tell me, Aleksey, what are our neighbors like?" Magdalena had caught a brief glimpse of *Swansgarten* as they drove up toward *The Walls*.

"You'll know soon enough," he answered. "We've been invited there to dinner tonight. They've been asking about you and Rebecca.

"You'll like them very much. Nice people. As a matter of fact, you might even know their grandson's nurse. She's from your village . . . and she spoils that child as much as they do. I can't blame them, though. He's as smart as a whip, that Carter."

"Carter?" Magdalena repeated, disbelieving her own ears. "Benton and Anita's son?"

Aleksey nodded. "Yes. Oh, I'd forgotten . . . you know them. Yes, their son."

Something warned her not to scream, not to tip her hand. But as sure as she was alive, young Carter Asheley was dead.

She'd seen the body herself, that awful night when it all came crashing down. When a drunken Benton Asheley had

58

fought with Tullio and her father. He'd killed his own son, then poor Mikel stabbed him in self defense. Before dawn she and Tullio had to flee to Orvietto. She never saw her father again. He and his gypsy clan were wiped out and everyone told her that included her baby, Stefano. But she never believed that. Only a few months before she left Italy a gypsy had renewed her hopes. *He is alive,* the old woman assured her. *You will be together soon.*

That evening Magdalena could barely contain her nervousness. She still had no idea what she would do if her suspicions proved correct. Could she confide in Aleksey? Would he believe her or would he dismiss her as a hysterical woman. She missed Tullio more than ever. He would know what to do.

Although *Swansgarten* was the adjoining estate, the great houses were more than ten miles apart and so they were driven to dinner by Aleksey's chauffer. A butler led them into a stately mahogany panelled library where the Asheleys awaited them. Magdalena's first impression was of a handsome white-haired couple. Earl Asheley resembled his late son, but his face reflected more kindness and character than Benton's ever had. He could be a good friend, she told herself. Mrs. Asheley was another matter. She fluttered nervously, making sure that they were all comfortable but never relaxed for a moment. Magdalena pitied her.

After the butler had served drinks and disappeared, Louise Asheley spoke. "I understand you knew my son Benton and his wife."

"Yes," Magdalena acknowledged. "They lived in a villa near my farm in Lombardy."

"Then you must know our grandson Carter." Louise rang for the butler and instructed him to bring the boy and his nurse.

In a matter of seconds they were standing in the doorway. Magdalena recognized the old nurse immediately. A tiny gray-haired woman in black, her large brown eyes wide with surprise and fear as she recognized Magdalena. But she was speechless, and had been all her life. She gripped her young charge's hand tightly. Magdalena stared at the little boy. Just as she had feared and hoped and dreamed. It was her Stefano.

"Mama!" he cried and she stood up. Then the room began to spin and went dark.

When Magdalena awakened, she was still in the library, but she was lying on a leather sofa. She was alone with Louise Asheley who held a cold compress to her forehead.

"There," she said. "That feels better, doesn't it?"

Magdalena sighed. "What happened? Where's Stefano?"

"Don't worry, dear," Louise said. "He's safe. My, we've had a lot of excitement for one day."

"I don't understand," Magdalena insisted. "How did Stefano get here? Why are you calling him Carter?"

"Your friend Mr. Kostenov brought him to us a few months ago. He honestly seemed to believe the boy was our grandson."

"And you knew he wasn't?"

Louise's eyes looked sadder than ever. "I wanted to believe that he was. But Anita, my son's wife, had written to me. She confided that our grandson was—not right."

"So you knew."

"I pretended I didn't for Earl's sake. He seemed so happy to have a grandson. I couldn't bring myself to tell him the truth."

Magdalena only needed a second to think. "Louise," she said. "Stefano and my daughter Rebecca have no grandparents. Won't you still be theirs?"

The old woman's eyes filled with tears. "You're very kind, Magdalena. But what will we tell Earl?"

"Let me talk to him. I'll think of something."

Louise left and a few minutes later Earl Asheley entered. He looked concerned.

"Are you all right, young lady?" he asked. "You gave us quite a scare."

"I had quite a shock."

"I'm sorry about that," he said and then explained how he

60

had learned the truth and why he had kept it from his wife.

Magdalena was touched. Each of the Asheleys had known the truth, but had tried to protect the other. They must love each other very much, she thought.

Without betraying the confidence of either one, she managed to convince both Louise and Earl Asheley that each would be able to adjust to the news that Carter Asheley was really Stefano Disanti, soon to be Stefano Disanti Barragatto. And the poor mute nurse looked as though a huge weight had been lifted from her shoulders. Aleksey Kostenov took a little longer.

That evening, after dinner, they were driven home to *The Walls* and Magdalena cradled a sleeping Stefano in her arms.

"I'm so ashamed, Magdalena," Kostenov repeated. "Can you and Tullio ever forgive me? How could I allow myself to be deceived?"

"You meant well," she assured him. "I know who did this. My first husband's cousin, Rosalia Disanti. She was after the farm Stefano inherited from Tomaso. It was simple greed."

And in time, she told herself, Rosalia would pay. That was the gypsy way.

In the months that followed, Magdalena delighted Aleksey Kostenov with the changes she wrought at *The Walls*. Before she came, the huge house had seemed dark and gloomy; now sunlight filled every room.

She had discovered a greenhouse on the grounds and all through the winter every table top had at least one china bowl of fresh flowers. Usually roses, he noticed. She was especially fond of roses.

"The gypsies believe that roses mean good fortune," she told him. And although Aleksey, who had seen many strange things in his travels, had never met a fair-skinned, red-haired gypsy girl before, he had to agree that the roses had brought him good fortune. For the first time since losing his beloved Anna, he felt as though he had a real home.

Tullio had allowed her almost unlimited funds to create a new home at *The Walls* and she took full advantage. She bought what she liked, where she liked: a gold and green malachite clock at an auction, a huge Tintoretto and a small Rembrandt at a Manhattan art gallery, two comfortable over-stuffed sofas at a modest store in the town of Jericho. She had covered them in fashionable green chintz and placed them in the drawing room. Aleksey Kostenov sat on one of them as he surveyed the room. Salvatore Crispino, Tullio's cousin, was waiting for them in the library, but he wanted a few minutes alone with Magdalena first.

The walls of the drawing room had been painted a soft rose color and the elaborate moldings were in contrasting cream. Most of the parquet floor was covered with a pale green Aubusson carpet. Heavy rose velvet draperies at the window had been pulled back to allow the last bit of afternoon sun to shine in. Plump red roses in Sheffield vases sat on the carved marble mantle over the fireplace where a fire was burning.

She has created a real home, he told himself. He tried not to think about how many years it had been since he had enjoyed a real home. Not since Anna. He heard Magdalena's footsteps and turned to greet her.

She was wearing a fashionable new "little black dress" and pearl and diamond clips shone at her ears. Her thick red hair was pulled back loosely and caught with a tortoise shell comb. Aleksey was relieved that so far she had resisted the fashionable new bobbed hair.

"You're the queen of *The Walls*," he told her.

She smiled. "You have that strange look on your face again," she said. "What in the world are you thinking about when you get that look?"

"Nothing special. I just like to look at you. I'm happy that you're here. I used to be lonely."

He was suddenly embarrassed. He wasn't used to exposing his feelings. It wasn't his way.

"Thank you, Aleksey. That's very nice of you. That's really

very nice. I'm glad we met, too."

"You do like living here, don't you?" he asked her.

"Who wouldn't? If only . . ."

"I know, Magdalena. I know. You miss him." He didn't say anything else, because whenever they talked about Tullio she would cry. He didn't want to see her cry this evening. She looked too pretty this evening.

"But, it's been so long, Aleksey. It's been seven months. I can't stand it anymore. What's wrong? You promised they'd get him out by now. What's gone wrong? You were all so sure you could buy that major. What's gone wrong?"

"These things take time, Magdalena. If you try to rush matters like this by saying or doing something hasty or foolish, you stand to lose everything. You've got to be patient. You've got to trust his cousins. They won't let him down. They'll get him out."

"You ask me to be patient. I am patient. I pick daisies and play children's games and make up dinner menus and have lunch with Louise and redecorate rooms and take English lessons. I am patient. But—God!—Aleksey! Tullio's not patient! And, the longer he's in Guidonia, the worse it will be. He'll blow up! He's the one who will do something foolish or hasty—not us—if we don't get him out of there fast! Then, he'll be in even more trouble!"

The two were so engrossed in their discussion that they'd both forgotten Salvatore. He'd heard Magdalena's outburst and was now standing in the doorway, a tall, good looking man, not quite as handsome as Tullio. "You make it sound as though we're not doing anything," he complained. "As though we've forgotten all about him. We're doing the best we can, as fast as we can. We can't do anything better than that, so there's no use in your carrying on like this. It doesn't help matters. It just puts everybody more on edge."

"I forgot you were here," she said.

"That's obvious," he snapped.

"Well, what *are* you doing?" she asked him. "Nobody tells

63

me anything anymore. If you have something in mind, I have the right to know. He's my husband!" She turned back toward Aleksey. "First, you were all so positive it would take only a few weeks . . . then, two months, at the most."

"Please, Magdalena, just be patient," Aleksey said.

She persisted: "You don't really have a plan, do you, Salvatore? You found out you can't buy that major . . . right? Is that what happened?"

"All right, Magdalena," he said, "you'll get the truth."

There was something in the lawyer's 'All right, Magdalena,' that froze her. "What happened?" she asked him, almost inaudibly. "What's gone wrong?"

Salvatore answered: "You. You and your stupid letters."

She turned toward Aleksey, but he said nothing.

Salvatore continued: "Because of you, we're at a standstill."

"What do you mean? Aleksey, what is he talking about?"

Magdalena had written her husband often, at least twice a week at the beginning. Meaning to bolster his spirits, she'd once mentioned that, no matter what the major demanded, they would pay; that, because of this, they would be together again very soon. Salvatore reminded her of this. He ended: "How could you do such a thing? What's wrong with you?"

She didn't understand. She was blank. She spread open her hands and turned up her palms. "What's wrong with encouraging him not to give up hope?" She looked from one man to the other. What were they saying? What had she done? "What's wrong with that?"

"You put it in writing!" He glared at her, then looked up at the ceiling. "How could you do such a thing? How?"

Her heart started beating faster. She was afraid to understand.

Aleksey said: "That's enough, Salvatore."

But the attorney continued: "The mail is censored, Magdalena!"

She couldn't talk. She closed her eyes and crossed her arms tightly in front of her.

There could be nothing gained by telling her what trouble that letter had caused; the information would grieve her, but the harm couldn't be undone. Therefore, Aleksey and Salvatore had agreed to keep silent about it. Now, the elder was seething; and, the two began arguing about it as though she weren't even there. One was accusing the other of trying to punish her. The other was furious, saying that he'd kept quiet long enough, and that, if it hadn't been for her stupidity, his cousin might be free by now.

"When my brother Ernesto walked into his office, the major had the letter on his desk. His clerk had already blacked out the sentences, but he'd told him what they'd said. And, only God knows how many other people he told. The man is scared half to death now. We can't get near him."

"What about the bigamy charge? Can't you threaten him with that?' she asked Aleksey.

"No. The wife in Rome died. The one that's left won't prosecute. She's not the type."

"How do you know?" she asked.

"We know!" Salvatore answered. "We know! Just take my word for it. We've already looked into it."

The impact of what she'd just learned kept coming and going. One moment, it was visible and overwhelming and heavy like a mountain; the next, it had no reality at all. It was like the pain-numbness-pain that comes right after a hammer-blow. There was shock. There was guilt. There was Salvatore's incredible question: How could you do such a thing? She said, "Oh, God! What I did!" and this is when the men stopped arguing.

Salvatore said, "I'm just as much to blame as you are. I should have told you all the mail is censored. How could you know? I just never thought of mentioning it." He took one of her hands in his. "I'm sorry, Magdalena, but the truth is that it looks pretty bad."

"There's no amount he'll accept?"

"He's scared. You have to understand the military mind.

Look, all his adult life, this major has had all his work planned for him by his superiors and by army manuals. He's never really had to do any of his own thinking. When he's not following some higher-up's orders, he's following the book. Not only that, but he has no trade, no real education, and no sense of business. He doesn't know how to do a single thing, and he couldn't make a living, outside the army. He's strictly a middle-ranking military man. He's good for nothing else; and, I'm sure he must know that.

"Can you picture all that must have gone through his mind when that clerk of his brought in the letter? There he was, with his whole life on one piece of paper. He's only a couple of years away from retirement, and he could probably see his whole pension flying out the window. That's the most important thing in his life, you know—his pension."

Magdalena tried not to hear what he was saying; but she had to—just as much as she didn't want to believe what she'd done; but she had to. In a little while, she left them and went to her room.

She thought of all the letters she'd written Tullio. They'd been personal, with words from her heart to his. They'd been lover's words, not meant for others to read. How horrible, strangers reading her feelings. How embarrassing. No wonder his letters had been so few. No wonder they'd sounded like he was writing to a younger sister. No wonder they'd been so matter-of-fact. He'd known others read what he wrote to her. Everybody had known, except her.

What's wrong with me? At a time like this, all I'm thinking of is my own embarrassment. That's not what's important right now.

She wondered if Tullio knew what she'd caused. If that particular letter had eventually been given to him. If he'd guessed what had been blacked out. But, she didn't know how to right the wrong she'd done him. During the next few months, she wrote as though to a brother; and, only at the end, would she pen: I love you and I miss you very much. Salvatore and Aleksey kept urging her not to give up hope; but, they

66

never offered her any, either. Soon, she no longer could think of a thing to write.

In mid-autumn, a year after she'd arrived at *The Walls of Jericho,* she was watching the gardener seed the lawn. It suddenly dawned on her: *The soil!* Security! What's more secure than a farm? A place to retire to! A roof over your head in your old age! She shouted it out to Aleksey.

"I don't know, Magdalena," he answered. "I don't know."

"Aleksey! If you don't try this, I swear I'll sail tomorrow and offer it to him, myself!"

"Don't even think of such a thing. You wouldn't even know how to approach the man. You'd wind up getting yourself arrested." He refused to listen to her anymore.

Then, she shouted it to Salvatore.

He said: "Magdalena . . . the farm . . . that might be the answer . . . Stefano's farm . . . that might work. That just might work!"

She screamed and stamped her feet and laughed. She was positive he'd accept a farm. She'd sail for Genoa at once. She'd go directly to Guidonia. She'd take him to Lombardy. She'd show him the fields. She'd bring him into the barn. He'd see the livestock. She'd show him the house. She'd light the fire for him.

"No," Salvatore told her. "No. Not that way. You stay out of this. I'll get in touch with Benedetto. He'll get to work on it. Is there anyone on the farm now?"

"There is someone," she answered, "my first husband Tomaso's cousin, Rosalia. She tried to steal the farm from my son and me." Magdalena smiled as she realized she could not only save Tullio, but also have her revenge on Rosalia. "The farm is legally Stefano's. She sent him away and took the farm for herself. She doesn't even know I've found him. She probably thinks that I've forgotten all about it. But, that's Stefano's land! And, I'm his mother. And I can sell whatever belongs to him! Right?"

* * *

More than a month later, Salvatore Crispino's letter arrived in Orvietto; but, Benedetto was in the Milan office at the time, so it waited for two more weeks for his return. When his servant handed it to him, he knew, immediately, that it must be important and personal; otherwise, his brother would have sent it to the office, and his secretary would have read it. He could almost feel its urgency as he slit it open. His grin became wider as he read it. . . . *it's still Disanti land. . . . and her name is Rosalia Disanti, or was, if she hasn't married by now . . . and the major's parents live at the southernmost tip of Calabria. . . . His father was a postman and has a very small pension. . . . a transfer of ownership, from Stefano Disanti to the father . . . You can even put it under his wife's name!*

The following morning, Benedetto left for Turin. He spoke to the major's wife. "What's one prisoner more or less?" he asked her. "If you talk your husband into accepting the farm, you can be comfortable for the rest of your life!" Then, he went to Calabria and spoke with the old postman. "Every year, your rent increases. Soon, you won't even be able to afford living in this apartment. If you can convince your son to take the farm, all your problems would go up in smoke." He never even had to go to Guidonia. The major came to him, in Orvietto. The transfer was effected. It had required several months for all the transfer papers and deeds to be finalized. But, it was done. He could expect that nothing would go wrong. He returned to Milan and sent a message to Genoa because an Asheley steamship was sailing that day. The ship's captain brought it to the wireless room. In mid-ocean, it was forwarded to another ship closer to New York, and then to the office of North American Distributors. Earl Asheley read it first and showed it to Salvatore Crispino who took it in to Aleksey Kostenov. Aleksey brought it home that evening and Magdalena found it on her dinner plate. It said:

PROPERTY TRANSFER SUCCESSFULLY COMPLETED. NOW WE MUST WAIT UNTIL NOVEMBER WHEN THEY TAKE POSSES-

SION AND MOVE IN. THEN ALL GATES SWING OPEN. LETTER
FOLLOWS.

She cried. That weekend, she gave her first dinner party. It
wasn't the regular Gold Coast type of party. There were only
Louise and Earl Asheley, Salvatore and his wife and children,
Aleksey, Rebecca, Stefano and herself. It was a very happy
party, though, and the food was good; and with the food, they
drank some *Barragatto Secco/Bianco* that had been smuggled in
on an Asheley ship.

On Christmas Eve, she received a letter from her husband.
He was in Orvietto. He asked her to stay where she was. He
would come to *The Walls of Jericho*. He'd be sailing in two
more weeks.

Chapter Three

There had been very little contact, lately, between Tullio Baragatto and the Crispino brothers; so, when a guard ordered Tullio to follow him to the chaplain's small office, he had no idea why he was being summoned. The only thing he could think of was that there might have been a death in the family; the chaplain was going to break the bad news. He knocked, and waited for permission to enter. He was surprised that the guard left him there. This was against the rules. No prisoner was left unescorted outside his cell. He knocked again. The door swung open.

"Let's go," Benedetto told him. He had a wide smile on his face and was holding a suit of clothes and an overcoat.

"Benedetto!"

"Well, let's go!"

"Where?"

"Home. We're going home."

"What?"

"You heard me. It's all over! You're out, as of now!"

"Out?"

"Yes! Out! But, I think you'd better put these on first. I hope they still fit you."

He'd thought of this day. He'd imagined it. He'd dreamed of it. He'd pictured himself jumping with joy! Shouting! Throwing his uniform out the window! Yet, here it was: *the* day—and he could barely move. He was dumbfounded. He was almost shaking.

Benedetto understood. "Come on," he said. "Let's get you out of that uniform."

"No, I can do it."

Benedetto wanted to yell at him: Believe it! Believe it!—but he didn't say anything. He only watched, very quietly; and it hurt him to see how awkwardly and how slowly his cousin was shedding the dark prison clothes he'd been living in for more than a year. Suddenly, he shouted: "Damn you! You're free!"

Tullio was so surprised by the young man's outburst that he started to laugh.

"Let's go!"

Benedetto led the way out of the little office and through the empty corridors.

"How do you know your way around in here so well?"

"You'd never believe how many times I've been here to see that major. I know this place like the back of my hand."

They passed some guards playing pinochle and, because none of the guards gave them a second look, Tullio asked: "Did everybody know I was getting out today except me? Nobody's stopping us. Nobody's asking any questions."

They crossed the front yard. It was sinking in. He was getting out. It was any moment, now. *Today! Now!* He started to laugh again, at first, slowly and alone; then, Benedetto joined him, and the laughter grew.

They got into Benedetto's car, and Tullio said: "Oh, my God! It's for real!"

Benedetto kept laughing also. Tullio knew that one reason was because of his baldness and that, had it been Ernesto who'd come to fetch him, he would be hearing plenty about it by now. He didn't care, though. It was great to hear Benedetto's laughter. It always had been. Now, it was music. *Musetta's*

71

Waltz. It was beautiful.

"Stop the car! I have to drive!" he shouted, and Benedetto slammed down on the brakes so fast that they skidded and he almost lost control of the car.

Tullio sat behind the wheel now, his own master for the first time in years. He stared at the wheel; fondled it. He sucked in an easy-sounding deep breath; maybe, a soft gasp. Then, he turned the ignition key and pressed very gently on the accelerator . . . once . . . twice . . . then, again . . . and Benedetto became silent—he mustn't spoil this moment; not these first precious, irreplacable seconds when he knew the freedom feeling was settling in and taking hold inside of every artery. If he were to speak, he'd kill the electric. He locked his door and braced one hand against the dashboard; and Tullio shifted gears and howled like an Indian. Then, they bolted from the little town of Guidonia like they'd been shot from a cannon.

Tullio headed due east, towards the Tiber, and didn't slow down until they had to pass over a wooden suspension bridge that didn't look like it could support their weight. Even Benedetto sighed with relief when they reached firm ground again. From the bridge, they followed the river north, riding along its bank, and avoiding the heavily-travelled main roads. He was driving quite slowly now, the first shock-wave of freedom having burned itself out.

"Do you want me to drive for a while?" Benedetto asked.

"Yes, all right."

They'd done almost no talking until now. It would have been useless. Neither could have concentrated on what was being said. Shortly, Tullio said: "I keep thinking this is some kind of dream, and that I'll wake up on that bunk again." He shook his head. He wasn't dreaming.

Benedetto didn't reply. He just grinned and offered his cousin a cigarette.

"Two years," Tullio continued, "two years. Two in there is like ten anyplace else."

"I know," Benedetto told him. He didn't say, but he'd heard, om others, about Guidonia. "I know."

"Why did it take two years?" he asked Benedetto. "Why so
ng?"

"No matter what we offered the major," his cousin replied,
e wouldn't take it."

"What did it finally cost?"

"Your wife's farm."

"Oh?"

"But, it was all her idea. Salvatore wrote to me, saying that
e major is probably afraid that, if he were to accept money
om us, we might trick him in some way and cause him to lose
s pension. She wanted us to offer him her farm. We did, and
was put under his parents' name. He can go live there in a
uple of years, when he retires. It was a good idea. It was the
nly thing he would go along with."

"That meant a lot to her, that farm."

Benedetto shrugged.

"Was there any trouble when they took it over?"

"A little, at first. There was some woman living there
lready. We had to kick her out. She didn't belong there, did
he?"

"No," Tullio answered, "she didn't belong there."

"I felt kind of sorry for her," Benedetto continued,
"because she'd already lost so much, the poor woman. First,
er house in town had burned down . . . and then, her
usband had left her . . . and then . . ."

But, Tullio Barragatto was no longer listening to his cousin.
He was thinking about his wife.

During the long two years at Guidonia, he'd often thought: I
know I still love her, but am I still *in love with her?* It was the
omance in their love that he'd wondered about, not the
everlastingness of it, because of that, he'd always been
ure . . . at least, from his own end.

He'd asked himself, also: Am I just blowing up her memory?
He'd realized how easy it is, and how natural, to idealize a
woman he hadn't seen for so long. It would be so simple, so

matter-of-fact, especially for an inmate in Guidonia, where a happy memory could be a life saver, and where fantasy was the only sure escape.

Then, there'd been the worst doubt of all: I don't know how long I'll be in here. Neither does she. Will she still want me when I get out of here? Really want me? What if they can't get me out? What if I have to serve the whole twenty years? How old would she be, then? Thirty-eight? Would she wait for me for twenty years? Could she? Could she even remember what I look like? What is she doing now?

It was raining very hard when they reached Orvietto, and it was colder than usual. There was almost nobody in the streets. "What do they know about me around here? Where do they think I've been all the while?"

"We told them that, after you got out of the army, you had to spend some time in a hospital; and that, from that hospital, you went to another one up in Switzerland."

"Switzerland?" His Crispino cousins had always been very inventive.

"For your lungs." Benedetto shrugged again. "Clear air, right?"

"You mean, I'm supposed to have been in hospitals for the past two years?"

"Well . . . you can say that, after you got out of the hospital in Switzerland, you decided to go travelling for a while."

"Is that what you told people? I just want to make sure we all have the same story."

"That's what I told them."

He grinned and shook his head, imagining all the covering up they must have been doing these past two years. "Switzerland, hah?" was all he said. He thought, also, of all the trips they must have made to the major's office. He wanted, very much, to say "thank you," but he couldn't, because that would embarrass Benedetto. He knew his cousin very well.

They drove more slowly now, because the cobblestones were wet and very slippery, and because the streets were narrow.

They passed the town hall; he noticed that its facade had recently been painted and that it had new shutters on its windows. They passed all the little shops around which he'd hovered as a boy; the proprietors' names were still the same. It was good, Orvietto. It was home. It hadn't changed.

All was as he expected when they reached his house. His aunts were waiting to welcome him back. Also, there were Ernesto and his wife and new daughter, and Benedetto's wife. Even the servants (whose families had served the Barragattos for generations) appeared individually and in small groups, spontaneously, each expressing his greetings. He felt the warmth of their genuine fondness for him, and they, his. There was no pretense; they liked each other.

He was very glad to be home. Despite the happy reunion, however, he wished he could be alone for a while . . . but, that would be too much to ask . . . and, anyway, he would have lots of time for solitude after today.

Orvietto exercised a special magic over Tullio. He couldn't imagine how anyone might ever want to leave it. There was a gentle antiquity about the place, a durability that tolerated today and defied tomorrow, but in a nice way: young women in chemise dresses and modern hairdos climbed ancient steps that long dead Romans had carved out of solid rock. There was a blending of classic paganism with the Church of Rome: remnants of Etruscan pottery and tombs painted and slashed into the hills that surrounded its cathedral, a bronze domed and spired building so beautiful that it was known to many as the Golden Lily. Everything about Orvietto was, at once, both old and new—ox-drawn carts shared its narrow streets with American Fords; and, old men and their grandchildren still walked and talked and worked together.

Orvietto is wine country. During harvest, the juice of the grape escapes from its orchards and valleys and knows its way to town. There, it slides in between the cobblestones and follows its fancy up and down every alley and piazza until the streets are tinted pink. The morning mist greets it then, and mixes with it, and all the air is filled with a rose-colored mist that lingers until noon, when it rises and hovers among the spires of the Golden Lily. The Angelus bells toll at noon, and the villagers stop, cross themselves, and look up at the pink cloud before they stop for lunch. The cafes are ready by now. The tables are prepared and the awnings are rolled out and new bottles are uncorked. Midday is very pleasant in Orvietto; it stretches through most of the afternoon.

In a town such as this, where everyone's livelihood is somehow dependent upon the vineyards, the whole idea of what the Americans called Prohibition was mind-boggling. It wasn't only because if affected them financially; it was because it was almost unholy. That's what a law is when it interferes with a way of life: unholy.

When Prohibition was enacted in 1919 there'd been a war raging. It was almost impossible to transport any luxuries, including wine, across the ocean because the ships were needed to carry munitions; so, it was the First World War, and not Prohibition, that had earlier dipped its hand into the villagers' pockets.

In European eyes, Prohibition was such an absurd law that many refused to believe it really existed. Lots of these people decided that it was only enemy propaganda. Others presumed that both the war and the law would end within a year—or two, at the most.

The war was over now, but this strange law, this Prohibition, still hung over them. It was robbing them of their most lucrative customer, the American market. It was hurting them very badly—not only money-wise: some of them were getting killed because of it.

Italy's organized criminal element, seeing the door that Prohibition had opened, took the advantage that was too obvious and enticing to be ignored. They pounced on the major wine growers, trying to force them into the illegal traffic of their product on American shores. When certain of the wine owers refused to deal with these criminals, their families ere threatened, many of their vineyards were destroyed, and ores of their workers were attacked and frightened away. The olence had already forced several of the major wine men to nd their families abroad, far away from the dangers at home.

Within a few days of his return to Orvietto, Tullio was ought up to date on all of these matters.

"You see," his cousin Benedetto told him, "how unwise it ould be for you to bring back Magdalena and the children? ther men are sending their families away . . . and here you e, thinking of doing just the opposite! Their safety would be sed as a weapon against you. Soon, you'd become so afraid for ieir lives that you would have to cooperate. How could you atch over them twenty-four hours a day? Keep them with ostenov for a while. At least, they're safe. Nobody knows iey're there."

"Where have you told people they're living?" he asked.

"In Switzerland."

"Switzerland, again," he said, and smirked. "Let me think bout it. I have to think about it."

He remembered now. Carmine Pace, a man who Tullio knew vas working for Italian based crime figures, had left Orvietto or New York upon the ratification of Prohibition. There, he'd pproached North American Distributors, offering to buy heir operation for an exceptionally high price. He'd even said hat the principals could remain working in their present ositions, and that the transfer of ownership would be a silent ne. From what he'd thought would be his death cell, Tullio aad written to New York, advising them to oppose Pace. While n Guidonia, he'd assumed that Pace hadn't completely orsaken his mission; however, he had no idea that the ituation had become so grave. He was sure that there was a connection between Mr. Carmine Pace's offer and the trouble n Orvietto.

"Let me think about it," he said again. "I have to think about it."

North American Distributors had three bases of operation in Italy: the vineyards and cellars in Orvietto, the central headquarters in Milan, and a branch office at the port of Genoa. Tullio spent some time in each place, working from just past dawn through late evening. Afterwards, he called several meetings with his cousins, managers and clerical administrators. He told them that he would be sailing to New York and that he'd be back very soon. Upon his return, he'd expect every procedure he'd denounced as slipshod to have been corrected. Also, he'd expect each innovation he'd just instituted to be fully operational. Nothing less was acceptable.

Tullio had been outwardly calm, and his wording, low-keyed, because this was his way in business; yet, whether his directives had been meant for one of the orchard foremen or for one of his own cousins, they'd been taken seriously. All knew how dissatisfied he was with what he'd found. Some of the orders he'd given Benedetto from his cell in Guidonia had not been carried out properly; for this, he blamed only Benedetto, because Benedetto was in charge of the Milan office. There had been some avoidable mishaps in the cellars; he held Ernesto responsible for this.

On the day he sailed, his cousin said: "If you continue the way you've been doing, you'll wind up like our fathers did, with ulcers. And, in the meantime, you'll drive us all crazy, too!"

He admitted, then, that he'd been extra hard on those closest to him. "I know it's no excuse for the way I've been acting," he said to Benedetto, "but, I think it's because I'm so damned angry I have to leave now. There's so much to do here. I really don't want to leave. How is it going to look to the workers in the vineyards? They see that my family isn't here. Now, they see me leaving, too. How can I expect them to stay and work, with all the violence that's going on here, if I don't even stay, myself?"

"It won't affect them," his cousin answered, "because they know you're coming back in a couple of months. I guess the only one who doesn't know is your wife." He shook his head. "She's going to be one furious woman! I don't know how you're going to keep her in New York when you tell her you're leaving again. I don't envy you that."

When the captain of the *Asheley Star* heard that his employer, Tullio Barragatto, would be sailing, he readied the most luxurious suite available. Tullio, however, was as bad a sailor as his wife, and, since the Atlantic is always choppy in the winter, he was miserably sick throughout most of the voyage. Because the water seemed to get rougher after sundown, he was never able to join the captain for dinner. After a while, the seaman—unable to fathom how anyone could be that seasick for such a long time—assumed that the accommodations, the crew, and everything else about his spanking new ship was unsatisfactory. The old salt was beside himself, and was almost sure that he was going to be fired when they docked in New York.

Once in a while, Tullio would venture out on deck and, like other freezing passengers, all wrapped in heavily fringed tartans, he'd just stare at the enormity of the dull, gray-green seemingly endless bulk of ocean. He'd watch it oozing up and down, and right and left. At this point, he'd surely believe that some of it had entered his stomach. No matter how far he tried to stretch his imagination, he could not understand what ever drove men to sea, and he cursed every wet drop of it. What aggravated him the most is that he knew he'd be repeating the trip in less than a few months.

Long after the engines finally stopped and the ship was safely in dock, he was still weak and his feet wobbly. He was flabbergasted: He held on to the railing very tightly and just stared ahead at the ocean of humanity crowding around them. It reminded him of a Sunday afternoon in St. Peter's Square;

at least, that was the only place, until now, that he'd seen so many peering faces. Most of them were looking upwards, their eyes squinting and their mouths slightly parted, as though they were awaiting a papal blessing. Amidst all the strangers, though, he immediately spied Magdalena on the pier.

It would have been difficult for anyone to miss Magdalena. She'd bought a least a dozen multi-colored balloons that looked as though they might lift her off the ground because it was such a windy day. They were flying to and fro so furiously in the gusts that others who'd come to meet the boat had to keep their distance from her. She may, very well, have been the only person on the pier who actually had three square yards of cement all to herself.

The gangplank hadn't been assembled yet, so he just stood at the railing, staring down at her. He knew that she couldn't see him from her vantage-point and that it would be useless to call out to her. She'd never hear him over all the other shouting voices. For the time being, he was content just to look at her. It seemed like hours, even though it was less than twenty minutes, before he could descend and put his feet on solid ground again.

Aleksey was several feet behind Magdalena, speaking with Salvatore. It was the men who spotted Tullio first and pointed her in his direction. Then, there was no holding her back. She ran his way, not caring how many people she rammed, and she almost flew into his arms. For several moments, she just hugged him very tightly, burying her face in his coat. She made no sound until he said, "Magda," and kissed her, and said, "Magda," again. Then, she began laughing and crying and wasn't able to talk at all. She barely spoke all the way home; but, she never let go of his hand either, not until she had to release it so he could take off his overcoat when they got into the house.

It was then, when he felt her fingers slipping from his own, that Tullio was positive that some of the questions that had plagued him since he'd last seen her had never had any basis at all.

It was her hand in his that had shattered his fears. Her fingers had squeezed and loosened around his so often that he'd known that she, too, could hardly believe they were together again. They'd even dug their nails into each other's palms—and no! they weren't dreaming.

It was her hand, just the touch of it. It had been soft and strong at the same time; and it had said all the words she couldn't because Aleksey and Salvatore were in the car with them.

His eyes were glued on her. The memory was real.

It seemed to the two of them that the long ride to *The Walls* would never end. Tullio talked most of the journey, telling Salvatore and Aleksey the latest news from the vineyards, but his eyes never left Magdalena's and he did not let go of her hand until they began moving up the driveway toward the big house.

Aleksey seemed to understand and allowed Tullio only the most perfunctory greeting to the household staff before releasing him and Magdalena to their private suite.

Tullio sighed loudly as he shut the heavy, gilded door to Magdalena's bedroom and gazed around the sumptuous furnishings, none more sumptuous than his green-eyed bride beside him.

"Very fine, Magdalena," he said with appreciation. "You've come a long way from the gypsy wagons."

Instead of answering, she stood on her tiptoes to kiss him. His lips met hers hungrily and even as they kissed his hands searched out the hooks of her dress. He opened them and the dress fell to the floor. As he had suspected, she was naked underneath. She looked at him boldly, once again the gypsy girl, and in one quick motion freed her hair from its clasp, so the fiery red mass spilled to her shoulders. His lips were on her again, when suddenly there was a knock at the door.

81

"I *told* Aleksey we wanted to be alone," she said angrily as he pulled away.

"It's for me," he explained and opened the door a crack. A downstairs maid was standing there with several green boxes.

"Signor Kostenov said you wanted these right away, sir," she said shyly.

"Thank you, Angela," Tullio said as he took the boxes from her. "And please remind Signor Kostenov that we are not to be disturbed."

He laughed as he closed the door again.

"Now, darling, we are truly alone. Let me look at you."

"Do you like what you see, Tullio?" Suddenly she was afraid she had disappointed him, but he quickly dispelled her fears.

"You are more beautiful than ever. America agrees with you." He had laid the green boxes on the bed and now stepped away. "These are all for you, Magdalena. Open them."

Eagerly she tore apart the wrappings and opened the largest box first. Inside was a dark black sable coat. She caressed the dark fur, then put it on, enjoying the feel of it against her nakedness.

"Oh, Tullio," she exclaimed. "It's beautiful."

He shrugged. "I heard that winters in New York are difficult."

A strange look darkened Magdalena's eyes. "They're difficult without you."

He said nothing, but pressed her to open the two smaller boxes. Inside one was a four strand pearl necklace, held with a ruby clasp. The other box held earrings heavily encrusted with rubies and diamonds. She gasped as she held them up to the light.

"Let me see how they look on you," he ordered and she obediently donned the necklace and earrings. He was pleased and he showed it by taking her in his arms again. His tongue and hands began to explore her body as he had so many times in his imagination during the lonely nights at Guidonia. But now it was different, now it was no pale shade of a dream he was holding, but his own flesh and blood Magdalena. Soon he was naked too and they were moving together on the floor, atop the softness of the sable coat. They had made love in many places, in the gypsy wagons, under the stars beside the banks of the Po, in his family's palatial mansion in Orvietto, but to Magdalena no hour ever seemed as precious as those they spent that night atop that sable coat.

Chapter Four

Tullio and Magdalena spent the first couple of weeks of his visit almost entirely within *The Walls of Jericho* because the children and the estate gave them all the entertainment they needed.

Afterwards, one of the first things Tullio did was to buy a pony for Stefano. They named it Big Babbo. Babbo means "daddy" in Italian. Within days, it was following the little boy all over the grounds and once, it pushed open the screen door and made itself quite comfortable in one of the enclosed back porches. The only problem the presence of Big Babbo really caused, though, was that Stefano immediately became so attached to it that he would have temper tantrums every sundown when the animal was returned to the stable.

For Rebecca, he bought a giant dollhouse. It was large enough for her and two other little girls to play in. All of its furnishings were scaled to her size and she loved it. It was her own dreamhouse and she spent hours rearranging its furniture and carpeting over and over again.

"Let's see your closets," Tullio said to Magdalena one evening.

She thought this a rather silly request, but obliged, not

knowing what he might be up to.

As he'd expected, her wardrobe was completely familiar to him. She'd not replenished anything at all since she'd left Orvietto. He took her to Manhattan the next day and more than made up for it, because, when they finished selecting everything from riding skirts to evening gowns, they had to bring in carpenters to build larger closets. She kept asking what she could possibly do with so many clothes, and no one was more flabbergasted by the new wardrobe than Aleksey, who kept asking the same question. This stymied Tullio because, as far as he was concerned, nobody could have too many clothes; and, as his Magdalena modeled each new item, he would think of something else that might compliment it—a different kind of hat, a special jewel, a small fur collar—and would order it at once.

It was Salvatore who showed them New York. He took them to Wall Street on a Sunday morning, when the place was a virtual ghost town, and then, again, during the rush hour on Monday. The contrast left them almost speechless.

He brought them to the Stock Exchange, a huge Corinthian structure on Broad Street, where hundreds of stocks were traded. Salvatore explained that they represented shares in all kinds of business: automobiles, steel, electricity and others. From the visitor's gallery it looked like total chaos.

The spectacle opened up a whole new way of gambling, though, for Tullio, and he had a ticker tape installed in the North American Distributors office, something which dismayed Aleksey Kostenov, but fascinated Earl Asheley and Salvatore Crispino. Aleksey wasn't one for speculation and totally distrusted the stock market. He was positive that any business which had to sell shares to the public must be too shaky to invest in. He refused to have anything to do with the machine and its long, thin ribbon that clicked noisily away.

Salvatore took them to some museums, also; then, to the ballet and opera, and even to the Palace for a vaudeville show. They thrilled Magdalena because she'd never seen performances of any kind, other than in a carnival; she'd never been in a theater.

One night, he surprised even Tullio. He brought them to a speakeasy. It was expensively furnished in stark white, with dark blue carpeting. The same dark blue covered its walls in velvet. It was lit almost entirely by candlelight in the dining area; but there were other rooms devoted to dancing and entertainment, and they were aglow with huge chandeliers. Kostenov and the Asheleys were with them that evening, and, after they ate, Earl suggested they visit one of the back rooms. There was gambling in these rooms, and after less than an hour, the men left the ladies at the roulette wheel, and headed for a baccarat game at the far end of the room. Magdalena sat with Louise and a half-dozen other women. This was when the owner of the speakeasy, Mr. Carmine Pace, first saw her.

His first impression was of a young red-haired queen surrounded by ladies-in-waiting. She was wearing an evening dress of pearl-gray satin that fit her like a second skin. The top was cut quite low and he noted that she had an excellent figure. She was wearing the pearls and ruby and diamond earrings that Tullio had given her and they glittered whenever she turned her head. She was laughing and seemed to be thoroughly enjoying herself. Compared to her, Carmine Pace told himself, every other woman in the room seemed pale and lifeless.

Pace watched Magdalena for a long time through a two-way mirror that separated the casino from his private office. She was enjoying a streak of beginner's luck and was very excited. She fascinated him—not only her looks, but her manner: it was fresh—and, as much as he wanted to seek an introduction, he decided against it. This evening, there were certain people present whom he didn't want to run into; his ownership of the place was secret, and they might guess about it if he were seen coming from the private office at such an hour. He asked about her, though, and the dealer answered: "I'm sorry, Mr. Pace, but I wasn't able to find out the lady's name. All I know is that she came in with Crispino, the lawyer. She was one of his party.

I couldn't even find out if she was with him or with one of the other men in his group. But, well, you know Crispino . . ." Pace agreed. The young attorney seldom lacked the company of beautiful women. "Yes," he said, "she's probably one of his. Thank you."

At one point, Salvatore began showing them so many different places that Magdalena felt guilty. She'd never left the children to their nurse so much and she believed she was neglecting them. She asked why they couldn't go someplace where they could take the children.

"Saratoga!" Louise suggested. "We'll go to Saratoga for the season!"

Salvatore had never thought of this, but the idea was very inviting. He even talked Aleksey and Earl into joining them, and this wasn't easy, because Aleksey and Earl never took a holiday. It would really be the first vacation any of them had had for several years; and the office staff at North American Distributors was aghast because of this. Once it was announced that all the principals would be away at the same time—for two whole weeks!—some of the clerks became afraid, and were already whispering, that they must be going out of business.

Tullio heard the rumor that was running through the office. He put the clerical staff at ease and convinced them that their bosses' coming absence was really just a vacation, and nothing more . . . just a well-earned vacation. He thought the whole thing was very amusing. He could not understand Americans. "They must lie awake at night," he said, "just thinking of things to worry about. When they have no work, they worry that they might not find any tomorrow; then, when they do have work, they worry that they might not have any tomorrow. All they do is worry."

There were so many things that Tullio couldn't fathom about Americans that, after a very short while, he just stopped asking. He had more important things on his mind, anyway; his visit to New York was running short, and he still hadn't told

Magdalena that he was planning to leave again. He'd received a letter from Benedetto, and the situation in Orvietto was worsening; therefore, he'd be sailing a lot earlier than he'd anticipated. He knew how excited Magdalena was about the coming vacation in Saratoga; but, he also knew that he'd be long gone by the time they went. He'd made up his mind, this morning, that he'd break the news to her that night. After they made love, he held her in his arms and began: "Magdalena, there's something I have to talk to you about."

"Yes?"

"I have to leave. I have to go back to Orvietto."

"What! What are you talking about? Why do we have to go back?"

"Not *we*, Magda. Just me."

She stared at him as though she couldn't believe what she was hearing. "No! No! You're not going back! You just got here! You've only been here for five weeks!"

"It will only be for a little while. I promise. I'll come right back. I wouldn't leave if I didn't really have to. I swear I wouldn't."

"Then, I'm coming with you, Tullio." She gave him a weak, but hopeful, smile and he felt more guilty. "That's what I'll do. I'll come with you. We'll take the children, too, of course . . . and their nurse. They'll be just as happy over there as they are over here. That's what I'll do. I'll come with you."

"You can't, Magda. You can't come. I'm going back alone. You're staying here."

"I'll just have to get used to Orvietto again. The last time, I'll admit, I really didn't give it a chance, but this time . . ."

"You can't come, Magdalena."

". . . but, this time, everything will be fine. I'm older, now, and I'll be able to handle your servants, and I won't argue with your aunts. It will be fine. You'll see."

"Magda, please. Don't make this any harder than it is."

"I'm going with you!"

"You can't come, Magdalena."

She wished he'd raised his voice, but he hadn't. She wished, so, that there had been anger in it, but there had been none. She knew this particular sound of her husband's voice. It was the kind he used in business. It was final. She couldn't gain anything by arguing, because he wouldn't argue back. It was as though he'd written a letter . . . he'd put down what he'd had to say . . . and now, he'd sealed the envelope . . . the dialogue was finished. She started to cry—not because she thought this would make him change his mind, but because she just couldn't hold back the tears. "Tullio, if I thought, for even one second, you might be in some kind of trouble, there would be nothing that would stop me from coming with you. I'd follow you right on the ship, whether you'd like it or not."

"I know, Magda." He did. He had no doubts about this, but it was very good to hear her say it. "It's just that I have certain duties that I must attend to, and I couldn't ignore them and still respect myself."

She crossed her arms in front of her and pleaded. "But what about me? Don't you have a duty to me? I'm your wife. There are duties that go along with being a husband, aren't there?"

"I'm fully aware of that."

"No, I don't think you are," she answered. "Oh, it's not that I thought we would continue the way we've been doing . . . what with going out to so many places and things. I realize that, very soon, you would have to get down to business . . . and go to work every day . . . and go to sleep early every night so you can get up the next morning. That's not what I'm talking about. That's not the kind of duty I'm talking about. That would be asking too much . . . and anyway, it would get very boring after a while. We'd get like the people at Capits Rock . . . they've done so much, already, that they have nothing left to do. The truth is, Tullio, that your duty to me is much more than putting food on the table and clothes on my back and taking me out in the evening. Your real duty is to be with me. You have no idea how lonely I was while you were away. You have no idea how many nights I just lay awake, wishing you were next to me."

"Magda, if there were any way possible that we could be together every day and every night of our lives, I'd make sure that it would be that way. But, it isn't possible. We can't just think of ourselves and say 'the hell with everything else' and you know that."

"And, while I remain here, by myself, what will you be doing? I don't believe you'd be all alone very long."

So, that was it. His wife was jealous. That was all right. There was nothing unusual about that. That was the way wives were. You had to let them get it out of their systems. She was just being a normal, average wife. That's what all this duty business was all about. It was his duty not to be unfaithful.

"You're no different from Salvatore. I don't know how his wife puts up with him."

"I haven't gone near another woman."

"I know you haven't. You haven't had the time."

"Magdalena, I'm going back to Orvietto because I have work to do, not because of any other reason. Now, I think we should both drop this subject." He rolled over and pulled the covers over his head.

"You're right, Tullio. Let's just drop the subject. Forget about your duty to me. It won't be hard. It's just like smoking."

Suddenly he was sitting bolt upright. "You've been smoking? You? Smoking?"

"No, of course not. What do you think I am?"

"Then . . . what's just like smoking? What are you talking about?"

"It's not important. It was just a thought."

"Tell me the truth. Have you been smoking?"

"No."

He sighed impatiently. "Okay, Magdalena. Okay. I'm wide awake. Now, tell me what you're talking about. What's just like smoking? Does Louise smoke?"

"Of course she doesn't smoke." Marvelous . . . she had his

90

attention again. "I only mentioned smoking because I suddenly thought about how unhappy you must have been in Guidonia. You told me that they gave you a pack of cigarettes only once a month."

"What made you think about that now?"

"Because you've been smoking so heavily again. Just look at this room. It's filled with smoke. How did you ever manage to get along with only one pack of cigarettes a month?"

As far as she knew, that had been the worst thing about Guidonia. It was only one of the things he'd ever mentioned about the place.

"It's a funny thing about smoking," he answered. "When you first get that pack, you can't stay away from it. As long as the temptation is there, you smoke. You can't even ration yourself to make the pack last the whole month . . . usually, you go through the whole pack in a day or two. After that, the first couple of days without a cigarette are really rough."

"And then?"

"And then, it gets easier. You see, you suddenly realize that the longer you stay away the longer you can do without it. After a while, you don't even think about it. At least, not until a new month rolls by."

"You mean you never think of it? You never want a cigarette during the rest of the month?"

"No, I didn't mean exactly that. There are certain moments when, for some reason or other, the thought of smoking suddenly pops right into your head. Then, you'd do almost anything for a cigarette. Any kind . . . fresh, stale, any brand, it doesn't matter."

"Then, I guess I was right," she said. "It's just like smoking."

"What! What's like smoking?"

"Sex." She'd never said that word before. But, there!—she had said it! And, in doing so, she'd surprised herself as much as Tullio. She felt brazen, now, so she repeated it. "Sex. It must be the same thing to a woman that smoking is to a man."

91

He lit a cigarette. The hour was late to be hit with such a statement. Magdalena was a decent woman, but look how she was talking. She'd been in America too long. "Would you repeat that?" he asked her. "You said that sex is to a woman like smoking is to a man? Is that what I heard you say?"

"Yes," she replied. "That's the only way I can think of describing it. You see, when we were first separated—when you went to Guidonia, that is—I felt like you must feel when you run out of cigarettes. It was like you said: really rough. But then, it got easier; and, after a while, the desire started to grow weaker. Oh, it's not that I wanted you any less . . . it's just that, the longer you were away from me, the longer I could do without you. After a while, I didn't even think about it. . . . So, like I said before . . . forget about your duty to me. I'm sorry I even mentioned it."

It was difficult to absorb what his wife had just hinted at. No! She'd more than just hinted. He couldn't have misunderstood her. She had actually said that she'd missed sex, that she'd thought about it, and that it was his duty to make sure she got it. She'd compared him to a guard giving out a pack of cigarettes . . . and now, he was leaving, and he wouldn't be giving her any . . . and he'd be shirking his duty. That was the duty she'd been talking about. That was his duty to her. Incredible. Women didn't ever think about such a thing—let alone, admit it. It was not indecent—Magdalena could never be indecent; but, still: it just was not done! A woman did not think about sex in the same nonchalant way a man might think about a cigarette! and a woman did not want sex in the same way that a man might want a cigarette because Nature hadn't made them that way!

But, he was not only surprised by this revelation. He was a little hurt, too. She realized this, so she kissed him and said: "But, there were moments, every now and then, that I would have done almost anything for that cigarette, Tullio. But, not any old cigarette. There's only one brand for me. I can't take any substitutes. You know that, don't you?"

This made him feel a little better. Still, there was an uneasiness about him, not because he thought she could be tempted into infidelity during his absence, but because there might be a basis for it. When he sailed, one week later, the vision of her looking up at him from the pier haunted him for a while. He'd jokingly left a pack of cigarettes under her pillow; he'd find it that night, wrapped in a note that said: Because I love you.

Before the giant vessel was out of American waters, he was steeped in his papers. There was a great deal to prepare before he got home.

During the prior year, 1919, as a result of postwar economic unrest, there had been a series of strikes in Italy. There had been, by official count, 316 industrial strikes during May, alone; and, a great many of them had hurt North American Distributors. In the turmoil, open fighting had broken out between the Socialists and Communists on one side and the Fascists on the other. Because of this, Fascism had become the avowed champion of conservatism and its leader, Mussolini, was amassing more support and popularity by the day. Hundreds of left-wingers had been killed by his ruthless, better-armed squads who were now uniformed and recognized throughout the country. Even a few American newspapers were starting to mention the little man and his black-shirted disciples.

The Italian peasants had been caught in the middle; between the postwar depression and the political chaos, they'd found no other way to survive but emigration. By hundreds of thousands at a time, they'd been leaving their country, mostly for America. There, they could feed their children, even if it meant squeezing two and three families into an apartment and accepting work for the lowest possible wages. Then the ax fell: the United States slashed Italy's immigration quota from 800,000 to 280,000.

The peasants, driven to desperation by the rising price of wheat, the political violence, and the tightened restrictions on emigration to America, had started to riot again and again. They'd been further incited by the Communists and Socialists, and had seized some of the big landowners' estates. Some of Tullio's friends' estates had already been destroyed, and the small town next to his had recently been left in rubble—so, although no violence had yet struck Orvietto, the Barragatto compound now resembled an armed camp. His cousins, Benedetto and Ernesto Crispino, didn't know whom to defend themselves against first: the peasants, who wanted to rip their orchards away from them; the left-wingers, who'd already left one bomb in the Milan office; or Pace's people, who not only controlled the port of Genoa, but were scattered throughout the land, like a pestilence.

While still in New York, Tullio had made full use of the publishing end of North American Distributors. Daily, he'd injected anti-Communist articles into the tabloids he controlled. Also, he'd devoted page after page of his magazines to the defense of Fascism. He'd have to intensify the propaganda, he now realized, not only stateside, but within Italy and her neighboring countries, as well. He knew, though, that he might have to employ other weapons besides words, and this bothered him tremendously; he'd already seen enough violence at the Front and in Guidonia to last him two lifetimes.

The Kostenov chauffeur reached Saratoga Springs in early afternoon. He checked his watch and was pleased that he'd made the long trip in record time. He entered the small town at the south end and drove up Broadway. The street was lined with ancient elm trees that half concealed some rambling hotels that had seen their heyday decades before. He continued to the fashionable center of town, where the streets were congested because it was August. Saratoga was in season.

Eight months of the year, Saratoga Springs was just a sleepy town in the Adirondacks, its main industry being the bottling of spring water. Beginning in June, it would start breaking out of its shell and stir with anticipation. By July, the mad rush to

94

the start of August was at a crazy pace, for August was the month of the races: the month when the town's population increased four-fold, far beyond the resources of its numerous hotels and uncounted rooming houses; the month when the principal occupation of the townspeople became the renting of quarters ranging from humble dwellings along Congress Street to palatial white gingerbread mansions gracing Union Avenue; the month when fortunes changed hands as quickly as the time required to cover a 1-⅛ mile oval of racetrack.

Before each race, the thoroughbreds would be saddled and paraded within the paddock. Here, socialites rubbed elbows with stable boys, politicians argued with farmers, and the famous drank with the infamous. The incongruous mixture which began in the paddock, though, didn't end there; it bled right through into the evenings because the night life was gay and diversified. It offered everything from Chopin to Broadway headliners to back-alley striptease acts. Gambling casinos flourished; the mad clicking of ivory balls spinning around roulette wheels, the flipping of case cards on faro layouts, the no-limit dice games, and the dusk-to-dawn poker games outdid the great old rooms in Monte Carlo and were on tap in every gambling hall, night club and roadhouse.

Saratoga boasted that it had something for everyone—the gamblers, the thrill-seekers, the beautiful, the lonely, and the bored—and they all came. It attracted confidence men by the droves. Publishers sent their best photographers, sports writers and gossip columnists. Matrons overwhelmed its spas and mineral baths. Socialites paraded their daughters like ripe vegetables. This was August in Saratoga, and all of the Gold Coast was there. So was Mr. Carmine Pace. He spotted Magdalena Barragatto as she stepped out of her limousine. She was with Salvatore Crispino, but this didn't matter, because he knew that she wasn't Crispino's wife; this made her all the more interesting.

When the final race was run on Getaway Day, the exodus from the little Adirondack resort would explode with a startling abruptness. For a few hours, the streets would be congested, the traffic would be unbearable and a person could hardly hear himself think; then, the place would be deserted with only an occasional horse-drawn hack trotting sleepily along in search of one last fare. Pace knew that, if he were to meet this lovely woman who'd enchanted him in his speakeasy, he must do so now, during these maddening two weeks, for after Getaway Day, he might never see her again.

Chapter Five

The smell of the Genoa docks attacked Tullio like a bull at a gate. He would have left the city at once, but, not yet having his land-legs, checked into a hotel. He was sure that, by morning, the vile, vast ocean that was swirling around his insides might subside.

This was not the type of hotel that Tullio would ordinarily stay in, but the taxis were on strike, and it was the most decent one he could find within walking distance of the pier. Ship personnel had carried his trunks through the streets and up the steps into his room. They'd told him that they'd heard the strike would end by midnight and that he shouldn't have any problems the next morning. He hoped they were right; if not, he'd have to pull his manager out of their local office, just to get himself transportation.

He was surprised at how quickly he fell asleep, and even more surprised at how much better he felt when he awoke later that evening. He was even a little hungry and, because the hotel restaurant was closed, he ventured out into the rain, seeking a cafe.

It felt good to have solid ground beneath him. Even the cobblestones, wet and slippery as they were, tranquilized him.

Soon, the rain started falling harder, but, since he wasn't swaying for the first time in—what was it now? . . . weeks? centuries?—he walked without rushing and didn't care about the downpour.

He stopped at a small corner restaurant. He was conspicuously better-dressed than its other patrons, and he felt many eyes on him and his pockets when he entered the place. He chose a table where he could sit with his back against the wall. From this vantage point, he could safely assess the whole room. Every now and then he would lean backward just enough to expose his shoulder pistol. Each time, it provoked a soft whisper from some of the other tables. He grinned, and he wondered if it was even loaded; he really should check it out when he got back to his hotel.

Meanwhile, he decided that he wouldn't rush through his meal. It was wonderful to have an appetite again, and he was in the mood for melon and prosciutto to start.

The place was noisy and filled with prostitutes and seamen at the bar and groups of dark-clad men at the tables. He guessed that the latter must be the dock businessmen: smugglers, paper-forgers, dope dealers and pimps. In the far corner, there were two young men who were obviously not from this part of town; they'd come here only for a chance to be together. The only other person in the room, other than himself, who was sitting alone was a man who would frequently catch his eye; it was disconcerting because there was something strangely familiar about him. Beyond them all, he could see some *scugnizzi* peeping in through the windows; he wondered whom they were sizing up: himself, or the lone stranger, or the two young men.

The *scugnizzi* had figured in Neapolitan folklore for centuries; now, because of the post-war inflation and population growth, they were becoming familiar to the streets of other major cities, Genoa included. They were street children, showing themselves only at night and disappearing, quite like fabled vampires, at sunrise. They ranged from about six years old to sixteen; and, whether they ran alone or in packs like wolves, they were looked upon without sympathy as "baby beasts." Most were of mixed blood and race, the discarded infants of prostitutes and the many sailors and soldiers who passed through the port cities. Born of diseased parents, many were disfigured. Those born whole were crippled by hunger and the streets. In the summertime, they slept under bridges; in the bitter cold months, they sneaked into basements where they could huddle closely to one another. They swarmed with vermin and lived off slops. They were used as pimps' and smugglers' messengers, as paid killers, and as lookouts for muggers; *Scugnare* means "to spin like a top"—and that is just what they did, these pathetic *scugnizzi:* they'd twirl without direction, and then stop and drop.

He ate a big meal and drank some good wine and the bill, because he was so well-dressed, was larger than it should have been. He didn't remark about the inflated price and left a good tip to the owner's wife. When he left the restaurant, he was sure he couldn't have eaten another morsel. He made note of the name of the place. If he should ever find himself in this decrepit part of town again, he'd come here to eat. The food had actually been good.

He'd barely turned the corner when he was almost hit in the face by a heavy piece of wool. Startled, he looked up. It was a wool scarf, and it was wrapped around the neck of a man who was dangling by his ankles from a window-iron. The man's hands were bound and his mouth was stuffed with the other end of the scarf. He was almost unconscious.

Tullio found a crate to climb on and untied the man, easing him down to the pavement as gently as he could. "Are you all right?" he asked.

It was the stranger who had been looking at him in the cafe; and again, he had that feeling of familiarity.

The man didn't answer for a while. He was still gasping for air.

"Are you all right?" he repeated.

"Yes, yes, I just have to get my wind back."

"What happened?"

"The *scugnizzi*," he rasped. "They set a snare. As soon as I stepped across it, it pulled me up by my feet. Then, they spun me around, shoving the scarf in my mouth and going through my pockets. They cleaned me out! And, they did it without making a sound!" He rubbed his bruised throat. "Devils! They were going to get whoever walked out first! A snare! They trapped me like an animal! With a hunter's snare! I'll kill the first one I see!"

It must have dawned on the both of them at once, because each suddenly saw the look of recognition in the other's eyes. It was the first time either had seen the other with a head of hair.

"Fallanca!"

"Barragatto! I *knew* I knew you from someplace!"

"What are you doing here?" Tullio asked him. "I figured you would have left the country long ago. Either that, or that they'd caught you by now."

"That's why I'm down here tonight. To buy some papers." He stopped, shook his head, and cursed. "When I think of what I did . . . just to get that much money together . . . and he never even showed."

"He set you up," Tullio said. "He had them waiting for you."

Giulio Fallanca shook his head again. "I just can't believe that I fell for such an old game. Me, of all people. I should have known better."

"Come on," Tullio said. "Let's go back to that restaurant and get a couple of drinks."

The owner's wife was very pleased to see Tullio again so soon and brought him some wine immediately. She was surprised to see who his new drinking partner was, though, and gave him a questioning look. "Bring another glass," he ordered. "Can't you see that there are two of us at this table?"

Giulio Fallanca shrugged. He was too upset to be insulted.

Tullio, however, had been thinking about something on the way back to the restaurant. Now, he asked, "Didn't you once tell me that your mother was German?"

"Yes," he replied. "Why?"

"Do you speak German?"

"Yes, I speak it fluently. Why?" He swished the wine round in his mouth and shook his head and cursed again. "I still can't believe that I fell for that game. I can't believe it."

"I can arrange for you to live in Germany. Would you be interested?"

Fallanca put down the wine glass. "I'm listening."

"I'm staying at a hotel not too far from here," Tullio said. "I'll get you a room there for the night. Tomorrow morning, I'll have one of my employees drive you to the French border. You can take a train from there. Here's enough money to last you until you get to Germany."

Fallanca was touched that Tullio had not even bothered to count how much he was giving him. He counted it, himself, and said: "I'll send it all back to you someday."

"I know. Now, here's an address to go to in Germany. Speak with Gerhard Moeller when you get there. He and I went to school together. His family owns Rhine vineyards and our families have been doing business with one another for ages, so I know him pretty well. Don't speak with his stepfather or with anybody else. Only with Gerhard, himself. Give him this note and tell him the story. He'll fix you up with German papers. You can even work for him, if you want."

Giulio Fallanca stared at the money and the note. If he were to remain in Italy, he'd surely be caught and returned to Guidonia. Tullio was offering him a chance for a whole new life. "Are you sure he'll do this?"

"He'll do it."

"If this works . . ." Giulio said, ". . . if this works . . ."

"It will. Whatever you do, though, don't cause him any trouble when you get there. He's a good man."

Tullio dreamed of Magdalena that night. One *scugnizza* had

reminded him of her.

Lately, Louise Asheley had begun to have spells when she mistook Magdalena for her dead daughter-in-law, and Stefano her dead grandson. Most of the time, however, she was quite rational. If matters should worsen, Earl had said, he could always bring her back to Jericho just as easily as he'd taken her away, and all had agreed.

Surprising even herself, Magdalena was already answering to the name of Anita, and Salvatore found this very amusing.

"It's not funny," Magdalena told him. "The children are very confused. It's not funny at all."

"Yes, it is," he answered. "She even has me calling you Anita!"

"Don't you dare."

She was sorry to act so cross with Salvatore. He'd been doing his best to cheer her since Tullio had left and she had to admit that she'd been less than cooperative. Besides that, she wasn't feeling well lately, and almost everything was bothering her.

No sooner had they arrived in Saratoga when a telegram was delivered from the New York office. An emergency had developed which required the immediate attention of Earl, Salvatore and Aleksey. All three men would be returning to the city the following day. She was very tempted to return, also, but knew that Louise would be too upset if she were to suggest such a thing; so, she remained silent, and she listened patiently as Louise told her all she knew about Saratoga Springs . . . Louise had been there often . . . it was such a fascinating place . . . she would love it . . . just wait and see.

She retired very early that first night. She was glad they'd rented a house. Marcello had taken complete command. The children would have a free run of the place and a large back yard, while she and Louise had quiet and privacy.

The paddock was crackling with life. Magdalena and Louise had left the children to their nurse and were admiring a light

102

gray horse called Lady-Lu. Later that day, it won a race and they discussed it over lunch. They'd go to the paddock the following day, they decided; and this time, they would actually place a bet. They asked the waiter for the check and were preparing to leave.

"It's been paid for, ladies," he said, and indicated a man at a table in the far corner of the room. "Compliments of Mr. Carmine Pace."

Magdalena stared at the man. He was dark and handsome, but in an oily way—not at all like Tullio. He was wearing a dark blue pinstriped suit with a navy blue silk shirt and white tie. He was sitting at one of the best tables in the room and it seemed that everyone who entered paused to pay their respects to him. He nodded when he saw Magdalena looking at him, then motioned with his fingers for permission to come to their table.

"Oh," the waiter said. "Mr. Pace is a well-known patron here. I'm sure he doesn't mean to be disrespectful."

"Well, it certainly can't harm anyone to be polite," Louise said. "Please ask Mr. Pace to join us."

The waiter followed instructions and Carmine Pace rewarded him appropriately. "How do you do, ladies," he began and Magdalena was immediately surprised. He had an Italian accent! "I hope you won't think it too bold of me . . . but . . . you see . . . I was eavesdropping on you this morning."

"How gallant of you to buy our lunch!" Louise told him. "I am Louise Asheley, and this is my daughter-in-law, Anita Asheley."

"How do you do. May I?" He gestured toward the chair.

"Oh, of course! Please sit down," Louise told him.

"I noticed you when you arrived in town yesterday. I was going to come over to say hello, but was distracted. You see, Mr. Crispino and I are old friends."

"Oh?"

"Yes. Where is he? Perhaps, you can all come to dinner with me this evening."

"He had to leave," Mrs. Asheley said. "As a matter of fact,

103

my husband had to leave, also."

"What a shame," he replied. Looking toward Magdalena, he asked, "And your husband?"

"He's not here, either," she said.

"What a pity. Two such lovely ladies should not be left alone. May I invite the two of you to dinner? After dinner, we can stop in at one of the clubs. I think it might be a very pleasant evening."

"Thank you, Mr. Pace," she said. "But I'm afraid Mrs. Asheley and I have other plans." She wanted to write Tullio a long letter tonight. She missed him already. But Louise cut her off.

"Nonsense. Your idea sounds lovely, Mr. Pace."

"Louise, really," Magdalena protested, but it was useless. Louise, well into one of her spells, was explaining to Mr. Pace that her widowed daughter-in-law needed to start going out again.

"I understand," Pace nodded. "And she's a good friend of Mr. Crispino?"

"Oh, yes," Louise assured him. "Salvatore Crispino has been very kind to us."

"Yes," he replied. "Crispino knows how to enjoy himself, doesn't he."

There was something in his voice that Magdalena didn't like. She suspected that his remark might have a double meaning—but what, she couldn't figure out. She dismissed it. The man, being a friend of Salvatore's, was just trying to be friendly.

"I'll call for you at eight, ladies," Pace said. Then he smiled, nodded, and left them.

Pace asked one of his men to find out about Mrs. Anita Asheley.

The man returned within the hour. "There's no such person, Mr. Pace. I checked it out with the biggest gossipers from the Gold Coast. Even with some society writer. There's no such person. Louise Asheley has no daughter-in-law. She

104

used to have a son, but he died. Maybe, he was married; maybe, he wasn't. I don't know. But, nobody knows of a daughter-in-law."

Pace was convinced, now, that the redhead was a very special friend of Salvatore Crispino's. One special enough to bring to Saratoga Springs. One special enough to employ the help of Louise Asheley to keep her true identity a secret. Perhaps, the redhead was Crispino's mistress . . . not just a special friend . . . Crispino had a lot of friends. Well, he'd play their game. He'd call her Anita Asheley. He didn't care what her real name was.

Magdalena was disturbed that she'd been introduced as Anita. She suspected, however, that they'd never see the man again after they left Saratoga. She might as well go by the name, she decided. What choice did she have? If she were to tell him her real name, he might think Louise was some raving maniac. She couldn't do that to Louise. *So,* she determined, *like it or no . . . I am Anita Asheley until we leave Saratoga . . . or until Louise snaps out of it . . . whichever happens first!*

They were ready when he arrived promptly at eight. The children were already asleep and the house was quiet. All was so peaceful that he remarked: "There certainly isn't any vacation atmosphere here, is there, Mrs. Asheley?" But, he guessed that it had to be this way—Salvatore could not have his mistress exposed to too many people, and that would be the case if he'd checked her into one of the hotels. After all, Crispino was a married man—runaround or not, he was still married, and had to keep up some kind of front.

"Yes, you're right, Mr. Pace. It's very quiet here."

"Well," he said, "we'll be sure to make up for it tonight."

They did. He took them to Sans Souci, the gayest restaurant in Saratoga Springs, a place where all the men looked handsome and wealthy and very debonair; where the women strode across the room like grand duchesses; and where the waiters moved about with a imperious air. Champagne, Prohibition or not, popped and fizzed from every quarter, and a small orchestra played waltzes continuously. The atmosphere was such that they could very well have been in Vienna, and not in a little Adirondack town that would close its eyes and fall fast asleep come September.

After dinner, he treated them to a Broadway spectacular. The whole cast had been transported north for these two weeks, and it received an ovation that it seldom got in Manhattan.

He was quite sure that, when he returned home to their house that night, he would be welcomed again, by both of them.

His first opportunity to see Magdalena alone presented itself when Louise Asheley mentioned she would be spending the next day at one of the spas. He found his Anita in the paddock. She was with a nurse and a blond boy, about five and a very dark little girl about four. It had never even entered his mind that she might have children. Crispino was certainly leading a double life! . . . but, maybe, they weren't Crispino's . . . she was such a beautiful young thing . . . and neither of them looked like Crispino.

He waited for the nurse to leave with the children before approaching. She'd not noticed him until now and was obviously pleased to see him.

"I see you decided not to go to the spa," he said. "Well, I can't blame you. There's nothing that those mud baths can do for you that nature already hasn't done."

"Mr. Pace, I was just thinking of you."

"I'm flattered."

"You know," she continued, "I'm sure I've heard your name somewhere, but I just can't remember when."

"Maybe, Salvatore mentioned me." He doubted this.

They lunched together and made arrangements to see each other that evening.

"We really are monopolizing you," she told him. "I feel a bit guilty about it."

106

"Shame on you, Anita! To say such a thing! Don't you ever say such a thing again!" He shook his finger at her. "Anyway, a woman with your looks should be used to having men rushing at you. I'm the one who should feel guilty, not you. I've been keeping you all to myself."

What a nice person he was. How wrong of her to continue this farce. She should really tell him her true name. Would that be so disloyal to Louise? No . . . of course not . . . he would understand. Louise was just . . . ill . . . and she had to play along. He would understand. "Mr. Pace," she began, "there is something I've been meaning to tell you. I hope you won't be offended that I've had to keep it from you, but it is rather difficult to explain. Once I do, though, I believe you'll understand."

He thought: *Well, here it comes. The whole story. But, why? Why? . . . Of course! I know why! I'm treating you better than Crispino does! That's why! And I'm not married, and he is! That's why! So, now, you're thinking of a change in meal-tickets! So sorry, my darling . . . as beautiful as you are, I'm not getting myself saddled with a woman who has two kids.* He said: "Whatever it is, Anita, I don't want to hear it."

"But, really, I should. You see . . . ."

"Ssshh! I refuse to listen."

"But, I owe it to you."

"I tell you what. Tonight, you come out with me alone . . . without Louise. Leave her at home. That's the only thing you owe me. Nothing else."

"I can't do that."

"Yes, you can."

"I can't."

"I'll send a car for you at eight."

"No, please, I can't do that."

He stood and before leaving, repeated: "I'll send a car for you at eight." He squeezed her hand. "Don't disappoint me, Anita. I've wanted to be alone with you ever since the first time

107

I saw you."

"Don't send the car. I won't come out without Mrs. Asheley."

"Where I take you tonight, nobody who knows Salvatore Crispino will see us. Don't be afraid. I would never get you in any kind of trouble with him."

"I'm not afraid of Salvatore!"

"Good. I'll send a car at eight." He walked away immediately, leaving her staring at his back.

She wanted to shout: Don't send it!—but she would have attracted too much attention. She turned on her heel and walked swiftly back to the rented house.

How dare he think I'm afraid of Salvatore! Anyway, why should I be? And, how dare he insist about tonight! What nerve! What absolute nerve! She was still thinking about this when she entered the house.

Louise had returned from the spa. Her face was as red as a beet. "Look what they did to me with that atrocious sunlamp! I look like an Indian! An absolute Indian! We've got to go home, Magdalena! We've got to go home as soon as possible!"

Magdalena stared at her friend. The only part of her face that wasn't bright red was the section that the eye goggles had covered. It looked awful. Also, she'd called her Magdalena for the first tir∼ in three weeks. "Yes! Yes! We'll start packing the first thing in the morning. But, don't worry . . . that will turn into a very lovely tan in a few days . . . and then, you'll look beautiful! Really! You will!" She felt very sorry for Louise. "Does it burn?" she asked her.

"No, not at all. But, I won't let anybody see me like this. I look like an Indian! An Indian!"

"I'll go send the wire right now," Magdalena said. "I'll be right back. I'll tell the cook we're eating in tonight, just we and the children. That should be nice. I'll be right back."

She found a Western Union office and sent the telegram. When she returned, Louise was already in her dressing gown.

"I know what I've put you through these past few weeks,"

Louise told her.

"What do you mean?"

"I know I've been calling you Anita again. I'm sorry. Stefano climbed up on my lap when I got back from the spa. He looked at my face and said: 'Grandma Louise!'—and I suddenly realized . . . this isn't my Carter . . . this is Stefano. I'm so sorry, Magdalena."

"It's all right, Louise. It hasn't interfered with our vacation one bit. We've still had a marvelous time. Haven't we?"

"Yes, we have, thanks to Mr. Pace. Oh, dear! You won't tell him, will you? He'll think I'm a silly old woman! You haven't told him you're not Anita, have you?"

Magdalena shook her head. "No, I haven't told him. We'll never see him again, once we get back to Jericho." She was glad, now, that she'd not blurted out the truth.

"He was here while you were out sending the telegram. I was really very embarrassed to be seen looking like this. I told him that, naturally, I couldn't accompany you this evening. I suggested that you two should go alone. He was very sympathetic."

Magdalena smirked. "I'm sure he was, but I have no intention of going out tonight. I'm suddenly in the mood for a picnic . . . right here on the living room floor . . . just us!"

"Oh, but I've already committed you," Louise replied.

"Louise, you're forgetting that I'm a married woman. It's one thing for the both of us to go out together with him. But, it's quite something else for me to go with him alone. Tullio would be furious if he ever heard I was out alone with a man. No, tonight, I'll stay home."

"Oh, Magdalena, this is the twentieth century! It's 1920, darling! Nobody condemns a harmless evening out. Anyway," —she poked her elbow into Magdalena's arm—"I promise not to tell. Go! Have a good time. Do it, if only as a favor for me, so I won't feel so guilty making you stay home on our last night in Saratoga."

Magdalena grinned, then said: "No, I think I'd better not."

"Look at it this way: He's a friend of Salvatore's. That means that he's a friend of the family." She gave Magdalena a motherly look and patted her on the face. "Enjoy yourself . . . now . . . while you're still young. The years fly so quickly, and then it's too late."

She knew Louise meant well. And, maybe, she was right. No harm could be done. It would just be an evening out.

"That's my girl! Anyway, soon, you won't be able to do much going out."

"Yes, I know."

Magdalena looked at herself in the mirror. In the last few weeks her breasts had swollen. The lavender crepe de chine chemise she was wearing was already quite tight on top.

"It's really remarkable how these chemise dresses hide everything. Besides you're carrying so small, it's a complete cover-up."

"Yes. The fashion came just in time."

Marcello the butler was at the door.

"Mr. Carmine Pace is here for the Signora," he announced.

A cat screamed outside and that awakened Magdalena. She was in her upstairs bedroom, still fully clothed but she had no idea how she'd gotten there or when she'd come home. Her head ached and as she struggled to sit up the room would not stop spinning. She looked down at her feet. Her silk stockings were torn and muddy, and her shoes were gone.

What happened to my shoes?

The half-memory returned. She couldn't concentrate on her shoes.

They are in Carmine's Rolls Royce. His chauffeur is at the wheel. She laughs. She tells him: "You have the thickest eyebrows I've ever seen. Really!"

"They're my trademark," he replies, "and that's very important, because everybody needs a trademark . . . especially where we're going tonight."

"Where's that?"

"The place doesn't have a name. It opens up only during racing season, in a different cellar each time . . . but, everyone from the Cotton Club will be there."

"What's the Cotton Club?" she asks him.

"What's the Cotton Club! Why, that's only the greatest little place in Harlem! That's what it is! Don't tell me you've never been to Harlem! Salvatore's never brought you to Harlem? You haven't lived, baby, you haven't lived! That's nigger heaven, that's what Harlem is. It's where you get the best music in the world. They look at you with those shiny black faces and those big yellow teeth and they blow the blues at you. And then, they serve up some yarddog and strings with a cup of white tea, and . . ."

"Carmine, what in the world are you talking about?"

"He's really kept you to himself, hasn't he. Well, yarddog means chicken. Strings means spaghetti. White tea can be gin . . . or vodka . . . depending . . . And they do it all with a smile. But, of course, don't let that smile of theirs fool you. They really hate the whites. Only, they'd do anything for our money. To them, we're the *oefay*. That's pig latin for 'foe'." He pauses. "I guess you don't understand pig latin, either."

Magdalena is in a very good mood. She's glad she's come out with him and she laughs. Pig latin. He must be kidding. "Okay, teach me pig latin."

"It's the easiest thing in the world," he says. "You say the word by starting it with the first vowel sound. Then, you take the beginning—the part you left off—and say it at the end of the word and add 'ay'."

She smiles broadly. Now, she's sure he's kidding her; but, he continues: "For instance, the word 'boy' becomes *oybay*. The word 'girl' becomes *irlgay*. Now, listen carefully, and see if you can figure out what I'm saying: *eThay oybay anray otay ethay irlgay*."

"Repeat that," she said; and he does.

"I know! It means: 'The boy ran to the girl.'"

"I knew you were smart, little lady! Now, let's see you tell

111

me something in pig latin."

Slowly, she said, *"ellWay, et'slay ogay!"* She feels especially confident. She adds: *"ouYay onlyay ivelay onceway!"*

"You better believe it, baby, you better believe it," he laughs. Then, he dismisses his driver and takes the car himself.

She struggled to the bathroom. Thank God she had her own, so that no one else could see her like this. She removed the ruined stockings and the dress as she struggled to focus on what had happened.

She began to run some cool water into the tub. How can it have started off so nicely, she asked herself, and end so badly?

They are in the cellar. It's so crowded that tables and chairs all have to be picked up for somebody to pass. She asks how they would ever get out if there were a fire, and he laughs and says, *"eWay on'tday, abybay. eWay urnbay."*

She asks him not to call her "baby" but he doesn't stop. She tells him that he isn't acting like himself. "Where is the Carmine Pace who was so gallant to Louise and me? What happened to him? Why are you talking like this? Why are you acting like this?"

"You can stop acting now. Mrs. Asheley isn't with us."

"I'm going home!"

"Sit down."

"No, I'm going home." But, she can't get through.

He looks crossly at a man who is about to make room for her to pass. The man seems to fear him and sits down again. She can't pass. "I said I want to go!" But she can't, because nobody moves for her.

"Sit down. Here, have some tea."

She doesn't know why, but she does. She has the tea, the white tea; then, she has more because he insists. After a while, she forgets she is angry with him. They are having a good time again. A short stocky Negro is collecting money for a man called Garvey. "The niggers' newest god," Carmine

112

explains, "that's who Garvey is." She doesn't know why she's having such a good time, but everybody else is, too, and she shouts: *assPay ethay athay orfay arveyGay!"*

She remembered Pace complaining that the teacup was too small; so, he'd started drinking from one of her shoes and she'd begun laughing at him. Then, she had started drinking from her other shoe. This had made the insides of both shoes so sticky that she'd walked back to the car in her stockinged feet.

She remembered how they'd sat in his car for a while, still drinking from the shoes, and how, soon, he'd begun touching the soft flesh under her toes and had said: "I know what the rest of you is going to feel like. If this part of your feet is so soft, the rest of you is like butter."

And she remembered trying to kick him away and hitting him with the heel of one of the shoes and becoming violently ill and crying. The memory would stop right there.

She's throwing up in his car and he's yelling, "Jesus Christ! Hold it in! Hold it in!" and she cries because she can't; so he jumps out, saying he's going for some rags to clean the car with.

"Don't leave me here!"

"I have to! How do you expect me to drive with this mess?"

"No, please don't leave! Wait! I'll come with you." She tries to get out, but she can't stand straight. Everything is swirling and she almost falls. "I can't."

"I know you can't!" he shouts. "Get back in." He is pushing her back. "Here! Here's a gun. Now, you don't have anything to be afraid of. Lock the car door. If any of those niggers comes to the car, shoot. Don't ask any questions. Just shoot first!"

"Don't leave me here! I feel so sick!" she keeps asking.

"I'll be right back. I have to get this mess cleaned up. Jesus Christ! I can't stand women who can't hold their liquor!"

He disappears. It's so dark out. She doesn't know how long he's gone. She tries to keep her eyes open, but they keep closing; and, each time she closes them, she becomes more dizzy. Where is he? . . . she feels so sick! Somebody is knocking on the car window and she is barely conscious because she's so sick. She screams: "Who are you? What do you want? Go away! Go away!"

The person is banging on the window.

"No! Go away! Go away!"

She screams and points the gun at the window and shoots through it. Then, she closes her eyes.

"Oh, my God, what happened?"

She tried, for a long time, to remember, but she couldn't. She thought: If I'd really shot through it, the glass would have shattered. Did it? I don't remember. The figure had been at the window. His hand had been pounding on the window.

Yes, I did shoot. It did shatter.

But, it had been so dark, too dark to see who'd been at the window. Who had it been? Carmine? Some innocent stranger?

"Oh, God . . . did I kill somebody?"

She buried her face in her hands. Who could she tell? Louise? No. No, not Louise. Perhaps, she should go to Pace's hotel to find out what happened? No, she couldn't dare go near the place. He might have been the one at the window.

"Oh, my God . . . don't tell me I killed that poor man!"

She could hear the children downstairs. Was it that late already? That meant Louise would be getting out of bed soon.

"Magdalena! Magdalena! Are you all right in there! Magdalena, answer me!"

"Yes . . . I'm all right, Louise . . . I'll be coming out soon . . . I'm all right . . ." *I'll tell Aleksey. Yes, Aleksey. He'll know what to do.* "I'll be right out. You go to breakfast. I'll join you in a few minutes."

She was noticeably upset at the breakfast table. It was just morning sickness again, she told Louise . . . just morning sickness. Then: "Louise, please don't let anyone know that we even met Carmine Pace. Please, Louise."

"Oh, Magdalena, don't tell me you feel guilty for going out with him last night."

"Please, Louise. Oh, please don't tell anyone."

"Well, all right, dear. If that's your wish, I'll tell no one."

As soon as they returned to New York, Magdalena confided in Aleksey all that she remembered of the whole Saratoga episode. He investigated: not only was Mr. Carmine Pace alive and well, but Aleksey could find no report of any shooting taking place in Saratoga Springs that week.

"I know I shot someone," she'd told him. "I know I did!"

"You might have shot at someone, but you missed," he'd told her. "I investigated thoroughly. There was no shooting in Saratoga that night, or, for that matter, any night during this season. Be at peace, Magdalena. You never killed anyone. There's nothing to be concerned about. Try to forget about it. Just be grateful that Pace never knew who you really were. He's a despicable character. He's an underworld figure. It just goes to show you what a low type he is . . . he never even came to that house you were renting the next day . . . that's the least he could have done . . . just to check if you were all right."

"But, it might have been him that I shot!"

"Magdalena, I told you the man is alive! Please, now, try to forget it. It's all over. Nobody got shot."

"An underworld figure? He's an underworld figure?"

"He is," Aleksey had told her. "He is. And, if Louise hadn't been in one of her spells, he would have known your real name. Now, thank God, he'll never know. And, you'll never see the man again, either . . . so, try to forget it."

The Leopard and
the Grande Dame

Chapter One

It was almost two years, now, since Tullio had sailed. Magdalena could hardly believe how quickly the days had turned into months—not the first several months, though, because she'd had a bad pregnancy, and she'd been forced to spend a great deal of it in bed.

She'd not forgotten about Carmine Pace. She believed she never could; and sometimes, she could see the hand pounding on the window, and then hear the shot and the glass shatter. She dared not speak to anyone about it, but she knew she would never forget.

The thought of her husband saved her. He would be returning soon. They would be together again. Everything would be beautiful again. Then, the bad dreams would stop.

Instead of Tullio, though, a letter had come, explaining the many reasons for his not being able to return yet.

She'd been sure that, once her time came, he'd return, if only to see his child. She'd never in her life been more disappointed in him. She'd never thought she could be so upset with anyone, for that matter. For a while, even Aleksey Kostenov tried to stay away from her; that's how bad-tempered and depressed her husband's letter had made her. If her pregnancy and birth-giving had not been such a bad one, and if it had not left her so weak for such a long time, she might surely have sailed to Italy, if only to scream out her feelings at him.

After those first bitter months of disappointment, Magdalena had begun writing her husband often. She'd named their new son Carlo, after his uncle, just as he'd asked her to do. She asked him when he'd either send for her or join her in America, for he'd assured her that one or the other was his intent.

Stefano and Rebecca, seven and six, respectively, could barely remember what Tullio looked like. Every one of his features was vivid in her own mind, though; and, countless times, she would try describing him to the children.

"When I first met your father," she would say, "he reminded me of the noblemen I'd heard about when I was a little girl. He was riding the most beautiful horse you can imagine. It had a golden coat and a long white mane and a tail that fluttered in the wind. And, he sat high and proud on the golden horse. And he was dressed in leather and silk. And I thought he might be a prince. I was very poor, you see. I lived on a farm, and I'd never seen any man dressed the way he was. He was so handsome, and oh! so elegant. I was almost positive he was a prince."

She'd continue, telling them how tall and how broad he was, about his dark brown eyes, how his thick black hair would curl forward, how he'd smile, and all the other details that were important only to her. The prince part would always thrill Rebecca the most, but the boys were more interested in the horse; so, even though the story of their parents' first meeting never strayed too far from the truth, its details would be altered according to which of the children fell asleep first.

She managed to hide her unhappiness and her loneliness from her children, and even from her closest friend, Louise; but, not from Aleksey Kostenov. To Kostenov, she'd cry.

Except to visit the Asheleys, and other than accompanying

120

Stefano and Rebecca to and from school—for she didn't even trust them to the chauffeur's exclusive care—she seldom left *The Walls of Jericho* anymore, her self-imposed imprisonment having resulted from a conversation with her husband's cousin.

"Magdalena," Salvatore had cautioned, "there are lots of people who, if they know you are rich, are so jealous that they want to harm you in some way. Sometimes, they attack you or throw things at you, for no reason at all. Sometimes, they even steal your children . . . and then, you have to pay to get them back again . . . and you don't always get them back. If I were you, I wouldn't leave the children unless Aleksey or Earl is around to watch over them. And, I wouldn't wander too far away from home, either. Unless, of course, you let one of us know where you're going to be."

"Who wants to hurt my children? Who?"

"Nobody, in particular, but . . ."

"Then, why are you saying such a thing? Don't you ever say such a thing again!"

He'd started to cough. "Please, Magdalena, don't be angry. I can understand that what I've said might upset you. But, you really shouldn't be angry with me. After all, I'm only trying to protect you. You know how much Tullio counts on me to take care of you while he's away."

"If your cousin were so concerned about his family, he'd be here, with us."

"But, Magdalena, you know that it's not possible right now. You know what this Prohibition has done. He has to give most of his attention to the vineyards in Orvietto."

"That's not true! Your brothers are there! They can take care of the vineyards! They know as much about grapes as Tullio does!"

"They might know a little about making wine, but they're not businessmen. Who would run the Milan office, if not Tullio? He has to see to things in Milan. He's grooming Benedetto for the Milan office . . . but, it takes time."

They'd spoken for a long time that afternoon. Salvatore had left with a hacking cough, none of his reasons for Tullio's long absence having convinced Magdalena; yet, his warning regarding her and the children had frightened her, and she'd repeated his words to Earl Asheley.

"Salvatore's a typical lawyer," he replied. "He's always worrying for no reason." And this, the businessman honestly believed, saying to Aleksey the next morning, "I'm going to give Salvatore a piece of my mind. He had no business upsetting Magdalena like that. He knows how impressionable she is."

Yet, Aleksey Kostenov, knowing the attorney better than his associate did, silently thought: Salvatore Crispino says nothing insignificant. Therefore, he approached the young man before Earl could get to him. Perhaps, Salvatore would tell him things he might hold back from Earl.

"Salvatore," Aleksey began, "I have no intention of trying to interfere between a man and his wife . . . this long separation between Tullio and Magdalena . . . that's their personal business, and I won't comment upon it or ask any questions about it. But, where the safety of Magdalena and the children is involved . . . that's a whole different story. They are living under my roof, under my protection . . . and, if there is any real reason for your frightening Magdalena the way that you did . . . you have no right to hold it back from me. She and the children, besides being my responsibility while Tullio is away, happen to mean a great deal to me."

"I didn't mean to really scare her. I wasn't even talking about any particular people. I was just talking to her in generalities. That's all. Just generalities."

"I know you better. And, I know your cousin, too. Remember, I brought him up," Aleksey answered. "I know that, for some reason, you have orders from Tullio to try to keep Magdalena within the estate. I can't imagine what the purpose of the order is, but I do believe it must be a very good one."

"You're making a mountain out of a molehill," Salvatore grumbled.

"I am not! We've been through this before! I know there's something you and Tullio are keeping from us! What is it?"

"It's nothing, Aleksey. It's nothing at all. I don't know what you're talking about."

"Do I have to go directly to Tullio for an answer, or are you going to give it to me?"

"It's what I said before, Aleksey. I was speaking only in generalities."

He knew how angry Kostenov was, but there was nothing more he could say without first consulting with his cousin.

That afternoon, Salvatore wrote to Tullio:

"I know we cannot tell Aleksey and Earl the truth, because the first thing they would do is go to the police. That would make the situation worse for everyone concerned. They'd get us all killed, for sure. But, Tullio, I cannot keep arguing with Aleksey about Magdalena anymore; and, I certainly can't keep watching over her, myself. I'm having a hard enough time trying to hide my own family. Try to come up with something. I know you can't bring her to Orvietto; it would be worse there. But, have you thought about a bodyguard, maybe? Whom do you know that you can trust? I can't think of anybody from this end."

On one of the rare occasions when Magdalena Barragatto accepted an invitation to Mrs. Asheley's club, it was because her friend was too upset to be refused. This was the third summer that there was no one in the Asheley guest cottage; and that was, to Louise Asheley, a serious social calamity.

From the moment the Kostenov chauffeur turned on to Capits Rock Road and through its massive iron gates toward the clubhouse, Magdalena regretted having come. There was not a single thing that she liked about the Capits Rock Club.

Not the famous golf course; the game bored her. Not the food; it was tasteless. Not the decor; there was none. Not the members; no! definitely not the members.

She arrived earlier than her hostess and was seated at a small, rickety white table on the rear porch dining room. She didn't like the table, either.

The Capits Rock Club had been one of the original "600" estates. Now, it boasted the finest golf course on the Gold Coast. Its huge clubhouse had been a guest cottage; its pro shop had been the chauffeur's quarters; its private dressing rooms and lockers had been converted from stables. One of the few things that had not been altered were its entrance gates: they were the original swinging barriers which the estate's first mistress had so painstakingly selected from the hundreds of drawings offered by aspiring architects of her time.

Like all other golf clubs, Capits Rock was a men's club; yet, the men were seldom there, except on weekends. The women who came were the members' wives; and it was they who constituted the true, if not the official, membership.

Aleksey Kostenov and Earl Asheley were members; but Magdalena, not the wife of one of the members, was ineligible for anything except "guest status." The situation caused her no anxiety at all, as the young woman possessed no social aspirations, disliked most of the other women members, and kept—unlike others who lived within the immediate area—mainly to herself, her children, and her home. Her aloofness was the cause of a great deal of speculation amongst the neighboring matrons.

All Capits Rock women looked alike to Magdalena. Their hair was side-parted and dark blonde. They were tall and schoolgirl thin. The older women wore more jewelry, drank more, and laughed more easily than their daughters, who tried very hard to be blasé. Despite the difference in ages, though, all of their hands (much to Magdalena's amusement) were much more darkly tanned than their faces or the rest of their bodies. They spoke the same, also, somehow managing to lose the last phrase of each sentence.

"You're shooting that disapproving stare at my friends, again, Magdalena."

"Yes, and no, Louise," she answered, glad that her hostess had finally arrived. "Anyway, they're not really your friends."

"They're important to me," Louise said softly.

"Yes, I know." *But, I'll never know why.*

They ordered, and ate tasteless sandwiches garnished with pieces of pickles and potato chips. Then, as Magdalena assumed might happen, they were joined by two other women, and their private conversation was abruptly halted.

"I hear you'll be traveling again, this summer," one said to Louise. "You're certainly developing an affinity for ocean cruises. Third year in a row, isn't it?" She sat back confidently, stretching out her legs.

"No," she replied. "I'm afraid I'll have to remain at home this summer. I have a guest who'll be spending some time with us. And, frankly, I'm not sure how long her visit will be. Perhaps, well into the fall."

Magdalena was discreetly astonished.

"Who?" the second intruder asked.

"I'm sorry . . . I can't . . . I mean . . . well, I hope you won't consider it rude of me, but, you see, the lady is traveling incognito."

The tanned woman sat forward. "Incognito?"

"Yes," Louise continued, "incognito. I'm sorry, but I can't divulge her name." She looked toward Magdalena.

"Yes," Magdalena improvised, "Mrs. Asheley and I were just discussing the lady's situation. She'd had such a hectic time of it lately, what with the scandal, the notoriety . . . well, you know."

"And, I've got to keep my word to her," Louise finished. "All she wants, now, is complete privacy."

The less Magdalena and Louise told of the guest, the more the others assumed they knew; and when the two women departed, Magdalena looked Louise squarely in the eyes and said: "Will you please tell me what's going on?"

"I'm sorry I should have warned you," Louise told her, "but I was afraid someone might overhear."

"Overhear what?"

Louise's face tightened. "That I've hired an actress."

Her young guest fell silent; and, as she listened to Louise Asheley's plan to enhance her social position with Gold Coast society, she began to feel more sorry for her every moment.

At the language instruction school she was attending, Louise explained, she'd befriended an Italian actress who was trying to master English. The young woman had been brought to America by a man whose reputation "is a little on the shady side." After several years, he'd deserted her. Now, with neither friend nor family in this country, the actress was almost destitute. "I had to do it, Magdalena," Louise ended. "I offered her my guest cottage. You understand, don't you?"

Magdalena sighed very deeply. "Yes, I understand." She sighed again and shook her head. "You're going to pass her off as European nobility . . . or, something like that. But, what about when they start talking to her? They're sure to question her. They're dying of curiosity."

"She speaks English very badly, but she'll pretend to them that she doesn't speak it or understand it at all. I know that nobody around here can speak Italian; so, actually, you and I are the only ones she'll ever really speak with."

"Louise, does she understand the situation?"

She nodded.

"Completely?"

"Yes. And, she knows that her fee depends on how well she plays her part. And, if I'm named chairwoman of the dance committee this year, she knows there'll be an extra bonus in it for her. She'll be moving into my cottage tomorrow morning. Her trunks were delivered this afternoon. Her name is Bella Modesto. And, guess what? She's from Orvietto. Isn't that a remarkable coincidence?"

Magdalena stared incredulously at her hostess. "Bella

Modesto? Bella Modesto, from Orvietto?"

"Oh! Do you know her?"

"No . . . I never met her . . . but, I know of her." And, because there was too much questioning in Louise's eyes not to continue, Magdalena added: "My husband is the one who knew her. He knew her very well."

Louise understood immediately, and her smile gave way to a look of concern. "Oh, Magdalena! Oh, I'm so sorry! I don't know what to say! I had no idea! How could I? Oh, of all the women in the world to have picked! Oh, Magdalena, I'm sorry! What can . . . ?"

At that moment, the intruders returned—a respite for Magdalena, since she didn't know how to answer Louise.

She listened to the women ramble on. Occasionally, she would nod, feigning interest in their conversation. She noticed Louise's eyes flit nervously from one face to another; and, the longer she sat at the table, the more she pitied her friend: should the sham be discovered, she realized, Louise would be laughed right out of Jericho.

But, she can't expect me to entertain one of my husband's old mistresses, can she? Bella Modesto! Of all people! Bella Modesto!

Louise Asheley's eyes were almost filling.

My God, I think she might be reading my mind! Look at her! She's a nervous wreck! Oh, damn it! She looked at her wristwatch. *I don't know what to do! Bella Modesto! Of all people!* "I have to go, Louise. My car is probably waiting for me by the gate." *Oh, Louise, please stop looking at me like that!*

"Magdalena?" Louise's voice was weak.

Magdalena looked from Louise Asheley to the other women. *They suspect something, already. Just from the tone of your voice, they know something's wrong. Look at them! Witches!* Then, she heard herself say: "I'll see you tomorrow morning. I'll come to *Swansgarten* and help you get your guest moved in." She smiled. "Okay?"

"Thank you."

"See you tomorrow." She thought that Louise Asheley was

about to cry with relief. "Thanks for lunch. It was nice seeing you again, ladies."

"Wait, I'll walk to the gate with you," Louise said.

"No. I know my way out. I'll see you tomorrow."

Magdalena didn't look back. She walked directly from the porch; through French doors to the main dining room; beyond that, through a small oak sitting-room; then, across a large entrance hall and into a vestibule. She'd not noticed doors being held open for her, or waitresses moving out of her way as she'd passed, or other guests and members nodding their greetings toward her. *Bella Modesto! Of all people!* And she was calling herself an actress now! That was a new one!

Aleksey's driver, as she'd suspected, had already arrived and was speaking with one of the club personnel. "Home, madame?" he asked.

"Yes. We'll be going straight home." *Not only is the whole idea crazy! Imagine trying to make them think she's some kind of nobility! Poor Louise! Oh, damn it! And, Bella Modesto! Of all women, Bella Modesto!*

They drove slowly through Capits Rock Road because it was narrow and winding, and because it was starting to rain; then, over the arched wooden bridge that crossed Capits Pond, and onto the highway. *If this scheme of hers doesn't work, it will be all over for Louise. Oh, that poor woman. How can she be so desperate for their approval?* She could feel the car speeding up once the chauffeur reached the highway. When they entered the gates of *The Walls*, she could see the children waiting for her on the lawn. But, *Bella Modesto! Of all people! Bella Modesto! With thousands of actresses in New York, Louise has to run into Bella Modesto!*

That evening, after a very quiet dinner, Magdalena told Aleksey of her meeting with Louise.

"I was wondering what was bothering you," he remarked.

"At first," she said, "I couldn't possibly imagine entertaining one of Tullio's women. As soon as I'd heard her name, I'd wanted to scream. But, then . . . well, Louise looked so

128

helpless . . . and I was sort of forced to think the whole thing over and change my mind. Just like that!" She snapped her finger. "Just like that!" She snapped again. "One look at those witches, and . . ." (snap! snap!) ". . . the way they were about to pounce on her! I had to agree to help her!" She paused: "After all, he used to see Bella, before we were married."

The businessman smiled wryly at his charge. "I'm very pleased with your attitude, Magdalena. Very pleased."

"And, anyway, she ran the most respectable house in Orvietto."

"House?"

"Oh, yes. But, I couldn't let Louise know the truth. That would really upset her; and, she's nervous enough, as it is, over this whole thing. You should have seen her, Aleksey . . . drinking one martini after another . . . that's all she and Earl would need now . . . for her to start drinking again . . . and, if this thing doesn't work out for her, that's just what might happen!"

"Calm yourself, Magdalena."

"Do you think it will work, Aleksey?"

"I would have discouraged attempting such a ruse. But, now, after the fact, all I can say is that it had better."

"But, do you think it will work? It would be so horrible for Louise if something should go wrong! Oh, my poor Louise."

He shrugged. "It is so outlandish that it might."

She'd needed his words. "Well, that's that," she replied, then noticed Julia, the children's nurse, standing in the doorway.

"The babies are ready for bed now, Signora," she said.

"I'll tuck them in, Julia," she answered and followed her to the stairs.

He watched her ascend the staircase.

He shouted up: "Magdalena, I almost forgot to tell you. Salvatore is coming tomorrow. He'll be spending the weekend with us."

"It seems the whole world is coming tomorrow," she

answered. "Maybe, I should take him with me to *Swansgarten*. He was a friend of Bella's, too."

"I think I'd like to meet the lady. She sounds very interesting."

To this, Magdalena hadn't replied. She'd just found a letter on her desk and was anxiously opening it.

My dear Magda,

Once again, I find myself forced to put off joining you. I've tried, in every way possible, to put things in order here so that I could be with you and the children on Stefano's birthday; but, believe me, it's absolutely impossible. I've come to a firm decision, though. It is that—no matter what!—I will definitely be there right after harvest. I swear that I'll be there by then. I know how many times I've promised and how many times I've had to break my promises, but not this time. This time, nothing will keep us apart. When harvest starts, I'll have them pack my trunks and send them to the ship. And, on the last day that the last grape is picked, I'll leave.

When you stop to think about it, it's really much better to do it this way. If I were to come this month, as we'd planned, I'd only have to return in a few months. It will be better if I put off my coming until after harvest—that way, I won't have to rush right back. I'm sure that, when you think it over, you'll agree with me.

I know how angry you must be about this. I know that you probably don't believe that I'll be there after harvest. I know, from your last letter, that you're starting to disbelieve anything I say. I can't help it, Magda. I'm telling you the truth. I would do anything to be with you. It's just not possible right now.

I'm sure you can understand that there are some things a man must do and certain duties to which he must attend which he cannot pass on to others. You do understand, don't you?

Kiss the children for me and give my regards to Aleksey and the Asheleys. I love you very much.

Tullio

She folded the letter into its envelope and placed it atop the others she kept in a drawer below her dressing mirror. She wondered why she was saving them.

She lay down, staring at the ceiling. She'd not told Stefano that Tullio would be home for his birthday party. *Why disappoint him again? I must have known all along. That's why I didn't bother saying anything to Stefano. Sure! I knew he wouldn't be here!*

She thought, then, about writing to her husband, but decided against it. She was too furious. She'd say all the wrong things. *Tomorrow . . . I'm going to sit down and have a long talk with Salvatore about this tomorrow . . . and I'll write to Tullio tomorrow night . . . after I speak with Salvatore.*

Tomorrow. Tomorrow's going to be some day. Well, maybe, it's better that he's not coming this month. I don't want him here while Bella is around. She's sure to be gone by harvest. Not that they ever meant anything to each other. Still . . . just the same . . . why should they meet again?

She suddenly became as angry with herself as she was with her husband, realizing that she was actually rationalizing why it might be better for him to stay away a little longer. Only, this time, Bella Modesto was the excuse—one was as good as any other.

In a few minutes, she rejoined Aleksey. She'd brought down the remaining mail and was uninterestedly skimming through it. There were invitations, the usual ones which she was annoyed to receive; each required a response.

There were always invitations for Magdalena Barragatto. Unlike Louise, she wasn't considered a social climber, because that label was reserved only for newly rich Americans; and, neither Magdalena nor Aleksey could ever be considered a part of that crass group. Kostenov and the Barragattos were foreigners. Europeans. Not immigrants. They were very wealthy, very cultured foreigners. A little unfriendly at times. But, they lent the immediate area a continental touch.

She had to think, now, before writing her usual refusals. Louise might have received some of these same invitations—at least, those for charity functions. If she had, she would be attending with her guest. Magdalena would have to be present to translate. Already, she mused, her life was being affected. *But, Bella Modesto, of all people!* She shook her head, receiving a questioning side glance from Aleksey.

Magdalena sighed deeply. Another story was beginning. She glanced at her wristwatch. It would be already past midnight in Orvietto, and she wondered what her husband was doing. She missed him more than ever.

Chapter Two

Nothing is so black as an Italian woman in mourning. When one loses a husband or a grown son, all of her clothing is dyed black. If she is poor, her stockings are thick cotton, and the black dye covers any trace of flesh beneath them; if she is wealthy, the stockings are silk, and the black dye doesn't adhere so completely or evenly, causing the shading to appear even more ominous. Her eyes fall deeply into their sockets, and creases appear around their ridges. The skin under her fingernails turns olive-gray and her complexion sallows; then, the whole of her succumbs to being a shadow. And, she will never again appear in another color until the day she is laid to rest, at which time, she will be buried in a soft, white shroud.

Tullio stared at his aunts and at Ernesto's young widow. He knew that, eventually, they might wear jewelry again—but that, too, would be only jet beads or ebony. All else would be stored in a vault for their daughters or daughters-in-law. He watched the women for a long time, not listening to the funeral prayers or the eulogies or the weeping. Ernesto, the youngest of his cousins, was dead; a hunting accident, they said. But Ernesto was an excellent hunter. He would not shoot himself with his own gun and the females in his family were as black as they should be. Throughout the requiem mass he could think only of how, just four years ago, Ernesto had saved his life.

He would remain in black only until after the funeral. Men don't mourn.

The next day, he invited young Guido to dinner.

"I've kept your dinner warm, Don Tullio. I knew you'd be coming back tonight," his cook was saying. "That's why I cooked so early. But, it's not ruined. It's not dried out at all."

He nodded. He had little appetite this evening, but, to avoid hurting her feelings, decided to attempt eating what she'd prepared.

"There's a letter for you."

"Thank you, Carmella." He put it in his pocket and stared at the table.

Each course was in a silver dish: the appetizer, soup, entrees, and salad arranged in a semi-circle from left to right. Two wine decanters and a pitcher of effervescent water stood guard. Nuts and other fruit, as well as cheese and pastries, waited on a sideboard with coffee and liquors. The bulk lessened his appetite even further. He'd just returned from Milan; there, people had been standing in bread lines.

"I'll serve myself," he said.

She grunted a "Good night."

"*Buona notte,*" he answered. "Oh, I sent for Guido. When he gets here, please send him right in."

"Into the dining room?"

"Yes."

"Even if you're still eating?"

"Yes." He waited, then, for her words . . .

. . . which came: "Your father would never have let outdoor servants come into his dining room. He would have let them wait in the kitchen."

She was satisfied. She had chastised him and would sleep well tonight, so he grinned and repeated, "Yes. Good night." He watched the door swing widely behind her as she left the room. Within minutes—he'd barely cut into his first piece of melon—a young man appeared. He was young, slight, but darkly handsome. As a small orphan boy he had helped Magdalena while Tullio was in prison and he cherished him for that.

"Excuse me, Signor Barragatto, but the cook, she said you wanted me to come in as soon as I got here."

"Come in, Guido. Sit down."

"Sir?"

"That's all right. Sit down. There's something I want to talk to you about. Have you eaten? Help yourself. There's too much here for one person, anyway. Go get yourself a plate from that china closet over there."

He watched Guido handle the platters: he knew that their delicacy intimidated him. Then, pouring wine, he said: "To your health."

"Thank you."

"How old are you now, Guido?"

"Eighteen."

"You look older."

Guido nodded.

"I've been hearing, lately, that, when it comes to automobiles, you're the best mechanic in the area. I hear that you're a very good driver, too. Is that true?"

"Well, I guess I am pretty good. I love a good car. It's something beautiful, a good machine."

"I've heard also, that you're pretty good with a rifle. How are you with pistols?"

"I'm better with pistols. But, usually, the shooting contests are only for rifles. I don't get many chances to use pistols."

Tullio left the table. "Excuse me. I'll be right back," he told the youth. "Stay here. Try some of that fish. It's very good."

Tullio returned with a pistol. He opened a window and pointed to a nearby tree. "Is that within this pistol's range?"

"Yes."

He handed the gun to Guido. "You see the four birds on that limb?"

135

"Yes."

"Let me see you hit them." Then, Tullio clapped his hands suddenly and loudly, and the birds scattered.

Almost simultaneously with the birds' movements, four shots rang out, three of the birds falling to the ground.

"That's not bad," Tullio said, trying to hide his astonishment. "Three out of four. That's not too bad."

"I'll try again."

"No, that won't be necessary."

They returned to their dinner. Later, over espresso and anisette, Tullio approached him. "Would you like to be my wife's personal chauffeur?"

"The signora's driver? Of course! I'd be honored! When is she coming home?"

"She's not. Not yet, anyway. You would be working for her in America, as long as she's there. Then, when she returns, you could return with her, if you like."

"America? I thought she was in Switzerland."

"She's in America," Tullio said. He put down his fork and continued: "And now, you are the only person, except for my cousin, Benedetto, who knows where she is. I don't want anyone else to know. Understood?"

The young man looked pensively toward his host. "Yes, understood." There was silence for a few moments. Shortly, he asked: "Signor Barragatto, does this have anything to do with the trouble in the vineyards? Is the signora in any danger?"

Tullio poured more espresso. "The situation is this. In America, they have an idiotic law which prohibits the manufacture or sale or importation of anything containing alcohol. That includes wine. We can't ship anymore of our wine to them. Whatever we make here, we can sell only in Europe. There's no more legal American market for *Barragatto*."

"A law that says men can't drink wine? That's ridiculous."

Tullio breathed deeply. "Nevertheless, it exists."

"But, what does that have to do with us? Or with the signora?"

"Before Prohibition came into effect—that's what the name of the law is, Prohibition—we opened vineyards in the United States, also. Our American wine is called *Piccolo Villaggio*." He paused, then, noticing a change in Guido's expression. *He's getting the picture*, he mused. "The American vineyards are going to waste."

Guido winced. This wasn't for the benefit of his host. This was an honest expression.

"So," Tullio continued, "*Barragatto Wineries* is in a very bad state because it's lost its best customer, the American market. And, *Piccolo Villaggio* might as well not even exist."

Guido leaned forward, his forearms resting on the table, his palms down, his fingers separated like the points of a star. A thought-veil obscured his face.

He understands. I'm sure he does.

"The *malandrini* . . . they're there? . . . In America, too? They stretch all the way across the ocean?"

"Yes."

". . . and, they know that *Piccolo Villaggio* and *Barragatto Wineries* are owned by the same people?"

"Yes."

"I see."

"What do you see?" Tullio asked him.

Slowly, measuring his words, Guido began: "They want you to make wine in your American vineyards again. Not only that, they want you to sell them *Barragatto*, too. They want to sell both wines illegally. You've refused. You've been fighting them." Hearing himself say the words cleared the picture. All was focusing. "And, that's the reason for all the fires in our vineyards lately. They didn't start by accident. And the reason for the shootings. And why some of the families have been leaving our vineyards . . . after their fathers, and their grandfathers before them all worked here . . . because they're afraid to stay."

Tullio Barragatto didn't reply, and his servant realized that he'd guessed correctly.

Guido continued. "And the recriminations . . . you're afraid that they might reach out for the signora, herself . . . That's why you're keeping her far away from here, and far away from yourself. That's why everybody thinks she's in Switzerland. You've been hiding her."

Tullio sat back. He'd studied Guido for months now. He'd assumed, but tonight he was convinced: *He thinks before he talks. And, he's Italian . . . he thinks our way. He'll do very nicely.*

"You know, Signor Barragatto, that your wife took me in when I was fourteen. I was an orphan. I never knew who my parents were. I owe everything to her."

Tullio nodded. This was another reason why he'd chosen Guido. Guido had no one to worry about. No family. No loyalties. No debts that might have been passed down through generations.

"My wife doesn't know anything of the situation."

"Of course not," Guido said.

"As far as she's concerned, you wanted to live in America, and I am sending you as her personal chauffeur. She's never to suspect anything else. You're to take her everywhere and wait until she's ready to go home. Never let another chauffeur take her anywhere. You do all the driving, no matter where she goes. Never leave and come back later to pick her up, either. Always wait. Understood?"

"Yes."

Tullio handed him a business card. "Go to this place tomorrow. He's my tailor. He'll make all your uniforms. Order a half-dozen to be ready by the twelfth. Your ship sails on the fifteenth. Order two winter coats to be forwarded to my office in Milan. I'll send them to you from my office."

"Three weeks? I sail in three weeks?"

Tullio continued, "Then, go to my gunsmith. I've already

placed my order with him. The order is ready. Here's his card. He's to give you three pistols. One, you'll keep in the car trunk. One, you'll keep in the glove compartment. One, you'll wear at all times."

"I sail in three weeks?"

"On the fifteenth, from Genoa, on the *Asheley Neptune.*"

"But, how can all those uniforms be ready by the twelfth?"

"They'll be ready."

"But, I have no birth certificate. No baptism certificate. I have no papers at all. How can I leave the country?"

Tullio placed a leather portfolio on the table. He watched Guido go through all the papers inside of it.

The boy was flabbergasted.

"Everything you need is in there. Your ticket. Your credentials. More money than you can possibly spend during the voyage. You even have a last name now: Fallanca. Oh, I noticed that they made a little mistake. They wrote down 'Giulio' instead of 'Guido'—but that won't make any difference, will it . . ."

Guido stared at the papers. "Fallanca. Fallanca." He liked it. "Guido Fallanca. Giulio . . . Guido . . . what's the difference . . . nobody's going to look at the papers except the immigration people. I'll still call myself Guido. Fallanca. That's a good name. Fallanca." He was shaking his head with amazement. "Guido Fallanca."

"When the ship docks in New York, you'll be met by my cousin. His name is Salvatore Crispino. He'll take you to where my wife is living. Consider whatever he tells you as though it were an order coming directly from me. Naturally, the signora isn't to know that, either."

"Very well."

"There's a question in your eyes. What is it?"

Guido replied: "Your cousin, Ernesto Crispino . . . how was he related to this Salvatore Crispino who'll be meeting me?"

"Ernesto was Salvatore's youngest brother."

"Was it really an accident?"

He'd already asked himself that more than a hundred times. "I don't know," he replied. "Are there any more questions?"

He shook his head. "I can't think of any right now." He was still staring at the portfolio. He'd never seen so much money at one time.

"There's something else. As far as anyone around here is concerned, you're moving to Milan. No one, not anyone at all, is to know you're leaving the country. I don't want anyone finding out where my wife is living by having you followed. You hear me? You're to tell nobody at all that you're sailing. If anyone wants to know where you're going, I've found you a job in Milan."

Guido smiled. "You've thought of everything, Signor Barragatto. All the preparations. The papers. The uniforms. The pistols. Signor Crispino meeting me at the dock. All that before I even knew I was going. Even a name . . . Fallanca."

"Does that bother you?"

"No, but it surprises me. I really do want this job. But, how did you know that I would?"

Tullio shrugged carelessly. At first, he replied as Guido would never have expected: "You used to have a crush on my wife when you were a kid. Now, you can be her bodyguard."

Guido fidgeted.

"Seriously, Guido, why in the world wouldn't you want the job? After all, I'm offering you a better position than you would ever get here. I'm offering you a chance to go to America . . . you may or may not want to come back . . . that's your choice, when the time comes. Anyway, what could you do with your life in Orvietto? You're no wine man."

"That's true. I've never thought about what I would do tomorrow."

There appeared, then, to be no more questions. Tullio said, "I'm going up, now. I haven't had any sleep in over twenty-four hours. If you'll take my advice, you'll get to bed, too. You're going to have a busy day tomorrow. You should try to get to the tailor's as early as possible. He'll have a lot of work to o with you."

"Yes. Yes. The tailor. The first thing in the morning."

"Oh, something else. Have your picture taken for the papers. It has to be put in the space next to your name." He showed him where the photograph had to be pasted. "Don't forget. That's important. You need a picture on it. Then, sign along the bottom of the picture. And, whatever you do, don't forget to write Giulio Fallanca, and not Guido Fallanca; otherwise, we'll run into trouble with all the other papers. There's the same mistake on all of them. They all say Giulio."

Guido stood. "Good night, Signor Barragatto. And, thank you. Thank you, very much."

Tullio nodded. "Good night, Guido." Pointing to the untouched pastries, he said, "Finish them, if you like. Carmella is a very good cook."

He left the young man in his dining room. He went directly upstairs, then; and, by the time he reached his bedroom, he suspected that he might fall asleep on his feet.

A bath had been drawn. Its warm, fragrant vapors escaped his bathroom and sneaked through his dressing room toward his bedroom. They were too inviting to ignore. He followed the teasing mist, dropping his clothes in a trail. In front of the tub, he smiled sleepily, stuck one foot in, then the other; then slid down, sinking into it.

Hours later, Tullio awoke, still in the white marble tub. The bath water had turned icy-cold and he cursed. For a few frightening seconds, he thought he was in the army again, awaking in the bottom of a trench filled with snow. The room was chilly—the fire had gone out—and he was shivering. Emerging awkwardly from the tub, he almost lost his balance as he wrapped a huge towel around himself. He cursed again, then, and got into his bed, still wrapped in the towel and still shivering. It was the start of another rotten day, he decided; but he'd stay in bed for a while—anyway, at least until sunrise.

This was his third day back in Orvietto. He'd remain two weeks, then return to Milan. That was the norm, now.

Alternating weeks. Two in the office and two in the vineyards.

Just before Ernesto's accident, he'd been considering devoting more time to the office. Unlikely, now. Unless it was an accident.

Benedetto would come by this morning. He'd fill him in. They'd not been able to talk about it during the wake or funeral.

Maybe, it really was an accident. Anything is possible.

No! Even Guido knows it wasn't. He wouldn't have asked about it if he didn't already know better.

His thoughts dwelled on Guido. He expected him to be a good chauffeur, a faithful bodyguard. He'd always been devoted to Magdalena.

Eighteen. That's a nice age. But, I'm only twelve years older than he is. How come I look more than twenty years older?

How old is Magdalena now? Twenty-two? Twenty-three? She's twenty-two. That's right. She was born in 1900. That would make her twenty-two.

Once he began thinking about Magdalena, he gave up trying to fall asleep again. He resigned himself to the start of his day, rotten or not, and was dressed and downstairs before the surprised Carmella had finished brewing the coffee.

In a short while, Benedetto arrived. He wondered why he couldn't sleep either. They breakfasted together. They reviewed the weekly yields. They studied the pedigree of a racehorse they'd been considering adding to their stables. They discussed the Italian economy. They speculated over the coming grape harvest. They commented upon the weather. Then, there was silence. They'd stalled as long as they could. They looked squarely at one another, then away. The silence was a long one; almost several minutes.

Benedetto brought it up: "They killed my brother."

Tullio had to ask: "Are you sure?"

"I'm as sure of that as I am that the two of us are sitting here."

"What happened?"

"More of your people were leaving. Ernesto went and spoke with them. He spoke to them right out in the open, in a mass meeting in the vineyards. You know Ernesto. Hotheaded! They'd burned some of the vineyards and flooded some of the cellars. He'd had enough. He said something to the effect that if anyone is trying to scare away our workers, he would put them straight. From what I've been told, he was talking as though he had a whole army behind him. He was so convincing that some pickers unpacked their wagons and moved back into their cottages. The next morning, Ernesto was dead. And, the pickers he'd talked into staying packed up their families again and left that very afternoon."

The cousins talked until lunchtime. As he was about to leave, Benedetto said, "Maybe, you've been right all along. Maybe, your way is the only way to deal with them."

Tullio didn't comment. He knew what his cousin meant. Tullio's way was political. It was Fascism.

During his university days, Tullio Barragatto had been no less impressionable than any of his fellow students and far more so than many of them because he was so idealistic. One evening, he and a friend had joined a crowd of thousands, feverishly applauding a twenty-eight-year-old socialist named Benito Mussolini. The speaker had cried out against injustice, poverty, and illiteracy, sentiments neither original nor innovative; yet, he'd been a spellbinding orator; he'd enraptured his audience.

Mussolini's sincerity was beyond question. His hatred for all kinds of oppressors of the weak—and, he'd singled out Italy's organized criminals—was as startling in its simplicity as it was courageous in its naming of names. Further, he'd reminded the students of the grandeur of Italy's past, and he'd shamed them by pointing out its miserable present; then—he knew his countrymen very well—he'd caressed their hearts, encouraging them to recapture their place in the world.

From that evening when he'd first listened to the youthful

143

orator, Tullio had become his disciple. When his idol, disillusioned with the socialists, broke with them to form his own party, *I Fascii*, Tullio had become a Fascist.

In its literal translation, *fasce* means a "band" or "bandage" or "swaddling band." Loosely translated, it came to mean a "banding together" or a "bandaging" of the wounds of the country.

The very first bands—or *fascii*—were almost like social clubs which turned, very quickly, into political clubs. They consisted of well-intentioned, highly-motivated individuals who were mainly political reformists and university students.

These young Fascists were so mindful of the greatness of their country's history that they were humiliated by the reality of her present. Daily, they were confronted with the truth: she was being governed by a weak king and a shaky cabinet; poverty and ignorance were everywhere; leftist agitation was destroying her, inch by inch; and corruption—the same kind that had been crippling her for centuries—was running unchallenged in every sector.

Infuriated by what they saw around them, Fascists called for a strong, centralized government. They committed themselves to the destruction of illiteracy, Communism, and organized crime.

It was in this original mode that Tullio Barragatto had become a Fascist. He loved his country too much to be anything else.

By the early 1920s, it was apparent to a large majority of the original old-line Fascists that their leader was changing, and, along with their leader, the very movement, itself; even its newest members were of a whole different breed. Whether the change had come about suddenly or gradually didn't concern them. What mattered was that there was a very definite and frightening shift—not only in the party's goals, but in its methods—and it was beginning to terrify the most astute and stouthearted of men.

To Tullio Barragatto, though, the changes didn't appear so

144

ominous. He could find a reason for everything of which he disapproved. Wishing to avoid another political argument, however, he hoped that Benedetto wouldn't persist.

"You heard what I said," Benedetto repeated. "I said that two wrongs don't make a right!"

Tullio was startled. "I didn't hear you say any such thing. The only thing you said is that my way is probably the only way to deal with them."

"Now, we send out one kind of killer . . . to kill another kind of killer. That's your way."

"For a few moments, there, I thought you were starting to see the light. What's wrong with you? Do you want your brother's murderers to get away with what they did? That's exactly what's been happening for the past few hundred years. Everybody's always been afraid to fight them."

"Nobody in our family has ever been afraid of them. Only, before, we used to deal with them ourselves. We didn't take our troubles to political clubs. We had too much pride."

"Vendettas have killed off more families than the plague."

Benedetto persisted: "We didn't hide behind political terrorists!"

"Enough!"

The cousins had separated in a huff that morning. Their arguments were happening too often lately and were seriously straining their friendship. The arguments were always over the same subject, Fascism. Afterwards, each man was disappointed in himself, feeling that he could have handled the other in a more tactful manner; but it was too late, because they didn't expect to see one another again for a couple of weeks. Benedetto would be going to Milan, now that Tullio was in Orvietto. Apologies would have to wait.

It had disturbed Tullio more than he'd allowed Benedetto to realize. This was not the first time his cousin had used the term, "political terrorists," and he took this as a personal insult. He was totally committed to the party, and that meant that his cousin was accusing him of terrorist tactics, also.

The rest of us can't be blamed for the actions of some lunatic fringe. There are fanatics in every movement.

There had been numerous bad episodes—that's how Tullio referred to them, as episodes; but Benedetto called them terrorist attacks. Brigades of black-shirted party members had attacked whomever they'd considered enemies to the cause.

The cause—to stamp out Communism! A vile, contemptuous way of life! It denied the individual . . . the artist in your soul, the one force that made men different from animals. There was no room in the land of the arts for such a manner of thinking . . . it would destroy the beauty . . . it would be such a waste . . .

The cause—a strong, centralized government! Who could deny the necessity? For the rich, it was the only way to regulate labor and tariffs . . . there would be fewer strikes . . . the leftists couldn't incite the populace so easily. For the lower middle class, it offered a way to control inflation . . . they wouldn't have to emigrate just to survive . . .

The cause—annihilate illiteracy. If this one, beautiful thing could happen, everything else would fall into place . . .

The cause—destroy organized crime! This had been the true ruler of the country for centuries . . . with neither crown nor written charter, it had outlasted governments of Europe and the Americas . . . and it had obligated the people . . . and now, it stretched across the ocean . . .

The change has got to be made. That time for change is now. Right now. Why can't you see that, Benedetto? You're not an ignorant man.

And, we're not terrorists, either. We're not. It's true—I won't deny it—we've had to use violence at times. But, that's the only way to deal with certain people. If you try to reason with them, they laugh right in your face. All they understand is violence. It's unfortunate, but it's a fact of life. I know that, now.

The prior year, 1921, Mussolini had gained the alliance of more respectable parties. Support for his cause had come to him from every level of society. Now, at 39, he'd become the youngest premier in Italian history. And now, the violence would subside, Tullio was sure, because Fascism was officially recognized. It was accepted. Benedetto was wrong . . . he was positive of that . . . and he would somehow convince him.

Tullio nodded and the new stablemaster grinned. The youth was learning quickly. He'd checked ahead and had been told his master was dressed in champagne and gray this morning; and, he'd readied the proper animal—the palomino, with the silver-gray saddle.

This was one facet of Tullio Barragatto's reputation. He was so fastidious about his appearance that he wouldn't even ride a horse of a color that didn't compliment his attire.

Tullio's nails were always manicured. The creases in his trousers were always sharp. The tailoring of his jackets was constantly perfect. All of his shirts were silk, and many were ruffled; and he favored furs and suedes and soft, fine leathers. He was lightly, but distinctly, perfumed; each scent had been developed expressly for him. And, even though some of his peers had more extensive—and a few, more expensive— wardrobes, his particular look had a specialness about it. It was never contrived, but it was complete. It was always masculine, but it wasn't afraid to be beautiful. And, it was uniquely, and undeniably, his own.

His appearance was not limited to his personal grooming. It included a fixed set of rules for everything connected with him: the manner in which the table was set in the evening; a specific choice of linens by the day and the season; the pedigrees in his stables; the respect his servants received from the townspeople.

Tullio's preoccupation with grooming and outward appearance wasn't all vanity on a conscious level. His grandfathers, uncles and father had been the same. He'd inherited the fundamentals; then, he'd gradually developed the finer points, tailoring them to his specifics. To his workers, now, whose parents had served him through the generations, he was just as a Barragatto should be.

It wasn't merely vanity. It was breeding. It was tradition. It was what a baby prince grows up with before he becomes a king. A very necessary self-esteem. A matter of survival.

Besides the physical finery, the Barragatto fortune had bought him finesse and charm and a broad education. Added to these assets were natural blessings—an abundance of good looks, a handsome figure, and a body language that was regal. And, as had his father, his uncles, and his grandfathers before him, Tullio Barragatto took full advantage of his virtues. They were his most powerful weapon.

It had been frightening for Tullio (still in his twenties when his father died) to have to accept all the responsibilities that were dropped in his lap. He had the unswerving loyalty of his cousins, the young Crispino brothers, and of Kostenov—but that wasn't enough. He was the head of the family. The victories and the mistakes would be his own. And now, on this morning of his thirtieth birthday, the obligations that made up his world were more awesome than ever. But, he dared not admit this to anyone.

Chapter Three

The day—what little there'd been of it—had gone well so far. In its wee hours, he'd settled the business with Guido. After breakfast, he'd smoothed Benedetto's feelings. Not a bad start, he decided. Perhaps, it wasn't going to be such a rotten day, after all.

He had no qualms about saddling Guido with the escapee's identity. Everybody had a price. Guido was not unique. Some day, he might be tempted to sell out . . . but, not if he knew that Guidonia would be the consequence . . . All he had to do was not betray the Barragattos, and no harm would come to him.

And, as for Benedetto: he was just a little confused, uncertain; he'd come around. He'd continue to speak for him at the meetings. He'd convince them that Benedetto wasn't really anti-fascist; just very, very confused . . . just confused . . . he didn't have leftist leanings . . . he wasn't a socialist at heart. He'd let no harm come to his cousin. This was in his blood, and he would, if necessary, defend him with his own. He'd made this very plain at the last meeting. He'd warned them, and those old-line fascists in his group knew that he would not make idle threats; it was the new members he was

149

concerned about . . . he'd have to watch out for them—some of them were merely thugs; they had no respect; they were the lunatics; they were why Fascism was getting a bad name.

It was definitely not a bad day, he decided; and there was no reason why the rest of it shouldn't go just as well.

At this moment, he was riding through the vineyards. He would have been safer inside his automobile driving over a paved road into town, but it was more impressive this way. To drive in would have served no purpose. It was better to go on horseback. His workers would have to look up at him. He would nod his greetings toward them. He would be all alone, out in the open, unprotected; and they would wonder if he were going to be shot like Ernesto—that would give them some drama. He would ride high and proud, like a nobleman, like an old Roman warrior; and they would admire him—that would supply the spectacle.

There is a gene that Italians have. Scientists have not yet discovered it or isolated it; but it does exist, nevertheless, just as surely as night follows day. That gene controls the soul of the Italian. It makes him crave drama and spectacle; if he is denied these two phenomena, he dies. The grand opera, a great orator, the history of Rome, some lines of poetry, a circus, a beautiful painting, a sporting event, intense love or hatred, violence, any high-pitched emotion, a mystery of religion, pride, a sky filled with stars—the drama and the spectacle intermingle and keep him alive. Recognize the gene, and you understand him; manipulate the gene, and you enslave him.

Tullio knew his people. The sun would be beating down on them at this time of day. They'd stop as he'd pass. They'd wipe their brows and squint to look up. The older ones would remember his father. The younger ones would wish they were he. They would all admire him. He was their landlord and their employer. And there was no doubt that—("Look at his grandness!" they'd tell themselves.)—he was their protector. He knew the gene very well.

When he reached the cobblestones of Orvietto, he was

certain, and rightly so, that his tour of the vineyards had been much more effective than poor Ernesto's mass meeting. He'd satisfied his workers' cravings:—none of them would be deserting the Barragatto fields this week.

He didn't dismount until he was directly in front of the cafe. There, the owner's son took charge of the palomino; and Tullio walked toward the open-air portion of the restaurant where a small group of men were already standing.

The men, an Italian, a Frenchman and a German, were quite a bit older than he. They'd done business with his father; and, although they'd never met Tullio, they'd recognized the Barragatto in him, and had stood to introduce themselves. When the amenities were concluded, the meeting started. Their questions began.

"Yes," he replied, "I'll tell you whatever I know about Carmine Pace. First, he's not an independent. Second, he's not just another middleman. He used to travel back and forth, between Palermo and Orvietto. He was being trained by the *patrono*, himself. I suppose he could be considered his protégé."

"And, this particular *patrono*," one asked, "how far up on the ladder is he? Or, is he just a local?"

Tullio answered: "He's local, but only in the sense that he lives just up the road from here. Actually, he controls this whole part of the country, and I'm sure that he answers only to Palermo." He knew that they had hoped not to hear this, but he had to make it clear. "He's not just a local."

Each of the men owned vineyards in Europe, as well as in the United States. Each had been trying to comply with the American law. And each had been approached by one Carmine Pace. Now, their prime suspicion was being confirmed, and by the newest Barragatto.

Tullio knew that each of his competitors had done business, at one time or another, with at least one of the local *patroni*. That's how they managed to survive. He knew that even his father had dealt with them. ... But, to do business with

151

Palermo—that was the bottom line, the final contract.
. . . And, to buck Palermo—it had never been done.

"Have you ever dealt personally with Pace?" another asked.

"No," Tullio said. "I met him once, a few years ago. He
introduced himself to me in passing. That's all. I didn't even
know who he was. Shortly after that, I went into the army, and
he left for America."

*. . . and Bella sailed with him . . . I wonder how Bella is
doing . . . if she's still with him . . . well, as Salvatore used to say:
Viva Bella!*

"Were you going to say something else?" the Frenchman
asked.

"No," Tullio replied. "I was just thinking about something.
It had nothing to do with this."

Could she still be with him? No. I doubt it.

"So," the Frenchman continued, "as we suspected, this
Pace is the American counterpart." He smirked. "Sort of an
ambassador."

That means we're all in the same position.

"It appears that way," the Italian said. "First our American
business manager or attorney is approached by this Carmine
Pace. Not just once, but a few times, in a very businesslike
manner. Nothing crude. No threats. No violence. But then, if
we do not agree to his proposals, our vineyards at home are
attacked. Then, our workers. And then, our families. Do you
see the pattern, Herr Beckmann?"

"Precisely," the German said. "There's been no deviation at
all. They've used the same method with each of us."

Tullio said: "So, it's evident that Carmine Pace has gone to a
great deal of trouble to make sure we know whom he
represents. And, they probably know that we're all meeting
here today to discuss the problem."

"Is that why you called this meeting, Tullio? Is that why you
wanted it here, in Orvietto, in this open cafe? To show them a
united front?"

"Yes," he replied. "That's exactly the reason. You see,

gentlemen, if my guess is right . . . they'll give us a little time to put our heads together and think about it . . . and then, Pace will contact our American operations again, if only to see what we've come up with."

Tullio continued. He spoke at length. He ended: "I intend being in New York the next time Pace approaches North American Distributors. I imagine that would be just after harvest."

"Why after harvest? Why not now?"

"Well, there's nothing they can do to us right now. They won't dare burn any more of our vineyards, because that would destroy the yields . . . and, with no crop at all, everybody would lose, including them. We'd have nothing to sell them. But, if they wait until harvest, they could attack our cellars. Then, they know they could ruin us all in one single night."

The elders listened to the words of this newest Barragatto. And they liked what they heard. His ideas mirrored his appearance. The phrasing was cautious, but it was firm. It was just like his shirt cuffs; they were laced, but they were also tailored. And, this pleased them, because he, the youngest in their midst, would someday be the oldest wine man; and he would be counseling their own sons at future meetings. It gave them a good feeling, a sense of security; the dynasties would survive. He was a worthy competitor.

They listened attentively to Tullio. They allowed him to speculate freely, considered all he proposed, and found it seldom necessary to object. When he departed, he did so as gracefully as when he'd first approached—high and proud in his silver saddle, the golden palomino trotting grandly away; and, his position and thoughts about the Pace situation were as concise and uncluttered as his picture. Also, because each of the elders realized that he'd discreetly withheld enough information to safeguard his own interests without compromising theirs, they respected him all the more.

He returned home through the same route. Sometimes, the

palomino would break into a trot, or a canter, at its own will, because it didn't like the cobblestones; and this made the horse look even more beautiful than it was, and Tullio even more a master equestrian than he was—the duo were a spectacle.

He crossed himself when he passed in front of the cathedral and bowed respectfully toward nuns who were sitting outside their convent door. He acknowledged greetings from the townspeople. He half-smiled at the ladies. He nodded to the merchants. He waved to the men in the fields.

By the time he reached the dirt road, he knew what Orvietto was thinking—

. . . Barragatto isn't afraid. They killed his cousin. But, he's not afraid.

. . . He wouldn't come into town on horseback, without even a bodyguard, if he were afraid. He wouldn't sit in open cafes, right under their noses, just like a target, not if he were afraid. And, he wouldn't smile as he does, nor ride as he does, nor look as he does, not if he were afraid.

. . . He might have already made a deal with them. Or, maybe, he's just too powerful for them.

. . . So, maybe, for a little while longer, I'll continue to pick his grapes, and press them, and bottle them, and cork them, and label them. Why should I run? Why should I be afraid, if he's not?

Not even Benedetto suspected the truth.

Tullio was relaxed at last. He could loosen his tie and roll up his sleeves. He could even slump into the soft leather of the great winged chair and kick off his boots. No servants would come into the study at this time of day. He was assured of his privacy.

He'd poured himself a tall glass of whisky, something he would not usually do, because he didn't like the taste of it. He'd believed he'd needed it, though; and it had helped. It had settled his nerves.

He'd not expected that anything might occur on the way to

the meeting, or even during the meeting. He'd known that Pace's people had wanted that meeting. It had been just as important to them as it had been to the wine men. It had been necessary that everybody concerned know with whom they were dealing. It would be after the meeting, when Tullio would have served their purpose, that they might attack . . . if only as a warning to the other wine barons. All of this, he had known from the beginning; and even Benedetto had been adamant about his not going.

"Call it off," his cousin had demanded. "Call the whole thing off. Go meet with them in Germany, or in France, or even in Milan. But, not here. You'd be like a sitting duck over here. All they want is for you people to get together . . . just to make sure you all know it's them you're dealing with. After that, you would be expendable."

He'd acted well. He'd convinced Benedetto that he didn't agree with him. Benedetto had been furious. He'd called him a fool and said that he'd wind up getting ambushed on his way home.

That is precisely when the fear had set in—during his return to the Barragatto compound. He'd not expected it to be so overwhelming. Only the movements of the prancing palomino had hidden his tremor. He'd managed, however, to fool everyone. Of this, he was positive.

The whisky had been a very good idea. He felt much better now. He'd finally stopped shaking. Yes, he was sure that no one had suspected.

With his legs sprawled out, he rested his elbows on the arms of the chair and steepled his fingers in front of him. It was a pose he would never assume with others nearby because it made him appear too casual; and, some people might confuse that with carelessness, or indecisiveness, or even a lack of authority. Yet, nobody could see him now; and that was good, because this was his favorite position for serious thinking. He pressed inwards on his fingers until his knuckle joints cracked. Then, he let them slide into spires again, and he stared through them at nothing.

He wondered: Did he know anyone, or of anyone, who'd ever really resisted Palermo? . . . *No, nobody.*

Did he know anyone at all, besides Mussolini, who would dare to even suggest it aloud? . . . *Yes, Ernesto.* But, Ernesto had done it the wrong way. He'd been impatient. . . . *Mustn't be impatient with them.* Ernesto had permitted others to see his true feelings. He'd shown his anger. . . . *Mustn't show anger, not before you strike.*

But, who else?

There was no other solution. There had to be a change, and it was already too long in coming. The fear had to be dispersed; and then, the custom—the resignation to their will—could be broken. Even if it were to begin with him, himself. He'd shown them, only this morning, that he wasn't afraid.

There had to be a change!

But, not Benedetto's way, either. I have a daughter and two sons now. And Magdalena. I can't. Not Benedetto's way.

He was certain that Fascism would destroy Pace's people. It would attack them at their very foundation. All it needed was a little more time. It would succeed. Palermo would be routed. Italy would be rid of the vermin. But, what of the *malandrini* who'd already reached America? Fascists couldn't fight them in America. The American politicians . . . the New York police . . . they were all the same . . . they'd sell their mothers for a glass of beer . . . Palermo already owned them, their price was so low.

Fascism would bring about the change that would save Barragatto Wineries. If North American Distributors were to survive, though, he could depend only on himself. All he had to do was stay alive. He poured another whisky.

The second whisky was even better than the first. It warmed his insides. It made him mellow. In America, they drank it with ice. He couldn't understand this: unless, maybe, it was to kill the taste . . . it was vile . . . they had to suffer through the taste to get the effect . . . that might be the reason—at least, it was the only one he could think of.

There would be a party tonight. His aunts always gave him a party on his saint's day. But, the people he'd want to be present wouldn't. Not Ernesto. Not Benedetto. Not Magda. Not Aleksey.

He'd commissioned an artist to paint Magdalena. She'd sent him the portrait as a birthday present. It showed her sitting next to a table with nothing on it except the silver cup he'd once given her and the pack of cigarettes he'd left under her pillow. He loved her even more for having thought of that. People might see the painting and would surely comment about the cup and the cigarettes; but he'd not tell them of their significance. One doesn't share his love letters. He was surprised, because he didn't think that he could love her more than he already did. He felt foolish, because he was tempted to kiss the painting. Men don't do such things.

He stared at the portrait. At Magdalena. Her green eyes. The cigarettes. The silver cup. The emerald brooch she'd had placed on it.

I've seen that pin someplace before. I know I have. I'm sure of it. Now, how did that story go? The brooch was her mother's . . . and her mother had come into the camp one evening . . . a complete stranger . . . and Mikel wasn't her real father? I think that's the way it went . . . or, something like that.

He admired the painting for a long time. He'd placed it, temporarily, in front of the bookcase opposite his desk. He'd bring it upstairs later. It would hang in his bedroom. He wouldn't share it. The artist had captured her. He wondered if the artist had questioned her about her choice of accessories; he knew she wouldn't have explained them.

Magda, if anything ever happened to you . . . You stay there . . . You stay there, with Aleksey.

He wondered if Aleksey had gotten used to the noise from the ticker tape machine yet. It had annoyed him so much. He shrugged and laughed about this. The old man would give the machine a dirty look every time he passed it; and once, he'd hit it when he'd thought nobody was looking.

Good old Aleksey . . . he's as steady as a mountain. But, he's so stubborn about certain things. There's nothing wrong with playing the stock market. It's not really just gambling, like he says. It's more than gambling. It's one of the quickest ways to make big money without working for it. Well, that's Aleksey for you. And as smart as he is in certain ways, he's hopelessly naive in other ways. If he ever suspected the Pace problem, he'd go straight to the police. He'd get us all buried within the week. Salvatore is right. Can't let Earl or Aleksey find out about Pace. Pace . . . there's got to be a change . . . starting now . . . a big change.

On the bookshelf directly above the portrait, he suddenly noticed a copy of *I Ching*, which translated, meant *The Book of Change*. How appropriate, he thought . . . *The Book of Change*. While Kostenov had still been his tutor, he'd insisted he study it. He reached for the ancient text. It was the same one from which he'd read as a child and Aleksey's notes were still mixed within its pages.

Tullio handled the yellowing pages carefully as he read:

> *"A Great Man accomplishes the change like a tiger; he is so confident that he does not need to employ divination."*

Kostenov's handwritten interpretation was noted in the margin. It explained: "To 'change like a tiger' means in a brilliantly civilized manner. Confidence that doesn't need divination means he is so certain that his convictions and methods are righteous that he doesn't require the counsel or approval of others regarding what action to take."

Tullio considered this for a while. Then, he read the next hexagram, which said:

> *"The Superior Man brings about the change like a leopard and lesser men promptly switch their allegiance."*

Alongside this passage, Aleksey had inked: " 'Like a leopard'

158

means that he does so in a manner that is exceedingly graceful. That 'lesser men promptly switch their allegiance' means they readily accept his lead."

Tullio returned the book to its shelf. Then, he resumed his thinking pose. He was satisfied that his present thoughts echoed the old Chinese writings. He'd made his position entirely clear to the wine barons; and, he'd employed almost every one of his virtues in doing so . . .

. . . his youth: "Am I still so ignorant and naive, gentlemen, that I am the only one of us who still has no intention of sacrificing principle for profit?"

. . . his continence: "You all knew my father. Is he so lacking in me that you fear my intentions, or my methods? Take a long, hard look, gentlemen. Do you see someone who would defile his name? For, that's what I would be doing if I were to demean you in any way . . . you, whom my father trusted and respected through the decades."

. . . his whole Barragatto: "What good is complete safety without pride? Why acquiesce so readily? I share your fear that they could destroy us in the end . . . but, why not at least *try* to resist them? And then, gentlemen, if, in the long run, they should win, we shall be able to look our sons in the eye and say that we did the best we could."

The elders hadn't replied. Yet, when he'd stood, they'd done so, also, as though they'd been dismissed.

He stared at his fingertips and smiled. His noble competitors would consider what he'd said. Then, the smile disappeared. Either they'd unite behind him, and he'd confront Pace on behalf of all of them—that would make him a leopard; or he would have to stand alone against Pace, and fight like a tiger.

The German, the Frenchman, and the Italian all came to Tullio's party. So did Benedetto.

"What are you doing here?" Tullio asked his cousin. "You're supposed to be in Milan."

"I missed the train. I'll have to catch it tomorrow."

159

Tullio smiled and poured a drink for his cousin. Now, he knew he hadn't been imagining things. Before the meeting, during it, and after it, as well, he'd been almost positive he was being followed by two men with rifles. (That was why Benedetto had missed the train, he realized. He'd never even gone to the station.) "You scared the pants off of me today. I thought you were some of Pace's people."

Benedetto looked at him innocently. His eyebrows and shoulders raised. "What are you talking about? What are you accusing me of now?"

Tullio slapped him affectionately. "Who was with you? Guido?"

Benedetto shrugged and walked away with the drink. He left Tullio alone and feeling very good.

But, I can't start going around with bodyguards, he told himself. That would be admitting weakness.

The wine men's presence really surprised him. He wondered who had invited them, because a saint's day party was usually just a family affair. Also, he'd not expected to hear from any of them until just before harvest since that is when they had agreed to give him their decisions.

"My stepson asked me to tell you that he met your friend and that he put him to work for us," Herr Moeller said.

"Oh, thank you," Tullio replied. "How is Gerhard these days?"

"Fine. As a matter of fact, he's just been engaged. He'll be married by this time next year." The man grimaced. "She seems like a decent enough girl, but my wife is a little upset."

Tullio could not imagine Gerhard being a husband. He'd never seen him with the same woman more than once.

The Frenchman approached him later. In hushed tones, he said, "Look at this," and handed Tullio a Swiss newspaper. He had underscored certain lines in a story about a party in Geneva. They read: ". . . and Magdalena Barragatto came to the masquerade ball as—what else? a wine fairy, and a very

160

beautiful one, at that. Mrs. Barragatto, one of our newest residents, has been a staunch supporter of our goal to . . ."

Tullio recognized the tabloid. It was a North American Distributors publication. Salvatore had probably planted the article. He feigned annoyance.

"If I can find out your wife is in Switzerland, just through some stupid society gossip column," the Frenchman continued, "so can others."

"Thank you for bringing this to my attention," Tullio replied. "Society functions . . . right in the middle of the Alps. Who could foresee such a thing? I'll have to move her to one of the other villages."

The man nodded and took back his paper before rejoining the other men.

Tullio thought: For you to react like that, you must be hiding your wife, too. We're all in the same position. This is a ridiculous way to have to live.

Last to engage Tullio in private conversation was the Italian. "I've been speaking with your cousin Benedetto," he said. "I'd like him to meet my daughter. You've met Cecilia, haven't you, Tullio?"

"A long time ago," he replied, "when we were children."

Tullio listened, as attentively as he possibly could, regarding the virtues of Cecilia; after a while, he realized that the only way to end the conversation was to say: "Let me see what I can do. I'll try to arrange a meeting between Benedetto and Cecilia. Let me see what I can do." He was relieved, and quite positive, that his cousin had not been talking politics with the wine man; in that case, the latter would never have thought of him as a prospective son-in-law, but only as an outspoken enemy to the Party.

He'd learned all he could about the three wine men a few months before he'd called the meeting. He was certain that, of all the choices, this trio had been the best to approach, not only because of their Stateside holdings, but because they, having

161

diversified their businesses and having become the wealthiest, had the most to lose.

"Tullio," his father had once told him, "find out as much as possible about the personal lives of the people you'll have to do business with."

He'd taken his father's advice.

Chapter Four

With her red hair, green eyes and creamy white skin, Magdalena had always made an unusual gypsy. Tullio had told her that the first time he met her. But by the time they were married, she had an explanation for him:

"I wasn't really a gypsy. I was only brought up by gypsies. You see, my mother wandered into their camp one evening. Something terrible must have just happened to her because she was half out of her mind. No one could understand what she was saying. She was babbling and crying and wasn't making any sense at all. The next morning, she gave birth to me and she died that very same day. No one ever found out who she'd been. But, they were certain she wasn't a gypsy, because her clothing and jewelry were too fine. I still have her brooch. See? Here it is. Mikel gave it to me. He saved it for me. No, she definitely wasn't a gypsy. For all I know, my mother might have been a queen. And, that would make me a princess!"

But, those years of lovely freedom when she could run happily alongside the wagons might easily have been part of a different lifetime, so seldom did she think of them or long for them anymore. Like it or not, she was now Magdalena Barragatto, and no longer a little gypsy who could swim and dance and imagine herself a princess.

Once in a while, though, she would finger her mother's emerald brooch and she would remember how sweet her life had been just several short years ago; and she'd wonder and smile.

She would think of her first husband, the farmer. He'd not been a bad husband, not as farmers go.

You look exactly like him, Stefano. Could you ever be a farmer, Stefano? . . . a landlord, maybe . . . but, a farmer?

She'd think, also, of how Tullio had come to help her with the farm, and how he'd taught her to read. Then, she'd fondle the silver cup he'd given her, the cup he would have used as a chalice, had he continued in the seminary.

Your grandfather was furious, Carlo! A Barragatto with a gypsy! They didn't like your mama very much, Carlo.

But, oh, how they resented Rebecca. The worst sin of all. They could teach me how to be a gentle lady, but how could they camouflage her?

The gem now covered the IHS oval of the chalice. Once it was put away, the memory would dispel, and she'd try not to look at it again for several weeks. Reverie did no one any good. She was convinced of that. It was just a waste of time.

Time! She mustn't be late! Not this morning! She has to get dressed! She has to be coiffured! This morning, she must, indeed, look the *grande dame!* If one must meet her husband's former mistress, isn't that the safest offensive?

. . . yet, she wasn't exactly his mistress . . . she had her own house . . . he just used to visit her.

She stood in front of a tall, tri-fold salon mirror. It was rose-hued, gilded along its edges, and supported by lion's-paw footing under a carved ebony platform. It had one shallow drawer the width of its platform. She kept Tullio's letters in this drawer.

Any woman would look beautiful in this mirror. It lies.

It was an antique, a present her husband had once sent her.
. . . in place of himself, damn him.

A lot! He used to visit her a lot! All the servants knew! Even his aunts knew! The whole town knew! Damn you, Tullio!

She scrutinized the image. She'd decided to wear a white linen suit in the new narrow style that clung around the curves; she had an excellent figure and the suit showed it to full advantage.

She grimaced then, realizing why it reminded her of him: the suit, like the valuable mirror, had also been an unexpected present.

There were so many gifts, all unanticipated in that they'd not arrived for her birthdays or wedding anniversaries or even at Christmastime. In a way, this pleased her. If he'd sent things only on special occasions, he'd merely been fulfilling a duty.

There were moments, though, when the gifts would offend her. She would assume they were Tullio's manner of easing his conscience for staying away so long, his way of paying for her patience.

Well, at least I know I'm on his mind, she'd conclude, *but, who's in his bed?*

Still, there was no time for reverie (or for any speculation) this morning. The suit was beautiful, frightfully expensive and perfect for today's task. It had even been accompanied by a handbag and shoes made of the same white linen. He'd forgotten nothing.

She emptied the stuffing paper from the handbag and found a note from Tullio. She giggled over the note, because it suggested she wear the suit for Rebecca's first holy communion and send him a photograph of "my two girls all in white."

Maybe, I should bring a camera with me to Swansgarten and have Bella Modesto put on a white veil. Well, he did ask for a photograph of his two girls. No, I'd better not.

Swansgarten was in bloom. Louise had a natural talent with flowers and her gardener had to do little of his own planning. Her rose arbors had already been cited by the local

165

horticultural groups as the North Shore's finest, and she'd recently received an award for a new tulip strain which now blanketed both sides of the long driveway to the main residence. Her newest innovation, though, a heart-shaped lily pond which reflected *Swansgarten's* outdoor dining area and which was lit at dusk by pink and amber lanterns, was even more striking. Four stately white swans glided over the water.

Louise Asheley was seated near the pond when Magdalena arrived. She was still in her blue brocade housecoat, having breakfast. She looked up, startled.

"Good morning, Magdalena. What a lovely surprise! My goodness, you look so absolutely beautiful today."

"Thank you, Louise. I gather she hasn't arrived yet."

"Who?"

"Bella Modesto."

"Bella Modesto?"

"Oh, dear God!" *The strain has been too much for her. She's blocked it all out.* "Oh, dear God, I should have known this would happen."

"What?"

At that moment, they heard a car turning into the driveway and Louise complained: "Oh, I'm getting company. Who in the world could it be at this early hour? I'd better get dressed."

Magdalena turned quickly from the sound of the motor toward her hostess; but, before Magdalena could stop her, Louise scurried toward the back entrance of the house.

"Oh, dear God, she ran away! Maybe, she hasn't blocked it out, after all. Maybe, she does remember what's happening today, and she just can't face it! What's wrong with me? Now, I'm talking to myself!"

Magdalena watched her friend's pale blue housecoat disappear behind the arbor while, less than fifty feet to the right, a woman was being helped out of the car and led into the house by the Asheley butler. She was too far away to see the woman's face, and this annoyed her.

Magdalena sat at the table at which Louise had just been

166

eating, unable to decide what to do—to run after Louise or to run away, herself. The minutes, themselves, decided; the Asheley butler approached.

"Mrs. Barragatto," he began, "Mrs. Asheley has suddenly developed a rather bad migraine. She would appreciate it if you would stand in for her and . . ."

She interrupted: ". . . and greet her guest?"

"Yes, madam. I've shown the lady into the parlor."

I don't believe this.

"Mrs. Barragatto?"

How could she do this to me?

"Are you ill, madam?"

She wanted to leave immediately, but decided she mustn't do this. She looked at Louise's breakfast, then at the pond; then, she shook her head and asked, "Has Mrs. Asheley been having these headaches often lately?"

"Yes, they have been occurring again."

"As badly as before? The same kind?"

He cleared his throat and replied, "Yes, madam. I'm afraid so, madam."

"I think it would be better if Mr. Asheley were to greet Mrs. Asheley's guest, and not I."

"He's not here, madam. He left a little while ago. I overheard him instruct the driver to bring him to *The Walls*. You might even have passed each other on the road."

There was a short, awkward silence. Magdalena looked at the lily pond; but, the butler would look at nothing else but her. He required an answer. She felt an almost uncontrollable urge to throw one of the breakfast dishes at him.

"Very well, I'll go meet the lady!"

He nodded, almost grinned.

"In the meantime, please bring the lady's trunks into the guest cottage! And, have your housekeeper assign a maid to her, if she hasn't brought her own! This lady will be staying for a while!"

The man cocked his head to the side as a young puppy does

the first time it sees a cat. He backed away from her. "Yes, madam," he said, and he left instantly.

Magdalena remained sitting where Louise had been. She looked down at the breakfast dishes. She looked at the lily pond again; then, back at the dishes. She poured the orange juice into the eggs, and this made her feel better. Foolish, but better.

She walked toward the house. Her gait was steady and uninterrupted by the butler and downstairs maid and French doors. She entered the parlor where the woman was standing, her back to Magdalena, as she stared out at the grounds. She paused, breathed deeply and said in Italian, "Good morning. I am Magdalena Barragatto."

The woman turned from the window. She was a few years older and a few pounds heavier than Magdalena, but the weight was in all the right places. Most of her blonde hair was covered with a purple cloche hat, decorated with a ridiculous purple feather. Her short purple chemise stopped just before her knees and she wore a fashionable diamond "dog collar" at her neck. The white toy poodle she held in her arms wore a matching diamond collar. The dog barked when it saw Magdalena.

"How do you do," said Bella Modesto. Her face was heavily made up and her lips painted in a bright red cupid's bow. She resembled a blonde Clara Bow.

"Mrs. Asheley is my closest friend," Magdalena explained. "I'm here to welcome you to *Swansgarten* on her behalf, because she's been taken ill today."

"Ill? Is it anything serious?"

"Yes." Anticipating the woman's next question, she added, "But, she doesn't have to be hospitalized, and she doesn't need a doctor."

The butler knocked and entered. He advised Magdalena that her instructions had been carried out. She asked him to serve coffee in the sun room, telling him that she and Miss Modesto would be in the sun room presently. It was a respite both women welcomed, since each had private thoughts that needed punctuation.

They entered the sun room as though they were retiring to it instead of just changing surroundings. They sipped the coffee slowly.

"Will you please draw open all the curtains?" Magdalena asked the butler. She realized that this would take at least a few minutes because the curtain tassels were difficult to reach. Louise had placed dozens of her newly potted tulips in front of each window.

Bella smiled, perceiving the purpose for the order. When they were alone again, she spoke first. "I think we should clear the air and settle the preliminaries. No?"

Magdalena's look was at once both suspicious and assenting. She'd—not for a single moment—anticipated that Bella Modesto would be, in any way, slovenly or crude, since Tullio wouldn't have taken her to the finest restaurants in Orvietto, had she been anything like that. Yet, she was still very different than she'd expected.

"When Louise told me that her closest neighbor and friend was from Orvietto, I was tempted to call this whole thing off. Then, when she told me your name, I was a little bit more than surprised. I'm sure you were equally moved to find out that I would be coming to *Swansgarten*."

Magdalena realized that there was no need to reply.

"You see," she continued, "I've read a great deal about the people of the Gold Coast, but I've never read anything about the Barragattos. It's almost as though not a single society columnist knows that you're here."

"This is my husband's wish. He doesn't want any publicity of any kind. He's very adamant about that."

"I just can't imagine how you've managed to purchase an estate and live here these years without any . . ."

"I really don't understand why our lack of publicity should bother you, Miss Modesto. It can't possibly have any effect on

169

the job you were brought here to do. Can it?"

"You're perfectly right. I'm sorry for prying. Now, to resume our original conversation. Since you are from Orvietto, you must know I ran a house there."

"Yes," Magdalena answered, "and, you must know that I was once a gypsy. All right?"

"There! Isn't it better that we've cleared the air?"

Magdalena relaxed. She almost smiled. "Yes," she said, "it's better." She wondered, though: *Do you know that I know about you and Tullio?*

"Have you told Louise the truth about me?"

"No."

"I think that was a very wise decision." She poured more coffee for them. *Do you know about me and Tullio?* "Yes, it's better that she doesn't know. It might make her anxious. And, I think it might be better if you don't mention anything to her husband, either."

"I have to tell him that you're an actress, and not visiting royalty. But, I won't say anything else."

They spoke for almost two hours—of the receptions Bella would have to attend; of the house in Newport, where Louise might possibly take her for a few weeks of the season; and of the women at Capits Rock.

"I know their kind," Bella said. "They play tennis, and when they get too old for that, they play golf. But, mostly, they lunch. I'll try to avoid them as much as possible. I assume that some of them will be at Carter's birthday party?"

"Carter's birthday party?"

"Yes. Her grandson's party."

Magdalena breathed deeply and looked upwards to the ceiling. "There is no Carter," she said. She closed her eyes and shook her head and repeated: "There is no Carter."

Bella became silent. She stared at her stand-in hostess.

"I'd completely forgotten to tell you about that, but it's another thing you've got to know about Louise, because it might crop up from time to time."

170

This was the first moment since Magdalena had set eyes on her that Bella looked ill at ease.

"You see," Magdalena continued, "Louise and Earl had one child. They'd not seen him for several years because he'd been living in Europe. He wasn't much of a son. Well, anyway, while in Europe, he married a British girl named Anita and had a son whom he named Carter.

"But, then, a terrible thing happened . . . an accident . . . a dreadful, terrible accident. Her son and daughter-in-law and grandson were all killed, before they reached America. And, Louise never got to meet her son's wife, or the little boy. And, all she had left was an old, faded photograph of her son before he'd sailed to Europe."

"But, she's shown me a picture of Carter! It's a very recent photograph. It couldn't have been taken more than a year ago."

"She probably showed you a picture of my son, Stefano."

"Louise thinks your son is her grandson?"

"Sometimes," Magdalena replied. "Sometimes, she calls him Carter . . . and, at other times, she thinks I'm Anita, her daughter-in-law."

Bella Modesto was mute with astonishment. Bella persisted. "She's planning a tremendous party for him."

"There are times when she's under stress . . . that's when she starts to drink . . . and those are the times when she starts with the Carter business all over again. She snaps out of it. You'll see—in a day or so, or maybe a week or so—she'll forget all about the party, and she'll be back to normal again."

A short while later, Bella Modesto retired to the guest cottage, and Magdalena went upstairs, to Louise's bedroom.

"You must hate me," Louise told her. "I don't know what possessed me to do that . . . to run away like that . . . to desert you . . . to put you in such a position . . ."

"No, I don't hate you. I understand how upset you must have been. But, I'm glad you're feeling better now. You are feeling better now, aren't you, Louise?"

"Yes."

"Anyway, Bella Modesto and I had to meet each other sooner or later. Now it's over with."

"Where is she now?"

"She's in the cottage, changing her clothes."

"I don't know how to thank you, Magdalena."

"It's all right, Louise. It's not going to be as difficult as I thought. She's very intelligent. It's not likely that she would make any mistakes in front of anyone. I think she might work out very well."

"Do you really?"

"Yes. But, there's one thing you've got to promise me."

"Anything," Louise answered.

"She must never suspect that either of us knows anything about her and my husband. I don't think I could deal with her if she did."

"I understand. It will be as though you'd never said a word to me about them."

"That's good, Louise. Now, why don't you put on some makeup and get dressed? It's almost lunchtime, and you have a guest."

"Will you stay?"

"No. I have to get home. Salvatore is coming, and I want to catch him before he and Aleksey leave for the club."

She would not have felt so compelled to leave *Swansgarten* as quickly as she had if Bella Modesto's posture hadn't been so erect; or, if her movements hadn't been so graceful; or, if she'd not been so softspoken and articulate. Magdalena admitted this to herself. Still, the woman was much finer than she'd expected. Worse yet, she was stunning; this, Magdalena couldn't deny, either.

What would she have been in the past? A queen? . . . no, too mundane. A painting by Gainsborough? . . . no, too boring. A courtesan? . . . possibly . . . quite possibly.

Bella Modesto had been only a name without form, an in-

172

angible with neither face nor body, just something she'd used
o throw up at her husband. It had been such a short, easy
ame with which to assault him, so effective during little
rguments.

She'd used the name, for the first time, to stop him short.

"It's all over town that you've been going in to see a fortune-
eller," he'd yelled. "How many times have you gone to see
er?"

"Not as many times as you've gone to see the Modesto
woman," she snapped back.

He'd been stunned. He hadn't replied. How long had she
nown?

She'd used the name, also, to make him feel guilty.

"I love you, *bella mia*," he'd whispered.

She'd turned away from him.

"What's wrong?" he'd asked.

"You mixed up my name with hers. How could you, at a time
ike this?" She'd begun to sob.

"No! I swear! I meant *bella!* Not Bella!"

He'd begun to stutter; and it had been so dark that he'd been
unable to see that she wasn't really crying.

She'd even used the name just to tease him.

"What should we call the baby if it's a girl?"

"Whatever you want," he'd answered.

"What do you think about Bella?"

No more. It was no longer just a name. It was something that
had to be far from *The Walls of Jericho* by harvest. Newport.
Perhaps, she could convince Louise to take Bella to Newport.

173

Chapter Five

Until this morning, Guido had been only two places. One was the tiny Lombardy village where he'd grown up in the fields and barns, an orphan abandoned to the sporadic charity of the townspeople. Then, the young signora had taken him to Orvietto, the second place; and there, he'd lived safely and comfortably within the Barragatto compound. But today, Genoa! And, he had three pistols and six sets of clothes, besides what he was already wearing! And, he had two valises! And soon, America! A passing angel must have kissed him when he'd been born; or somebody must have rubbed garlic into his navel; one or the other! or maybe, both!

Giulio Fallanca. Soon, Guido Fallanca. A very good name, he decided. A strong name.

637 . . . 638 . . . 639 . . . yes, this was his cabin . . . 639 . . . the door was unlocked.

"Signor Barragatto! I didn't expect you to be here!"

"Come in, Guido. Come in. The ship will be sailing soon, so we don't have much time, and we have some last minute business to talk about. Come in. Close the door behind you."

"I didn't expect the room to be so nice. I see another bed here. Will I have a roommate?" He sat across from Tullio.

174

"No. It's all yours."

"It's beautiful!" He stood, overwhelmed by the thought of the cabin.

"Sit down, now. I have a few things to say to you."

"Yes, Signor Barragatto."

"Have you already signed on as Giulio Fallanca?"'

"Yes. Now, I am legally Giulio Fallanca. Why? Is anything wrong?"

"No," Tullio said. "Now, we get down to business. In the first place, you already know that nobody is to know where you'll be working."

"Yes. Just like you told me. Nobody even knows I'm sailing. I told anyone who asked that I got a job in Milan."

"That means you won't be in touch with anyone, either. No letters to anybody over here once you reach New York."

"Naturally," Guido agreed. "Anyway, there's nobody here that I would ever have to keep in touch with."

"Okay. Now, we have two things to settle. The first concerns something I don't expect will happen. But, just in case . . . we should get it straight right now."

"Yes?"

Tullio leaned forward, resting his elbows and forearms on the table that stood between them. This made Guido sit farther back in his chair.

"When my wife first brought you into my house, you were thirteen and she was seventeen. You followed her around like a lovesick puppy."

"Signor Barragatto, I admit that I had a little crush on her . . . but, I was only a child. Surely, you don't think . . ."

Tullio held up one hand, then replaced it on the table. "Let me finish."

The youth nodded, and said, "Sorry."

"As I was saying," Tullio continued, "it was obvious to everyone how you felt about her. Don't get me wrong. I'm not upset about that. It didn't bother me then, and it doesn't now, either. It was taken just for what it was—a harmless schoolboy

175

crush, and nothing else."

The younger gestured and grinned—a mime, giving a *yes, of course*—but he was embarrassed and he sat up straight in his chair.

"But," said Tullio, "you're not a boy any longer, and she's not seventeen anymore. She's twenty-two now, and you're eighteen. You're both all grown up. And, you're going to be alone with her a great deal."

A pause, now, and a change of position—these were necessary for the rest of Tullio Barragatto's message. He slid his arms from the table and sat back in his chair. He crossed his legs in the figure-four position—like American men sit—it made one look like a ruffian in European eyes.

Guido's expression sombered.

"Remember what I told you? No matter where my wife goes, you bring her, you wait for her, and you take her home. She's never to be taken anywhere by anyone else."

"Yes, Signor Barragatto, I remember."

"Guido, my wife has grown more beautiful than you remember. And, she's lonely, which is my fault. There could arise an occasion when, because of that, you might be tempted to get a little too friendly with her."

"But, I swear, I'll never!"

"Well, there are times when an unexpected situation can develop. Don't think I don't trust my wife, because I do. But, you'll be together a lot."

"I'll never touch her! I swear! It will never happen!"

"That's right, Guido. It will never happen. Because, do you know what would happen to you if it did? The same thing that happens to men who bother little schoolgirls."

He didn't answer.

"Do you know what they do to men who bother young girls?"

"Yes."

"What do they do to them? Tell me, just so I'm positive you understand. Because, that's exactly what would happen to you."

In a very low voice, Guido replied: "They cut off their balls."

"That's right. I'm glad you understand." He could uncross his legs now. "Now, so much for that, and we go on to the next point of business: money."

"Money?"

"Yes, Guido. Money. It's the most important thing in the world. It's what keeps women beautiful. It's what makes men powerful. It causes wars. It turns loyal people into traitors. Money. That's what we're going to talk about next. Money."

"Yes?"

"These people from whom I'm hiding the signora . . . they might, someday, possibly approach you and offer you a great deal of money to sell us out."

"Never. I'd shoot them between the eyes, even before they'd finish the sentence."

"Maybe you would. Maybe you wouldn't. Nevertheless, I'm going to tell you what would happen, just in case they should offer you more money than you'll be getting paid from me."

"Signor Barragatto, I can understand that you had to say the things you did before . . . about the signora, I mean . . . that's a husband's right. But, this thing, this thinking I might betray you . . . that's insulting . . . and you have no right to insult me."

"I don't think you'll betray us, Guido. If I did, I never would have given you this job. But, money betrays the best of us. Look what it did to one of the Apostles."

"I won't sell out. I know who you're fighting. I've seen what they do to our people."

Tullio was very tempted to say, "Thank you. Have a good trip." but, he didn't; he had to finish what he'd come for. He continued: "Once, there was a man, a friend of mine, who was sent to Guidonia."

"You mean the stockades?"

"Yes."

177

Guido shook his head. "I've heard a lot about that place."

"Probably, not the whole of it," Tullio replied. "Well, anyway, this particular person had an especially hard time of it in there—worse than most other prisoners, because he'd killed a brother of one of the guards before he'd been arrested. That guard made life more miserable for him than you can imagine. Later on, to make matters even worse, one of that guard's cousins started to work there, too. So, when this friend of mine wasn't getting hell from one of them, he'd be getting it from the other. Between the brother of the man he'd killed and the cousin, there wasn't a day or night that went by when my friend didn't wish he was dead."

"How come," Guido asked, "either the brother or the cousin didn't kill your friend? I'm sure they could have done it. I'm sure they could have made it look like an accident."

"Because they didn't want him dead. That would have been too easy on him. You see, these particular cousins were sadists, in every sense of the word. But, to make a long story short . . . one night, only one of them came into his cell . . . it was the cousin . . . and my friend . . . he was so insane that particular night that he broke the guard's neck . . . and then, he slit open his throat, just for good measure. After that, he took the keys and escaped."

"Did they ever catch him?"

"No, not yet. There's a rumor that he made it all the way to America, but nobody's sure."

"Can they bring him back to Guidonia if they find him?"

"Yes."

Noticeably uncomfortable, Guido asked, "What does this have to do with me?"

"You remind me of him. He's a little older than you . . . but, then, you look older than you are. Yes, you certainly do remind me of him. As a matter of fact, you two look so much alike, that you can pass for one another."

"We do? We look alike? That much alike?"

"Yes. I'll bet that, with your head shaved, nobody would

believe you're not him."

It was Guido who put his elbows on the table this time. Then, he cupped his hands together and rested his chin on them. Presently, he asked: "This prisoner friend of yours . . . what was his name?"

There was no reason to answer.

Guido walked away from the table and toward the porthole. "I don't know why you did this." He opened the window. "I don't know why." He closed it again, but continued looking through it "God, I don't know why. I wouldn't have sold you out." He turned sharply. "I can walk out of this cabin, right now, and tell them the whole story."

Tullio reached back and opened the door for him.

"First, you threaten to cut off my balls! And then! Then, you threaten to send me to the stockades! Why in hell did you hire me for the job, in the first place?"

"Because I trust you. And now, I can trust you even more."

"I probably saved your life when you met those wine men that day! Me and Benedetto! We were watching out for you! You didn't know that, did you! This is the gratitude I get! Threats!"

"Have a good trip," Tullio told him. "And, be careful when you drive. Don't speed with my wife and children in the car."

"What would you have done if you *didn't* trust me? Slit my throat?"

"I wouldn't have hired you if I didn't trust you." Tullio stood, but before leaving, added, "Someday, when this mess is all finished with, I'll make up for the precautions I've had to take today, and for everything that's had to be said today. Maybe, by that time, you'll have your own family to take care of, and you'll understand."

"I don't know, Signor Barragatto, if what you've just said is an apology or an excuse, but . . ."

"It was neither an apology nor an excuse." He glanced at his wristwatch. "It was a reason. Think about it." He left without further conversation.

179

As he stepped from the gangplank, the final whistle blew, and all other visitors left the ship. He hoped Guido would not hate him for too long. He liked Guido. He could not dwell upon this, though; he was running late, and he didn't want to keep Pire waiting. Jean Louis Pire was the first of the wine men to contact Tullio since their meeting.

"I am certain you didn't expect to hear from me so soon," the small, dapper Frenchman said, "but, since I was going to be here, in Genoa, I thought we might take this opportunity to discuss something that might be beneficial to the both of us."

"I'm glad we could get together like this," Tullio replied. "And, yes, I really am surprised to hear from you so soon. I didn't expect an answer so quickly."

"Well," Pire said, "it isn't over the Pace situation that I requested we meet. It's about something else."

"Oh."

"Don't be disappointed, Tullio. Just because I'm not here to talk about Pace today doesn't mean that I've decided against what you'd suggested. I'm still considering that, only it's a very important decision, and I'd like to think about it a little longer."

"Of course," he answered. "Of course. It's an important decision. It requires time."

After they ordered dinner, Jean Louis Pire said: "Your father and I enjoyed a partnership of sorts for a long time. It was a good, profitable business."

"I know."

"I wasn't aware that you knew about it."

"My father wasn't ashamed of it, and neither am I. He told me about it a long time ago, long before he died."

"Then, it doesn't bother you."

"No, of course not. I can't see anything wrong with clean, honest brothels. They're just as necessary as schools and churches."

The Frenchman nodded. "Yes," he said, "that's a good way

180

of looking at it. They are just as necessary. It's true."

Tullio said: "But as far as I knew, my father had gotten tired of it. He told me that it was too much work, what with the formation of North American Distributors. He told me you bought him out."

"Yes. That's what happened," Pire answered. "Now, however, I would like you to consider coming in with me. You see, I'm thinking of expanding, perhaps to the States. There's a big market for good houses over there. From what I saw the one time I went to America, they don't have anything decent. I didn't see a single establishment that I would ever patronize over there. Did you see anything decent?"

"I don't know anything about American houses. I have no idea of what they're like." He wondered how Pire knew he'd already been in America. "However, when I go after harvest, I'll be glad to do some investigating for you, if you'd like."

"What I would like, Tullio, is a lot more than investigation. I've already done that, and I'm convinced my findings are right. What I need is someone to watch over the operations. A manager of sorts. Not an investigator."

"A manager?"

"Very well. A partner."

Tullio still had a question in his eyes.

Pire responded: "A full partnership. Right down the middle. But, that wouldn't include any of the houses here in Europe. Only the ones in the States."

"Monsieur Pire, I'm quite astonished that you would offer me such a proposition. I have no experience in running that kind of business. Also, to do it properly, I would have to be living there, in America . . . and, I have no such plans in my future . . . I've never, ever, considered leaving Orvietto permanently. Please don't think me ungrateful, but, I just cannot understand why you would come to me with such an offer. Ther are so many others who would be better suited to it."

"I have no brothers," the Frenchman answered, "and I have

181

four daughters and only one son . . . and he's only fifteen. To whom else should I go, besides my former partner's son? We might have been competitors, all of these years, when it came to our wines . . . but I can't think of a better partnership than the one we had with the houses."

"I'm overwhelmed," Tullio told him, "and, again, please don't think me ungrateful . . . but, I just don't know if I would be able to handle it properly . . . and, frankly, in a way, it would be very unfair to you."

"How is that? How would it be unfair to me?"

"Well, most of my money is tied up in North American Distributors, so you would have to finance the houses at first. And then, of course, you would have to send us your best ladies to get the houses started on the right footing. Things like that."

Pire grunted. "Well, all businesses require an investment at the beginning. This is no different, I guess."

"I'll give it very careful consideration, Monsieur Pire . . . yet, there are so many questions I have that . . ."

"Formulate all of the questions, and I'll answer each one. You'll see, Tullio, that this isn't a proposition to turn down."

Tullio shook his head. "I don't know . . . I'm afraid I might not be able to give it the time it would require."

It was getting too late for Pire to remain and talk any longer. He had to catch the only train leaving that day for Paris. "Before you sail for New York," he told Tullio, "we'll see each other again. At that time I'll let you know what I've decided about Pace, and you'll let me know about this."

Tullio returned to Orvietto that afternoon and told Benedetto all that had happened.

"How could you have done such a thing to Guido?" his cousin asked. "And, worse yet, how could you have let him know what you did? That's like rubbing salt in the wound."

Tullio answered: "It will keep him honest. Consider it a forewarning. Would it be better for me to wait to see if he would turn on us, and then lower the boom? Isn't it kinder to him, in the long run, to warn him about what would happen if

182

he should get any wrong ideas?"

Benedetto shook his head. "Sometimes, I can't figure how you think. You're devious . . . yet, I think that you really believe you did the right thing."

"I did. I like Guido. He's a smart boy. But, he's still just a boy, and his head can be turned by a good offer from the wrong people. This way—my way—he'll think very carefully before he ever does anything wrong. It's protection for us—sort of insurance, if you want to call it that—and for him, too."

Benedetto shook his head. "You really believe you're right. You really do."

"Well, I am. Listen, in years to come, I intend making full use of Guido. He's smart. He's quick. He sizes up a situation like lightning. When the time comes that Magdalena doesn't need a bodyguard anymore, I'm going to offer him a very good job."

"If he stays with you that long," Benedetto snapped. "He probably hates your guts by now. You made an enemy out of a friend. I hope you're satisfied. Anyway, I don't know what kind of work you might have in mind for him. All he's interested in is women and cars."

Tullio smiled. "I know."

"I don't trust that look you have," Benedetto said. "What are you up to now?"

"Nothing. I was just thinking that, perhaps, he might be just the right person to run the Stateside houses."

"Houses! Houses! You're not serious! You're not considering going in with Pire!"

He shrugged. He'd expected this reaction from Benedetto, and he almost laughed. "Well, it's very inviting. There's a lot of money to be made. It's worth considering."

"No, it isn't."

He became serious now, and said, "There's a lot of money to be made in it. And, if we don't do it, somebody else will. Why not us?"

"You're kidding, aren't you?"

183

He shrugged again.

"Tullio, prostitution is just as illegal in America as selling our wine would be."

"Not really. Prohibition is a federal law . . . but prostitution, that's just a minor infraction, nothing serious."

"Everything you do is a contradiction. You defend your right not to break the Prohibition law, and you actually put your life on the line over it . . . and then, you turn right around and consider opening up houses."

"But, Benedetto, don't you see the difference? With the wineries and brewery, Pace's people are actually trying to force us to work with them. With Pire, it's a whole other thing . . . just an offer, one that we can refuse or accept with equal freedom. Can't you see the difference? In one case, it would be because we want to do the business . . . but, in the other case, it would be because we're being forced into it. It's a matter of principle."

"A matter of principle?"

"Yes, exactly. Our fathers had a partnership with the Pire houses for a long time. It was a good business, strictly private, and nobody got hurt over it."

"Yes," Benedetto replied, "but they sold out to him a long time ago."

"But, that was only because they didn't want to be bothered with it any longer. They were too involved with North American Distributors and they were both too sick to continue with all the work that it involved. But, there's nothing wrong with our health . . . and, we have a lot of good years ahead of us."

"Now, let me get this straight, Tullio. The only reason why you won't sell the wine is because you would have to work through the *malandrini* if you did?"

"That's the main reason, not the only one. The other reason is because the wineries and the brewery are part of North American Distributors. Anything involved with North American Distributors has to be strictly legal. We couldn't implicate

184

the corporation by messing around with anything that isn't above reproach. We would have too much to lose."

"But, you wouldn't involve the corporation with the houses? You would keep that private? Just you and Pire? Aleksey and Earl wouldn't even know about the houses, right?"

"That's right. It would just be Pire and us."

"Who do you mean by us?"

"You, and Salvatore and me. Who else?" Tullio responded. "It would be a perfectly clean operation. Nobody could tell us how to run it. It wouldn't do any harm to anyone."

"So, we should obey an unholy law and not sell our wine . . . and, at the same time, consider breaking another law by opening houses. And, we can call the whole thing a matter of principle."

"That's right, because that's exactly what it is. I won't deal with Palermo, and I know that Salvatore won't either. It's the principle of the thing."

"Bravo. The perfect Party member. Typical Party thinking."

"Party thinking? What does politics have to do with this? I'm talking about wine and women, and you're talking about politics. Anyway, what do you mean by Party thinking?"

"Whatever you want to do—legal, illegal, moral, immoral— you go right ahead and do it. But, first, you find a few good reasons for it, so you can call it a matter of principle. That's Party thinking."

Chapter Six

Aleksey Kostenov was not given to gossip, but he was so pleased with Magdalena's attitude regarding Bella Modesto that he spoke of it to Salvatore.

"Can you imagine that?" he asked. "Not only is she raising Tullio's daughter by another woman, but she's actually agreed to entertain a past lover of his!"

"Well," Salvatore replied, "Tullio and Bella were never exactly lovers. They might have had some good times together, but they were not what you would call lovers."

"Nevertheless, isn't it remarkable? You've got to admit that she's a remarkable young woman, don't you?"

The young attorney listened quietly for a while. He successfully hid his consternation from Aleksey, and the elder continued in his praise for his charge until Salvatore asked:

"How long do they expect Bella to remain in *Swansgarten?*"

Kostenov shrugged. "I guess Magdalena will have some kind of idea after speaking with her. She should be back soon."

Their conversation ended, then, because Earl Asheley arrived. They decided to play some golf at Capits Rock, but Salvatore advised them that he had an errand to attend to, and that he would join them as soon as he could.

Salvatore drove directly to *Swansgarten*. When he arrived at the Asheley estate, he went, unnoticed, to the guest cottage; and, finding the door unlocked, he entered and was determined to wait for Bella Modesto, no matter how long he might have to sit there.

Bella, of all people. Wait until Tullio hears about this.

Through the window, he could see that Bella and Louise were having lunch by the pond. He hoped they weren't just starting, because it was very warm in the cottage.

His lungs had always troubled him. Recently, he'd developed an almost ever-present cough. When he was particularly anxious about something, the cough would become worse, and his breathing more difficult. At this moment, he could barely catch his breath; he felt as though he'd been running uphill. Almost exhausted, he made himself as comfortable as possible in an overstuffed club chair, his chest heaving from the effort to breathe. He pulled a hassock close to the chair and propped up his legs. He felt like a very old man and cursed and thought: *Less than a year ago, I was as strong as a bull. I can't believe this is happening to me. I must be dying, but I'm too young to die.* Then, disgusted with his waning health, he closed his eyes and fell asleep. When he awoke, Bella Modesto was sitting opposite him. She had undressed and was wearing a yellow silk kimono, the same color as her hair.

"Have I stared you awake, Salvatore?"

She was a very nice vision to awake to. "You haven't changed a bit, Bella," he said as he reached up and playfully tousled her hair.

"Thank you. I'll accept that as a compliment."

"That's just what it was. I guess you must be surprised to find me here." He tried to stretch, but the chair was too soft; it made his movement clumsy and the hassock tipped over.

She laughed when the hassock fell. "You haven't changed, either," she said; and, "Yes, I am surprised." She grinned then, and added, "I certainly never expected Magdalena Barragatto to tell you I was here."

187

He shook his head. "She didn't tell me. She doesn't even know I'm here. And, I'd appreciate your not mentioning it, either."

"Well, how did you know I'd moved in?"

"What's the difference how I knew? Anyway, I'm here because we have a couple of things to talk about."

"It sounds serious."

"It is."

"How long has it been since we've seen each other?" she asked him. "Years, I'll bet."

"The last time we saw one another was on the ship, when we sailed from Italy."

She nodded. "Yes, that's when it was. About four years ago."

He continued: "We could have had a good time on that ship . . . except that you were travelling with Carmine Pace."

"There's no need to be nasty. Anyway, you had your wife and kids with you, or don't you remember?"

He smiled because they both knew he would have managed a few free evenings. "Well," he asked, "what happened? How come you're not with him any longer?"

"Carmine and I had sort of a disagreement . . . over a dancer, if you must know. We haven't seen one another for almost two years, now."

"And, you've never kept in touch?"

"No, not a word. I don't even know if he's still in New York."

"He is."

Trying to change the subject, she asked: "How's Tullio?"

"You'll find out for yourself. He'll be here in a few months."

It was obvious that this pleased her. She asked: "Salvatore, why did you come here today? What are these things we have to talk about?"

"I want to talk to you about Pace, Bella."

"Oh?"

"Yes, I'd like some information from you."

188

"Like what?"

"Well, the last time you saw Pace . . . what was he involved with, besides liquor? I know about the speakeasies, but was there anything else?"

"Oh, some gambling rooms, nothing big; one or two clubs in Harlem; a casino in South America."

"They're really branching out," he muttered. "Where in South America?"

"I don't know."

He mused. "That's very interesting. From South America to Harlem."

"We used to go to Harlem a lot. He was always so busy when we went up there."

"I thought you just said he had only one or two clubs."

"Well, it wasn't just the clubs that kept him busy. There's the numbers, too . . . and, there was this man Garvey. He . . ."

Salvatore interrupted: "Marcus Garvey? The colored guy who's trying to take his people back to Africa? That Garvey?"

"That's right," she replied. "He's the one. He's trying to get them to set up a whole new country over there. Or, something like that."

"He's mixed up with Pace?"

"No, not Garvey, himself. But, some of the people working for him deal with Carmine. You see, a lot of contributions are coming in for Garvey's cause. The money is being held by a small group . . . I'm not sure who they are, or how they're connected with Garvey . . . it's rather complicated. Anyway, Carmine used to meet these men a lot, these men who work for Garvey, and I know that, when they used to come and talk, it was all in secret, behind closed doors. Garvey doesn't know."

"Did you ever hear what they spoke about?"

"No, but once, Carmine laughed, and said: 'Pass the hat for Garvey, brothers and sisters! Keep passing that hat!'"

This interested Salvatore; still, it wasn't all he'd come for, so he asked: "Is there anything else Pace might have been into?"

She shrugged. "Like what?"

"Oh . . . like houses, for instance. Things like that."

"Well, I don't know if there was anything else, but I'm sure
he wasn't into houses. Not at that time, anyway. After all, he
would have spoken to me about that, wouldn't he? No, I'm sure
he wasn't running any houses. He would have asked me for
some advice."

Salvatore had no reason to doubt anything Bella was saying.
The liquor, the gambling, Harlem, Garvey; possibly, Pace
couldn't have hidden those ventures from her. Yet, he
wouldn't have gone into detail about them, either. Who would
discuss business with women? So, maybe the casino wasn't
even in South America; it might be in Central America, or in
the Caribbean.

*They really are branching out. Looks like there's no stopping
them. Jesus, she's a good looking woman.*

"Bella, are you sure you never heard anything about
houses?"

"I'm positive."

Most of the time they'd been talking, she had been
undressing. Now she lay back on the divan, teasing him boldly
with the ripe pink curves of her body. She said, "We have to
cut this short, Salvatore. I have to change. Louise and I are
visiting her club this afternoon. She's going to show me off to
some of the vultures."

He winked. "Are you really in that much of a hurry?"

"Yes, I am."

"Okay, just one more thing."

"What's that?" she asked him. "Please hurry, Salvatore. It
will be very embarrassing if Louise were to find you here."

He nodded. "It's just this: under no circumstances do we
want Pace to know that Tullio's wife is living here."

"Why?"

He didn't answer. He continued, "As a matter of fact, we
don't want anybody at all to know that she's here. If, for some
reason or other, you and Pace should ever run into each other
again, don't ever mention you've met Magdalena, or that you

190

now anything at all about her."

"Why in the world would I?"

"And, don't mention that we had this talk today, either. Don't let him know you've seen me or that I was asking any questions about him."

"Salvatore, I don't expect to see Carmine again. I haven't heard from him in a couple of years. As far as he's concerned, I could be dead and buried already."

"For your own sake, you should keep it that way."

"I intend to."

He kissed her goodbye and left to join Earl and Aleksey at the club. "I'll probably see you there," he told her.

While driving, he reviewed their conversation. He was convinced—more now, than before—that men should never talk business in front of women. He shook his head. As vague as it had been, the information Bella had just volunteered could send Pace away for a few years.

Numbers and clubs . . . that's good money in Harlem. And, this thing he has going with Garvey's boys! Whew!

During the war, blacks from the southern states and the Caribbean had resettled in the northeastern section of Manhattan, the area called Harlem; within a couple of years, it had become a city within a city. Very quickly, it had deteriorated into a black ghetto, a hell-hole whose inhabitants (mostly illiterate) were unable to find jobs or decent dwellings. The environment shackled and crippled its people, who were unwelcome in other parts of the city. The one man who was giving them a sense of their own dignity was Marcus Garvey.

Garvey had come to Harlem in 1917 and had begun publishing a weekly called *Negro World*. He was unschooled, but highly intelligent, a skilled orator and a clever organizer. Because he appealed to racial pride, the first real mass movement among American blacks was beginning. Half out of love for his own people and half out of hatred for the whites, he'd gone to the League of Nations to attempt settling a colony in Africa and had entered into discussions with Liberia, trying to negotiate the return of American blacks to Africa; but his efforts failed. After that, he'd tried to force whites out of that continent by founding several organizations, all of which could not find enough backing to succeed.

Marcus Garvey, however, was persistent. Determined that Harlem be left to the rats, he established the African Orthodox Church and promised blacks a utopia under the African sun. A shrewd psychologist, he soon had more than a half million followers, and many were hailing him as God. Between 1919 and 1921, he'd already collected more than ten million dollars as donations for his movement. He intended setting up steamship companies, manning the vessels with black crews, and transporting his people to his empire in Africa and the West Indies.

And Carmine Pace, Salvatore realized, might very well have been receiving a generous piece of the pie.

Salvatore shook his head again, and grimaced. If the right people should discover how much Pace had allowed a woman to know, they'd put an end to him very quickly.

No, that would implicate Bella. I can't let that happen.

It was hard to imagine Carmine Pace having been so careless. With a woman like Bella, it was always necessary to warn her what she must not repeat, because that was the only time she would keep her mouth shut. She was a natural talker, always had been, even in Orvietto.

He smiled when he tried to picture her at Capits Rock that afternoon. She would not be able to speak to anyone, because she wasn't supposed to know English; she was really going to be flustered. He smiled even wider when he remembered what she'd looked like while undressing. *Jesus, she's gorgeous! Trouble, maybe; but, gorgeous!* And wider, still, when he began reminiscing about some of the times they'd shared in Orvietto. Finally, he almost laughed aloud when he thought of Tullio's reaction; he couldn't wait to tell Tullio who their new neighbor was.

192

He sobered quickly, though. He mustn't get carried away. He and Bella had had good times. Tullio and Bella had had good times. But, Pace and Bella—that was a whole different ball game—Pace had taken her to America; and they'd lived together for a couple of years; they must have cared for each other. Yet, here she was, rubbing elbows with Magdalena.

He tried to review what Aleksey had told him: how Bella had met Louise in a language instruction class . . . how and why Louise had hired her . . . why Magdalena would have to play the translator.

It was all too compact, too smug, too coincidental.

He pulled off the road and on to a soft shoulder to think.

Coincidence, after all, does happen in this world. If it didn't occur, there would be no need for the word. But, this was the reasoning of a lawyer trying to argue a case against a gnawing inside of him. It was not effective enough to put him at ease, and he remained on the shoulder long enough to finish two more cigarettes. When, finally, he did make a U-turn and head for Capits Rock Road, he was still bothered.

The strike was over because it was Wednesday. Whenever a holiday falls on a Tuesday, Italians invariably find a reason for a nationwide strike on Monday. Reconciled to this fact of life, Tullio Barragatto had put off returning to Milan until after the four-day weekend. The office was already humming with activity when he walked in. The clerks and secretaries were rested and smiling. The typewriters were clicking and ringing their bells; and the filing cabinet drawers were opening and closing like acrobats' legs. The windows were open, and the street noises almost drowned the buzz of the ceiling fans. He was tempted to turn around and return to Orvietto; but, this was only his first day back, and he had thirteen more to go before he could again retreat to the sweet murmurs of the vineyards and village. He quickly resigned himself to the next two weeks and, after exchanging greetings with his employees, went directly to his private office, where his secretary, Sr.

Pavetto, had already ushered his visitor, Cosmo LoGiudice. The second wine man was a stout balding figure with a thick gray walrus moustache.

"Good morning, Signor LoGiudice. It's good to see you. No, please don't stand," he said. "Stay seated. Be comfortable. I've just asked Signor Pavetto to have some coffee sent in to us."

"Ah, yes . . . Signor Pavetto . . . a fine gentleman, very efficient. I wish I could find somebody like him for my office."

"Yes, he is very good at his job," Tullio replied. "It's funny, but when I was a child, I was frightened of him."

They continued with small talk until after the coffee was served, at which time, the visitor asked: "Well, Tullio, tell me, have you received any response from Pire or Beckmann?"

"Not yet."

"Well, I am here to give you my answer. It is yes, because, as you so aptly put it during our meeting . . . it is time for a change, and we owe that change to our children."

"Needless to say, I'm very pleased with your decision. Also, I'm grateful that you would trust me to represent you."

"You deserve trust. I haven't come to this decision lightly. I've heard quite a lot about you, all very good things, and from reliable sources. You've earned people's trust."

He nodded a "thank you," and smiled slightly.

"I'll give you whatever authority you need, and I'll instruct my New York manager to put himself at your disposal."

"Thank you. That should be sufficient."

"Now, there is something else. The touring company you started, Magdalena Tours . . . I have been thinking of going into that business, myself."

"Oh?"

"Yes. However, where Magdalena Tours doesn't go any farther south than Rome, my outfit would use Rome as its northernmost city, branching all the way down to Reggio de Calabria. So, you see, we wouldn't be competing; on the contrary, if we can work out some sort of arrangement, our tours could complement one another. They could provide an entire package, north and south Italy. Right now, there are no tours that bring people south."

"None at all?" Tullio asked him.

"That's right," Sr. LoGiudice said. "The only travellers who get to see anything south of Rome are millionaires and businessmen. Why, most people don't even know that islands like Capri and Ischia exist! The nobility—they've kept places like that all to themselves . . . they maintain their own villas there . . . so, it's almost impossible to find a decent hotel."

The longer LoGiudice spoke of his idea, the more details he filled in.

At length, Tullio replied: "When passengers reserve tickets on our ships, we automatically give them pamphlets describing Magdalena Tours. We can add your outfit's literature to the packet and work it from there. If they agree to start off with one tour, and continue on to the other, we can offer them a special rate, a good discount. It might work out very well."

"We can iron everything out," LoGiudice said, "and, by next year, we should be able to move on it."

"What about accommodations?" Tullio asked. "Magdalena Tours uses only the best hotels. You, yourself, just said that there isn't a decent hotel south of Rome. What would we do about that? We would have to keep the southern part of the trip comparable to the northern part, where quality is concerned."

"Ah, I was just coming to that," the wine man said. "Beckmann gave me the idea, and he would be willing to come in on it."

"Beckmann? What would he have to do with the tours?"

"Nothing, but his factory is in the midst of a new thing. It's called prefabrication. His stepson . . ."

"Gerhard Moeller?"

"Yes, Gerhard . . . he's very inventive, you know."

Tullio nodded.

LoGiudice continued. "Gerhard Moeller believes he can prefabricate parts of a hotel, ship them to the location, and assemble them on the chosen site. The hotels would be only two stories each. And, each room would have its private entrance leading out to the roadway. They have something like that in America already. They call them *motels* over there."

"I can't imagine anything like that," Tullio replied.

"That's all right. Gerhard could explain the whole concept to you. What Moeller's idea is, is that we supply the patrons, and he pays the touring company a percentage of the income."

"We would receive a percentage of what? of the money he makes from the people from our tours?—or of the receipts from *all* travellers?"

"We would have to guarantee him a certain number of reserved rooms per season. If we meet that guarantee, we get a percentage straight across the board. If we fail to meet that number of patrons, though, not only would the percentage be lowered, but it would be based upon the receipts of only the patrons we supply."

"That's reasonable."

LoGiudice continued: "I realize that this whole thing might be a little too much to absorb in one sitting and that you need time even to formulate your questions properly. That's why I'm only skimming the surface. In a few weeks, you get in touch with me again about this, and we can talk about it in more detail."

"But, can it be possible to build parts of a building in one country . . . then, ship them to another country and put them together, just like a jigsaw puzzle?"

"You speak with your friend, Gerhard. He'll explain the technicalities."

"Leave it up to Gerhard to come up with something like that. Has it ever been done before?"

"What in the world hasn't been done before?" the elder asked. "And, if it hasn't, does that make it impossible?"

Tullio wished he could assume his thinking pose, but he dared not. Also, he wished he could grin from ear to ear, because the proposition sounded so good; but, this, he would never do, either. He had to show a little hesitancy. "Very well," he said. "I'll talk to Gerhard. If he can convince me that such a thing can be done, then, you and Herr Beckmann and I can sit down and discuss the financial aspects of it. At that point, I'll bring the proposal back to Kostenov and Asheley. If they'll go along with it, my cousin, Salvatore, will meet with Herr Beckmann's and your attorneys in New York, and iron out all the rough spots."

"Fine," LoGiudice replied.

Tullio added, "It looks like each of us has a lot to think about before harvest, Signor LoGiudice. I hope we all come to the right decisions."

"Do you believe in destiny?"

"Yes."

"Then, we will come to the right decisions."

When LoGiudice left the office, Tullio sent for Sr. Pavetto. He instructed the secretary: "Write to Signor Kostenov, please. Tell him I would like him to set up a whole campaign in praise of southern Italy." He looked at his secretary's questioning glance. "That's right, Signor Pavetto. I said *southern* Italy. Tell him I want a whole public relations program. First-person articles in the magazines. Reminiscences of some society women's holidays. Biographies of local artists. Pieces on the castles, the palaces, the cathedrals, everything. And, whatever he does, tell him not to forget the folklore. That'll get them, for sure! The folklore!"

"Get whom, sir?"

"Anybody who can afford a steamship ticket."

"Sir?"

"We're going into the motel business, Signor Pavetto."
Now, to break the news to Aleksey and Earl.
Pavetto was puzzled.

"Motels are baby hotels," Tullio explained. He paused for effect, then repeated. "Baby hotels."

When Pavetto left, Tullio wrote to his cousin, Salvatore. He addressed the envelope to his home, not the office, and marked it "Personal." He recounted the Orvietto meeting with the three wine men. He wrote, also:

You were right about Pire. He's definitely interested in opening houses in the States. However, I did not mention the subject to him, as you had suggested. Instead, I waited for him to come to us. When he did, I acted as surprised as I could be about his proposal. It seems that he would be willing to finance the whole thing and even get us started with some of his own ladies. Still, Salvatore, I'm not so crazy about the idea. (And, Benedetto—he's really against it.) Are you still that much in favor of it?

Now, for the very good news. Do you remember Gerhard's ideas about prefabrication, and about our hopes to apply the principle to small hotel units? Well, it's all coming to fruition. Gerhard has managed to convince his stepfather (it's a pity that those two have never gotten along) to build the parts in his own factory. It is obvious, at this point, that Herr Beckmann knows nothing about our arrangement with Gerhard. However, once the manufacturing starts, some of the first prefabricated parts will be coming to the States. Then, we can proceed with the motels we were planning in the New England ski areas.

I don't know how in the world LoGiudice ever thought he might be able to keep his touring venture a secret from us. In any event, he has now decided not to buck us. It's probably been made obvious to him that Magdalena Tours has the whole northern portion of the country tied up. So, he's decided to concentrate on the south.

Salvatore, LoGiudice needs us; so we can easily tie our outfit in with his. Our expertise, media, and transportation facilities—we'll supply all of these—and, he'll get all the headaches, because he'll have to deal with the southerners, himself. In other words, we would attend to the travellers, and he would have to contend with the hosts and staff in the south. I don't envy him.

There are other facets of his proposition that are also very good for us. But, they are too complicated to go into in writing, so I'll explain it all to you when I get to New York.

The letter continued, touching on various subjects with which the cousins were involved, and ending with:

. . . one of our most pressing issues, that of Carmine Pace and his associates. I have only one reply so far, a positive one from LoGiudice. No response, yet, from either Beckmann or Pire, and I really can't guess, at this time, how they might go. I hope that Pire's answer doesn't depend upon what we decide about his houses. He might possibly be using that as a wedge.

Tullio was satisfied with his day's work, and he was especially elated over Cosmo LoGiudice's visit because he and Gerhard had been waiting, so long, for the prefabrication idea to materialize.

Gerhard Moeller intended establishing his own business (quite apart from that of the family's) and exporting the units for the New England ski areas would be his first step in that direction. It was his wish that it be kept confidential, though; and Tullio suspected that this was one way of Gerhard's striking out against his mother, whom he'd never forgiven for having remarried so quickly after his father's death.

Tullio wondered if Gerhard's plans to marry might be another way of punishing Frau Moeller. This was Gerhard's personal business, though; and, as much as Tullio would like to have seen his friend accept his stepfather, he would not dare interfere by suggesting it. He would wait until Gerhard broached the subject again. He was sure he would do this the next time they'd meet, because Gerhard confided in Tullio more than in anyone else.

Chapter Seven

Magdalena was irked because she'd not arrived before Salvatore had left for the club. She'd wanted to ask him some things, questions that had not even occurred to her until she'd spoken with Bella Modesto.

She wanted to know, why there had never been any publicity about the Barragattos, why Tullio had demanded it be kept that way, and why Salvatore had gone to such lengths to see to it.

North American Distributors owned tabloids and magazines. Publicity was hers for the asking. What society clutched after, she had within the palms of her hands; yet, she was denied its advantage.

She remembered, now. When Carlo was born, Louise had had an argument with Salvatore because he'd forbidden his society editor to print the birth announcement. Magdalena had not cared about it then; she'd been too ill and too angry with Tullio to be concerned over such a matter. She wondered about it at this moment, though. What harm could there be in announcing a child's birth? Why should her husband's cousin have been so set against it?

I hope he has a good explanation for that!

And, what about when Stefano and Big Babbo won the "Little

Equestrian Cup?" There were lots of reporters there, but nothing ever appeared in the papers about it. I wonder if Salvatore stopped that, too.

She halted, then. It might not be fair to confront Salvatore with these questions. He might simply be carrying out Tullio's orders. Why jump to conclusions and put his back up against the wall again? Poor Salvatore . . . he was always the buffer. She'd wait, she decided. She'd wait; and then, she would have a very serious talk with her husband.

She could hear the children's squeals. They were playing hide-and-go-seek with their nurse, and she was tempted to join in their game. She changed her mind, though; Bella Modesto would never play children's games . . . she was too sophisticated . . . real women don't play children's games.

She looked at her hands, and at her fingernails; and she grimaced.

I will never bite them again. And, I'll never have to hide them again.

There were other things she must attend to. She'd always considered them such trivialities. But, they weren't; they were important. They were what made real women. Bella was the proof. Bella had never ignored them. That was because Bella Modesto was a real woman.

They were things like . . . perfumes, all kinds, for all occasions . . . and hairpins that matched your hair color . . . and manicures, with red polish . . . and mascara . . . and hand creams . . . and night creams . . . and, maybe, even a little rouge!

And, there were those other matters, the things Tullio's aunts used to preach about . . . like sitting up straight . . . and knowing clever stories to tell . . . and nodding, instead of bobbing her head . . . and oh, so many other things!

My eyelashes are absolutely invisible.

She hung the white linen suit in the closet and inspected everything else she owned. She had to admit that Tullio had impeccable taste; and, to her surprise, anything he'd sent her was just now starting to appear in the fashion magazines. She definitely had a head start, she decided, because Modesto's wardrobe couldn't possibly be so voluminous and up-to-date.

Yet, she believed herself very far behind in every other way. A wardrobe could take one just so far. It was only the wheels to get you someplace. What really counted was how you arrived, in a carriage or a cart. That's what those other things would do for her: they'd give her her carriage.

She looked out from her bedroom window. She wanted to play with the children, but she didn't. She just smiled at them and waved.

Capits Rock was its busiest on Saturday afternoons. The Grill Room was always especially crowded at that time, because most early golfers, having completed their games by then, would come to this room for lunch, drinks, and to trade excuses about their swing. Aleksey and Earl had been here for a few hours already when Salvatore arrived. He had not played.

Capits Rock observed the Prohibition law and so no alcoholic drinks were served. That did not prevent most of its members from bringing their own liquor, usually in silver flasks hidden away in expensive purses or jacket pockets. By this time of the afternoon the club had all the ambience of a speakeasy.

The Grill was "hopping," as the members would say. Mrs. Cheshire, an octogenarian who'd just gone nine holes, was feeling her oats and was draining her fourth martini. She began singing and plunking away at a baby grand at the far end of the room, and the god-awful sounds forced the other members to shout to be heard. Her father-in-law had been one of the club founders and she was now the undisputed matriarch of Capits Rock. There was generous applause after each of her songs. But, even the clapping halted when Mrs. Earl Asheley entered with her guest.

Louise beamed while introducing her husband, Aleksey and Salvatore to Bella, and the whispers from other tables gave her even more satisfaction.

The men were captivated by Bella Modesto, even if for different reasons.

Earl spoke no Italian. Fearing that other members might realize his guest could speak English, he dared not exchange a word with her. He just stared at her, poured her drinks, and grinned.

Aleksey was both curious and fascinated. This was the most famous lady of Orvietto, and he quickly determined that she deserved her reputation. His young rooster—(this was how he still sometimes secretly alluded to Tullio)—had tasted the best of two worlds, he decided. He smiled. *Yes, between her and Magdalena, he's had the best.*

Salvatore, who conversed freely with her in their native tongue, was thoroughly amused. He'd never known she was such a fine actress. He could hardly believe—judging from her present deportment and from the Bella Modesto he knew so well—that this was the same woman who, in her cottage just a couple of hours before, had been talking to him while sprawled boldly naked across a divan. He would be propositioning her right now if it were not that Aleksey could understand Italian. She seemed to understand, and nodded a sweet promise toward him.

They left the Capits Rock Club together, without introducing their stunning blonde guest to anyone, not even Mrs. Cheshire. Louise Asheley knew she was treading dangerously, but she was the happiest clubwoman in the town of Jericho.

Magdalena wasn't as garrulous as usual during the evening meal. Aleksey Kostenov noticed. Having met Bella, he could imagine what was going through his young charge's head, so he tried to keep the conversation as light and as whimsical as possible. Despite his attempt to avoid the subject, however, she brought it up.

"Well?" she asked. "Tell me the truth. What's your opinion of Bella Modesto? Your honest opinion, now. The truth." She didn't look at him when she spoke. She tried to make herself sound as casual as possible.

"The truth," he replied, "is that she is beautiful, an excellent actress, a superb conversationalist, a delightful mixture of the finest geisha and courtesan I can imagine"—he paused, then, for the effect—"and absolutely no competition for you."

"What?"

"You heard me," he said. "Now, don't you ever ask me such a foolish question again. After all, what you really want to know is what I think of you, not what I think of her. Isn't that the truth? Now, admit it. And, from my opinion, you might try to gauge how your husband would compare you two. Do you think that Tullio and I think the same way? Well, sometimes we do, and sometimes we don't."

She flushed. She didn't know she was so transparent.

"Do you expect me to answer that she's not beautiful? Well, I won't, because she is. But, so are you. Did you want me to call her a dullard? Well, I won't, because she's intelligent. But, so are you. And, certainly, I could not possibly say she isn't desirable."

"I really feel stupid now."

He patted her hand. "If she's still here when your husband returns, there won't be any problem at all. You'll see."

"You really think so?" She hadn't meant to ask that aloud. She felt even more foolish now.

"Yes, I do. That's because you're a lady. A real one. A *bella donna*. And, it's about time you realized it."

He'd stunned her and he would not have said it, otherwise. He admired Magdalena more than any female he could think of; and sometimes, she even reminded him of his beloved Anna, because Anna, too, had been unsure about herself at times, and he'd had to encourage her in the same way.

The older Kostenov grew, the more he was thinking of Anna. He could still remember how she'd looked the last morning he'd left her to go to work. He dismissed the memory, though;

it was reoccurring too often; it was a sign of approaching senility to remember too much, he decided, and he must stop it.

After the nurse had ushered the children to bed, Magdalena said: "Thank you for saying what you said before, Aleksey. About my being a real lady, I mean. That was really very nice of you."

"You're very welcome, but it was the truth, not just a compliment."

"Nevertheless," she continued, "I realize that there are a few things I've got to do about myself. Improvements. Changes. And, you'll see . . . there will be a difference . . ."

He replied with a smile, "Well, don't change too much. We like you this way."

Germany's Main Valley resembles a beautiful and delicate table scarf; instead of a crocheted lace edging, though, it is fringed with golden-leafed vineyards. Through the Main runs the picturesque *Romantische Strasse* (or "romantic road") which leads southward through Rothenburg, a perfectly preserved medieval village. This was Gerhard Moeller's favorite place and he'd recently built a house there.

Tullio had agreed to spend some time with Gerhard in Rothenburg before leaving for New York. The moment he reached the hamlet, he felt as though he'd just lost a couple of centuries. He could understand Gerhard's attraction for the place because he believed that his friend should have been born somewhere back in the early 1700s. Gerhard believed this too, and sometimes, he was positive he'd been reincarnated and had been drawn to Rothenburg because he'd lived there in his past life.

Tullio had to leave his car outside of Rothenburg because the streets were too narrow to accommodate it. He didn't mind, though, because he enjoyed looking at the buildings and because the town was so small he could walk its breadth very easily. He followed two young boys who carried his valises to the Moeller house. They'd refused money, but had accepted a pack of American cigarettes. He'd made a habit of carrying a supply of cigarettes with him lately. He'd found them very useful in the smaller villages where bartering was still an art form.

He could feel eyes peeking at him from behind half-closed shutters. Visitors were such an oddity here, he guessed, that the people had the right to spy upon him. He suspected that they would question the boys about him as soon as their job was completed; and, for this reason, he spoke to them very little—he was good with languages, and he decided he should leave them guessing what country he'd travelled from. By the time he turned the last corner leading to the Moeller house, the town was quiet with wondering about him. Only one voice could be heard—Gerhard's—because he'd spotted him from an upstairs window and called out to him. When Tullio looked up he saw that Gerhard was not alone. A young blonde girl was beside him. This was the first sight of Nicole Grynszpan.

She was not at all the fiancée he would have expected from Gerhard. His friend was quiet and shy, while Nicole was gay and vivacious. And although Gerhard kept referring to the young Belgian as his "little schoolgirl," to Tullio she seemed quite clever and sophisticated. Later that night, over a dinner of roast spring lamb, she entertained them with tales from her convent school in Antwerp. She'd escaped this weekend by telling the Mother Superior that she had to attend to a desperately ill old aunt in Rothenburg.

Later the three of them took brandy in the library, and Gerhard and Tullio joked a lot about private things from their past, things that Nicole knew nothing about; often, she couldn't figure out why they were laughing and very little was explained. She didn't seem to begrudge them their secrets, though, and was amused by them. She excused herself at midnight, and the two men remained talking until dawn.

The next morning, their conversation turned to the serious side. They'd known one another since childhood, had always

206

been very good friends, and now were on the verge of a partnership.

Gerhard was the only person outside the family who knew where Magdalena was living. Gerhard expected to travel to America on his honeymoon. They would spend some time together, they agreed; Magdalena and Nicole were sure to get along.

A few days before coming to Rothenburg, Tullio had been advised by Herr Beckmann and Monsieur Pire that they wanted him to represent them in the Pace matter. Tullio was elated but Gerhard was against it.

"They wouldn't stick their necks out for you," he warned. "Not one of them."

"What you don't understand," Tullio responded, "is that it is to my advantage for Pace's people to know that I'm not alone. Pace will be easier to hold off if he sees we wine men are united. I'm not sticking my neck out for anybody but myself . . . only, this way, I'll have backing, even if it is only on the surface."

"I don't like it. I still don't like it. What do you have, lately, some kind of great passion to be a leader of men?" Gerhard toasted him with his beer stein. "*Il Duce*, the Second!" With this, he left them at the table.

Tullio turned to Nicole. "Do you think we'll see him at dinner?"

Nicole shrugged. "He's completely spoiled," she said. "Completely! But, I'm used to him by now, and I guess you are, too."

Tullio grinned and nodded. He knew that Gerhard would not be back for at least a few hours. When Gerhard didn't agree with someone, he would not argue; he would go away and sulk. "Yes, I guess we both know him."

Tullio didn't mind Gerhard's absence. Nicole was lovely to look at, witty and (what impressed him greatly) the only woman he'd ever met who was interested in politics. She had opinions about almost everything, and she softened them with humor. The more time they spent together, the more he liked her. By noon, she was teaching him how to make *crepes*. By mid-afternoon, she was coaching him in Flemish. And, by early evening, when Gerhard finally did rejoin them, he was almost relieved. She was a most attractive young woman.

She came into his room that night. The blonde schoolgirl braids were loosened and her hair hung to her waist. She looked like a fairy princess. Rapunzel perhaps. In hushed tones she said, "Gerhard is asleep. He drank too much. He won't wake up until morning."

Tullio steepled his fingers in front of his face. "You can't be sure of that."

"I am sure." She waited a few seconds, then asked, "Do you want me to leave?"

"No. No, I don't want you to go. I've been waiting for you."

"Thank you for saying that."

"It's true," he answered, and he felt suddenly guilty.

"I don't know what I'm doing here. I love Gerhard very much. Believe it or not, I really do."

"Why should it matter to you whether I believe you?"

"Because I don't want you to tell him about this, and I have a feeling that you might. If you tell him, I'll lose him. To me, that would be losing everything."

"Then, why did you take such a chance by coming here?"

"I don't know."

"You can leave, if you want. I'll understand."

"I don't want to leave, Tullio."

"Then, don't talk anymore."

She came closer and kissed him and said, "Please don't tell him."

"I won't."

Her hand was already boldly on his trousers. In seconds she had removed his pajamas and pushed him back on the massive oak bed. She explored every inch of his body with her lips and tongue, he was her prisoner, moaning in ecstasy as she took his rigid shaft in her mouth. Finally she allowed him to respond in kind and soon the two of them were united in a rhythmic movement as old as Eden.

Her experience took him totally by surprise. Could Gerhard have taught her all these things? He doubted it. Perhaps his friend was getting much more than he could handle. Certainly she was a match for Tullio. And at dawn, when she sneaked back to her fiancée's bed, he heaved a sigh of relief.

Nicole told Gerhard that she'd awakened during the night and had gone out for some air. He had no reason not to believe her; besides, his head was aching because he was hung over, and the throbbing was the only thing he could think about. He never noticed that, when Tullio came to breakfast, nobody's eyes met. He was usually very observant, but not today; today, he wished he had never woken up.

Nicole was so obviously nervous that Tullio was positive she would give them away. She spilled the coffee, and then the tray. She tripped more than once, and even Gerhard remarked that something must be bothering her. On the verge of tears, she finally excused herself, claiming a headache. Some aspirins and a couple of hours of sleep might help, she told them, and Tullio agreed with her.

"Wait, I'll help you with that tray," Tullio said.

"No, I can manage."

"Let me carry it inside for you." He took it from her and followed her into the pantry. When they were out of Gerhard's earshot, he said, "Look, I feel the same way that you do. Last night never should have happened, but it did. It's over. And, it won't happen again. Now, go upstairs and get yourself a nice hot bath and relax. You'll feel better."

"Do you believe that it won't happen again if you remain here? Do you really believe that?"

He skimmed his fingertips along her chinline and over her lips and throat. "Go upstairs, Nicole. You'll feel better after some sleep."

That evening, he told Gerhard he would be leaving the following afternoon. He would like to remain in Rothenburg longer, he explained, but there were just too many matters to attend to in Milan.

Gerhard accompanied him to the edge of town where he'd left his car. "How did you like Nicole?" he asked.

"What do you mean?" Did he suspect? Had she already blurted out the story?

"Just that. What do you think of her?"

"I think she's perfect for you," he lied.

"I'll bet you thought I was marrying her just to aggravate my mother." He chuckled. "You did think that at first, didn't you?"

"It entered my mind. But, I know better now. I think she'll make you a very good wife. And, you won't have much trouble if you keep her and your mother apart as much as possible."

"I know." He shrugged and helped Tullio load the valises into the car. "I'll see you in New York," he said. "And, for God's sake, watch your step with that Pace thing."

Tullio drove from the Main Valley more slowly than usual because it was too pretty a place to hurry through. He passed some of the little-known landmarks that Nicole had told him about and pictured her at each one of them. She'd described each one with an excitement that seemed to push its way into most of her conversations. Yet, everything about her was exciting, he decided, not just the way she talked. He liked the way her eyes lit up when she had new ideas, the way she laughed, her accent, her walk; and her face, and blonde coloring, and form—she reminded him of a Dresden figurine. He couldn't find a fault with her, and was amused with himself, because he was trying to. He liked the way she'd kissed him goodbye, in front of Gerhard, and the sweetness and relief there had been in her smile.

Why did she think I would tell him? So I could clear my own conscience? Maybe.

Or, maybe, to stop him from marrying her, because she might be an unfaithful wife. She thought I might try to protect him from that. She doesn't know Gerhard very well if she thinks he needs any protecting.

210

I hope she knows what she's doing.

He thought of lots of things during the long motor trip back to Italy. It would be harvest soon . . . and, he would leave Orvietto, and he would be with his Magdalena again, and then he wouldn't need anybody else. He thought about the portrait he'd sent him and about the pack of cigarettes on the table . . . and he was certain that they'd still be sealed when he returned to *The Walls*. He thought about Beckmann and Pire and LoGiudice. He thought about Carmine Pace and what he would say to him. And, he thought a lot about Nicole Grynszpan.

Chapter Eight

The invitations to Carter Asheley's birthday party, sent out during Louise's "spell," had to be honored.

She'd asked Stefano: "What would you like for your birthday?"

He'd answered: "A circus! That's what I want! A circus!"

The *Swansgarten* grounds, therefore, housed a full-blown carnival. There were striped tents; and inside of them were knife throwers and tightrope walkers and trapeze artists. There were large tables set with foods of all descriptions. There were clowns and fortune-tellers. There were even souvenir hawkers and booths where the shell game was played.

The little boy didn't mind being called Carter by all the well-wishing strangers who were meeting him for the first time. All he cared about was that whenever he heard, "Happy birthday, Carter!" a present followed. He loved being Carter Asheley.

News of Mrs. Asheley's mysterious house guest had spread rapidly through the North Shore, so very few who had been invited did not attend. Louise was gloriously happy. It was a sign of better things to come.

Bella and Magdalena stayed together throughout the affair, avoiding the crowds and reporters who swarmed over the state like hungry and curious ants. No matter where the two women wandered, though, Guido was close by.

Guido looked especially handsome in his chauffeur's uniform and he was a little embarrassed because some of the matrons' daughters were obviously attracted to him. His foreign mannerisms, mixed with the fact that he could not speak English, added to his allure. Magdalena noticed how the young girls glanced toward him and did not resist teasing him about it. He took his bodyguard role very seriously, though, and he upset her when he refused to take the children home after the birthday cake ceremony.

"I will take them home when you are also ready to leave, signora. I will take you all home together."

"That won't be necessary, Guido. You're my driver, not my bodyguard. Now, do as I say, and bring them home. It's far too late for them to be up."

"Signora, if you insist that the children go home, I'll ask Signor Kostenov's driver to take them. But, I, myself, will wait here for you."

"Guido, what's wrong with you? I appreciate your concern, but I'll be fine. Now, you drive my children home, and I will come home later."

Salvatore Crispino was within earshot. "Thank you, Guido. Please take the children home. I will take care of the signora."

He nodded to the attorney and, as though nothing had happened, said: "Fine! I'll go collect the children."

Magdalena was incensed, not only because her orders seemed meaningless to the youth, but because he had challenged her in front of Bella Modesto. "He has a lot of growing up to do," she said. "Apparently, he thinks he's still in Orvietto. I'm going to have a very serious talk with him the first thing in the morning."

"How long has he been your chauffeur?" Bella asked.

"He arrived a few days ago. My husband sent him. Until now, he's been living on my husband's estate."

"That might be the explanation," Bella told her. "Perhaps,

your husband told him to escort you everywhere. It possible." She looked toward Salvatore. "Do you think th could be it?" she asked him.

"He was just doing his job, Magdalena. Don't be angry wit him. Come, the show's just starting. Let's enjoy ourselves.'

Salvatore was very pleased with what he'd seen. He wa satisfied that Guido would do what he'd come for, and sav him a lot of worrying. He could spend less time on the Islan now. He'd met the young man at the dock, had driven him t *The Walls*, and had helped move him into the chauffeur' quarters; and there, he'd reiterated Tullio's orders.

Guido's room was attached to the main residence. He had private entrance from the back garden and could also ente from the kitchen. He was grateful that he was close to th kitchen because he'd always had a ravenous appetite. He wa thin and tall, though, and didn't show the huge amounts o food he consumed; the cook took great pleasure in feeding him After having been here only twenty-four hours, he was in he full graces. When he brought the children and their nurse back from the birthday party, there was a snack awaiting him.

"Why don't we all have something?" he asked them.

The nurse blushed and hesitated, but Stefano and Rebecca were thrilled by his suggestion, and because they pleaded with her, she permitted it. The cook joined them, put a birthday candle in a cupcake, and they had their own, private party. He couldn't know that the reason the children were so happy was because they'd never been allowed to eat in the kitchen before. For them, this was a special treat, a picnic, something just as exciting as the grand carnival their Grandma Louise had given them. Rebecca asked him to be her husband when she grew up, and he promised her he would, but only if she stayed as beautiful as she was now. Stefano asked him to ride with him on Big Babbo, and he promised he would; at least, he would watch, he said . . . he'd never learned how to ride a horse.

"It's remarkable," he said to the nurse. "The birthday party they had today . . . at home, we could have fed a hundred

milies for a year with what this one party must have
ost . . . it's remarkable."

"You haven't seen anything yet," she told him. "You
aven't seen anything."

During these final weeks of waiting for her husband to
eturn, Magdalena Barragatto began her changeover to what
he believed would make her more attractive to him. The fact
hat he'd always found her more desirable than any other
voman didn't faze her. She was looking to the future. The
eauty she had now would disappear with her youth, she
ealized. It was the second kind she was after, the kind that
loesn't come naturally, the kind that one must cultivate.

How had Bella put it? "When you are very young, depend
pon your beauty. Later, upon your brains. And in the end,
ou can depend upon your money." This was Bella's bible.

Magdalena and Bella had become surprisingly friendly in the
hort time they'd been forced to associate with each other.
Their mutual fondness amused Aleksey Kostenov and relieved
Louise Asheley. Still, friendship or not, Magdalena was in the
process of cultivating her brainpower: she was determined that
Bella Modesto be miles away at harvest time.

Louise brought Bella to Saratoga in August. Magdalena did
not accompany them and was grateful that Louise had kept her
promise, and never mentioned their adventure with Carmine
Pace. Before the two women went to Saratoga, Magdalena
suggested Newport.

"I really think it advisable that you take her to Newport,
Louise. Everyone who's anyone will be there. You should go
directly from Saratoga. Don't even bother coming back to
Jericho first."

"Do you think so?"

"Yes, Louise, I really do. You've got to follow the seasons,
you know. Then, after Newport, you might find that you don't
even need her services anymore. It's not that I don't like Bella,
because I really do . . . but, after all, you can't keep up this

pretense indefinitely."

"Yes, Magdalena, you're right. So far, our plan has worke[d] out, but I might be pushing my luck a little too far to extend [it] for too long."

During the second week of August, Magdalena read in th[e] first paragraph of *Social Doings:* "Among the most noteworth[y] ladies gracing the paddock this morning were Mrs. Ear[l] Asheley and her mysterious house guest, known to all the Gol[d] Coast as The Visitor."

Magdalena was happy for Louise, and she admired Bell[a] Modesto for the job she was obviously doing so well. She didn'[t] feel guilty for suggesting that the farce end because Bella ha[d] recently been hinting that she was tiring of her role.

Kostenov said to Magdalena: "I have a feeling that Mis[s] Modesto has had a better offer; but, being a woman of honor she doesn't want to abandon Louise until her mission i[s] completed."

"I hope you're right, Aleksey. I would not like to see Bell[a] with nowhere to go."

"I don't think that will be the case," Kostenov laughed. "O[n] the contrary, I believe she can't wait for this job to end. The last time I ran into her and Louise at the club, she looked completely bored."

Magdalena smiled and asked: "Who could possibly blame her for being bored at Capits Rock?" She added: "I'm surprised Louise took her there without me. They couldn't speak to each other in front of anybody. What did she do? Just sit there in silence?"

"No, Salvatore was with her."

"Oh, I should have known." She shook her head. "I should have known. He hasn't wasted any time, has he?"

The man shrugged. "Well, you know Salvatore."

The weeks were speeding by much too quickly for Tullio Barragatto. He didn't know how he could attend to everything that had to be done before his scheduled sailing. He was used to keeping up a frenzied pace during harvest; but, this year, all the problems involved with the growing of crops seemed to have been multiplied by the dozens. Parts of his cellars had been flooded again and some of his best pickers had left during his last trip to Milan. He'd been forced to hire migrant workers and had had to arrange for their transportation from their home towns to Orvietto; then, he'd had to provide housing for them. He was almost tempted to put off his sailing for a later date; were it not for Benedetto's intervention, he would have done so.

In addition to his problems in the orchards, he was not anxious to leave Italy at such a time because one of his dreams was about to blossom, and he expected that he might be in mid-ocean when it happened. Mussolini was threatening a "march on Rome," something for which Tullio and other party members had been crying out during their midnight meetings. Tullio had hoped to be a part of that "march;" now, he knew he would not even be here to see it. He placated himself, though, because he was convinced that all the hard work and time he'd devoted to the cause was its own just reward. The weak, corrupt government would soon topple . . . Once that occurred, the healing process would start . . . and that would be just the beginning.

He was right about the timing. While he was lying seasick on his stateroom bed, the news reached him. It had already spread through the ship like wildfire. The Italian king, Vittorio Emanuele III, had refused to sign a Cabinet decree ordering Italy's army to suppress the threatened blackshirt "march." Instead, the monarch had sent Mussolini a telegram, inviting him to come to Rome to form a new ministry.

Tullio was jubilant, but he was sadly disappointed to find that so many of his fellow passengers opposed the man whom he believed would be his country's salvation. It was a pity, he told them, that Mussolini was so grossly misunderstood; but, the young politician would prove himself very quickly— Tullio was positive of this—and they would all regret having given him such a hard time.

At home, there were riots and killings because of the "march;" but, Tullio Barragatto could not know about this because it wasn't widely publicized. What he could not know, also, was that Mussolini's famous "march" was actually a comfortable train ride in a sleeping car from Milan, and that the train was followed by the straggling arrival of 25,000 largely unarmed blackshirts.

The day after the "march," Orvietto's local *patrono* was murdered by some of the Fascists from Tullio's club. That same evening, still drunk with the excitement of their leader's new found power, they attacked Benedetto Crispino because his anti-Fascist feelings were well-known, and because his cousin wasn't there to speak out for him and protect him; they left him barely alive, then turned their wrath on other dissidents. But, Tullio could not yet know about any of this, either.

When Tullio's ship docked in New York this second time, his attention was drawn to a woman who was so exquisitely dressed that she stood out in the crowd. She was wearing a pale blue velvet greatcoat trimmed with chinchilla, and her hands were hidden within a huge muff tipped with the fur tails. Her hair was completely covered by a turban that tilted higher to one side.

"She looks like something out of a Russian novel," a fellow-passenger said.

"Yes," Tullio replied, not knowing until then that others were also admiring her.

At that moment, the woman turned, and he realized: "God, that's my wife."

He didn't try to call or wave to her. He only stared at her. He moved closer to the rail so he could see her face more clearly. "That's my wife," he repeated, not caring that the man with whom he'd just been speaking couldn't hear what he was saying.

He could see that she was anxiously scanning the waves of passengers at the rail. He doubted she could spot him from her vantage point and he knew it would be senseless to try calling to her because he was too far away to be heard.

Up here, Magda. Look up this way, Magda.

He was standing on the uppermost deck because he'd just walked out of his cabin. It would be several minutes before he could even get near the stairway. He would have to wait for a while. He hoped she would think of looking up toward him.

For a few endless minutes he kept staring at her. He was astonished because she looked so different than the young wife who'd run to him with balloons in her hands a couple of years before. And, certainly, he could see no trace of the gypsy girl he had made love to in Mikel's wagon. He hoped she was still there, hidden somewhere under the finery. She could not have changed that much, he told himself; not on the inside, not his Magdalena.

The long, empty minutes brought the wagon back to him. He could see her, now, in the old wagon; and what he remembered made him smile because he felt a tickle inside of him. He took a deep breath and grinned and stood very still. He thought he touched her, but it was the rail.

Up here, Magda. Look up here. Look up.

His thoughts kept fluctuating between the glow in the wagon and the bleak New York dock. It had been very warm in the wagon.

He'd let her pierce one of his ears while they were in the wagon. It had been pouring that night; there had been a summer storm, and the lightning had frightened her, so she'd hidden her head under the blankets. He'd laughed at her, but she'd continued clinging to him for protection.

God, it's been a long time, Magda.

He kept watching her. She turned her head toward the left; then, toward the right; then, she looked upward; and they were the same eyes that had met his in the wagon. They were glowing.

I love you.

She was saying something. He tried to read her lips. He

shook his head, letting her know that he couldn't understand what she was saying. She smiled and pursed her lips toward him. He nodded.

The deck was beginning to clear now and he started toward the gangplank. He wondered why he hadn't even waved to her. He wondered why he'd only nodded. He wondered what she'd been saying. He didn't know if he was amused by her self-control or surprised by it: even though her eyes were following him every inch of the way, she was not making a move toward him; she was actually waiting for him to come to her this time. He was amazed with himself, also, because he was so suddenly excited that she could very well have been lying next to him, rather than fully clothed and hundreds of feet away. Despite the cold, he took off his overcoat and carried it folded in front of him. He almost laughed out loud because he'd had to do this and he suspected he must have a very stupid grin on his face.

Guido was directly behind Magdalena, visibly annoyed by the confusion and shouting that surrounded them. Tullio wondered if the young man still hated him; he'd soon find out, he told himself, because Guido had never been any good at hiding his feelings. This, too, almost made him laugh; and he was very grateful that he had the coat.

It seemed like ages before he could reach her, there were so many people between them. When he did, he stopped short, a foot or so away from her. He felt awkward because they were both speechless.

She stepped forward and kissed him.

It felt very good to hold Magdalena again, especially because he realized that her heart was beating as quickly as his own. He knew, now, that the girl had grown up, but that she was still there, cleverly camouflaged from everyone else but him, and he wished they were already at home and alone, and not on the dock.

Magdalena stood aside while Guido greeted Tullio, but she would not take her eyes off him for a moment. He turned back to her and looked around.

"Where are you hiding the others?" he asked.

Magdalena laughed. "Aleksey and the children are waiting for you at *The Walls*. I wanted you to myself for a while."

"And you shall have me," he agreed.

Guido had finished loading Tullio's bags in the trunk of the limousine. Now he was standing at the open door awaiting further instructions.

"There's been a change of plans," Tullio announced as he and Magdalena settled in the rear seat. "The signora and I will be stopping first at the Plaza."

If Guido was surprised, he showed no concern. The desk clerk inside however did raise an eyebrow when the two well-dressed strangers checked into a suite with no luggage. The eyebrow returned to position when Tullio ordered champagne to be sent up immediately.

"And roses," Magdalena whispered. "I want to make love in a roomful of roses."

The roses filled the room when the bellhop let them in.

The champagne was waiting for them in a silver bucket of ice and the roses filled the room. Magdalena walked to the window as Tullio filled two glasses. The room looked down on Central Park and she could see it was covered with snow, the frozen lake filled with ice skaters.

"Come see, Tullio," she said. "It's beautiful."

He joined her, handing her a glass. "Yes," he agreed. "But not as beautiful as Italy."

"Oh, Tullio, do you miss it already?"

He didn't answer, but continued staring thoughtfully at the skaters.

"Really, Tullio," she persisted. "I'll go anywhere you want. We don't have to stay in America. I would go back to Orvietto tomorrow if you wanted me to."

They were getting into a dangerous area. He was not going to discuss his reasons for sending her away, for keeping her in seclusion on Long Island. Instead he put his fingers gently to her lips.

221

"Enough talk, Magdalena," he whispered and he kissed her hungrily on the lips. In his fantasies during their two years of separation he had dreamed of taking her gently, tenderly, but now he surprised himself with his own eagerness. She responded in kind, and they were both undressed and on the bed in seconds. He seemed to want every inch of her at once as his hands and tongue explored her body. She matched him caress for caress, stroke for stroke, kiss for kiss. She was a new Magdalena, a hungry, almost insatiable woman utterly abandoned to the act of love.

During a brief respite, as they caught their breath and sipped champagne, he mentioned it to her.

"You've changed, Magdalena," he said. "You're getting more American."

"Do you like that?"

He hesitated. The truth was that he wasn't sure. He liked a woman who was sexually aggressive. He'd certainly enjoyed Nicole. But his wife was different. Especially when he would have to leave her alone again soon. He remembered her ideas about smoking and lit a cigarette for himself.

"What are you thinking about, Tullio?" Magdalena finally asked.

He reached out and took her in his arms again. "I'm thinking that I'll ask Guido to come for us in the morning"

Three in the Morning

Chapter One

In winter, the trees on Long Island are bare and the ground, when it isn't iced over, has a muddy look. The rolling hills aren't high enough to break the monotony of the gray-white sky, and the colorlessness is staggering. This one difference between Orvietto and Jericho hit Tullio Barragatto like a whip; he had suddenly come from a gallery of oil paintings to a study in charcoal.

Not only did his eyes require refocusing; his ways needed some readjustments also. Magdalena realized this, and it worried her.

Whether in Milan or Orvietto, Tullio spoke with several people before he started his work day—the speaking was with servants and neighbors and children and fellow merchants; it was an exchange of pleasantries, a recognition of others, and, even though it might be a simple comment upon the weather, it was people saying, "Hello, I'm here and I know that you are, too." But, in New York: the cook would serve the morning coffee, ask "Is there anything else you would like?" and disappear before he could answer; Kostenov's chauffeur would nod and drive to the station in silence; the conductor would take his ticket and grunt; and nobody ever spoke in the

225

elevator, so, for eight stories, he would stare ahead silently at other men's haircuts.

Equally disturbing was the matter of the midday meal. In the best restaurant he could find close to his office, the waiter would write up the check while he was still ordering dessert; and the headwaiter would, at this point, already begin eyeing his table for the next patron. At home in Italy he could peruse the menu and speak with the chef; he could relax and savor his wine; he could exchange thoughts with his waiter; to rush someone while he's eating is almost a sin.

"My husband isn't happy, Aleksey."

"Oh, he just has a lot on his mind. He'll be his old self soon."

"No. He's homesick."

"If I got used to America, he can."

"Suppose he doesn't want to?"

Kostenov shrugged. He didn't care to admit that he'd recently been wondering about the same thing. "It's the winter," he said. "He's not used to our New York winters. You wait until spring comes."

Tullio didn't complain about his growing dislike for his surroundings. He had no idea that it was so visible. He thought he'd managed to hide it very well, and was quite surprised when Magdalena said:

"Why don't you get away from this place for a while? Why don't you and Salvatore go hunting or something?"

"Hunting? In the middle of winter, with all this snow?"

"Oh, I didn't think of that."

"Well, the next time, think before you talk."

She left the room, rather than argue. But, she'd given him an idea. He would get away for a while, he decided. He'd take a look at *Piccolo Villaggio*. He'd not seen it during his first trip to America; he hadn't had the heart to look at vineyards going to waste. He informed Salvatore the next morning.

"You might as well go," his cousin told him. "There's nothing you can do about the other thing until Pace gets back."

226

"That's right . . . though I have to admit that I still have some reservations about it . . . maybe, Benedetto is right . . . maybe . . ."

"There's good money in it," Salvatore said. "Good money."

"Yes, I know."

"I wonder who the new *patrono* will be."

"Well, whoever it is, it's certain that Pace won't be back until he meets him and gets his orders." He paused; then said: "Yes, I might as well go upstate."

"When are you leaving?"

"Tomorrow. I think I'll take Carlo with me."

"Magdalena's letting you take him?"

"She doesn't know yet."

That night, he and Magdalena argued over his decision to bring Carlo with him. She acquiesced when he finally agreed to take the nurse, also; she was immediately sorry she'd given in, though, as she watched the car drive toward the road. Three or four days . . . a week at the most, he'd said . . . and she missed the baby already.

The ride upstate was more exhausting than Tullio had thought it would be. He'd never expected that the roads would be so icy. He would not admit it, but he was glad the nurse was in the car, because Carlo became very restless after an hour or so, and he would have to have stopped a few times, rather than drive straight through. Magdalena had packed sandwiches and juice for the baby; Tullio had not thought of that, either. They reached *Piccolo Villaggio* at sundown, and he was very grateful not to have been at Carlo's mercy during the long, grueling trip. He'd never had any idea that such a little child could be so demanding and he was astonished when the nurse remarked about how well-behaved Carlo had been during the ride. He decided to increase her salary; no matter what it presently was, it couldn't be enough. The next morning, he told her: "I'll take him today. You take the day off. Here's my car keys. Go into town if you like."

She was rather surprised, but accepted the free day without

question. It amused her to wonder how her charge and employer would fare with one another; neither was very patient, and she expected it would be a day each would remember for a long time. She watched them walk toward the main residence, then drove away. She wondered why they'd had to sleep in the guest cottage; perhaps, the large house hadn't been readied, she told herself; this could be the only reason.

Tullio waited until the car disappeared and until he could no longer hear even a trace of its engine. Then, he rang the doorbell and said to the butler, "Will you please tell Miss Modesto that Mr. Barragatto is here?"

About five minutes passed before Bella came downstairs. She looked like she hadn't aged a day, a little heavier perhaps, but it was difficult to believe she'd been a longtime friend of his father's. Salvatore had told him to expect this, but he commented upon it, anyway. It was Salvatore, also, who had told him about Bella's stay in *Swansgarten;* Magdalena had still not said a word about it, and he'd thought it best not to bring up the matter, either. Knowing his wife as well as he did, he expected that she would approach the subject sooner or later.

Bella stooped down and held out her arms to Carlo. She was thrilled because he remembered her, and she swung him around as she used to do before she'd left for Saratoga. For the first few minutes, she ignored Tullio completely. She finally said: "It's been so many months since he's seen me! I can't get over how he could remember me!"

"Well, you're not easy to forget."

She laughed and said, "I see you haven't changed much, either." She gave him a friendly kiss, then, and added: "Your cousin telephoned me yesterday. He said you were coming here. How did you get rid of the nurse? Are you sure she doesn't suspect I'm here?"

"I'll keep her in the cottage . . . and you behave yourself, and stay indoors for a few days . . . and she'll never suspect a thing."

"I hope so."

"She'll be in town all day long. It will work out very well. She probably won't get back until dark . . . and then, you and I can go out and get ourselves something to eat. I passed a couple of restaurants not far from here, and they looked pretty good."

They began to talk business. She'd asked Salvatore to set up this meeting, she explained, because she had heard he was discussing going into business with Pire. She had a better proposition.

"You remember my house in Orvietto," she said. "Your father gave me the money to start it."

Tullio nodded. Bella had run the finest brothel in the city.

"I'm not getting any younger," she continued. "And I'm getting fat." She patted her rounded hips. "Soon I'll be a fat old woman and I'll wear black dresses and stockings all the time."

Tullio tried not to laugh because she seemed so serious.

"I don't mind getting old, Tullio," she said. "But I don't want to be poor."

Slowly, and in great detail, she laid out her idea to him. They spoke all through the rest of the morning, stopped only for lunch and continued throughout the afternoon.

The entire vineyard of *Piccolo Villaggio* could be turned into a resort, she said. A resort for men only. The thirty bedrooms in the main residence could be converted to two-room suites. The shortest stay would be for a weekend, the longest for a week.

"It would be a spa, a hunting lodge, a gambling casino, and a house, all wrapped up in one package," she said. "All the girls would be selected by me and answerable only to me. There would be guest cottages for those who want special privacy."

The more he listened, the more excited Tullio became. It would be a way to use *Piccolo Villaggio* and take care of an old friend at the same time. No one knew how to run a house better than Bella.

"Just make sure the girls are clean and have some brains,"

he cautioned.

Bella Modesto smiled. "Give me one year," she said. "Just one year . . . and, when you come visiting, you'll think you're back in Orvietto."

He wondered: Did it show that much? "Have you ever thought of going back to Orvietto?"

She shook her head, and she knew that he was a little disappointed.

Two days later, Tullio drove back to Jericho. He'd surprised himself, as much as Bella, because he'd returned to the guest cottage each night.

"You've really turned into a husband," she'd told him. "Who would have guessed it would happen to you."

He'd shrugged and grinned, but he'd not answered. He'd not thought of it until she'd spelled it out. But, there it was: as long as Magdalena was within reach . . .

But, she's not within reach! What's happening with me, passing up somebody like Bella?

He'd been snapping at Magdalena. He'd make it up to her when he got back. He promised himself this.

The roads were more icy on the return trip then they'd been going north. The nurse gasped a few times, because he skidded; he wished she'd just fall asleep because she was getting him nervous. He didn't reach *The Walls of Jericho* until after midnight.

Magdalena was asleep. He wanted to awaken her, but she looked too peaceful. He slipped into bed as quietly as he could and kissed her. He thought she smiled.

The winter weeks went slowly and the only difference between Jericho and Manhattan was the shade of gray from dark to light. Tullio had forsaken the railroad and had begun driving to the city. Earl and Aleksey would accompany him, but they would usually fall asleep before he'd even turn on to Capits Rock Road, so he'd continue the long, dull trek in silence.

The offices of North American Distributors were humming with prosperity. The ticker tape machine gossiped endlessly and Aleksey never stopped complaining about it. He was very absorbed with the public relations campaign for southern Italy, though, so he did not venture out of his own office any more than was necessary. Salvatore disappeared for a few days almost every other week, and the elders were delighted that he'd suddenly taken such a deep interest in the upstate grape crops. Earl became so involved with details and plans for the New England motels venture that he stopped noticing the Fascist propaganda Tullio was injecting within their publications. There was complete harmony among the four men because each was so engrossed with one facet of the business that he had no time to interfere with the other.

At the end of February, there was a snowstorm, and this was the only morning that none of them went to work—Salvatore, because he was at *Piccolo Villaggio*, and the others, because the roads were impassable.

Tullio called the office and was relieved that some of the staff had managed to get in. "Are there any telephone calls?" he asked his secretary.

"Just one," she replied. "A Mr. Pace. He didn't leave any message."

Tullio had become so involved with other matters, lately, that he'd neglected going over the passenger lists of the Asheley Steamship Line. Carmine Pace always used the Asheley Line; he'd known that for a long time; that meant the man would have docked only yesterday. Pace was certainly in a rush to contact him; or Pace was *being* rushed.

He tried to figure the timing. For Carmine Pace to have returned so quickly, he could not have remained in Italy for more than a week. His orders must have been waiting for him. They must have been very precise.

"Are you still there, Mr. Barragatto?"

"Yes . . . yes . . . I'm here. Did Mr. Pace ask for me or Mr. Crispino?"

"He asked only for you."

"Oh."

The secretary didn't know whether or not the conversation was over. Deciding she shouldn't end it herself, she sat silently for almost a half-minute, just holding the receiver to her ear. It wasn't until she cleared her throat rather awkwardly that Tullio said:

"If Mr. Pace calls again, tell him that I'll be back in the office tomorrow morning."

"Tomorrow's Saturday."

"Oh . . . well . . . that's okay . . . just tell him I'll be there tomorrow."

"Should I tell anybody else that you'll be here tomorrow?"

"No, only Pace. And, do me a favor, will you?"

"Yes?"

"Before you leave the office, call me at home and let me know if Mr. Pace calls again."

When he finished speaking with the young woman, he sat, quite numb, for several minutes. He had nothing on his mind. It was totally blank. It was as though he were a student again, walking into a classroom just before a written examination; all the studying and last minute cramming had been for nothing . . . which test was this? . . . for which course? . . . what would he say to Pace?

"Magda!"

She was there, standing at the foot of his bed. Tullio said to her: "Sometimes, when I was in the trenches, you would suddenly pop into my mind. And, I could see you very, very clearly at first. But then, your face would become sort of blurred, and soon, I couldn't make it out at all. And the more I kept staring at it, the more blurred it would become. It was uncanny. I could see everything about it . . . I could see your eyes . . . I could see your mouth . . . I could see your nose . . . your hair . . . everything . . . but nothing came together right. It was a face, but it wasn't a face. It was like a head that didn't have a face. I kept trying, but I couldn't remember what you looked like."

"You couldn't remember me?"

"No! It wasn't you that I couldn't remember, it was your face!"

"My darling, what's wrong?"

I don't know who the new patrono is. I knew how to deal with the old one. "I'm sorry. I swear, I'm sorry. I don't know why I yelled at you. I don't even know why I was talking about that ... the trenches ... your face. It was stupid. I don't know what made me think of that."

"Were you dreaming? You were really fast asleep. You might have been dreaming about it."

"I don't know. What time is it?"

"It's only one o'clock."

She would have called me if he'd called back. Or, maybe, she's waiting until just before she leaves the office, so she can give me all the messages at the same time.

"Do you dream about that a lot?"

"About what?"

"About the war, the trenches."

"No."

"You've never told me anything about the war. Was it really very bad at that front?"

"I might have to go into the office tomorrow."

"On Saturday?"

"Well, I'm not sure yet."

He drew her closer and she knew that he didn't want to talk anymore; but, she knew, also, that any physical desire he'd had earlier had now vanished, and that all he wanted, right now, was to hold her and to think his secret thoughts. He would cling to her, she knew, in the same way the children would when they needed a mother's arms—Tullio did this sometimes; so, she cuddled him as she would a baby. Then he smiled and kissed her, and he buried his face in her until he fell asleep again. It was very nice, she decided, and she wasn't disappointed, because this was the closest kind of love.

More than an hour passed before the telephone interrupted them. Tullio jumped to answer it. He said: "He did call again? . . . Will he be coming to the office tomorrow? . . . Thank you."

She saw him hesitate before replacing the receiver. She saw his mood change. She saw him stare out the window at the snow. He hated snow.

"In one of the Eskimo languages," he said, "there is no word for *snow*. They have words for *freshly fallen snow;* for *snow that fell yesterday;* for *soft, wet snow;* for *snow that's turned to ice* . . . they have a word for every one of its conditions . . . but they have no word for *snow*."

Chapter Two

To Tullio, it was a day that had no reason except to wait for tomorrow. He should be preparing for tomorrow, he thought; but he could not. He wondered what had become of all the fire that had surged within him on the day he'd met with the three wine men. He'd been prepared for Pace then; he was sure he'd been. He was sure then.

. . . funny . . . there's no word for just plain snow.

He drew the curtains tightly closed so he wouldn't have to watch the large flakes come rushing at the windows.

He could hear Aleksey coming in with Rebecca and Stefano. He'd stay upstairs. He wanted the quiet. He'd take a bath; a good, hot bath. Then, he could think better. He would know how to confront Carmine Pace. All he had to do was collect his thoughts. One *patrono* wasn't much different from another. Why hadn't Benedetto written and told him who the new one was? He was supposed to have written.

The old *patrono* had finally paid for Ernesto. He guessed that the old man must have realized it was coming. Everybody pays, sooner or later, one way or another.

But, why had they attacked Benedetto? They knew he was harmless. *I'm going to get the ones who did that.*

Pace . . . he's just a messenger, a go-between . . . what I say to him will be in answer to somebody else . . . but, who's the somebody else? How can I deal with somebody if I don't know whom I'm dealing with? The old patrono *. . . I knew his ways . . . he knew my father . . . my family . . . maybe, I could have made a deal . . . for old times' sake. But, who's this new one?*

He checked the lock on the bedroom door. He didn't want anyone coming in. No one. He sat on the little chair in front of Magdalena's dressing table. The tub was taking a long time to fill.

. . . have to get rid of this tub . . . have to get a black marble tub . . . maybe, green marble . . . tubs shouldn't be white . . . they're like trenches filled with snow . . . God, what in hell's wrong with me . . . it's just a tub . . . it's a tub . . . a tub.

Why didn't Benedetto write yet? Maybe, he hasn't found out who the new one is! Maybe, he did write. Maybe, he just found out. Maybe, he just found out . . . and he just wrote . . . and the letter might have come in on the same ship with Pace. . . . I should have it by Monday, in that case. What good will it do me on Monday? I have to meet him tomorrow.

He looked around at the little dressing room. There were traces of Magdalena in every corner. It even smelled of her. The silver chalice he'd given her years ago sat within a glass domed box to one side of the table. He'd once suggested she donate it to a church, but she'd become upset with him. She'd just had her mother's emerald affixed to it, she'd told him, and she would never give it away. He stared at the emerald.

That damned brooch . . . I'm positive I'd seen the same one a long time ago . . . long before she'd shown it to me.

He stepped into the tub. It felt just right. It had been worth waiting for.

"Where's Tullio?"

"He's taking a bath."

"Oh, well, that's that. I was hoping for a good chess game."

"Aleksey," Magdalena said, "something is wrong. He's

acting very funny. He's talking about the war, and about not remembering what I looked like, and about words in some Eskimo language. I don't know what, but there's something . . ."

"Eskimo?" He raised his eyebrows. He'd taken to smoking a pipe lately and was having trouble lighting it. "He's always been good in languages."

The telephone rang. Magdalena answered it. It was Tullio's secretary. She felt guilty, she told Magdalena, because she'd left the office much earlier than she'd planned.

"The storm was getting so bad, you know, that I thought I'd better get started and get home before it became even worse. So, Jerry—he's our new office boy—he promised to call Mr. Barragatto for me before he left. He was supposed to tell him that Mr. Pace called again."

"Mr. Pace?" she asked. "Pace? Carmine Pace?"

Aleksey said: "Pace? Is he on the phone?"

"Mrs. Barragatto?" the secretary asked. "Are you there?"

"Yes."

Aleksey asked her again: "Is that Pace on the phone with you?"

Magdalena didn't answer Aleksey. She held the receiver tightly.

The secretary continued: "Did Jerry call? He promised he'd call for me."

Magdalena uttered: "Somebody called."

The young woman said, "He was supposed to tell Mr. Barragatto that Mr. Carmine Pace called again. I just want to make sure that Mr. Barragatto got the message. Mr. Pace said he'd meet him tomorrow morning."

"Mr. Carmine Pace?"

"Yes, Mr. Carmine Pace. Will you give Mr. Barragatto the message?" Again—the secretary thought—again! Why do they keep me on the telephone without answering me? "Mrs. Barragatto?"

Magdalena said to Aleksey: "It's Tullio's office. Carmine

237

Pace called his office. He's going to meet Tullio tomorrow."

"Mrs. Barragatto?"

"Yes," Magdalena said. "Yes, he got the message. Thank you."

"Give me the phone," Aleksey told her.

Magdalena hung up. She'd not heard Aleksey's request.

Aleksey threw his pipe into the ashtray in disgust. He lit a cigar. He said: "There could be a hundred different reasons why the man is calling Tullio."

"What does he want!"

"Don't panic, Magdalena. Just stay calm. Let me think. Let me handle this."

"No!" she said. "He's going to tell him about Saratoga! I can feel it. He's going to tell him!"

"Magdalena, do you think, for even one moment, that the man would contact your husband just to tell him he was with you a couple of years ago? Really, Magdalena! You surprise me!"

"But, why else!"

"Magdalena! Stop that! Men don't call a meeting with other men for such a reason!"

"Aleksey, please! What should I do? Should I tell him, myself? Yes, I should tell him, myself. No! No, he'd never understand!" She stopped short. "How did Pace find out who I was? He thought I was Louise's daughter-in-law. How did he find out?"

"Magdalena! Stop this! Stop this foolishness! I don't know why he's calling him, but it can't possibly have anything to do with you!" He huffed and glared at her. "Now, you calm yourself. You act like a grown-up—or you'll be starting trouble for no reason at all."

She sat down and stared ahead and said: "I'm afraid of him, Aleksey. I'm so scared of him. He might. He might say something."

"Let me speak to Tullio," Aleksey replied. "He must have some idea of what Pace wants. Then, I can . . ." He looked at

238

the chair where Magdalena had been sitting. She'd left the room.

Tullio was almost finished dressing when Magdalena came into the bedroom. "What's wrong?" he asked her. "You look as white as a ghost."

"Nothing."

"Who just called? I heard the phone ring."

"Your secretary."

"Well? What did she say? Does she want me to call her back?"

"No. She's home already. She said to tell you that Mr. Carmine Pace called you and that he'll meet you tomorrow. She said somebody else was supposed to have told you and that she was just checking to make sure you got the message."

"Oh. Yes, I got the message."

"What does he want?" she asked him.

"What does he *want?* What do you mean by that? It's business."

"What kind of business?"

"But, since when, all these questions?"

"He's a criminal, Carmine Pace. I know about him. You can't believe anything he says."

"What do you know about Pace?"

"I know about him. I know about him. From somebody I know. A friend of mine. I know her very well. And, she told me things about him."

Who's she talking about? Bella? He shook his head. "Well, you shouldn't believe everything you hear, so just forget about it."

"He's a criminal. Not only that—he's worse. I know. I know. You see . . . this friend of mine . . . she wouldn't lie."

"Okay. Okay."

"She wouldn't lie, Tullio. I know her very well. I've known her for a long time."

"Magdalena, you're dying to tell me what she said, so, say it, and get it over with."

"This friend, she went out with him one night. He took her to a place where there were all colored people. He made her drink a lot. He made her get drunk."

"He made her get drunk? What did he do? Force the drinks down her throat?"

She glared at him. "She wasn't used to drinking."

"Then, she shouldn't have drunk so much . . . so, anything that went on after that was her own fault."

"She didn't lead him on."

"Look, what are you trying to say? That he attacked her? What?"

"She's not sure. He might have . . . he started to . . . but, she was vomiting, because she was sick from the drinks . . . she doesn't exactly remember what happened. She remembers some things and she can't remember other things. She might have passed out for a few minutes."

"Well, whoever she is, don't bother with her anymore. Stay away from her."

"Why? She didn't do anything wrong. It was him!"

"Magda, if this friend of yours is telling you that he assaulted her, or that he even tried to, she's lying. He wouldn't have done anything to her unless he knew damned well that she'd wanted it. Probably, after she got her kicks, she changed her mind . . . only, it was a little too late by then. So, she got whatever she deserved."

"How can you be so sure?"

"They don't rape."

"Who's *they?*"

"People . . . people like Pace."

"Why are you defending him?" she asked. "You're so quick to condemn her, but you're defending him."

"I'm not defending him. I just know that there are certain things his kind wouldn't do. I'm certainly not defending him."

"He's a criminal, an underworld figure. Why are you meeting him?"

"Magda, I don't like all these questions, and I want them to stop right now."

"There won't be any more questions, if you'll just answer this one. I want to know what you have to do with him."

"Okay. I have nothing to do with him," he replied. "I have to go to the office tomorrow because I'm behind with a lot of paperwork. He asked to meet me to talk about a couple of things, and I'm just extending him the courtesy, since I'm going to be there, anyway. That's all there is."

"But, why does he want to meet you? What does he want to talk about?"

"Enough!"

"This woman . . . this friend of mine . . . she's a very respectable woman. She has three beautiful children. She has a good husband. He could have ruined her life."

"She's married?"

"Yes."

"And, she went out with Pace, anyway?"

"She's not what you're thinking."

"Where was her husband all this time?"

"He was away, on business."

"Very nice. You know what? I hope Pace did a job on her. She sounds like a real winner. Her and that jerk husband of hers, both."

"Why are you calling the husband names?"

"Because he should have known what he was marrying."

I was right, Aleksey. He would never understand. He wouldn't allow himself to. "I'm going downstairs. Dinner will be ready in about ten minutes."

He didn't look up because he was already engrossed in an editorial he was preparing for one of their publications. He didn't know she left. Had not Stefano come upstairs to call him later, he would not have remembered to come to dinner.

Rebecca spoke a great deal during dinner. She usually did. She talked about everything that happened during the week. She didn't care if anyone was listening. Stefano said very little because he enjoyed eating so much and didn't want to

241

interrupt his chewing with unnecessary conversation. Carlo made inarticulate sounds now and then, and was interested only in imitating his father—he put down his fork, wiped his mouth, and drank whenever Tullio did. Aleksey noticed that neither Magdalena nor Tullio said a word. It wasn't anger, he realized; it wasn't that kind of silence; it was more like a muteness to conceal thoughts.

After Magdalena took the children upstairs, Aleksey poured a drink for Tullio. "What's weighing you down so heavily?" he asked him.

Tullio would have liked, very much, to have said: "Nothing. Why?"—and then, to have made a joke of it and laugh; but, he knew better than that. He would be insulting Aleksey. His old faithful tutor knew him too well; and there was no sense in pretending there was nothing wrong.

"There are times," Kostenov said, "when little things start to pile up, and, if you try to tackle them all by yourself, they seem insurmountable. But, if you share them, even if you just talk about them, they somehow shrink back to their proper size."

"Aleksey, there is something that I cannot share with you. I wish I could . . . but, if I did, it would only make it worse. Believe me, that's the truth. I appreciate what you're saying. I really do. I know how sincere you are. But . . . right now . . . this thing . . . I think I have to handle it myself."

The room was dimly lit, and the shadows around Tullio showed more of him to Kostenov than daylight would.

You look old, my rooster.

I know, Aleksey.

I would like to help you.

I know.

He dropped a heavy, steady hand on Tullio's shoulder and said, "Very well. If you should change your mind, you let me know." He left him, then, and climbed the high stairs to the bedrooms. At the middle landing, he turned back and looked down, and Tullio was still looking up at him. He said: "You

242

ok just like your father."

Tullio grinned and nodded. *I know, Aleksey. I know.*

Tullio remained downstairs for a while longer, then went up, to his own bedroom, where the lights were already turned out. He sat in a deep clubchair near the window. He put his feet up on the table in front of him, and rested his elbows on the tufted upholstery arms; then he steepled his fingers before him and stared through them at nothing. He wished that Salvatore were here to talk to, or Ernesto, or Benedetto. He wished his father were alive, or his uncle Carlo. Because Aleksey Kostenov could never understand.

He tried to think of the morning. He would have to allow more time to get to the city because of the snow. There wouldn't be a problem parking right in front of the office; there shouldn't be any problem on a weekend; that part of town would probably be deserted. Then, he'd do some work; Pace would arrive a few hours later, and there should be plenty he could accomplish before the meeting. Yes, Saturday was better than a regular weekday because there would be no interruptions, no telephones; he could work straight through, right up until the minute Carmine Pace walked in.

He tried to remember the first thing Nicole Grynszpan had said when she'd walked into his room. He could still see her. He thought, for a long time, about Nicole. But, he thought of Nicole very often, not just tonight.

He thought of a lot of things while he sat in his deep chair; but he could not think of a thing to say to Carmine Pace.

The door opened and Magdalena came into the room. "Where have you been?" he asked her. "I thought you were in bed all the while."

"In the kitchen," she said. "I was hungry. Are you coming to bed?"

"In a little while."

Long after he thought she'd fallen asleep, Magdalena lay quietly beneath the covers, thinking of tomorrow. She'd just come from speaking with Guido. He was to have the car ready early, she'd told him; he was to drive her to the city.

The weather was threatening again and the morning was as dark as sundown. From her window, Magdalena watched Tulli push open the huge iron gates of *The Walls of Jericho*. When h drove away, she rang for Guido.

"This is a day for funerals," the chauffeur said. "Look a how black that sky is. Are you sure you want to go to the cit today, signora?"

"Yes. I have to go in today. I want you to take me to m husband's office."

"But, he just left a few minutes ago."

"Yes, Guido, I know he did. But, I have some shopping to do That's why I didn't drive in with him. Okay?"

He shrugged.

It had rained just before dawn, and there was a sheet of ic over the snow that covered the roads to Manhattan. Guid drove slowly and carefully, much to Magdalena's relief. He wa disturbing her, though, because he was, as usual, inquisitive At times like this, his questions seemed endless and she' imagine herself back in Orvietto, having to explain her action and movements to everyone from Tullio's aunts to the gatekeeper's son.

"Does Signor Barragatto know you're driving in? I'll bet he doesn't know. He would tell you to stay home on such a bad day. Do you have to go shopping that badly? He doesn't know you're going in, does he?" He continued asking and answering his own questions and, soon, Magdalena realized there was no need to reply. No matter what her comments, he would keep talking, nonetheless.

Magdalena had not slept at all during the night and had suspected that Tullio was also awake; she'd assumed that, in her husband's case, it was because he'd slept too much during the day. Now, she wasn't even sure why she had decided to drive in. She knew it was to see Carmine Pace, but she didn't know what she would say to him. She'd thought, at first, of

244

offering Pace money, but she couldn't guess how much his silence might cost. For a while, she'd considered telling Guido the story; he might talk to Pace on her behalf—she had no doubt that he'd do it, he was devoted to her. Later, she'd mulled over telling Kostenov the whole story—all the details she'd omitted the last time—and he, too, might have been able to help. She'd even been tempted to telephone Louise and ask for Earl's advice. Yet, by sunrise, she had discounted each person to whom she might turn, and knew only that she must keep what happened in Saratoga from Tullio and his cousin.

The roads were a maze of sharp turns under tree branches bent heavy by snow and icicles and the young man was driving more cautiously than before. They passed two accidents where ambulances and police cars had already arrived, but Guido continued steadily, and she admired his driving skill. She was afraid that Pace and Tullio would meet before she could reach them, but she dared not ask Guido to hurry. They reached Tullio's office building almost two and a half hours after they'd left *The Walls of Jericho.*

"We beat him in, signora!" Guido told her. "See? There's only one other car on the block and it isn't his."

"Yes. That's right. I'll go wait upstairs in the office for him. You can go get yourself some breakfast, if you like. I might be a little while." She got out of the car before he could open the door for her. She said: "You did a beautiful job with the driving, Guido. A beautiful job. Thank you."

"Thank you, signora," he answered, but he wasn't used to compliments and was embarrassed. He waited until the watchman familiar to him admitted her into the building, and then he returned to the car. He was hungry and was tempted to walk to the corner coffee shop to eat, but he decided not to do so. He would not leave the signora and come back; he would wait right there, no matter how long her visit, and then take her shopping and then, back to *The Walls.* These were the orders given him in Orvietto and repeated by Sr. Crispino on the day he'd arrived in New York. He'd never ignored those

245

orders yet, and would not this morning, either.

He glanced at his wristwatch. He knew that, if Tullio Barragatto were coming to the office, he would have arrived by now, because he, too, was a very good driver. He grinned, then he suspected that Tullio had used working on Saturday as an excuse to get out of the house. He was almost sure his employer was actually visiting a woman friend.

Guido began to speculate. He wondered how long Magdalena would wait upstairs. Then, he wondered how Tullio would explain his absence from the office to her. This should be very interesting, Guido decided, and he was looking forward to seeing his mistress return to the car in a huff.

"Don't move. We'll get you out soon. Don't try to move at all." This was the first thing Tullio heard when he regained consciousness. The second accident Magdalena and Guido had passed had been his car.

"Are you in any pain?" a policeman asked him.

"No," he said, and he sat still, watching them try to pry open his car door. He could see the driver of the other car being put on a stretcher, and now, he remembered what had happened. A branch heavy with snow had fallen on the approaching stranger's hood. The man had braked, skidded, and pushed him off the road. Upon impact, one of his own tires had blown, and that had made his car flip over on its side. Then, all had gone blank.

Several more minutes passed before the police could get Tullio free of the wreckage, and they were as shocked as he was that he appeared completely unharmed.

"I guess you weren't meant to die young, mister. It's incredible how you can walk away from a wreck like that."

"Yes," he answered. "It's incredible. That's the word . . . incredible." He stared with disbelief at his automobile. "It looks like an accordion, doesn't it," he said.

They took him home because he refused to go to a hospital. It wasn't until Tullio had removed his overcoat and was again alone that he remembered: "Pace!"

It was especially unusual, but there wasn't a single automobile on the estate grounds. Kostenov and his chauffeur were off somewhere with the sedan. He presumed that Guido had taken Magdalena to some hairdresser's. The gardener's car wasn't around. Even the handyman's pickup was gone. He questioned the cook and the children's nurse, but neither had any idea where anybody was, or when they would be returning. Then, he called the Asheleys to borrow one of their automobiles, but neither Louise nor Earl was home. He was infuriated. He glared contemptuously through the windows at the snow. There was no way he could leave *The Walls*, and he felt like he was in prison. He pictured Carmine Pace standing outside of his locked office door, just waiting and thinking that he'd backed down. Then, his head began throbbing, and his vision started to blur; and any discomfort he'd been too dazed to feel until now forced him to lie back and try to rest.

But, to rest requires freedom from complicated thought; so, this, Tullio could not do. There was a telephone in the night watchman's office. He would call that number, he decided, hoping that the watchman was awake, or close enough to it to hear it ringing.

Chapter Three

Boris Pachenker spoke the same dialect that Aleksey Kostenov did when he was a child. This, Aleksey admitted, was the main reason he'd hired Boris as night watchman. It was very nice the old tongue now and then. Sometimes, it made him feel like a boy again.

Pachenker and his wife lived within a four-block island of White Russians. All of the local merchants and each of his neighbors had migrated from the same area, so he'd never found it necessary to learn English. His children spoke it, and that was enough. If he should ever receive some important mail—if anybody would ever be thoughtless enough to write to him in English—his sons could translate it; but, that was not likely to happen. He'd found the perfect job, too: he didn't have to converse with anyone; he was the only person in the building during his tour of duty. He was very satisfied with his life, and he was thinking about how fortunate he was. Then, the night bell rang. It startled him, because nobody ever came to the building on Saturdays.

"Will you let me in, please? I'm Mrs. Barragatto."

"Barragatto?"

"Yes, will you let me in please?"

"Barragatto? Barragatto no come. Come Monday. Monday."

"No," she said, "I am Mrs. Barragatto."

He unlocked the doors and said again: "Barragatto no come. Come Monday. Monday."

Magdalena pointed to the elevators and he assumed she didn't believe that Barragatto was not in his office. He would have to prove it to her, he decided, and he took her to the eighth floor.

"No come. No come. Come Monday Barragatto," he said. Then, he showed her that the door to Barragatto's private office was locked. "No Barragatto," he said. He assumed, at that point, that the woman would permit him to escort her to the elevator again and out of the building.

"I realize that you don't understand what I'm saying," Magdalena told him. "I will sit here and wait for him." She pointed to a wooden bench in the corridor. "I will wait here," she repeated, and she sat down.

"No Barragatto! Barragatto Monday!"

"Don't get upset," she told him. She patted the bench. "I will wait here. Don't worry. I'll be all right. Go downstairs. I'll wait here."

Did this strange woman expect to wait for Barragatto until Monday? What could he do? He couldn't throw her out bodily. He looked at her and sighed. She would get tired of waiting, the poor thing. He motioned to the elevators and to himself, and she understood that he was going downstairs, leaving her sitting on the bench. He got out on the lobby floor and walked down the extra flight to the caretaker's office. He felt very sorry for the woman. Barragatto must have done something wrong to her, and now, she'd come to confront him. But, Barragatto wouldn't be in until Monday.

This was the first time Boris Pachenker's Saturday tour had ever been interrupted. He'd have to tell his wife about the woman—the poor thing. He'd always suspected Barragatto was a little evil.

The telephone rang. This was really too much. Who would

be calling him? It had never rung before. It couldn't be his wife. They had no telephone at home. He stared at the instrument. It kept ringing. It would not stop ringing. He lifted the receiver to his ear, but didn't say anything.

"Pachenker? Is that you, Pachenker?"

He recognized Tullio Barragatto's voice. "Yes."

"This is Tullio Barragatto."

"Yes."

"Listen carefully, Mr. Pachenker. I'm expecting somebody to come to the office today. A Mr. Pace. A Mr. Carmine Pace. Do you understand me? Mr. Pachenker, can you understand what I am saying?"

"Barragatto?"

"Yes. Yes. Did you understand what I said?"

"She come. She come," Boris said. His heart was beating fast, because he couldn't understand a thing Barragatto was saying to him. Yet, he had to tell him the woman was there. He repeated: "She come." He was sure that this was what Barragatto was calling about. He hoped Barragatto could understand. "She come. She come."

"He's there already? Pace is there?" Tullio was sure the watchman was mixing up his pronouns. "He's already come?"

"Yes, she come." He said nothing else, but he was feeling the same frustration that Tullio was feeling. He knew the man was trying to tell him something. Something that might be important. He might lose his job because of this. He should not have answered the phone.

"Mr. Pachenker, go get him. Bring him to the telephone. Pachenker?"

"Yes, Pachenker."

"Oh, God, this is impossible." Tullio held the telephone receiver and sat mute. He could make himself understood when speaking to the watchman in person. He could use gestures. Mime. Anything. But, this was impossible. He tried a few words in Italian; some in French; some in Spanish; then, he tried German. He hoped Pachenker could understand a

250

little bit of one of them. It made matters worse, though, because the barrage of strange sounding syllables confused the man even more. He was wondering how to get across his message, how to get him to bring Pace to the telephone, when he heard a click. Pachenker had hung up.

The night bell had rung. Another person wanted to come into the building. And, there had been Pachenker: talking on a telephone with his boss, unable to understand a word he was saying one moment, and now, listening to him say nothing at all. What else was there to do, Pachenker had asked himself, except to hang up the telephone and go answer the door? Who could it be this time? This was a terrible Saturday.

Tullio Barragatto stared stupidly at the receiver. Boris Pachenker would not have purposely hung up on him. He must have accidentally cut himself off. That could be the only explanation. He dialed the number again.

Tullio let the phone ring more than a dozen times. Pachenker must have walked out of the office, he realized. He'd have to try again, in a few minutes.

But, a few minutes might be too late. If Pace were already there, he might still be there. In that case, he must make Pachenker understand and put Pace on the telephone. He called the watchman's number again. He would keep ringing, he decided, no matter how long it might take Pachenker to answer.

"Will you unlock the door, please? I have an appointment with Tullio Barragatto."

Pachenker threw his hands up into the air and let Pace into the building. "Barragatto come Monday," he said. "Monday."

"No. He'll be here today. We have an appointment." He walked past Pachenker and read the building directory. It showed that the executive offices were on the eighth floor. "Do you know how to run this elevator?" he asked Pachenker. "Oh, never mind. I'll manage. Your phone is ringing. Aren't you going to answer your phone?"

"Barragatto come Monday! Monday!"

Carmine Pace didn't have enough patience to act out his wishes to the watchman. He smiled, nodded, and walked into the elevator.

Pachenker remained in the lobby, watching the elevator's floor indicator go toward the eighth floor. He shook his head. Now, there were two people waiting for Barragatto. But, they were safe enough, he concluded. Very well dressed. They wouldn't rob anything. They couldn't. Every door was locked. They'd just sit on that bench and wait. And soon, they'd get tired and leave. And everything would be back to normal. If only the telephone would stop ringing.

Tullio slammed the receiver into its cradle. The throbbing in his head was worse now and he lay back, hoping it would subside.

Magdalena heard the elevator begin moving. Tullio's office was at the far end of the corridor, too far away from the elevators for her to see the floor indicator; but, she knew no other office was in use over the weekend. She knew, therefore, that whoever was using the elevator was coming to the eighth floor. It was either her husband or Carmine Pace. She hid in one of the door recesses. Tullio must not see her before she could speak to Pace.

The elevator stopped. She heard the footsteps. They weren't Tullio's. She listened as they came closer. Then, they seemed to hesitate, and she suspected that he must be wondering which was Tullio's office.

The footsteps started again, more quickly now, and all the courage Magdalena had just had a few minutes ago disappeared. She could not go through with it. She could not say a thing to him. She would stay hidden. She would wait right there, she decided, until her husband came to let the man in. Once both were in Tullio's office, she would slip away; and nobody would ever know she'd come.

The footsteps stopped. She heard Pace knock on the private office door. Her legs felt like jelly and she began to breathe very heavily.

Suddenly, Pace shouted: "Who's there! Who is it!"

She didn't know if he'd heard her breathing, or shuffling, or if he'd seen her shadow; but, she had to stand out in the open now. Slowly, she stepped out of the door recess. She stared at him.

Carmine Pace's back was up against a wall and one of his hands was reaching for something in his pocket. He looked as scared as she was. Then, all of his features relaxed and he said, "Oh, my God, I can't believe it! It's you! You, of all people! What in the world are you doing there in the corner? What are you doing here?"

He remembered her. He remembered her very well, but he could not remember her name. He could even remember the older woman she'd been with, but he couldn't remember her name, either.

Magdalena's voice was very low. She said: "I want to talk to you . . . not here . . . someplace else."

"Well, I have an appointment. I can meet you later."

"No. I want to talk to you now, but not here."

He looked at his wristwatch. "Okay," he replied, "it's a little early, anyway . . . I don't think he'll be here yet . . . if it's that important, we can go somewhere and talk." He glanced sideways at her, then, and asked, "How did you know I would be here today?"

"There's a coffee shop on the corner," Magdalena said. "We can go talk there, if it's all right."

He held out his hand and said: "After you." He was trying very hard to remember her name.

She hoped she could get him out of the building before Tullio arrived. She wondered what was taking Tullio so long to get there. She walked ahead of him; she held her head high and her stride looked certain and confident, but she didn't know what she was going to say to him; she didn't know how to begin, or what to offer, or what to promise. She didn't know if she should ask or demand his silence. She didn't know if she should threaten or beg. She wanted to run away, to start the

253

whole day over again. He was talking to her; he was acting very pleasant, like the first time she'd met him; but, she didn't hear a thing he was saying. Perhaps Aleksey was right: a man wouldn't call a meeting with another man to tell him he was with his wife!

It impressed her that he knew how to run the elevator. She felt foolish, because it was such a silly thing to notice . . . it wasn't such an achievement . . . anybody could run an elevator . . . all he had to do was watch how it was done. *What am I thinking about such a stupid thing for? So what! So he can run an elevator! So what! God, what am I doing here!*

"Were you actually waiting for me? Or, were you waiting for Crispino? Is he the one who told you I was coming?" He was trying very hard to remember her name. He wouldn't feel so awkward, if he could just remember her name. "What's the matter? Why don't you answer me?"

"Crispino?" she asked.

"Yes . . . Crispino . . . you're still with Crispino, aren't you? That's why you're here . . . right? You were waiting for Crispino. Or were you waiting just for me?" Because she looked at him blankly, he asked: "Look, what's going on?"

He thinks I'm one of Salvatore's girlfriends! He doesn't know who I am! God, he doesn't know who I am! Oh God! That means he wasn't going to tell Tullio! Oh, my God! Oh, thank God!

The elevator stopped. They'd reached the lobby.

"What's wrong with you?" he asked her. "What's the matter? What are you looking at me like that for?"

. . . and he wouldn't be talking to me so calmly if I'd taken a shot at him . . .

"What kind of game are you playing?" he asked. "Say something!"

"Whom did I shoot at that night?"

"Oh, for God's sake! Is that what this is all about? Is that what's worrying you?" He drew his arm around her. "Don't you worry about that. Carmine took care of everything. Don't you worry another minute over that."

254

She pulled away from him. "Somebody was shot that night! Who?"

"I just said not to worry about it. I took care of everything. Now, just forget about it." He put his arm around her again.

Pachenker came into the lobby.

"Why don't you answer that phone?" Pace asked him.

Magdalena asked Pachenker: "Will you unlock the door, please?" Then, she said to Carmine Pace: "Please keep your hands off me," and pulled away from him a second time, because he had, once again, put his arm around her.

The rebuff would not have bothered Carmine Pace so much if they had not been in front of the night watchman, and if he had not seen the watchman's indignant glare. He said to Pachenker: "Is something bothering you? Mind your own business and go answer that damned telephone."

Magdalena pointed to the door. "Will you please unlock that door?"

Boris Pachenker shuffled for the proper key—there was a double lock—and, all the while, kept looking at Pace. His eyes were saying: Take your hand off her shoulder! She doesn't want to be touched!

This aggravated Pace all the more and he said to Magdalena, "Let's get out of here. Let's go to that coffee shop."

"No," she replied. "We don't have anything else to talk about. I just wanted to find out about that shooting. That's all. You told me all I needed to know. There's nothing else that we could possibly have to say to each other."

"You mean that you're dismissing me,"—he snapped his fingers—"just like that? I want to talk to you! I don't want to talk to you! Who do you think you're dealing with? Another Crispino?"

She stepped out of the building. "I'd like to set you straight about that," she said, "about Salvatore Crispino, that is. I am not his mistress . . . or one of his lady friends . . . or anything at all that you might think in connection with him. My relationship with Salvatore Crispino is nothing like you can possibly imagine. And, I resent your presumption that it's ever been anything along your line of thinking. Not that I have to explain anything to you, because I don't. Frankly, I don't even know why I'm bothering to talk to you at all."

"Get off your high horse," he told her. "You're not fooling anybody."

"Mr. Pace, I'm not trying to fool anybody . . . because I don't have to. Now, if you'll just step aside, I'll be on my way."

"Whoa!" He held up both hands. "Look, I don't know what you're mad about . . . but, maybe, we can start all over again."

She gave him a disgusted look. "After what you did!"

"What I did! What did I do?"

"In the car! That night! In the car!"

Magdalena marveled at the surprised look he gave her. Either he was a magnificent actor, or he was crazy! But, right now, she didn't care either way. All that was important at this moment was to leave before Tullio arrived. She wondered what was taking him so long.

Pace remembered then: her name was Anita . . . Anita something . . . only, she wasn't really that older woman's daughter-in-law . . . she'd given him a false name . . . whatever . . . he'd call her Anita. He said, "Anita, just exactly what was I supposed to have done that was so terrible?"

Boris Pachenker had stepped from the building to the sidewalk also. He was standing right behind them, as though listening to every word, even though he didn't understand what they were saying.

"Didn't I just tell you to mind your own business?" Pace said to him.

When he heard Pace's voice raise, Guido got out of the car and walked toward Magdalena. He wasn't sure what to make of what was happening. It was obvious that his mistress knew the man. She'd just been talking to him. So, she wasn't being annoyed by some stranger. Still, she definitely was annoyed. That, too, was obvious.

"Signora? You want to go now, signora?"

"I want to talk to you, Anita," Carmine Pace said.

Magdalena looked from one man to the other. If she were to walk away from Pace, he might get angry . . . he might say something he shouldn't . . . he might even pull her back. If anything like that should happen, Guido might say, or do, something hasty.

No! There mustn't be a scene! Tullio should have been there by now; he might be turning the corner at any moment. There mustn't be a scene. He mustn't find her here.

"We're going to that corner coffee shop," she told Guido. "We won't be long." She gave a sideways look at Pace and said: "Well? Have you changed your mind?"

They walked briskly toward the corner. Theirs were the only footsteps in the snow. Guido followed them in the car. When they went into the coffee shop, Guido also went in, and he sat on a counter stool from where he could see every one of Pace's movements through a mirror lining the wall.

"Anita," the man said, "about that night, that last night in Saratoga . . . all right, I should have stayed with you until you could get into the house . . . but, after all, you didn't want me to . . . and, if I'd insisted, you would have woken up the whole neighborhood. That's what you're mad about, right? That I didn't stay with you until you could get in the house? You feel I just dumped you there? Is that what it is?"

Magdalena said: "This is ridiculous, this farce!"

"For God's sake! If it's not that, what is it? Tell me."

"How do you want me to tell it to you? In English, Italian, or pig latin?"

He smiled. "That's right," he said, "I was teaching you pig latin that night. Yes, I remember."

"Then, I'm sure you must remember everything else . . . including what you did to me," she replied, "so, there's no more that we have to say to each other."

Magdalena stood up. If there were to be any kind of scene here, she could not care less. Even if Tullio were standing in front of the office building—(he had to have arrived by

257

now)—he couldn't possibly see anything that might be goin
on in this coffee shop. That was all that mattered: that, an
that Carmine Pace still had no idea who she really was.

"What did I do to you?"

"You know what you did. You're a low-life."

Pace said, in a very low voice, "Sit down." And, becaus
Guido had stood when Magdalena had, he added, "And, if yo
don't want to see that kid's head broken, tell him to stay righ
where he is. Tell him not to make a move."

The man seemed, suddenly, very quietly vicious, and sh
became frightened of him again. She motioned to Guido t
remain at the counter and she slid back into the booth sea

"We'll probably never run into each other again," he began
"but, since you know my name, there's a chance that yo
might go around saying things about me that aren't true. So
you listen to me, now. And you listen very carefully. And, yo
remember what I'm saying."

She kept staring only at the coffee while he was talking
She'd not noticed the waitress bring it to them.

He continued: "That night, I couldn't have treated yo
better if you were my own sister. I don't know what kind o
distorted fantasies you've made up in your own mind, bu
that's the truth. Now, I have a feeling that you *really* think
tried to attack you, or something like that . . . otherwise, yo
wouldn't have called me what you just did. So, I'm going to tel
you exactly what happened."

Magdalena still would not look at him. She kept staring a
the coffee cup.

"First," he said, "you got cockeyed drunk . . . so drunk tha
I had to take you out of that nightclub because you wer
getting too loud. You were embarrassing the hell out of me.
knew a lot of people there."

You shouldn't have gotten me drunk.

"Then, when I finally got you back into the car and tried t
get you to sit up instead of falling over, you started screamin
that you were pregnant. You were acting like I was attackin

258

you, or something! And, the next thing I knew, you were vomiting all over the front seat! I went to get some rags to clean up that mess you made . . . I left you perfectly safe . . . I'd locked the doors . . . I'd even given you a pistol for protection! And, what kind of thanks did I get? You started shooting at us when I got back! You know, you're crazy!"

"Us? There was someone with you?"

"Yes, there was. I'd paid a guy to clean the car. I started knocking on the window. I was going to get you out of the car while he cleaned it up . . . and, the next thing I knew, you were pointing that gun at us. A couple of seconds later, you blew almost his whole ear off."

Magdalena sat back. She didn't know what to make of these things Carmine Pace was telling her. Was it the whole truth, or only half-truth and half-lie? "What happened to him? That man."

"Well, in the first place, I'd thought you'd shot him in the head . . . he'd gone straight down when that bullet hit him. I pulled him away from the car because I didn't know if you were going to start shooting again. Then, you ran out of the car and headed back toward the house you were renting."

"And, you let me go . . . just like that . . . in the middle of the night."

"Well, what did you expect me to do? I had a man on my hands who I thought was dying!"

"What happened then?"

"I put him in the back seat and brought him to some doctor I know up there. That's when I finally found out it was only his ear, so I paid him off and left him there. Then, I came back to look for you. You were walking along the edge of the road and you wouldn't get back in the car, so I followed you back to that house. You insisted on sitting on the porch swing . . . but, you didn't want me on the porch with you . . . and, before you decided to get violent again, I thought I'd better leave. You see, it was almost daylight by then."

"And then, what?"

"I gave you a whole day to sleep it off. I came back the next afternoon, but you'd all packed up and left. And, that's everything."

"Is there anything else you want to say? Are you finished?"

"Yes, I'm finished," he replied. "That's all there was. Nothing else. So, think twice before you start calling people names the next time."

Carmine Pace stood and threw a dollar bill on the table. Then, he left the coffee shop. He did not bother to look back at her again.

Magdalena did not know what emotion she was feeling. It might be outrage, because he could be lying and confusing her even more than she already was about the events of that night. It might be remorse, because, if he'd been telling the truth, she'd condemned and insulted a man who had tried to help her. Or, it might be just embarrassment, because, as Aleksey had advised, she should not have pursued the matter, in the first place. For several minutes, she quietly pondered what he'd said. Then, Guido approached.

"Signora? You want to go back to the building?"

I should have listened to Aleksey . . . But, no! . . . If I'd listened and stayed home this morning, I never would have found out that he still has no idea who I am. . . . That's the important thing . . . the most important . . . nothing can ever get back to Tullio.

"Signora?"

"Let's go home, Guido."

"I heard that man call you Anita. Why was he calling you Anita?"

"Please, Guido, no questions. I just want to go home."

"You know, signora, when I first saw you talking to that man, I thought he looked familiar. Now, I know where I saw his face. It was in the newspapers, just a few days ago. What's his name? Is he important?"

"What did it say about him?"

"I don't know. It was an American newspaper. Who is he?

260

What's his name?"

"Oh, Guido! Why do you ask me so many questions all the time! You always have so many questions!"

"But, I think I know him from someplace else, too. It's not only from the newspapers. Someplace else. But, I don't remember where."

They drove through the street in front of the North American Distributors building. The Saturday mail was being delivered. Pachenker was just opening the door for the postman, but he was refusing to allow Pace into the lobby again. Pachenker and Pace were arguing, each in his own language. Pace was on the outside, in front of the door; Pachenker was on the inside, looking out at him through the upper glass portion. Neither noticed Magdalena's car pass by, but both she and Guido could hear the men's rising voices. It disturbed her that Tullio's car was still nowhere in sight.

"We'd better get right home, Guido. My husband should have gotten here by now. I think something might have happened to him."

Guido didn't think so, but he didn't say anything.

Chapter Four

"How can you possibly say I should calm down? Look at thi
nonsense! He can't go printing something like that! He's not i
Europe, he's in America! The United States of America! Wh
can't he get that into his head? If he keeps printing this kind o
junk, we'll go out of business—or get bombed out of it! One o
the other's sure to happen!"

"Let me take a look at it," Aleksey said. He'd been so bus
lately, that he'd not been reading Tullio's editorials. "In th
meantime, just calm down."

Earl continued: "Do you have any idea how many reader
he's losing us? American's don't want to read Fascis
newspapers! People are cancelling subscriptions! We'r
receiving all kinds of hate mail! We're getting bomb threats!"

Aleksey said to Earl, "Look, either you're going to kee
yelling, or you're going to be quiet for a few minutes so I ca
read what he said that's so terrible. Do you want me to read i
or don't you?"

"Yes! Read it! Read it!"

"Then, stop fanning the air with it, and give it to me."

Earl handed the tabloid to Aleksey. Then, he folded hi
hands behind his back and started pacing. He would loo

sharply toward Aleksey each time he turned, hoping to see some reaction. Aleksey realized this and purposely maintained his best poker face—he even feigned a yawn; but, he understood why Earl was so upset. He read:

Last night, Senator Richard Jaysen told the graduating class of Condon that "Democracy is the only way of life that offers dignity," and that "we shouldn't rest until every government of every man, woman and child on earth embraces it!" Then, he went on to advise those youngsters: "And, if their governments won't give them democracy, let's shove it down their throats!" The students applauded him wildly. They're so young and naive. What else could they do?

Democracy, Senator Jaysen, is *not* right for every man, woman and child on earth. On the contrary! In nations where the populace is neither well-educated nor reasonably content, democracy is suicide. It's a pity that someone who yields as much power as a United States senator doesn't know that.

Would you trust decisions concerning national defense to the beggars of Arabia? Or economic strategies to an Umbrian shepherd? Or foreign policy to an embittered war veteran? Would you grant your own youngest children complete self-rule?

There are times and places, Senator Jaysen, when a strong, centralized government is required, and, at the head of that government, a benevolent dictator or triumvirate which will look to the future and enact not only the current, popular legislation, but that which gives the most far-reaching benefits to the greatest number of its people.

If you shove democracy down the throats of those who are not ready for it, they might choke and spit up all over you. It's already happened more than once. Study some history, Senator.

Aleksey folded the paper and said, "Tullio majored in political history. He was very good in it."

"Is that all you have to say?"

Aleksey held back a grin because he knew how seriously disturbed his friend was. He replied, "What Tullio was saying is that the same way of life isn't necessarily the best way for everyone. That no medicine is a cure-all. That fire gives warmth to some, but, that in the hands of infants, it kills."

"Our readers don't interpret it that way."

"So? Who is to blame for that? Tullio or our readers?"

"Aleksey, I'll have no more of it. And, I mean that."

"Very well, I'll speak to him about it. I don't know what good it will do, but I'll try."

Aleksey Kostenov was more worried about Tullio's political views than he would admit. He did not expect that Tullio's ideas would change, and he wasn't totally against them either, but Americans were essentially parochial thinkers, and this, Aleksey realized, was costing the company money. He'd spoken to him about this already; but he'd known, even then, that Tullio had listened quietly only as a courtesy.

What was more important to Aleksey than a loss of revenue was the ever-growing breach between Tullio Barragatto and Earl Asheley. The two had to be made to understand one another. This one difference between them was affecting their entire relationship. It was spilling over into other matters and a wall was emerging; it had to be broken down before it became too thick and too tall to overcome.

"Attack irresponsible voters," he'd advised Tullio, "not democracy, itself. And, for God's sake, don't use words like 'dictatorship,' or even 'benevolent dictator.' They're abhorrent to Americans. You should know better."

Tullio had nodded. For a while, he'd even altered his choice of words. But, that hadn't lasted very long, and it was obvious, now, that Aleksey must speak with him again. Or, maybe, he would talk with Salvatore, and have Salvatore approach Tullio. The cousin had a way with him that no one else had. Yes, this is what he would do. Salvatore would be returning from *Piccolo Villaggio* this afternoon. He'd have the young attorney sit down and have a good heart-to-heart with Tullio. That might do the trick.

Salvatore Crispino was, at that moment, enroute to Jericho. He was deeply engrossed in thought—not about the relationship between Tullio Barragatto and Earl Asheley, over which he was already quite worried—but about that which might exist between Carmine Pace and Marcus Garvey . . . or, more likely, between Pace and Garvey's associates.

Salvatore had spoken to Bella once more; and now, he was almost positive that Pace was very intricately involved with some of Garvey's people. Also, he was sure that Garvey didn't even know of Pace's existence. There was too much money connected with Garvey's Back to Africa movement for it not to have attracted the underworld element; and Mr. Carmine Pace, was undoubtedly, not one to ignore millions. Salvatore suddenly pitied Marcus Garvey.

If, somehow, Garvey were to find out about Pace—Salvatore reasoned—Pace would have lots of trouble up in Harlem.

Lots of trouble.

So much trouble, that he'd be forced to ease off the pressure on North American Distributors, because he wouldn't have the time for it.

But, Salvatore would have to look at the situation from all angles. He'd have to confer with his cousin the first thing Monday morning.

No! He shouldn't wait for Monday. He should drive directly to *The Walls*. It wouldn't matter—his wife had already told him that she didn't care whether or not he came home anymore.

Yes, he'd go right to Tullio, that very afternoon. This was too important to put off. It might be just the opening they'd been looking for. And, the timing was good: perhaps, they could work out some kind of strategy before Pace returned from Europe.

Thousands of blacks hailed Marcus Garvey, literally, as God. Yet, some of God's high priests were mixing with a known criminal. Why? Could it be that those priests were stealing some of God's money? The hard-earned money donated by poor people? Money that was meant to buy them their salvation?

Oh, there could be so much trouble in Harlem.

Magdalena sat back. She was relaxed and comfortable. She was safe. Pace still didn't know who she was . . . and he never would . . . so, Tullio would never find out about Saratoga, her one indiscretion. It was warm in the car, and the snow was clean and beautiful to look at. She rolled down one of the windows and breathed in the crisp air. The world was very nice again. She caught Guido's eyes through the rear view mirror and she smiled at him. Guido wasn't talking for a change. Even Guido was giving her some peace.

And, surprisingly, Mr. Carmine Pace had turned out to be not such a monster at all. On the contrary, he'd been very nice to her. Very patient. She'd insulted him, but he'd been the perfect gentleman. What the man did for a living was none of her business. What counted was that he'd been very, very nice to her.

She grinned. She tried to remember some of the pig latin he'd taught her. How did it go?

Yes, I remember . . . Pass the hat for Garvey! assPay ethay athay orfay arveyGay! Yes, that's how it goes . . .

They'd had some fun in Saratoga. She'd teased him about his eyebrows. Those big, bushy eyebrows of his. He'd been charming, and rather attractive in a mysterious sort of way. He still was. And, he was really very nice.

"Guido, what do you think happened to my husband?"

He shrugged.

"Do you think he could have had a flat?"

"That's possible, signora."

"Can you imagine my husband changing a flat tire? Getting his hands all muddy and dirty?"

"No, signora, I can't. I really can't."

In mid-January, while Carmine Pace was still in Italy, Benedetto Crispino had received a dinner invitation from Orvietto's new *patrono*.

Benedetto knew what to expect, and he'd already done what custom demanded. Representing the Barragattos and Crispinos, he'd sent greetings to the new neighbor, welcoming him to Orvietto. He presumed that, this evening, the chieftain would wine and dine him, then ease the conversation toward business, and, at that point, issue the ultimatum: either North American Distributors cooperates or Barragatto Wineries ceases to exist. Nothing would come forth crudely or obviously; there would be no threats made or even inferred; but, the ultimatum would be very definitely understood, nonetheless. This was the way of the *malandrini*.

Benedetto had been able to learn very little about his host. The previous *patrono* had left no male heirs, so this new one had not come about through the natural order. He'd been sent, instead, by his superiors in Palermo; and, since he'd arrived, he'd been having difficulty with the old chief's wife. The woman was, at times, quite senile; at other times, literally mad; and, during other occasions, as sharp-witted as Borgia. She'd refused to relinquish the house to the new chieftain and, having barricaded herself in the upper story of the big mansion, she would hurl bottles and pieces of furniture at anyone trying to climb the stairs. The only one permitted up the steps was an old nun, whom she'd allow to bring her her meals. Though the new *patrono* offered her triple the property's worth, and though her own married daughters begged her to come live with them, she refused to sell and move. It is not that the house belonged to her—(it was never really her husband's, it was the organization's)—but one does not put an old woman out in the street. This was not the custom. This was not the way of the *malandrini*. The man had finally moved into the house, but he confined himself to the bottom floor, never walked anywhere near the staircase, and tried to ignore the insults and curses that flowed down the echoing walls daily. In this way, having shown all of Orvietto that he adhered to custom, he had gained a degree of respect from the townspeople and they'd already begun calling him "Don Italo."

Besides the above, which he'd learned through local gossip, Benedetto knew only that the man was originally from Genoa; that he was a widower; that he had one unmarried son and one married daughter, neither living with him; that he'd had to flee the country for a while; and that his name was Italo Filippo Fallanca.

Promptly at eight, the *patrono's* personal driver arrived at the Barragatto compound to bring Benedetto to the big house on the hill. This was something he'd not expected; he'd not even been told the chauffeur was coming.

"You didn't think I'd let you come alone, did you?" the chief asked him. "After all, you can't be too careful nowadays."

"I appreciate your concern, Signor Fallanca, but I wasn't aware that I should have anything to fear."

"Well, I heard about your unpleasantness. The Fascists, I mean. I heard about what they did to you." He shook his head. "They're bad people. You have to watch out for them."

"Oh, that unpleasantness."

"Yes, what else?"

"I thought you might be referring to Ernesto, my brother."

"Did they attack him, too, the Fascists?"

"Ernesto was murdered. Not by the Fascists, though. By your people." He knew that neither Tullio nor Salvatore would have brought this up. They would be too interested in the present negotiations to cloud them with the past. Yet, he could

268

think of no reason to be that polite and not mention it. This was, after all, a business dinner, not a social event; and, the sooner they could get down to business, the sooner he could leave.

"I didn't know about that."

That might be possible, but Benedetto doubted it.

Fallanca continued: "My condolences."

That wouldn't bring Ernesto back. He didn't reply.

"You must realize, though, that what took place before I came here was none of my doing." The man waited, partially for effect and partially for Benedetto to say something. When his guest remained silent, he went on: "I, myself, am against violence of any kind, because most of it can be avoided. I'm a businessman. An entrepreneur, of sorts."

The meeting was starting. Benedetto looked at his watch. It had taken two and a half hours to begin. His stomach was bothering him.

Italo Filippo Fallanca was smoother than Benedetto had expected. He started talking about politics . . . about misunderstandings among politicians . . . and about how those misunderstandings can lead to civil wars, and eventually, to wars among the nations. He cleverly tied the bickering politicians' blunders into hunger, then into disease, then into international trade. From there, he very easily slid into the subject of foolish, unnecessary laws; and, from there, to unholy laws, like Prohibition.

"Yes, I agree with you, Signor Fallanca,"—Benedetto absolutely refused to call the man "Don Italo"—"the American and Canadian Prohibition law has got to be the stupidest thing ever devised. And, yes, it has hurt Barragatto Wineries tremendously. However, there's nothing we can do about it. The law is the law, and my cousin refuses to defy it, either through his wineries or his breweries." He thought it wise to add: ". . . and, my cousin's partners, and my brother Salvatore and I are all in agreement with him. So, if any misfortune should befall my cousin, the position of North

269

American Distributors in this matter would remain unchanged."

Fallanca said, "Perhaps, after you've all had a chance to give the idea more thought, you'll reconsider. To change one's mind isn't a sign of weakness. It's done every day. As a matter of fact, statesmen and kings do it all the time . . ."

You know very little about Tullio.

". . . especially when they stop and think about the long-term ramifications of their decisions—for everybody involved. For themselves . . . their associates . . . their families." He stopped and poured some liquor. "It would be a shame if a wrong decision were made because of old prejudices. There's lots more profit to be made from Prohibition."

Benedetto looked directly at his host.

Sr. Fallanca continued: "When you don't make money where you can, it's the same as losing it. And—as far as I'm concerned—when certain people stand in the way of your making money, it's the same as if they were stealing it from you." He paused, this time, only for the effect. "Would you or your cousin step quietly aside while someone was stealing from you? Would you expect me to?"

This was the *either/or* which Benedetto had been waiting for. Now that it was said, the meeting should soon be over. He checked his watch; it had been a very long night, and all had gone as expected. The meal had been lavish. His host had been very generous. The script had flowed freely, and the ultimatum had been served with the after-dinner drinks. Therefore, he could never have anticipated what was to come next: the butler announced that Sr. Carmine Pace had arrived.

Benedetto was more than surprised. He'd not heard that Pace was in Orvietto.

"Signor Pace represents me in New York."

"Yes, I know," Benedetto replied. How could he not have known the man was in town, unless he'd just arrived that very day? He wondered about this. Also, he wondered why Pace had been summoned to this meeting. This was very unusual, because a man like Pace—one who merely carried out orders—was not customarily included in the talks. It could mean only that Pace had risen to a much higher position since he'd left Orvietto.

As though reading Benedetto's mind, Fallanca said, "The reason Signor Pace is here is because I don't want there to be any misunderstandings in this matter. So, I'll say what I have to say now, with both of you present."

Neither man knew what to expect.

"Tullio Barragatto saved my son's life . . ."

Benedetto tried to hide the impact of the revelation, but Carmine Pace had a harder time of it—his eyes opened widely.

". . . and, the Fallancas have always paid their debts." He stopped, lit a cigarette, and continued: "Therefore, I am offering Signor Barragatto the opportunity to join forces with us and make more money than he's ever dreamed possible. He has the Asheley brewery, the vineyards in New York State, and the vineyards right here, in Orvietto; and they're all tailor-made to this American Prohibition law. He even has the ships to transport the stuff.

"Carmine, when you return to New York, I'd like you to approach him about this again. Do everything in your power to convince him that it would be best, in the long run, for everybody involved. I want you to tell him, also, that the decision is entirely his own. Entirely his own.

"If he still decides against joining us . . . tell him that Giulio Fallanca's father wishes him good fortune, but that I would always be ready to listen, in case he should change his mind. What you tell him will be confirmed, I'm sure, by Signor Crispino."

Turning then, toward Benedetto, Fallanca said: "I assume your report of this meeting should reach him about the same time Signor Pace returns to the States."

Benedetto nodded and said, "I'll write to him the first thing in the morning." He left shortly afterwards. He'd not ever made the connection between the new *patrono's* family name and the name of the inmate Tullio had once helped flee to Germany; but, everything fell into place now. It had been a very productive evening.

Carmine Pace was furious. He'd sailed across an ocean to meet his new superior, only to find that all the effort he'd put into bringing North American Distributors into the fold was in vain. Though he could not dare show his dismay in front of Crispino, he was sure that Crispino was aware of it. After Crispino left, he said to Fallanca:

"Don Italo, perhaps the debt can be cancelled in a different way. You see, a lot of time and energy have already been invested in this Barragatto issue. The old *patrono* . . . he . . ."

". . . he is dead. I'm here now. And, if anyone should ask about this, tell them that Tullio Barragatto is under the protection of Italo Filippo Fallanca. That's all they have to know."

There was no more to say. He'd come to Orvietto. He'd met his new chief. He'd received his new orders. There was no more to do except sail back to New York. He wondered how Barragatto had saved the man's son's life; but, he really didn't care because he was too disheartened. He wondered, also, if Fallanca's bosses in Palermo were aware of what he was doing. He dwelled upon this last question for a very long time; yet, there was no safe way for him to find out.

Every now and then, Guido would glance toward the rear view mirror. Magdalena noticed the serious look on his face. She wondered what was on his mind. She finally asked: "Okay, Guido. Tell me what's wrong."

"It's that man, signora. The one you had coffee with. The one whose picture I saw in the newspaper."

"What about him?"

"When we were coming back from the coffee shop . . . when we had to pass your husband's office building again . . . that's when I remembered where I saw him before. When he was yelling at the watchman . . . his dialect . . . he's from Or-

272

vietto. Didn't you recognize it? The dialect, I mean. I remember him from Orvietto. And, he's not the kind of person Signor Barragatto would want you to speak to."

She glared at the young driver. "You're never to mention it to my husband, Guido. You're never to say I met that man today. You understand? Never."

He drove along silently for a while. This man was one of the people he was supposed to be protecting the signora from. She should not be talking to him. She shouldn't even know him. And, he most certainly shouldn't know her. He would have to think about what she'd just said. He'd have to think about it very carefully.

"Guido, you didn't answer me."

"I heard what you said, signora."

She knew that Guido could ruin everything—just now, when she felt so safe for the first time in years. "It's rather important to me that no one knows we went to the office today, Guido. No one."

His eyes replied: Yes, very well. Still, he had not actually said it, and the look about him left her uneasy.

The trip back to Jericho was as slow-going as the morning's ride and the roads seemed more icy than they'd been earlier. They rode along quietly for almost an hour. She wished Guido would say something because his unusual silence disturbed her. She thought it better not to pursue the subject, though, so she didn't ask him again not to mention her encounter with the man from Orvietto. She'd not known that Carmine Pace was from Orvietto; perhaps, that was why he was visiting Tullio— he might just be looking up an old friend from home.

Midst her thoughts, she happened to glance toward the side of the road. They were passing one of the wrecks they'd seen that morning. Her heart almost stopped and she shrieked: "Oh, my God! That's Tullio's car!" She started pounding on the window.

Guido stopped short. It did look like the Barragatto car, or what was left of it. When he saw the license plate, he was

273

certain it was. He sped the rest of the way home and he'd barely stopped in front of the house when Magdalena almost jumped out of the car. He followed her in.

Aleksey and Earl were standing in the foyer and Magdalena shouted:

"Where's Tullio? What happened to him?"

She'd startled the men.

"He's upstairs, in the bedroom. He's all right," Earl said, "he's all right. The doctor just left."

She ran up the steps before he could finish the sentence.

"We just saw his car on the road," Guido told them. "We just passed it. I thought, for sure, he must have been killed."

"Well, he was very lucky," Aleksey answered. "Very lucky."

Magdalena closed her eyes for a second before entering the bedroom because she was afraid of what she might find. She tried to compose herself, then walked in slowly. She half-laughed and half-cried when she saw Tullio calmly staring at the snow which had begun to fall again.

"I thought you were dead."

"Well, I'm not. All I got was a bad bump on the head. Where were you all morning? Never mind, it doesn't matter anymore."

"When I saw that car, I thought you were dead."

"Well, I'm not! Everybody's making such a big thing of it. I just have a bad headache. That's all."

"What did the doctor say?"

He shrugged. "The same thing I just told you. Only, he charged for it."

"It's good that you called him. There's no sense in taking chances."

Tullio silently wondered who'd called the doctor. The last thing he could remember was listening for Boris Pachenker to answer the telephone. He guessed he'd blacked out. Then, the doctor was there, and Aleksey and Earl. He didn't know how he'd wound up in his bedroom. All he knew was that, now, the

274

pain in his head was throbbing again and that the room was darkening and that his wife was somewhere nearby. He said, "I think I'll lie down for a while."

She came closer and hugged him.

"There's nothing to cry about, Magda. I'm fine. Now, come on, stop that."

"I love you so much, Tullio, and I thought you were dead. I don't know what I would do. I don't know."

He eased himself away from her as gently as he could and lay down again.

"I'll leave you alone so you can get some sleep. I'll leave the door open. Just call me if you want anything. I'll hear you. I'll be right in the next room. I'll hear you."

Carmine Pace waited in front of the North American Distributors building for two hours. Before getting disgusted and leaving, he rang the night bell and Pachenker came to the door again.

"No Barragatto! Barragatto Monday! Monday! Monday!"

Pace motioned that he didn't want to come in any more, but that he wanted to leave a business card. Pachenker took it from him, and, satisfied that he'd won the battle, nodded to the disgruntled visitor. Then, Pachenker slipped the card under Tullio Barragatto's door. He hoped he'd never have a Saturday like this again.

Carmine Pace had never been stood up before. He was angry enough to spit. He didn't know what kind of game Barragatto was playing. He was positive he hadn't gotten the message wrong. The secretary had definitely said Barragatto would come in on Saturday. Barragatto had purposely done this. Barragatto was giving him the runaround. Barragatto was trying to make a fool of him. Barragatto was pushing his luck.

Chapter Five

Tullio found Pace's card on his desk on Monday morning. It sat atop a pile of unopened mail. It read only: CARMINE PACE. There was neither address nor telephone number nor handwritten note on it, but the message was clear: when Pace wanted, Pace would contact him.

The card held Tullio's attention. It was not a business card, it was a calling card. He'd not seen one in a long time. They were seldom used in New York, except by troubled society matrons; but they were commonplace in Orvietto, where such subtle things were still preferred. He'd not used his own for years and wondered if he had any left. He was still looking at it—admiring it—when his secretary announced Mr. Carmine Pace.

Tullio was surprised that the man would come without even calling first, and he certainly hadn't expected that he would return so quickly. He stood to welcome him and he apologized to him for Saturday.

"There was just no possible way for me to get here," he told Pace. "I even tried calling the night watchman, but everything went wrong. There might have been something wrong with the telephone."

The explanation seemed to satisfy Pace. He grinned and told Tullio how many times he'd heard the telephone ring; and Tullio was relieved that Pace didn't think he'd been avoiding him. He'd saved face. They both had.

When Tullio cleared the desk for an espresso tray, he suddenly noticed an envelope addressed to Salvatore from Sr. Pavetto, his secretary in Milan. Pavetto's handwriting was unmistakable. PERSONAL/CONFIDENTIAL was sprawled across its front in bright red ink. Still, a quick glance showed no mail from Benedetto.

He poured coffee for Pace, then said, "My cousin, Salvatore Crispino—he's told me you two have already met—he's asked to sit in with us, if it's all right with you."

Pace nodded and Tullio rang for his secretary.

"If Mr. Crispino is in yet, will you please tell him that Mr. Pace is here?"

Salvatore joined them within minutes, and Tullio handed him Pavetto's envelope, which he put aside.

Pace said, "I presume you've already heard from Benedetto Crispino."

Neither replied. The silence was strong and effective.

Pace continued: "So . . . we all know, or think we know, where we stand. That's all the better. It saves a lot of time. Nothing needs to be repeated."

"We've been empowered to represent the LoGiudice, the Pire, and the Beckmann families," Tullio said. He knew he'd just dropped a bomb, and he admired Pace's composure.

The visitor poured himself more coffee and scrutinized the cousins. Could Fallanca have agreed to this? Had it been determined before he'd joined Fallanca and Crispino that night? Had it been part of the earlier talks? Had the old man simply forgotten to mention it to him? How could that be? How could such a thing possibly have happened? To forego the Barragatto label would prove very costly—but the other three, also? Palermo would never permit this. Fallanca was insane. Either that, or very powerful; more powerful than even Pace, himself, had thought.

Salvatore took this moment of silence to open his letter.

Yet—Pace theorized—Fallanca might not be aware of this and, if that were the case, Barragatto could merely be taking advantage of Fallanca's protection.

Not knowing where the truth lay, Pace knew only that he must continue talking just as though Tullio Barragatto had never said a thing about the other three wineries. He musn' show surprise at the revelation, nor any trace of disagreemen with his new *patrono,* nor any agitation of any kind.

Tullio admired Pace more every second, because he couldn' guess at all what the man might be thinking. He said, "Th proposition you've brought to us in the past has been ver carefully considered." Motioning toward Salvatore, he added "My cousin has explained it in every detail. We've looked at i from every angle. We've gone over every one of its pros an cons. And, there's no question in our minds that it's a mor than generous offer. But, our position is unchanged. W simply can not take the chance."

Pace said, also looking toward Salvatore, "Yes, I'm sur you haven't left out any details."

Something was wrong with Salvatore. Tullio saw his fac tighten, and his eyes close slightly. He wasn't sure, but h thought Pace might have noticed it, too.

And, because it was obvious that Salvatore wasn't going t speak, Tullio continued: "Perhaps, if the situation wer different . . . if there weren't our other companies so closel involved with the wineries . . . the publications, the steam ships, the tourism . . . they'd all go down the drain . . . they' all be implicated if North American Distributors got involve with Prohibition . . . maybe, then our response would be different one. The way it is now, we just can't afford to go i with you."

This is not what Tullio had wanted to say. He'd wanted to tel Pace: No! Not now! Not ever! You people have had your way for too long! Times are changing! . . . But, Salvatore had warned him against it. . . . Go the calm, businesslike route, Salvatore had said. He already knows you hate him, so what good would it do to spit in his face?

Pace replied, "I'm sailing for Havana this afternoon, but I'll be in touch with you again, when I return. In the meantime, I think you should reconsider."

Tullio's secretary knocked. Before Tullio could tell her that he didn't want to be disturbed, she blurted out: "Signor Barragatto, your wife just called! She couldn't hold on, because Stefano was crying so much! Her chauffeur had to shoot Big Baboo because he broke his leg!"

"What! He broke his leg!"

"Yes. Your son, Stefano, he sneaked the horse out of the stable so he could ride him along the road. The horse slipped, and . . ."

"Is Stefano hurt?"

"No, no, he's not hurt. It was only the horse. But, Mrs. Barragatto wants you to call her as soon as possible."

Salvatore, said, "He'll call later. Leave us alone right now."

"That's a shame," Pace said. "But, as long as nothing happened to the boy. You can always replace a horse, but not a son." He picked up his hat and said, "I'll see you again, gentlemen."

Ordinarily, Tullio Barragatto would have seen his visitor to the elevator. Not this time. He nodded to the man, as did Salvatore, and their secretary showed him to the exit.

"Now, he knows they're not in Switzerland. If he ever thought that, in the first place." He turned toward his cousin. "Well, that's the end of . . ."

"My brother is dead." Pavetto's letter was crumpled in Salvatore's hand. "Jesus Christ, my brother's dead." He buried his face in his hands and let the letter drop to the floor.

Tullio picked it up and read it.

It was food poisoning, Sr. Pavetto explained. Don Benedetto had dined with Don Italo. Everyone had gotten sick. But, everyone had recovered except one of the kitchen help and

279

Don Benedetto. All of Don Italo's staff had been very, very
sick. Don Italo had almost died, too. It was so unfortunate
about Don Benedetto. Only he and the young kitchen girl
couldn't be saved. There was some talk that the previous
patrono's wife had been trying to kill Don Italo; then, she'd
have the house to herself again; but, of course, this was only
idle gossip, only speculation. Most likely, it was just a very bad
case of accidental food poisoning. They'd had shellfish that
night. They'd had pork, too. One can't be too careful when
cooking pork. It's happened before, but usually in summer, if
the meat's been sitting for a while . . .

Salvatore mumbled, "I wasn't at Ernesto's funeral. Now,
Benedetto."

The cousins felt the loss equally. They'd all grown up
together. In a way, Benedetto was as much Tullio's as he was
Salvatore's brother. They didn't console one another. It wasn't
necessary.

They were even thinking the same thoughts. That the
youngest ones had died first, that it wasn't supposed to be that
way. That the family was growing smaller.

"I'm the last Crispino."

Tullio didn't respond to this, but he'd also been thinking it.

"And, all I have are daughters."

Salvatore left Tullio alone then. He passed Earl Asheley,
who was very excited about something that had just come
across the ticker tape machine; but, he didn't respond when
the older man said something to him. Then, he passed Aleksey;
the secretary was just telling the man about Big Babbo. Then,
he entered his own office and locked the door behind him and
cried.

Aleksey walked toward Tullio's office; but Tullio's door
was also locked.

Later that afternoon, Tullio said to Salvatore: "You're going
back to Orvietto for a while, aren't you?"

"Yes. I'll take a look at the graves. Put some papers in order.
Maybe, my wife will come with me. Maybe, we can start all

280

over again."

"She might. I think she might go with you."

"I won't be gone long. Just for a while."

Tullio Barragatto had never felt so alone as when his cousin Salvatore left for Orvietto. He did not feel lonely; he felt alone. He couldn't feel lonely—he had Magdalena and the children, and Aleksey Kostenov, and Louise and Earl Asheley, and a myriad of business associates who admired him; so, he couldn't be lonely, even if he tried. Nevertheless, he was alone. For the first time, he was in a country without someone who was his friend and his peer and his blood all at once; and that is very different than being lonely: that is being alone. But, there was a business to run, and, alone or not, he had to hold tightly to it and master it as he would a defiant stallion. This, he did very well.

Tullio had a gift—(at least, this is how Earl described it to Aleksey)—a special talent that kept him making the right decisions and opening up areas of progress that others might overlook. He could walk into a meeting room where all the participants were decades his senior and command the floor and wean each of them to his way of thinking. The greater the challenge, the more persuasive he would be, the more velvet his touch. His name was becoming very well known in the tighter circles.

He gambled ferociously in the stock market; but he was good at it, or lucky, or both. What he sold, others sold; and what he bought was quickly in demand. Yet, of all his business dealings, the market was the one he took the least seriously. It was strictly a diversion to him, just gambling on a larger scale than horse or dog or auto racing; and, no matter how much money he reaped from it, he could very easily forget his broker's name from one day to the next.

Midst all the good fortune and success that ran to him and stayed by his side like a faithful dog, he remained, though, very much alone. Without Salvatore—without at least one of his

281

cousins nearby—there was no one to share a private joke or a common problem. It is not that he didn't want to share his thoughts with Aleksey or Earl; he just didn't know how to. And Magdalena: she was always there, always responsive, always ready to listen; but, she was just a woman, and he couldn't talk to her of anything more serious than their love, or their children, or their home.

He and Salvatore had agreed that neither Pace nor the new *patrono* should discover Benedetto hadn't had the chance to write about the meeting. Obviously, Benedetto must have said something right at that meeting, because there had been no attacks on the vineyards since that night; but, they couldn't imagine just what he had said, or what he had agreed to. They would have to play for time. They both knew by now that the man's name was Fallanca, but this didn't mean anything to them, because Fallanca was a very common name.

Carmine Pace approached Tullio more often now. He met him at the racetrack, and at speakeasies, and at restaurants where he'd stop for lunch. The man was everywhere. Sometimes, he would come over and talk. Sometimes, he would only nod. Tullio started to wonder if he might be following him; but, then, he realized that this was absurd . . . Pace simply knew where to find him, whenever he wanted to. It was unnerving.

It was just a matter of time, Tullio decided, before Pace's people became too impatient to wait any longer; and then, Pace would make his move. He had to protect himself. He had to be ready for anything. He should start working on the Garvey angle now, he realized, before it was too late.

But how, without implicating Bella?

He pondered this for a while. Then, it started to fall into place. He'd use Salvatore's Manhattan apartment. He'd need it, because he would have to spend some evenings in the city. He would go there late, when Harlem was just waking up, long after the Gold Coast fell asleep. He wouldn't go near the clubs

282

where he might be recognized. He'd stay clear of the clubs, keep to the seedier parts of town . . . drop a word here and there to the right people, Garvey's people, his real people, his followers . . . the right word, just here and there . . . just the right word . . . and the word would travel fast . . . and it would explode in Pace's face.

He was planning the first night when Magdalena said, "You have a look on your face that I don't like. It makes you look evil."

"I was just thinking of a few things I have to do."

"What's the suitcase for? Where are you going?"

"I have some late meetings scheduled this week, so I'm bringing a few changes of clothes to the apartment. It would be too late to come home each night. It'll be easier to stay in town. It'll only be for two or three days."

She sucked in the sides of her cheeks and said, "Uh-huh."

"What the face for?"

"Nothing. Dinner will be ready soon. Coming down?"

"In a little while," he answered. He thought it better not to say anything further, as long as she didn't.

After dinner, Magdalena asked him: "How come Salvatore didn't get rid of the apartment? After all, he's going to be gone at least a year."

"He signed it over to the company. It might come in handy. You know . . . for late meetings . . . things like that."

"Well, since it belongs to the company, you won't mind if I have a key to it, will you? You know . . . for when I want to freshen up while I'm shopping in the city . . . things like that."

He grinned and handed her an extra key. Then, he purposely buried his head in a newspaper. He devoured the international news first, then the business news, and then, the closing market quotations. He was just about to put the paper down when he noticed Marcus Garvey's name in a small headline.

Tullio was shocked. Garvey had just been indicted for mail fraud in an attempt to raise money for the steamships for his Back to Africa movement. He read the article over and over.

He realized that the timing was perfect. Garvey's followers would be up in arms.

To a bootblack who'd donated his pennies, he could say: With all the money Pace has been making on that deal, I'm surprised they didn't indict Garvey a long time ago!

And, to a bartender, he could very easily comment: It looks like Carmine Pace is going to need a new meal ticket with Garvey gone.

Just a few words. Just here and there. Just the right words to the right people. And Carmine Pace would have much less time for North American Distributors.

The next morning, Tullio brought his suitcase to work. It was Tuesday. He said to Magdalena, "I'll see you Friday night."

"Uh-huh."

He never could figure what she was thinking when she said that.

Blacks hated whites more than whites hated blacks, so white men didn't usually walk through Harlem, especially alone. There were some exceptions, though. A crooked detective could stroll in and out of any storefront, alleyway or building to pick up his bribe money without being attacked. Also, anyone known to be connected with the rackets was relatively safe. Other than that, all white men knew enough to stay clear of Harlem. Tullio knew this also, but he had no choice. He certainly could not hire anyone to do such a job for him.

The first night Tullio meandered down 125th Street, he went with a loaded pistol, ready for anything. He felt black eyes burning through his clothing. Even the smallest children squinted as he passed by. They knew he wasn't a detective; his coat was too fine and his shoes were shined. They realized, too, that he wasn't some small-time crook; he was wearing a gold wristwatch. Whoever studied him came to the same conclusion: this man was way up there in the rackets . . . don't go near him . . . there'd be hell to pay. So, Tullio Barragatto was

284

given clear passage, even as muted whispers followed him through the streets.

Tullio had not been to Harlem in several months and he'd almost forgotten how filthy it was. He doubted that any number of garbage trucks could ever keep up with the mountains of trash its residents threw into the streets. He hated the place, and he hated the people who lived there because he blamed them for its condition. He couldn't wait to finish doing what he'd come for. He was glad when, having carried out his plan for three consecutive evenings, he had no more reason to return to Harlem in the near future. Now, he had only to sit back and wait; and he would soon find out if he'd succeeded or failed in his mission.

The first time Tullio had visited Salvatore's apartment he laughed. It was exactly the hideaway he would have expected from Salvatore. That is, it looked like a brothel. He wondered if Bella Modesto had given his cousin decorating advice or if he'd just been inspired by his own adolescent fantasies. It was a small apartment, a living room, bedroom and bath on one side and a kitchen and maid's room on the other. Both the living room and bedroom walls were covered in deep red flocked wallpaper. Thick oriental carpets covered the floors. The huge art deco bed had a pale pink satin upholstered headboard and on the ceiling overhead was a large, gilt framed mirror.

But it was the bathroom where Salvatore had really outdone himself. Floor, walls and sunken tub were all carved from pink-veined Orvietto marble. The tub itself was the size of a small pool.

Tullio was thinking about the tub and the relaxing hot bath he planned when he arrived home Thursday night, his second in the city. He was tired and preoccupied. He let himself in and the first thing that caught his eye was the fresh bouquet of red roses in a crystal vase on the snow white marble mantlepiece. He recognized the roses from *The Walls*.

Then he heard the familiar laughter and he followed it to the bathroom. The tub was filled with suds and the scent of *Joy* and amid it all, looking for all the world like a red haired mermaid, was his wife.

"Magdalena!"

"Surprise!" she laughed.

His heart leaped. It was as though she had anticipated his needs even before he did.

"Well don't just stand there," she teased. "Can't you swim?"

Rising to the challenge, he soon proved he could do that and more in the right tub with the right woman.

Hours later, exhausted, the two of them curled together on the art deco bed. That's when it came to him.

"You came here because you wanted to see if I had a woman here, didn't you?" he said accusingly.

She didn't answer.

"What if I had?" he asked. "What would you have done?"

"Tullio, that never entered my mind."

"What never entered your mind? That I might have had somebody here . . . ?"

She shrugged.

". . . or, didn't it enter your mind about what you might have done if you'd found someone?"

"My darling husband, only God and I know how many times you've kept me guessing. Now, it's your turn to guess."

"Come on, Magda, tell me the truth. I'm serious."

"So am I," she said.

"But, suppose I hadn't come back to the apartment all night?"

"Well," she replied, "I'd have fallen asleep, I suppose. So, I guess it wouldn't have bothered me that much. Right?" She looked around the room. "You know, Tullio, this is really a very beautiful place. I'm glad the company is keeping it. We can always make good use of it."

In the morning, as he was getting dressed to leave for the office, the doorbell rang.

'"That will be Guido," Magdalena said. "He has Stefano and Rebecca with him. We're bringing them to the circus today."

He grunted. He wasn't ready for the noise of excited children.

"What's wrong?" she asked him. "Another headache?"

He shrugged. "It's not a bad one. It'll go away soon."

Since the car accident, Tullio had been suffering headaches. Usually, he would know when one was coming on. First, he would feel a little lightheaded. Then, within minutes, the throbbing would begin. When the pain was very bad, he'd have to lie back. During the worst, everything around him would darken to shadows. This last phase frightened him because he thought that, someday, his sight might not return when the pain left. He'd already visited several specialists, but no one could find anything physically wrong. He'd almost hit one of the doctors who'd suggested that the pain was all in his mind.

Magdalena handed him some aspirin. "Why don't you skip the office today?"

She was quietly disturbed when he agreed. She'd not suspected that the headaches were that bad.

"When you're finished with the circus," he told her, "come back here, and I'll ride home with you."

"Guido can take them, himself. I'll stay here, with you."

"No. Go to the circus. I'll get a little sleep, and, by the time you get back, I'll be fine."

Chapter Six

Weeks melted into months and it became apparent to Tullio that his strolls through Harlem had reaped some rewards. Carmine Pace was approaching North American Distributors less and less often. The New York offices of Pire, LoGiudice and Beckmann hadn't seen or heard from Pace at all. Also, Tullio read in the newspapers that two speakeasies he knew to be owned by Carmine Pace and his associates had been firebombed.

Stoking the fires even more was the news that Marcus Garvey had been found guilty of using the mails to defraud and had been sentenced to five years in the federal penitentiary in Atlanta. Enraged, Garvey's followers were playing havoc with any establishment even remotely connected with Pace. Pace's numbers runners had to be heavily guarded, and some of his high-stakes back-room games had been held up. The high rollers were fleeing to his competition.

All of this was happening in Harlem, and it was still only springtime. A long, hot summer loomed.

The Stateside managers and attorneys for Beckmann, LoGiudice and Pire praised Tullio Barragatto. They reported to their superiors in Europe that, somehow, Tullio had managed to keep Carmine Pace from their doors. They couldn't imagine how the young man had done this—the problem had seemed insurmountable until now—but he had; and they could not speak highly enough of him. There was an inconsistency, however, which they could not understand, and neither could Tullio. It was that all of their home vineyards in Europe, with the exception of the Barragatto Winery, were still being harassed. Could it be, they asked, that Pace and his *patrono* might be working independently of the bosses in Palermo? It was worth looking into.

Tullio basked in his success. Often, he wondered what he'd done right—or what Benedetto had agreed to—but neither he nor Salvatore could even venture a guess. He enjoyed every moment of it. He'd played the leopard.

Still, Tullio was not completely blind. He considered this victory over Pace just a temporary one, a respite, a play for time, and not something of any lasting significance. He knew that, eventually, Harlem would calm down, Pace would be on top again, and the vicious circle would resume. He refused, therefore, to be tempted into any fatal sense of security. In this vein, he focused some of his attention on *The Walls of Jericho*.

Now, since Pace knew they were in New York, it seemed senseless to continue this kind of ruse. They had to be protected, Tullio decided. *The Walls* had to be fortified. It had to be impenetrable.

The original owner had named it well. A wall of cement and stone surrounded it, completely enclosing the property, except for the huge wrought iron gates that gleamed at the entrance.

Tullio studied the wall and the gates. The first was high and thick, but could be easily scaled. As for the gate, it had been designed more for ornamentation than for practical use—anyone could force open its lock. The surest way to offset this, he decided, would be not to depend upon the wall, alone, but to fortify it with armed guards. He hired twelve men, each in a group of four, working an eight-hour shift. Three guards would travel the property and overlook the wall, and one would always remain at the gate. Each man had a trained dog with him and a walkie-talkie and was required to check with the others every hour. At sundown, the estate was floodlighted. Had it not been that so many other Gold Coast residents also employed armed guards for their estates, Kostenov would have accused Tullio of paranoia; since it appeared to be the common idiosyncrasy of his neighbors, though, to protect themselves from God-knows-what, the elder simply tried to ignore the whole situation.

Even so, Magdalena could not dismiss it. It infuriated her. She disliked the guards, who never spoke to her, but nodded respectfully toward her from a distance; and she was afraid of their dogs.

"Those dogs are killers," she told her husband. "I can tell that they are, just by looking at them. They never even bark. They only look at you. Dogs that don't bark are dangerous."

"They're supposed to be dangerous," he replied. "That's what they're here for."

"There are children here, too. Or, don't you remember that?"

"They won't hurt the children. They're very well trained. And, anyway, they're always kept on leashes. They can't get anywhere near the children."

They argued often about the dogs, but Tullio would not be dissuaded. Eventually, Magdalena stopped talking about them. She kept her resentment to herself and would not discuss them, even when Louise or one of the other club ladies would remark about them. There were other things about which she refused to be quieted, though.

Without having consulted with Magdalena, Tullio had withdrawn Rebecca and Stefano from school and had hired tutors for all their lessons. Then, to offset any boredom or lack of friends this might cause the children, he'd convinced owners of a few of the nearby estates to send their own children to *The Walls* for their primary schooling, after which he'd converted one of the servants' houses into a small, very private, very exclusive schoolhouse. Now, every afternoon, a line of limousines waited outside the gate to bring the students back to their respective estates when the day's lessons were done.

The schoolhouse was almost an acre away from the main residence, so it didn't create a noisy situation. Nor did Magdalena object, in any way, to having the twenty-odd children on the estate; on the contrary, she welcomed them. She liked children. She enjoyed looking down from her bedroom patio, watching them scamper about the grounds during their recess periods. Also, she liked being able to join them during lunchtime; she and Carlo would make a picnic of it. Moreover, it was so convenient just to send Stefano and Rebecca walking through the fields each morning, rather than having Guido drive them back and forth from their previous school which had been a few miles away. No, she definitely did not disapprove of the little schoolhouse. It was the reason behind it that bothered her.

"It's as though you don't ever want them off the estate grounds," she told her husband. "It's cruel. It's not fair to them. How will they ever know what the rest of the world is like if they never see what goes on beyond that wall?"

"They'll know everything they have to know," Tullio answered, "when the time is right for it."

"And, when would that time be?"

He was becoming more and more impatient with her lately. It seemed they were always arguing about this matter. He slammed down the report he was reading, and said, "I was brought up entirely on my father's estate. I shared the same teachers that his pickers' children did. When I was twelve, my father hired Aleksey, and, it wasn't until then that I . . ."

"Twelve! You expect to keep them as prisoners until they're twelve?"

"Prisoners? Did you say prisoners? They have horses, dogs, cats, maids, tennis courts, swimming pools, private teachers! They're spoiled rotten, and you consider them prisoners?"

"Well . . . well . . . they have no freedom. That's the same thing, isn't it? It's the same thing as being in prison."

He would not listen to her anymore. Though she kept talking, she knew none of her words was reaching him. He did make one concession, however, and this was due to Kostenov's intercession. Whenever possible, he would take them to the city on a Saturday morning. There, he would expose them to the finest restaurants, to museums, to the ballet and to the opera, and to any entertainment he considered necessary for their near future. This excluded puppet shows and circuses and zoos and ballgames; but Magdalena dared not complain about this, because half a victory was better than none.

Whether or not Rebecca and Stefano enjoyed these outings, Tullio either didn't care or didn't notice. He was doing his duty; and, when the activity was one which he thought Carlo might understand, he would bring him along, also. One thing Tullio did notice, though, was that Stefano was not only answering more and more to the name of Carter, but that he was referring to himself as Carter.

"Why do you say your name is Carter?" Tullio asked him. "That's not your name. And, you know that I don't like when you do that."

"It's for Grandma Louise," the boy replied. "Grandma Louise gets confused."

"Grandma Louise isn't with us right now, and your name is not Carter. So, stop it, once and for all."

Rebecca usually protected Stefano at times like this. "He likes it better than Stefano," she said. "Carter sounds more American."

"What do you mean, American?" her father asked. "It's not a long name. It's a very nice name."

"Well, the other boys . . . sometimes, they laugh at him. They say: 'Stefano! What a name!' . . . Then, sometimes, they tease him. But, they don't laugh when he says his name is Carter."

Magdalena knew of the problem her son was having with his

292

foreign-sounding name. This was, after all, the North Shore, and his playmates were its children. "We can call you Steven, if you'd like. Or Stevie. Or Steve. Would you rather that instead of Stefano?"

Yet, the little boy wanted Carter. At times, he absolutely refused to answer to anything else. He was usually careful enough not to do this in front of Tullio, however, because each time he did, he would be punished; and, this was another source of friction between Tullio and Magdalena.

"You're rougher on Stefano than you are on Rebecca or Carlo. You let them get away with murder."

"That's not true," Tullio said. "The truth is that every time I correct Stefano, you remember that he's not my real son, so you think I'm picking on him because of that."

"That's not so. As a matter of fact, you're the only one who ever brings that up. If you'll notice, I've never said anything about that. It only goes to prove, though, that it's probably on your mind, and that you might resent him a little for it, without even realizing it."

They were discussing this very subject one afternoon while in a restaurant. Stefano had stayed at home with Aleksey and Carlo. Only Rebecca was with them, but she'd left the table to go to the ladies' room.

Magdalena excused herself to see why Rebecca was staying away so long. She left the large, private back room where they'd been eating and was passing through the front restaurant section when she bumped into a man. She looked up to apologize and saw that it was Carmine Pace. She'd almost fallen into his arms.

Pace looked more surprised than Magdalena. "This is destiny," he said. "The way we keep running into each other. It's got to mean something. It has to be for some purpose."

"It's just coincidence," Magdalena answered, "just coincidence. I'm sorry for being so clumsy."

"Are you here alone?" As he asked her this, he kissed her hand. He did it gently. She liked it and she smiled.

"You're a very unusual man, Mr. Pace."

"Why so formal? My name is Carmine. Remember?"

She'd not taken her hand back from his. "Yes," she said, "I remember."

"Don't you think it's time you told me yours? I can't go around thinking of you as Anita for the rest of my life when I know that it's not your real name."

"What does it matter?"

"It matters to me." He kissed her hand again.

Magdalena cocked her head. She said: "I am Magdalena Barragatto."

"Barragatto?" He shook his head and half smiled. He repeated, "Barragatto. Of all the . . . I should have known . . ."

"I'm Tullio Barragatto's wife."

"My Anita."

"Please. Don't say such a thing. I'm Magdalena Barragatto. My husband is inside. He's waiting for me. I just walked out here to look for my daughter."

"Tullio Barragatto's wife," he said. "Tullio Barragatto. That name. Of all the men on earth. Barragatto."

"I have to go now," she said. She left him there without another word. When she returned, Tullio said:

"What's wrong?"

"Nothing. It's just a little warm in here."

"Where's Rebecca?"

She'd forgotten. She answered: "She'll be right out. The ladies' room is a little crowded. That's why she's taking so long."

This was Rebecca's birthday. Tullio was taking them to see *Sleeping Beauty*. Magdalena was relieved, because she wouldn't have to talk for a while. She could sit quietly back during the performance and think.

Sleeping Beauty had been Rebecca's request. She'd liked the story so much when her nurse had read it to her. She'd not wanted a party. "Just me and you, Daddy," she'd said. "That's what I want for my birthday. Just me and you."

"What about your mother and your brothers?" he'd asked. "Don't you want to share your birthday with them?"

"Well, just Mommy. Leave Carlo and Stefano at home. Promise, Daddy. Promise."

"If that's what you want for your birthday, that's what you'll have. But later, we'll have a birthday cake at home, and everybody can join us. All right?"

"I love you, Daddy. I love you more than Carlo does. You love me better than him, Daddy? You love me better than Carlo?"

"I love you all. You, Carlo and Stefano. But, you're my only princess, so you'll always be special."

Magdalena relaxed in the soft theater seat. She closed her eyes and tried to remember the last time Tullio had kissed her hand. It had been such a long time.

She mentioned it that night.

"You want me to kiss your hand?" he asked her.

"Oh, Tullio, be serious."

"Who was that man who kissed your hand in the restaurant, Mommy?"

They were both startled. Magdalena said: "Rebecca, how long have you been standing there? You're supposed to be in bed."

Tullio asked: "A man kissed your hand in the restaurant? Who was he? Why did he do that?"

Stefano was directly behind Rebecca. "A man kissed Mommy?"

"Both of you are supposed to be in bed," Magdalena said. "What are you doing up? Also, you both know better than walking into this room without knocking."

"Who was he?" Tullio asked her. "Why'd he kiss your hand?"

"Just some old man. I bumped into him . . . or he bumped into me . . . anyway, he apologized and kissed my hand. He was just some old stranger. I don't know who he was."

"Oh, so that's what this was all about. That's why you want me to kiss your hand."

"Forget it," she said.

She ushered the children to bed. When she returned, Tullio was thumbing through a magazine. "I don't think you should read if you have a headache," she said. "It might make it worse."

"I don't have a headache."

"Then, what are those aspirins doing on the night table? You just took some, didn't you?" She held out her hand and he gave her the magazine. "You're taking too many lately, Tullio. You go around swallowing aspirin tablets like other people eat candy. It's too much."

He smiled. "A couple of minutes ago, you were a neglected wife. Now, you're a doctor."

"I never said I felt neglected. That thing . . . about kissing my hand, I mean . . . I was just being a silly woman."

He surprised her, then, because he did kiss her hands, just the way he used to; and he said: "No matter what in the world you've ever been, you've never been just a silly woman. Not to me."

There were other things he began to say and to do, little things that he hadn't said or done for such a long time. If it was romance his Magda wanted tonight, it was romance she would get. Even he enjoyed it, which surprised him a bit. He hadn't known he'd missed it, too.

All the while, Magdalena wondered why she couldn't tell him it had been Carmine Pace she'd bumped into that afternoon. She seemed absurd to herself.

If he's a business associate of his, there certainly can't be anything objectionable about my bumping into him in a restaurant!

Still, she did not want to tell Tullio; and it bothered her because she didn't know why.

Louise had edged the *Swansgarten* pond with yellow tulips.

The effect was so pretty that she invited Magdalena to come see it. "We'll have a late breakfast," she told her, "right next to the pond. Wait until you see how lovely it looks."

When Magdalena arrived, Louise knew there was something on her mind. "What's bothering you?" she asked her young friend.

Magdalena told her of the chance meeting with Carmine Pace, and ended: "Yet, I don't know why, but something deep inside wants me to keep it a secret. Why should that be, Louise? We certainly didn't do anything wrong, just meeting by accident like that. This whole thing is so silly. It makes me feel like a schoolgirl. Why should it bother me like this?"

Louise wasn't as quick to answer as usual. When she finally did, she started: "Magdalena, I won't baby you. I'm going to tell you what I really believe."

"Which is?"

"That you're bored with your marriage, and that you're looking to have an affair."

"What! That's not so!"

"Yes, dear. I'm afraid that it is. You're so bored that you're actually pretending that you had some kind of illicit affair yesterday afternoon and have to hide it. To keep it a secret. To cover it up. I'm sure you don't realize it, but that's the truth. Take it from me. We women get just as bored with our husbands as they do with us. The problem is that we don't like to face up to it. It's improper, or so we've been taught. Yes, improper. That's the word. Improper. We're not ever supposed to be bored with them."

"That's not so with me, Louise. Other women might feel that way, but not me. There's nothing about Tullio that bores me. Nothing. I love him more than I can say."

"Oh, I know you love him," Louise answered. "I know that, and . . ."

"And I would never think of being with another man. Why, such a thought never even occurred to me."

"Hasn't it? Never? Not even once?"

"No, never," Magdalena replied.

"Then, why the secret over meeting Mr. Pace again? Why the guilt?"

Magdalena didn't answer.

"You might not be ready for an affair, not a real one, not yet, anyway. But, you're pretending you had one. Or, that you're about to have one. You're fantasizing. There's nothing wrong with that. There's no harm to it. I wouldn't be concerned about it if I were you."

Louise had spoken softly. Her voice had been gentle, and she'd patted her young friend's hands all the while; and Magdalena could take no offense at what she'd said. Still, she believed Louise wrong. A change of subject might be the best thing, she decided. She said, "Tullio's friend, Gerhard, is arriving today from Germany. He's on his honeymoon. He and his wife will be staying with us for a while."

"Have you ever met them before?"

"No."

"Well, I don't envy you. It's always difficult to entertain strangers. But, I can help you with the wife. We can bring her to the club. She might enjoy that. Does she play golf?"

"I don't know. I don't know anything about her, except that her name is Nicole and that she's from Belgium." She looked at her watch. It was almost noon. She left shortly.

Guido talked all the way home, but Magdalena could not remember a word he'd said. She'd been wondering about what Louise had told her. Maybe, there was an element of truth in it—not on her part, she decided, but on her husband's. Maybe, he was bored with her. Maybe, it was just an automatic thing to him. Maybe, it didn't still thrill him the way it did her.

But, she bored with him? No. She fantasizing over another man? No. She pretending she'd had an affair? Or was about to have one? No. Louise had to wrong. She had to be.

She was a little sorry that Gerhard and Nicole Moeller were arriving just this day. She'd received a telephone call from Bella a few days before. Bella would be in the city this afternoon, and she'd invited Magdalena to go on a shopping spree with her. Bella had been out of town; she hadn't mentioned where, and Magdalena hadn't thought to ask. She would have preferred to spend the afternoon with Bella. She liked her—so long as Tullio didn't know the woman was around. She wondered, now, what kind of work Bella was doing, and for whom and where; but, she was sure Bella would not tell her. It didn't matter. Bella would be here only a couple of days, though; and she wished she could see her; she'd been fun. She sighed deeply. She hoped Nicole Moeller wasn't going to be difficult to please.

No, I'm not bored with Tullio. You're wrong, Louise. I know you're wrong. And, he's not bored with me, either. No, he's not!

Chapter Seven

Bella Modesto's *Piccolo Villaggio* was flourishing. The "regulars" came from the northeastern section of the country; but, when businessmen were visiting from the south and west, they, too, having heard of the unique house from their New York associates, flocked to it. They came through recommendation and with reservations; and, so far as Tullio could see, they left satisfied, this, he decided, having been proven by their return visits. They were bankers and judges, and politicians and entertainers, the famous and the infamous. They were among the wealthiest men in the country. Anonymity wasn't necessary, because each felt secure, having seen the other. They greeted Tullio Barragatto as another guest when he was there, none of them ever guessing he was Bella's backer.

Tullio journeyed upstate every month or two to go over the books with Bella. He was glad when she came to New York on her shopping sprees because it saved him the long trip. She was to meet him this day in his Manhattan apartment. On the way to the apartment, he stopped in at Serge's, the restaurant to which he'd taken Magdalena and Rebecca.

"I'd like you to reserve a table for two," he told the

headwaiter. "We'll be here about 2:30, 3 o'clock."

"Certainly, Mr. Barragatto," the man replied. "We'll see you then. Oh, by the way, did Mr. Pace find you the other day?"

"Mr. Pace?"

"Yes. He asked if you'd been around lately. I told him that you were here, in the private dining room."

"Oh, no, we didn't see one another."

"I'd assumed you had, since I'd seen him speaking with Mrs. Barragatto a few minutes later."

Tullio took a cigarette from his case, and the headwaiter lit it for him. He said, "No, I didn't see Mr. Pace."

When he arrived at the apartment, Bella had already let herself in. A few hours later, she told him, "It's so ironic. You and Magdalena are just about the best friends I have in this country, and I can't be with the both of you at the same time. I still can't get over the fact that Magdalena has never told you that she and I have met. It's hard to believe."

"Then, you don't know her very well."

"Do you?"

"Sometimes, I wonder," he replied.

"What do you mean by that?" she asked him.

"Ah, it doesn't matter."

"Come on, now. Since when do you hold anything back from Bella?"

They'd spent most of the morning in bed. They'd just started working on the books. He gave her an honest smile. "You're one fantastic woman," he said. "Nobody can ever take that away from you."

"And we're friends, right? So, what's on your mind?"

He could always talk more easily with Bella than with anyone else. "Bella, how come you and I can always be so open with each other? I mean, I always know where I stand with you, and you with me. For instance, here we are, just finished having some terrific sex, and we're talking about my wife. Just look at us. A man who loves his wife is lying with her friend.

We should feel some kind of guilt, shouldn't we?"

"Why?" Bella asked him. "You have no intention of leaving Magdalena for me. And, certainly, I have no intention of trying to break up your marriage. So, why should anybody feel guilty about anything? What's the harm in a little sex between friends?" She sat back. "You know I would never do anything to hurt you or Magdalena, don't you? I purposely called her first. It's only when I was positive she would be too busy to come to the city that I even suggested meeting you here. I would never have taken the chance that she might pop in. You know that."

"I know that, Bella. I know. And, that's exactly my point. You're so honest with me. And, I know how honest you are about never wanting to hurt Magdalena, either. That's what I meant before, about my wondering how well I know her. I think I know you better than I know my own wife. She's not as honest with me as you are, and I don't know why."

"What's wrong? You caught her at something?"

"Something like that. And, you know, it's a funny thing, but I don't think there was any reason for it."

Bella answered, "Tullio, Tullio, Tullio . . . you might be a great businessman, you might make millions . . . but, when it comes to women, you're so unsophisticated."

"Why?"

"Why? Because you should know that there's always a reason when women lie. It might not be an important reason, but, nevertheless, there's always a reason."

"You think so?"

"I know so," she said, "and it's usually a good one."

"How can it not be an important reason, but be a good reason, both at the same time?"

"That's the way a woman thinks, Tullio. I can't explain it. Just take my word for it."

It was already two o'clock. They left for Serge's and, after their late lunch, they said goodbye. Then, he drove to the pier to meet Gerhard and Nicole.

Tullio wondered why Magdalena had lied about Carmine

302

Pace. Why had she told him it had been *just some old stranger*? They couldn't be total strangers if the headwaiter said they'd been speaking to one another. And, nobody would describe Pace as old. Why had the meeting sent her back to the table so flustered? How long had she known Pace, and how well? Where could they possibly have met before? He remembered how she'd spoken about Pace the night before the car accident. She'd said she'd heard about him . . . she'd read about him . . . but not that she knew him. Why in the world had she kept it a secret? Was that why she hadn't wanted him to meet Pace that Saturday morning? Was it because she hadn't wanted him to find out they knew each other? It didn't make any sense. What was she trying to hide?

How long had Pace known Magdalena? All this while, Tullio had been trying to protect her and the children from him . . . but, all the while, he'd known who she was. All the while? What did that mean? Weeks? Months? Years? No, it couldn't possibly be years, because that would mean they'd known each other while Tullio was still in Italy.

He could simply come out and ask her . . . but, she'd already lied about it once . . . a confrontation might lead to another lie to cover up the first. No, that wouldn't do. It wouldn't accomplish anything except to make him sound like some jealous husband.

It needn't be taken as jealousy. It could be plain, ordinary concern. Carmine Pace, after all, was an unscrupulous character. Even she had mentioned the bad reputation Pace had. Any husband had the right, and the duty, to be concerned if his wife consorted with such people.

Consort? That wasn't the right word. She wasn't consorting with him. She'd met him . . . they'd spoken . . . he'd kissed her hand. But, why had she lied about it? *Why'd he kiss her hand?*

I'm acting like an ass. She has the right to have friends who happen to be men. I have friends who are women. Look at me and Bella. No, that's ridiculous.

* * *

303

He could hear all the commotion as he got closer to the docks. Besides the arriving passengers, a politician was giving a speech, and the crowds were milling around him. They were lapping up every word the man was saying, and they were laughing because he kept telling jokes. His name was Jimmy Walker, according to the large banners that loomed overhead. Tullio didn't know too much about him, but he suspected he'd be hearing more of him; it was obvious that he was a crowd pleaser. He jotted down the man's name in his notebook. He'd have one of his reporters interview Walker. It might make for some interesting reading; maybe a whole spread—photographs, quotes, family background—a human interest feature, if nothing else.

Customs men were blasting instructions through a loudspeaker, but they were being drowned out by Walker's band and by other's hawking balloons and postcards.

Less than a hundred yards away, a skirmish was just ending. Several communists had been carrying some protest placards and a group of stevedores had attacked them. The police were still trying to separate them. One of the communists was lying on the ground, nose bleeding. Tullio watched the man being stomped. Then, he saw a billy club land, cracking open one of the stevedore's heads. He felt like he was in Milan again, with its Bolsheviks and Fascists, only the policeman wielding the billy club was definitely Irish. No, this wasn't Milan; it was the New York dock. But, what were communists doing on the docks? They usually clustered around Union Square. Then, he recognized Gerhard Moeller's high, shrill whistle, and he turned away from the bodies and his memories of Milan and he walked toward the lowering gangplank.

Gerhard had always looked as though he'd been put together loosely. Sometimes, it appeared that his arms and legs might fall away from the rest of his body, he was so gangly. He wore eyeglasses now, and their dark, heavy rims were the only contrast one could see on him; his complexion was pale, as were his eyes—they were light gray—and his hair fell forward like a stubborn hank of hay. He could be a cartoon strip. Nicole stood to his right, still and silent.

There was a building that Tullio had once seen in Florence. It was a corner building that housed a handbag factory in its two upper floors and a cafe at street level. He'd been leaning against it, waiting for Aleksey. Its walls had become hot, baking under the sun, and were rough to the touch, so he'd backed away from it, and that is when he'd first looked at it. It was constructed of large cement blocks. The surface of each block was completely chisel carved in a tiny fleur-de-lis pattern. It was incredible, almost as though somebody had pasted lace over its breadth, and he'd had to trace his fingers over it to believe what he was seeing: the entire building was a sculpture! Good God, he'd thought, who had the stonecutter been? Had he signed his name somewhere, that old master? Or, had he died anonymously? Nicole reminded Tullio of that little building in Florence, that masterpiece that couldn't be seen unless it was studied; she was too beautiful to be noticed casually.

Magdalena had done wonders with the guest cottage. Everybody said so. She'd decorated all of its rooms in pastels of pinks and lavenders and apricots and it looked like a showplace. The Moellers were impressed.

This was the first time Magdalena had been called upon to entertain her husband's friends. Other men brought home business associates for the weekends, or, at least, invited people to dinner occasionally, but Tullio never had. Except for the Asheleys, nobody ever came to *The Walls of Jericho*. She was going to prove, now, the kind of hostess she could be. Her guests would want for nothing. She'd seen to that, she'd been preparing for their visit so long. And this would be her chance, she'd decided, to change her way of life.

Gerhard, she found, was exactly as Tullio had described him, even down to his favorite expressions. She could often foretell what he was about to say. She knew which look meant he felt like another ice cold beer, what glance meant he was hungry, and which of his movements meant he would be wandering off on his own. An immediate empathy developed between her and the tall German.

"The little *frau* is a doll," Gerhard said to Tullio, "a real living doll. You're a rich man, having somebody like her."

Tullio was pleased, because he knew compliments never flowed easily from Gerhard and because he realized Gerhard was sincere. He told Magdalena what his friend said and how proud he was of her. She seemed to take it in stride, as though she expected nothing less.

"If only his wife were as friendly and outgoing as he is," she said, "it would be a lot easier."

"Nicole?" Tullio asked. "She's not unfriendly."

"That's true. I didn't use the right word. She's friendly enough. It's just that she holds back. It's as though she's thinking something completely different than what she's saying. There are moments that I'm sure she's carrying on a conversation only to be polite. Have you noticed?"

Tullio knew what Magdalena meant. Nicole was as quiet as a church mouse since she'd arrived. He suspected it was because of him. She'd avoided looking directly at him on the docks, and had spoken only when necessary since then. He understood. He hadn't said very much to her, either. He couldn't. He replied: "Well, this is the first time she's ever been away from home, and she's on her honeymoon, and, I guess everything in her life is suddenly changing. Maybe, the whole thing is overwhelming her."

"You're probably right," Magdalena answered. "She'll come out of her shell soon."

He hoped so. There was tension whenever he and Nicole were in each other's company. He was afraid that the others were going to sense the awkwardness.

It wasn't only the silence which was causing the strain; it was also that Tullio found himself staring at her when nobody

306

was looking and quickly turning guiltily away. He wished he could stop doing this, but it kept happening, and, there were moments when he was positive that she was looking at him in the same way. It made him feel even worse.

One evening, after Nicole and Gerhard had retired to the guest cottage, and after Magdalena had left to put the children to bed, Kostenov said to Tullio: "That young woman makes me yearn for the old days."

"The old days?"

"Yes," Kostenov said, "the old days. My youth. Clean Alpine snowdrifts. Viennese waltzes. Windmills. Dresden figurines. She resembles a Dresden doll, you know. It's a pity that she's so troubled. Ah, well . . . so goes all of Europe . . ."

"Troubled?" Tullio put down his snifter. "I wasn't aware that she was troubled about anything. She shouldn't be, anyway. There's no reason to be. No reason. She's just married into one of the wealthiest families on the Continent, hasn't she?"

"That's right," Kostenov replied. "She should not be troubled."

"No," Tullio repeated, "there's no reason."

"Are we saying exactly the same thing?" the elder asked. *You old fox.*

"You know, Tullio, this reminds me of a tale from ancient China."

Why can't I ever fool you?

Aleksey continued: "Once, there was a king who called together all the lords and generals and top-servants of his kingdom. 'There is trouble in our land,' he told his subjects. 'In some parts, there is famine, and in all parts, there is poverty. Worse yet, we are about to go to war, so we must now conserve everything we have for our soldiers, and not waste a single kernel of corn. Mend your ways, or there will be no way to avoid disaster.' When the king dismissed his subjects, they were, naturally, very downhearted . . . because, after all, nobody likes being told to watch his step . . ."

You just won't let up, will you, Aleksey?

"Well, anyway . . . among his subjects was the Keeper of the Royal Monkeys. The monkey keeper went directly to his cages. He told the animals what his king had decreed. Then, he said to them, 'From now on, instead of giving you three peanuts in the morning and three peanuts in the afternoon, you will be receiving three peanuts every morning, but only two every afternoon.' Oh, there was a terrible ruckus in the cages. The monkeys jumped up and down and started slamming themselves agaisnt the bars and walls, and the poor old keeper was afraid they might hurt themselves, they were carrying on so much. He couldn't sleep all night long, because he knew he would be beheaded if any of the royal monkeys should die. Then, as dawn approached, an idea came to him. He rushed out to the monkey cages. When the animals saw him coming, they started the commotion all over again, but he held up his hands and said, 'Wait! Wait! A great thing has happened. Everything has been settled. From now on, each of you will receive two peanuts every morning, and three every afternoon.' The monkeys were satisfied, and the man was not beheaded."

Tullio did not say anything.

Aleksey Kostenov scrutinized his former student. "Are you trying to make a monkey out of me, Tullio?"

Again, Tullio said nothing.

"Well, are you?"

"No, Aleksey."

"Then, don't say the same thing that I am saying in a different way. Don't try to placate me with a play on words. Don't ever try pulling a *Three in the Morning* on me, because I've known you too long, and it won't work."

"That wasn't my intention."

Kostenov continued: "And, don't make the mistake to assume that the other people in this household are monkeys, either. If I've already noticed the stolen glances that keep bouncing back and forth between you and Nicole Moeller, then, it's possible that the others have, also. Those looks of

308

yours . . . they're far from discreet."

He could act dumb. He could open his eyes very wide and hold out his hands and exclaim: Looks? Looks bouncing back and forth between me and Nicole? I don't know what you're talking about, Aleksey!

Or, he could deny it outright.

One look at Aleksey's expression warned him to do neither. He asked, instead, "Has anybody said anything?"

"No. No one. Not yet."

Tullio had not been chastised so by Aleksey Kostenov since he was a teenager. He'd almost forgotten what it was like. "It's not what you might be thinking," he said. "We're not having an affair or anything. It's nothing like that. It's . . ."

"I don't want to know, Tullio. That's your business. But, when there's indiscretion involved, it becomes everybody's business, because then you, yourself, make it everybody's business. All I must say, though, is that you had better tread carefully. There's more involved here than a pretty face. The lady isn't only your good friend's wife; she's your wife's guest, and she's living under this roof. Make sure she's not troubled!"

Aleksey Kostenov had said what he'd been wanting to say for days. There was no more he wished to add. He said goodnight.

How indiscreet had they been, Tullio wondered. They? Then, he'd been right. Nicole had been watching him, too. Before, he'd only suspected. Now, he was sure. Kostenov had confirmed it.

It was better when I wasn't positive, Aleksey. You shouldn't have told me. I had a feeling it was that way; but, you shouldn't have told me. You should have let me go right on thinking that it might be my imagination.

Hey, what the hell! We're not doing anything wrong! Is it a crime to look at someone? That's all it is. Just a look, now and then.

When Magdalena called down to him, he went upstairs without dawdling. It suddenly dawned on him that he'd been spending too much time in his study these past few nights—not tonight—so, he climbed the stairs without hesitating. And,

309

when he walked into their bedroom, he did not loiter near the window; he did not glance through the panes toward the guest cottage to see if those lights had already gone out—not tonight. And, when he drew his bath, he did not linger in it any longer than was necessary—not tonight. There was nothing to wonder about tonight.

Tonight—right here, right now—he was with Magdalena.

Magda.

His Magda.

The girl he'd met on that little farm by the Po.

The beauty he'd travelled with in Mikel's wagon.

His Magda.

His bride.

His wife.

The woman he loved.

Not somebody he'd slept with only once, a year ago. A year-and-a-half-ago? In a make-believe place called Rothenburg.

He was with Magdalena.

Where he should be.

He felt better now.

Chapter Eight

Since Bella Modesto's stay in *Swansgarten*, Louise Asheley's popularity had zoomed. Every now and then, the ladies of the Gold Coast still whispered and speculated about "the visitor" who had left the North Shore as mysteriously as she'd appeared. Louise had been chairwoman of the club dance committee for two years already and, had it not been customary to "change for the good of the club," she would most certainly have been elected a third time. She was as content as she could be. Her occasional lapses into thinking Magdalena and Stefano were Anita and Carter Asheley didn't trouble those close to her, and she no longer sought her abandon in a bottle. She was now one of Capits Rock's most honored members.

Tullio had finally agreed to join the club also. Magdalena could now go there on her own, and not only as Louise's guest. Because she was always in Louise's company when she did go, however, she, too, was considered one of the club's elite.

Louise and Magdalena brought Nicole to Capits Rock often. It is not that Magdalena had ever learned to like the club or its women, but this appeared to be the easiest way to entertain her house guest. Nicole Moeller was quite good at golf.

Gerhard spent a great deal of his time in the office with Tullio. There were so many details involved with the New England motels venture that his new bride saw as little of him as Magdalena did of Tullio. It wasn't what she'd expected her honeymoon to be like and Magdalena felt sorry for her.

Magdalena, chided Tullio for keeping the newlyweds apart so much, but it did no good. He would reply that men had to work and that women should understand . . . that he wasn't twisting Gerhard's arm . . . that a "working honeymoon" had been Gerhard's idea . . . that, if Gerhard had not wanted to spend so much of his time in the office, he wouldn't. Lastly, he told her that it was none of her business . . . that the Moellers were adults . . . that the amount of time they devoted to one another was strictly up to them.

"Has Nicole been complaining about it?" he asked.

"No," she replied, "but she doesn't have to. It's obvious that she's not exactly the happiest bride I've ever met."

"Well, that's her concern and Gerhard's, and not any of ours," he said, "and I don't want you to go upsetting the applecart by bringing it up."

To her surprise, Louise agreed with Tullio. They could discuss it freely this morning, because Nicole was out on the course with the other golfers. It had rained these past few days, and all the women wanted to catch up on their game. When Louise replied: "He's right, Magdalena, it's none of our concern," Magdalena merely shrugged. She would have challenged Louise about it, but not right now; at this moment, she was too excited about her plans for Tullio's birthday.

"His aunts back in Orvietto always threw parties for him on his Saint's day. They were supposed to be surprise parties, but he was never surprised. They did the same thing every year. This one will be for his birthday, more American. A real surprise."

"I don't know how you've managed to keep it from him all this time," Louise said.

"It hasn't been easy."

"I hope you know what you're doing, Magdalena. You know how much Tullio is against notoriety. Just a small party, okay . . . but, all those people! And newspaper coverage! My God, you're brave."

Magdalena grinned. "Well, I've reconsidered one point—the publicity—I'm not having any publicity. I told his society editor to forget about covering the party. Unless, of course, Tullio will agree to the publicity."

"Magdalena, either there will be coverage or there won't be."

Magdalena nodded. "The society editor is invited. If, during the party, Tullio says it's all right for the man to write about it, he will. But, that will be the only decision Tullio will be making. For all the rest, I'll be calling all the shots."

Louise toasted her. The birthday party was forty-eight hours away—Saturday afternoon.

"When do you intend breaking the news to him?"

"Gerhard will tell him he wants to play some golf. He'll get him out on the course very early on Saturday. Then, by the time they get back to *The Walls*, everything will be ready. All the guests will have arrived. Tullio won't suspect a thing until he walks right into it." She sat back and smiled and felt very smug. "It will be the best party these people have ever seen, Louise. They'll never stop talking about it. Tullio will never forget it. And—you'll see—after this party, our whole life will be different. Tullio will realize how much he's been missing. He'll start bringing friends home. We'll start entertaining again, just like we used to do in Orvietto."

"What about those dogs? One look at those dogs, and your guests will faint away."

"Oh, Aleksey's taken care of that. He's already told the guards about the party, and he's told them they should take the whole weekend off. Only one will remain, the one at the main gate. This way, when Tullio gets home from the office tomorrow night, he won't get suspicious, because the guard will be right there at his post—dog and all. Then, on Saturday morning, right after Tullio and Gerhard leave for the club, even that guard will leave."

"Well, it looks like you've thought of everything," Louise said.

"You'll see, Louise. It'll be the best party the area has ever seen. I'll really show them how to entertain. They'll talk about it for a long time. Tullio will love it."

Tullio no longer drove the men to work. The reason was that he feared one of his headaches, and the loss of vision that very often accompanied it, might occur while he was driving. This wouldn't affect him so much if he were driving alone, because then, he could simply pull over to the side of the road for a few minutes; he just didn't like the idea that it might happen with the others sitting in the car with him. He'd already admitted to himself that it was ridiculous vanity that made him hide his condition; it didn't alter his decision, though, because to advertise a weakness wasn't the Barragatto way. To cover up, he told the men: "It's better that we ride the railroad. This way, we can find out a lot more about what's going on. Everybody talks on the trains."

It made sense to Aleksey and Earl—especially to Earl, who learned a great deal about the stock market during his morning journeys. Aleksey enjoyed the evening rides better, because he found some rather good pinochle players among the other commuters. Gerhard didn't care one way or the other; he slept the entire trip, whether it be by car or train.

On the night before his party, Tullio suffered an especially bad headache. Magdalena massaged his temples until the pain lessened, and she was beside herself because he refused to try a new doctor she'd read about. A little while later, he left her asleep in bed while he went to take a swim.

The pool water was heated and it was one of the things Tullio enjoyed most about *The Walls of Jericho*. There'd been no swimming pool in Orvietto. No one had ever thought of such a luxury. He dropped his robe and dove in naked, swimming with abandon, grateful that the awful throbbing behind his eyes had finally stopped. He was in the warm water less than ten minutes when he decided to step out for a cigarette. He lay back on one of the lounges, admiring the view and listening to the soft cooing of some nearby doves. Then, he noticed Nicole. She was sitting on the lounge beside him, sipping from a tall glass.

"How long have you been here?" he asked.

"Long enough," she said, staring at him appreciatively.

"How come you didn't turn the pool lights on? Why were you sitting here in the dark?"

"Perhaps, for the same reason you swim in the dark. It's sexier."

He shrugged. "I guess that's part of it. The crickets . . . the doves . . . all the other little animals of the night . . . they bring a lot of things into perspective that the daylight manages to mix up."

"Like they're talking to you? Giving you advice?"

He grinned. "It sounds a little silly, doesn't it."

"No," she answered. "It doesn't sound silly at all. On the contrary, it makes a lot of sense. I'll bet that owl over there knows a lot more about life than you or I do."

He studied Nicole, the same way he'd studied the little building in Florence. Again, he liked, very much, what he saw. Her blonde hair, which was usually braided like a tiara, was brushed out. It fell fully and loosely below her shoulders. Her green silk wrapper was open and he could see she was naked beneath it. It was time to leave, to go back to the house; but he did not move. And Nicole, knowing he was looking at her, stayed very still.

"Is Gerhard sleeping?"

"Yes, he's fast asleep. And Magdalena?"

"I think so."

"What now, Tullio?"

"I don't know."

"I've been asking Gerhard to leave. I've been telling him I

315

want to see more of the States before returning to Germany, but he keeps saying he has too much work to do here, in New York."

"That's true. We have a lot of things to iron out with the motels."

"Well, I just want you to know that I've been trying to leave," she said. "I've been trying. I know it hasn't been easy for you having me here. It hasn't been easy for me, either."

"I can't say that I'm sorry you're here, Nicole, because that wouldn't be true."

"What are you telling me, Tullio? That you want us here?"

He shook his head. "I don't know what I want anymore."

She gave him a quiet smile. "Only children know what they want."

"Perhaps, that's true," he said. He pulled his robe tightly around him. "Perhaps, that's true."

"You know, Tullio, this is the most we've had to say to one another since I've arrived."

He nodded. "I'm fully aware of that."

"Do you think it's because it's so dark out here? Is that what's making it easier for us to talk?"

"I don't know. It could be."

He could barely see Nicole's face because the selfish moon was so dim and directly behind her. He wanted to see it, though. He wanted to get closer to her. He wanted to sit at the foot of her lounge and touch her. He wanted to study the building in Florence. Quite unexpectedly, he held out his hand. His sudden gesture surprised even himself.

"No, Tullio."

"Please."

"No."

"Why?" he asked her. "All I want is to hold your hand. Nothing else. I swear. Nothing else."

"No."

"Why?"

"Because it means too much to me, and because it doesn't

316

mean enough to you."

"You don't know how I feel, Nicole. You don't know any of the things I'm feeling right now. You might think you do, but you don't." He withdrew his hand and shook his head. "God damn it. What in hell did you come down to the pool for?"

"I was here first," she answered angrily. "I didn't follow you. I had no idea you'd be coming here tonight. I'm sorry. I'll leave."

"No. I'm sorry I said that. I didn't mean it. Really, Nicole, I didn't mean it." He paused.

"On the lung . . . on the tongue . . ."

"What?"

"Never mind. Never mind. It's an old German expression. It loses in the translation." She rose. "I'll leave now, Tullio. Go jump in the pool and cool off again."

"I said I was sorry! What else do you want me to say?"

She sat down again. "We are acting like children, aren't we."

"About before," he said, "I just can't understand why it would be so terrible for you to have held my hand. But, it's all right. Forget about it. It was stupid. Just a stupid thing I suddenly wanted to do. Just for a few seconds. That's all. I don't even know what made me think of such a thing. Here we are, two friends, just . . ."

"We aren't friends, Tullio. We could never be friends."

"Why not? We're certainly not enemies, are we?"

"No, not enemies. But never friends, either."

"Why are you saying such a thing, Nicole?"

"Because I love you. And because I see the way you look at me. So, we can't ever be friends. Not just friends. Let's not kid each other. You can be friends if you've never been lovers . . . and you can be friends if neither of you feels anything for the other any longer . . . and you can be friends if there's no harm in being lovers. But us? We can't be friends."

"You don't know what you're saying. You'll see things differently in the morning."

317

"I know what I'm saying," she answered. "I know exactly what I'm saying. And, so do you."

He wished she would turn so he could see her face better. He said: "I didn't know you felt that way."

"Yes, you did."

"All right. All right. So, I did know how you felt. At least, I had an idea. And, now, I'm trying to make the best of a difficult situation, but you're not helping any."

"Tullio . . . please . . . I want to leave New York. I want to go home. I want you to convince Gerhard that you can handle the motels on your own."

"I can't do that, Nicole. There's hundreds of thousands of dollars invested in this thing. The prefabricated parts . . . everything is so technical . . . I'd mess up everything right now. Gerhard knows that. I need him here . . . at least, for a few more months just until things get rolling. Then, I can take it from there. But, not until then. We'd lose a fortune."

"A few more months? Months? He never told me we would be staying that long."

"What can I say? That's the way it is. It will take months. Not less than two more. More likely, three."

"How cold you just sounded," she said. "How business-like. How matter-of-fact."

"I'm sorry, but there's nothing I can do about it. And, if you should try talking Gerhard into leaving, I might as well warn you, right now, that I'll convince him he has to stay. That's how important these motels are, Nicole. Neither he nor I can afford for him to leave at a time like this."

"But, I can't afford to stay," she answered. "Please. What do you want me to do? Beg?"

"Stop it, Nicole."

"Please! I'm trying to save both our marriages. I'm trying to avoid a lot of grief. I'm trying not to hurt anyone. You just don't understand."

"Yes, I do."

"No, you don't. I know what will happen if I stay here."

318

"Nothing's going to happen," he said.

"I know what will happen," she repeated, "and, this time, it will be all your doing, not mine."

"Stop it!" he shouted.

"Okay, Tullio. I'll stop. But, only if you can look me straight in the eye and say you don't think about me. Only if you can say you don't want me. Only if you can say that you don't look toward my window at night to see if the lights have gone out. Or, try saying that you've never, ever dreamed about me. Or that you've never relived that night. Or that you've never been afraid you might call your wife by my name. Say these things . . . even one of them . . . and I'll stop. Can you tell me even one of these things, Tullio? Can you?"

Under his breath he muttered, "What in hell's the difference," but she heard him, and said:

"So, it's as I thought. Just as I thought."

Now, he was glad he couldn't see her; and he made sure that he couldn't by turning his back to her.

"I love you," she said again. "I know it was insane, coming to you like that . . . in the middle of the night, with Gerhard just a few rooms away . . . But, you wanted me to come. You'd been begging for it all afternoon. Oh, of course, you would never commit yourself. You would never come right out and say it. You could never be that honest. But you wanted me, just as much as I wanted you. It was written all over you. Now you act like I threw myself at you."

"Well, you did, didn't you?"

"But, it was you who did all the urging. It was you who did all the teasing. It was you who did all the promising. You didn't care about the consequences."

"I don't know what kind of consequences you're referring to," he said. "You're the one who was so positive that Gerhard wouldn't wake up."

"I wasn't talking about Gerhard. I was talking about *me*. And you, too, Tullio. Believe it or not. I was talking about how it might affect you, too."

319

"It didn't affect me at all. There were no consequences to me at all."

"Who are you kidding?" she laughed bitterly. "You're not that good an actor. You weren't then; and you're not now. It might have started out as just a fling but it didn't end that way. That's why you had to leave Rothenburg. You couldn't stay another day. Because you felt something inside of you. Because you felt too, too much. Because it was scaring you. You ran. You ran all the way home. You're still scared. You're as afraid of me as I am of you. Tell me that's not true! Say it. Say it."

"I'm going to make myself a drink," he told her. "Do you want one, too?"

"Yes, please. I'd like another one."

Tullio walked into the pool house without looking back. He closed the screen door behind him so the bugs wouldn't fly in and he felt along the wall until he found the light switch. He squinted because the light was so bright.

The cupboards were stocked with almost every brand he could think of. He was surprised. He hadn't thought Magdalena knew so much about liquors.

Louise must have told her what to buy . . . what are all these cases for . . . who's going to drink all of this . . . what's she getting ready for . . . a party . . . a war?

He wondered how the poor were faring during Prohibition.

They must drink something!

He shrugged.

Who cares? That's their problem. I have my own right now.

He shook his head. *No, I can't say even one of those things. Not even one. She's right.*

When he returned to the pool, Nicole had gone.

He looked stupidly at the two glasses. Well, he'd drink them both, but not until after another swim. He placed the glasses alongside the pool's edge so he could reach them and drink a little between laps. Then, he dove in.

He tried to swim. He tried to forget what Nicole had said. He

320

tried, very hard, to simply swim. But, it was like trying to make a hole in water; so he pulled himself up and out of the pool and sat next to it, dangling his legs over the edge. He watched the ripples for a while, but they reminded him of his thoughts because they wouldn't stop; so, he looked away from them. He sipped a little of the whisky. He didn't like it; he was too Italian for anything but wine. He lit a cigarette. He inhaled so deeply that he felt a little dizzy.

Then, it happened: the barking, then a woman's scream.

He stumbled to his feet. "Jesus! The dogs! Nicole!" He began running toward the sounds. "Nicole! Nicole!"

There were gunshots and howling; then, more barking; and then, an abrupt quietness.

Tullio froze in his tracks.

Suddenly, screaming resumed. Screams that made his blood turn to ice. Then, still more gunshots. And more screams, until they ripped the air out of the night. He began running again.

He kept running, but he could barely see where he was going.

He could hear Guido shouting. He could hear some of the guards cursing. He was getting closer. He could hear Nicole. At least one dog was howling. Others were barking. Over everything, her screams wouldn't stop. And, he could not stop yelling: "Nicole! Nicole! Nicole!"

He ran, stumbling through thickets and over bushes and shallow mud ponds. When he reached them, at last, he found himself in a clearing behind the stables. It was nowhere near the guest cottage. He fell to his knees, trying to catch his breath.

"She must have gotten lost," Guido said. A pistol was still smoking in his hand.

Tullio stared at Nicole. She was sitting on the wet grass and sobbing. She was rocking back and forth, her whole body trembling. Her robe was torn and bloody.

"It's not all her blood," one of the guards said. "When Guido shot the dog, it fell on top of her. It's mostly his blood—

the dog's."

"Anybody would get lost on such a dark night," Guido said, "but, I don't know how she wound up all the way down here. It's so far from the cottage."

The guard said, "She shouldn't have been down this way."

"Nicole? Nicole? Are you all right, Nicole?" He bent down. "Are you all right?" He turned toward Guido, then, and said, "Hurry, go call a doctor."

She didn't answer him. She kept rocking and sobbing.

He carried her to the little schoolhouse because it was the closest building that had beds in it. One of the guards followed and one retreated with two of the dogs on leashes.

"Nicole? Are you all right? You'll be okay. You'll be okay. We're getting a doctor. He'll be here soon. It's all over now."

"We always let the dogs exercise for about an hour or so at night," the guard was saying. "We can't keep them tied all the time, Mr. Barragatto. We never expected anybody to come walking down this way this late. We couldn't help it, Mr. Barragatto. How could we know she'd come down this way?"

"Nicole? Talk to me. Say something. It's okay now." All the while he was talking, he was looking to find if and where she'd been bitten.

When Guido returned, Aleksey Kostenov was with him, still in his nightshirt and robe. Kostenov became a little queasy. There was so much blood on her—and Tullio, also, because he'd been carrying her—that he thought they'd both been mauled.

"It's the dog's blood!" the guard shouted. "It's mostly the dog's blood!"

"Oh, my dear God!" Kostenov said. "What's happened here?"

"The driver shot the dogs," the guard said. "He didn't have to shoot them. One word from me, and they would have retreated. He didn't have to shoot them."

"Shut up about those dogs! They shouldn't have been loose!" Tullio shouted. "Get the others off the grounds! I don't want any more dogs here!"

Kostenov sat on a bed opposite Nicole. He hung his head in his hands. He said, again, "Oh, my dear God," and wiped his forehead. "How bad is she?"

"I don't know," Tullio answered. "I can't tell. There's so much blood that I can't tell."

"And you?" he asked Tullio.

"Me? I'm all right."

Aleksey looked around the room. The guard was standing near the door. Guido was by the window. "Where's her husband?" Aleksey asked them. "Where's Herr Moeller?"

The guard gave him a sly look and shrugged, but he didn't say anything; then, he left, and Guido followed him out.

Aleksey Kostenov stiffened.

Nicole stopped sobbing for the first time since Tullio had lifted her from the grass. She sat up.

"You're feeling better now?" Tullio asked her.

She nodded.

"Where were you bitten? Where did they get you?"

"My legs, most. And here." She held up her arm so he could examine her wrist. "They came from out of nowhere. I started screaming. I tried to run away from them, but they began pulling at my robe. They were all around me. I couldn't see where I was running. And then, all of a sudden, Guido was there, shooting at them, and . . ."

"It's all right, Nicole. It's all right. It's all over."

"Oh, God! Thank God Guido got there!"

"Try to relax now. The doctor will be here soon."

"I had to leave, Tullio. I had to," she said. "I had to leave. I had made such a fool of myself, that I couldn't stay there any longer. All those things I said! I'd held them in so long, but I couldn't any longer! Suddenly, I had to leave. I had to run away. I had to."

"Sssh, Nicole, I understand," Tullio said. "I understand. It's all right. It's all right."

"I love you so much . . . I had to say those things. I had to get it all out. I . . ."

"Sssh, Nicole, please . . . Aleksey's here."

"What! What!" She turned sharply and saw Kostenov. She'd thought he'd left with the other man. She looked from him to Tullio. She began to cry again. "Oh, God, no."

"It's all right, Nicole. It's all right. It's all over," Tullio said again. "It's all over."

"Oh, God, Tullio, everything was happening so fast. I'm sorry. I'm sorry."

"I know," he answered, and he kissed her. He didn't care whether Kostenov saw this or not. He knew he should care, but he didn't; and he kissed her again. He kissed her lips; then, her eyes and her throat; and where she'd been bitten on her wrist. "I know," he said, "I know. It was all my fault. I made you run away."

Nicole tried and failed to avoid Kostenov's glare. It made her begin sobbing again, almost as violently as before. She rasped: "Stop, Tullio, stop."

"It was all my fault," Tullio repeated, "all my fault. I was cruel. Any woman would have run away."

Kostenov shouted: "Damn you, Tullio! Don't you have any shame! Get away from her! Her husband might walk in any second, now! Don't you have any brains? Forget about shame . . . carrying on like this . . . right in front of me . . . as though I weren't even here!" He threw his arms up in the air. "You're so wrapped up in yourself that you don't even care how you're embarrassing her, either!"

Tullio eased away from Nicole. He said, "I'm sorry." He stood, and he walked to the far end of the room and stared out the window. He could see Guido coming back. Gerhard was following closely behind and Magdalena was running to keep up with them.

"Where in hell's that doctor?" he asked. "What's taking him so long?"

Chapter Nine

Tullio left the little schoolhouse even before the doctor arrived. He didn't want to watch Gerhard Moeller caress Nicole again, or comfort her. He didn't want to see him next to the bed, brushing her hair from her face. He didn't want to see them together. Nor did he want to hear Aleksey's angry silence. He didn't want to look at Magdalena, either, because he was afraid she might see through him. He returned to the pool and dove into the water to wash off the blood. He didn't care if anyone had noticed he was gone.

From his vantage point, he could see that almost every light on the grounds had been switched on. The gunshots and screams had probably woken everyone, he guessed. Even the nursery and the servants' quarters were lit. Only the pool area was still in darkness; and this is the way he wanted it; he wanted the darkness.

He was lying on one of the lounges when, almost an hour later, Kostenov appeared.

"So, this is where you've been sulking all this time," Aleksey said. "Well, I must admit it's very peaceful here, and you must have a great deal to think about."

"To tell you the truth," Tullio replied, "I wasn't thinking

about anything. I was just relaxing for a while. I like it here. It's as you said, peaceful. Has the doctor gotten here yet? How is she?"

"He's been here and gone. And Frau Moeller is back in the cottage. She's all bandaged up. She got some nasty bites, but it wasn't half as bad as it had looked. It was just as that guard said: mostly the dog's blood. Frau Moeller was more frightened than hurt. He gave her some sleeping powders."

A long, thin shadow crept over the pool area. They looked up and saw Magdalena.

"Well," she said, "it looks like we're all wide awake tonight."

Tullio said, "I can't understand why those dogs were loose. And, why were there only two guards with four dogs? Where are the other guards?"

"They were in the midst of putting the dogs in the run for the weekend," she responded. "We were giving the guards the weekend off. Two of the men had already left, earlier this evening."

"The weekend off?"

"Yes," she replied. "You might as well know, now. I was giving them the weekend off because of tomorrow. We're having a party for you tomorrow. A birthday party. It was to be a surprise. Gerhard was going to keep you at the club until all the guests arrived, then bring you home. But, he'll never leave her alone, now. Not tomorrow, anyway."

He sat up straight. "A party? With guests? How many guests? Is that why there's so much liquor in the pool house?"

"Yes. I thought I might as well tell you about it now. You'll be here tomorrow morning, and you'll see all the comings and goings, all the preparations. You might as well know now, instead of early tomorrow morning, when the caterers get here."

"Caterers! How big a party is this going to be?"

Kostenov replied: "A big one." His eyes had opened wide as he'd said that, and he'd gestured with his palms apart.

"You seem to be more annoyed than surprised," Magdalena told Tullio. "You are annoyed, aren't you?"

"No, no, I just didn't expect anything."

"Well, I thought you might like it. Something different for a change."

He looked at his wife and was genuinely sorry he'd snapped at her. He apologized. He was doing a lot of apologizing tonight, he thought—maybe, too much; but maybe, not enough.

"What do you say we pour ourselves one now?" he asked them. "We'll start our own private party, right now."

"It looks like you two have already started," she said. She'd noticed the glasses at the pool's edge, but neither Tullio nor Aleksey realized that.

"Well, I don't know about him," Aleksey said, "but I've not had anything all night."

"That's right," Tullio said. "He just got here, just before you. What would you like, Aleksey?"

"Some vodka, please. Just vodka."

Tullio looked toward Magdalena. "And you?"

"Nothing. I'm going to bed." She didn't say anything else. She left them abruptly.

"Magda! What's wrong!" He looked toward Kostenov. "What's she angry about?"

"I'm not sure."

Tullio left the pool area and followed her. He called to her and she stopped. "What's the matter with you?" he asked her. "Why'd you leave like that? What's wrong?"

"I think there's a lot wrong, Tullio." She pulled away from him. "A lot! And, it just hit me! Like a bolt of lightning!"

"What?"

"I was just speaking with Gerhard. Just a few minutes ago. Just before I came down to the pool. He told me that this wasn't the first time his wife has gotten out of bed in the middle of the night. He told me that he wakes up sometimes, and finds her gone. He said he has no idea why she does that. Right in the middle of the night. She just gets out of bed and goes

327

wandering." She glared at him. "But, you know why she does that, don't you, Tullio? And now, I know, too. It's to meet you, isn't it?"

"No."

"You were together tonight, Tullio. Don't deny it. Somebody was with you at the pool tonight. It wasn't Gerhard . . . he was fast asleep when Guido went to call him. And, it wasn't Aleksey either. It was Nicole. You and Nicole. Why were you down here together . . . in the middle of the night?"

"We weren't together."

"Since when do you drink from two glasses at once?"

"What?"

"Oh, stop it. I've seen those looks you give her. I've tried to ignore them. I've tried to reason them away. I've tried to give you every benefit of the doubt. I've told myself: No . . . it can't be . . . it's my imagination . . . she's his best friend's wife . . . he wouldn't sink so low!"

"Lower your voice, Magda," he hissed. "Listen to me."

"No. And, if you don't let go of my arm this second, I'll start screaming. And then, I'll go straight to your friend and tell him all about his darling little bride and my husband. I won't wait until the morning to tell him. He'll get the whole story, right now!"

"You're not going to him with any story . . . there is no story."

"Let go of me, I said!"

"Okay! Just calm down. Go back to the house and calm down. I'll be in in a minute. We can talk then."

"Don't come to the house," she told him. "I don't want you there."

"Now, you're really acting like a child."

"And, make sure she's off these grounds the first thing in the morning. If she's not packed and gone, I'm going to tell Gerhard everything. And, don't think I'm bluffing, either. I want them out of here! It's them or me. Take your choice."

He knew that Kostenov had heard everything. He shouted back to him: "Aleksey, see what you can do with her! I give up!" He pushed her aside, harder than he'd meant to, and she fell. He stared down at her, but he didn't help her up; he hurried away, instead, and walked toward the house, his head throbbing worse than ever. He looked back once, and Aleksey had already run to her.

Aleksey Kostenov was good with words. He'd always been, since the days he was a professor, spouting Plato to unreceptive students—but, he didn't know how to approach Magdalena. He'd never imagined he would find himself in such a situation. How does one convince a wife of her husband's fidelity when one doesn't believe in it, oneself? He would try, though. He had no choice. He cleared his throat and shook his head and asked somberly, "Magdalena, aren't you ashamed of yourself?"

"I? I have nothing to be ashamed of. It's him. Him."

"No, it's not. It's you. I'm astounded. I never expected such unreasonable behavior from you. From any other woman, maybe . . . but never from you."

"Oh, Aleksey, please."

"Go right ahead and cry. You have good reason to. Not that Tullio's given you any reason to. You've brought it on yourself. Here you are, accusing your husband of betrayal just because a young woman walks in her sleep—or something like that—and just because you see some glasses by a pool."

"Walks in her sleep?"

"It's not impossible. There could be dozens of reasons why Nicole Moeller walks around at night. Who cares what they are? If you ask me, it's probably something very personal between her and her husband . . . After all, they are newlyweds. They might have a lot of things to iron out . . . if you know what I mean. You do know what I mean . . . don't you? Do I have to spell it out?"

"Do you really believe that, Aleksey?"

"What do you think?" he replied; but, not waiting for her

answer, continued: "And, that observation you made about those glasses! For heaven's sake, Magdalena, they could have been sitting there since this afternoon! Anybody could have been drinking from them. I certainly would not want to be a defendant with you as a member of my jury. You would send me to the gallows, just over some circumstantial evidence such as glasses! How do you know how long those glasses were at the pool? When was the last time you, yourself, were down at the pool?"

Magdalena looked at him blankly. This was the time to stop, he decided. He shouldn't press his luck. At least she was guessing now. At least she was trying to believe him.

He took her by the hand and said: "Come, let's go in. We've all had a bad night. What went on tonight was enough to unnerve anyone. Besides, you already had the party on your mind. You weren't yourself. At least, one good thing's come out of it, though—there will be no more dogs on the estate."

She began to cry again. "But, he still looks at her in a way that I don't like, Aleksey."

"Man is a hunter. Do you think Tullio is any different than any other man? So what! So, he looks! So what!"

"Oh, Aleksey, I don't know what to say to him."

"Don't worry about Tullio. He'll understand. We were all a little nervous tonight. He'll understand."

"Oh, God, I don't know what to say to him."

"Don't say anything. Not tonight, anyway. Let it all blow over."

"You expect me to walk in there and say nothing at all, just as though nothing's happened? Be realistic, Aleksey."

"If he should say anything, just tell him that there's a chance you might have been mistaken, and that you can talk about it some other time, but not tonight. I guarantee you: he'll jump at the opportunity to drop the whole subject."

It isn't easy for any man to confront himself. It was especially difficult for Tullio Barragatto; but, tonight, he had

330

to. Tonight, it was necessary to take stock. He thought back to the Main Valley, and to the *Romantische Strasse*, and to Rothenburg. It was as though Nicole had cast a spell on him that night. Every gesture and touch and look had been an invitation, and he'd not cared about the consequences. He'd simply had to have her, so, he'd charmed, and he'd promised, and he'd allowed himself to be seduced.

She'd been, in every way, more than he bargained for. And, when she'd left his bed, the thought of her had lingered. It had followed him all the way back to Orvietto. It had come back and forth into his dreams and had reappeared when he'd awakened in the mornings. It had clung tightly during the ocean voyage; and, there were times it had even stubbornly interfered when he was with Magdalena, here, within *The Walls of Jericho*.

But, how could she have known? he wondered. Did women have a sixth sense about these things? He hadn't been sure about how she'd felt, not until tonight; so, how could she have known what was gnawing at him? Had she known it from the very beginning? And, if she had, why had she agreed to come to *The Walls* on her honeymoon?

Was that why she'd asked him: "What now, Tullio?" Was it because she'd already reckoned with the truth?

What now, Nicole?

I've been keeping Gerhard here, purposely. There! That's the truth! I can manage without him. He's already shown me everything I need to know. I just didn't want you to leave. If you did, I might never see you again.

"Tullio. Tullio? Are you awake?"

He was startled. He hadn't heard Magdalena walk in. "Yes, I am."

"About what just happened out there," she said, "maybe, I was jumping to conclusions, and . . ."

She was very surprised when he answered, "Okay, just forget about it. Forget about it. It's all over."

She was more than surprised. She was perplexed. Kostenov seemed to know her husband much better than she did. Tullio

331

was reacting just the way Kostenov had predicted.

"Look at that," she said. "It's almost dawn already."

Tullio Barragatto's birthday celebration was a Gold Coast party. There were bootleggers in dinner jackets and judges in golf pants. Ladies brought their pets: they brought birds-of-paradise and monkeys whose pelts had been dyed to match their dresses; they brought Great Danes and dragged baby cheetahs on jeweled leashes. There were so many limousines coming and going that no one could keep count. When there was no more room in the driveway, the automobiles spread over the lawns until it looked like a vast parking lot. Chauffeurs sat on top of the roofs of the polished vehicles, watching their employers frolic in the grass and at poolside and in the back seats of their stretched-out sedans; and waitresses with trays of bubbling champagne and waiters with truffles and sweetbreads were everywhere. It was a conglomeration of old money and new money and guest-cottage guests and guests' guests. It was worthy of the North Shore and of the twenties.

It began sanely enough, with all the guests crowding around the luncheon tables behind the main residence—but, it was August, and it was hot and hazy and humid; and the iced cocktails were so cooling; and the pool was so refreshing; and the high-ceilinged rooms were so very inviting, that, before early evening, the party had spilled into every quarter of the estate. A jazz quartet took over a dressing room. A *ménage à trois* claimed the nursery. A brunette playing Lady Godiva romped through the kitchens on a polo pony. Lovers slid under tables; and queens came out of their closets and dared their wives to indulge.

It was easy, amidst the pandemonium, for journalists from competitive publications to mix with the invited guests. They sprawled on the patios, and over the steps atop divans, and into the bedrooms; and they melted, like globs of candlewax, into every niche and corner they could find. They recorded everything that they heard, and everything that they saw, and everything that they surmised, and everything that they imagined. It was the easiest party they'd ever crashed; all the guards had been dispersed, and no one was at the gates, checking invitations.

After the first few hours of the party, Aleksey Kostenov had retreated to *Swansgarten* with the children and their nurse. He'd not returned. Magdalena, wide awake and tipsy from drinking and the excitement, had not even noticed they were gone. The music thrilled her, especially the tunes being played by the Latin band she'd hired. They reminded her of the gypsy music in the caravans. One of the guitarists played flamenco style, and this started her dancing. She spun around and stamped her feet and clapped her hands above her until dozens followed her, urging her to quicker and wilder tempos; so, she snapped her fingers and clicked her heels and shouted, "Did anyone here ever know I used to be a gypsy! Well, I was! And, it wasn't so long ago! And this is the way we danced, and we courted, and we made love on our wedding nights! With the dance! This is the way we did it!" And Tullio had to pull men away from her who were reaching out as she'd swirl in front of them; but she was teasing them purposely, and didn't care how angry this made him.

Finally he could stand it no longer and pulled her angrily away. "Stop it!" he whispered angrily. "You're not a gypsy anymore, you're my wife."

"You don't want me to be a gypsy, and you don't want me to be too American," she snapped back. "What do you want, Tullio?"

"I told you, I want you to behave like my wife."

All the while they were arguing he was carrying her upstairs to her room. She only offered token resistance; the truth was she had had enough of champagne and dancing. He laid her on the bed and she fell asleep immediately. He locked her in for safety. He did not trust the Gold Coast guests.

As he made his way back downstairs he barely missed stepping on various bodies in clusters of two or more. It was worse on the main floor and he was glad to make it out to the garden where the night air was fresh. He found some flat champagne, drank it straight from the bottle, then threw the empty bottle into a fountain, relishing the sound of glass shattering. Then, he lay flat on his back on the dewy grass and stared up at the sun and guessed it must be almost four. After a few minutes, he rolled over and started to crawl in circles until a grasshopper jumped in front of him. He heard, "Follow me. I'll show you the way." He began creeping after it, and after he'd gone about a hundred yards, he saw the guest cottage directly ahead. That is when he stood and half-walked and half-ran the rest of the way. When he reached it, he fell into the little foyer, and he stumbled through the other rooms until he reached the bedroom. Nicole was sleeping in the bed; she'd not come to the party. Gerhard was in a club chair, into which he'd fallen unconscious after drinking all night long. Nicole jumped awake.

"Tullio! Oh, my God! Get out of here!" Her voice was hoarse.

"I don't even know how I got in here."

"Get out!" she rasped.

"I'm going. I'm going," he answered. "I'm going." He held up his hand and gestured to assure her and repeated, "I'm going." But, he did not back away; he moved closer, instead, and lowered his hand to her breast.

She raised her hand and held it on top of his. Then, she told him, "Please leave now."

He stepped back and turned away, and walked out of her bedroom, through the outer rooms and away from the cottage. He was unsteady on his feet and he stumbled a few times. He didn't bother going back to the house because he didn't think he could reach it. He lay down under a shade tree and slept until he felt Gerhard and Guido lifting him to his feet. By then, it was six-thirty, Sunday evening; all the guests had left; Kostenov had returned and Rebecca was crying because she'd never seen her father in such a condition; and Nicole

Grynszpan Moeller was directing her personal maid on how to pack her trunks. So ended the first party at the *Walls of Jericho*.

"Are you proud of yourself?" Kostenov asked him.

Tullio didn't answer. He just sat down quietly where Gerhard had placed him. He heard Guido snicker before leaving, but he didn't comment upon that, either. His head felt like it was bursting.

Kostenov continued. "It's not every day that a young girl comes home and finds her father sprawled out in a drunken stupor, totally exposed."

"Exposed?" Tullio said.

"You've made quite an impression on your sons, too. They're the ones who found you, you know. The children. Stefano thinks it's all very funny. Carlo doesn't know if he's supposed to laugh or cry. But, Rebecca, she's the one who's really upset. Imagine what she must think of you. Tch, tch, tch." He picked up a newspaper, then, and walked out of the room in disgust.

Tullio remembered, now: when Gerhard was waking him up, Guido had been saying something about fastening his trousers; but, he could not remember having opened them. As hard as he tried, he could not remember.

Gerhard was now sitting opposite him, smiling from ear to ear. He knew that, at any moment, hilarious laughter would come spilling out of him; and it did.

At that second—as soon as Gerhard started laughing—Tullio remembered having gone into the guest cottage. He wondered if he'd opened his zipper while he'd still been in their bedroom, if he'd shown himself to Nicole, or if he'd waited until he'd left. This part of his night was a total blank. A lot that went on at that party was still very clear, some was fuzzy, but this escaped him completely.

Tullio looked so bewildered that Gerhard could not stop laughing.

"Do you think you'll make it to work tomorrow?" Gerhard

asked him. Then, he threw his head back and started laughing again.

"Where's my wife?"

"She's sleeping it off," Gerhard answered. "I sure have to hand it to her. She really knows how to throw a party. And, she's some dancer! I didn't know she could dance like that! You should have seen your face when she was dancing! You were turning green. You do remember that, don't you?"

"Yes, I remember."

Aleksey stormed in again. He slapped one newspaper down in front of them. The reporters who'd left the party early had already printed what they'd seen. "For somebody who doesn't like publicity, you certainly have made a turnabout," he said. "And, you should see what they've written in the other tabloids!"

"They didn't waste any time, did they?" Tullio grunted.

Gerhard grinned. "It serves you right for reading the competition," he said. "Stick to your own papers the next time, Aleksey."

Aleksey was in no mood for jokes, though, and he left the room again.

Chapter Ten

Tullio did not see Nicole again until Tuesday. It was the
Feastday of the Assumption, and he always closed the office on
holy days. He would have gone to Capits Rock, but it was
raining; so, he loitered about the estate. Magdalena went to the
hairdresser's and Gerhard had wandered off by himself.
Aleksey left for *Swansgarten* to play some chess with Earl. They
found themselves sitting at the lunch table all alone.

"I'm sorry about the other night," he said.

She nodded.

"Gerhard told me that you're almost all packed and that
you'll be leaving this week. I think you should wait until the
bandages are off. There's no use in rushing. A few more days
wouldn't make any difference."

"Please, Tullio. Let's not go into that."

"Well, I suggested the same thing to Gerhard."

She looked at him with a plea in her eyes.

"I'm not going to try to talk you into staying," he said, "and
I won't try to convince Gerhard to stay, either. But, I really
think you should wait until the doctor can take off those
bandages. That's all. I promise. After that, I won't say anything
at all. You'll just leave, and that will be that."

"Just like that?"

"Yes," he answered. "Just like that."

"How easily you can turn it on and off, Tullio. It must be very nice to be a water faucet. On, off. On, off. On, off. Do you run hot and cold, too? One night, you deny that there's anything at all between us. A half-hour later, you're almost making love to me in front of Aleksey. Two nights ago you come stumbling into my bedroom. Now, you say I can leave, and that will be that. You are remarkable." She put down her napkin and poured some coffee for the both of them. "I wish I could be like you," she added, "but, I can't be that way. I know what I feel. And I say what I'm really thinking, if at all possible. That means not denying what's on my mind. Not denying it to myself, especially. But you: either you're living in and out of a dream world, or you're what I said, a water faucet."

"I didn't deserve that," he said. "Right now, all you're doing is throwing stones."

"Am I? Well, I'm going to tell you something, Tullio. Please listen to me very well, because I'm sure I'll never say these things again."

"All right, Nicole. But, when you're finished talking, I have a few things to say to you, too."

"After you left Rothenburg, I told Gerhard I wasn't in love with him, and I broke our engagement. A few months later, he came to Antwerp, and we got together again. I'd had time to sort things out by then. I'd come to the conclusion that, perhaps, I hadn't fallen in love with the stranger I'd met . . . that, perhaps, it was some kind of ridiculous obsession. At least, that's what I'd talked myself into thinking. I'd told myself: After all, he's the only man you've ever known besides Gerhard . . . and he's so different . . . so exciting . . . get hold of yourself . . . you'll never see him again. But Gerhard is someone real, someone you can count on to be there when you need him, and you can learn to love him, all over again, the way you used to . . . or, the way you used to think you did. So, I agreed to marry him.

338

"I did tell him the truth, though. Oh, I didn't mention anything about you, because that would have hurt him too much, but I did tell him the truth. I told him I wasn't sure. He said: 'That's all right, Nicole. I'll *make* you love me. You let *me* worry about that.'

"I remember how upset I was when he told me we had to come to New York on our honeymoon. But, he told me how necessary it was. He started talking all about the motels, all about those damned motels. I calmed down. I thought: Well, here's my chance to see if I'm really over it. Here's my chance. It's now or never. The past is the past. And I'm married now. And, he's very good to me.

"Well, I was wrong. I knew I was wrong from the very minute I saw you on the dock."

Gerhard came into the room. They looked at each other, not knowing if he'd heard anything.

He was holding a bottle of beer. He said: "Judging from the expressions on your faces, you two must have been talking about something very serious." He faced his wife, then, and said, "You've told him, right?"

"No," she answered, "I haven't."

"Then, I'll tell him, myself," he replied. Turning toward Tullio, he said, "We're going to have our marriage annulled. We decided that this morning. No, I shouldn't say that we decided that. It's all Nicole's decision. It shouldn't be too difficult. It was a civil ceremony, you know. It shouldn't be difficult at all."

Since this was the most unlikely announcement he could have anticipated, Tullio was speechless.

Nicole excused herself and left them.

Gerhard said to him, "You look absolutely flabbergasted."

"I am."

"Well," Gerhard added, "if it will make you feel any better, so am I. Don't let my outward appearance fool you."

"An annulment," Tullio said, as though he were talking to himself. "An annulment?"

"I figure that the best thing to do, at this point, is to go along with her. Leave here. She'll come to her senses. She's just a little mixed up. I know Nicole. All I have to do is give her a little time to think it over." He also left then, just as abruptly as his wife had.

What was there to do except to pour himself some wine; and more, when that was finished? He wondered if Nicole were going to tell him of her decision, or if she were just going to leave *The Walls* and disappear. She had to have realized that Gerhard would have told him—if not now, then, certainly, when the annulment was a fact. What then? Had she intended waiting, and getting in touch with him when the annulment came through? And, if that were her intention, what could she hope to accomplish? Of course, there was also the possibility that she was just about to tell him when Gerhard walked in.

Yes, that's it. She was going to tell me, but Gerhard did it for her. That's what happened. Gerhard did it for her. I think that's what must have happened.

He wondered what he would have said to her if she'd told him while they were still alone. Then, he wondered what else she would have said to him.

There was no point in speculating, because he had no answers. He wanted an answer, though. He wasn't sure why, but he wanted an answer.

Salvatore Crispino would be returning to America soon. He'd made sure the news would reach the *patrono,* because he still didn't know what the deal between the old man and Benedetto had been, and he didn't want to come back to Tullio with no information.

Hoping to run into the chieftain, Salvatore had made himself available in all of the man's known haunts. He could be seen at all hours in the cafes of Orvietto, as well as in its gambling rooms; and, each time he went home, he asked if he'd received any messages, hoping to find an invitation to the house on the hill. Still, he'd made no contact, and by now, he was starting to give up hope.

He was mulling over a glass of wine one evening in a cafe, wondering how he could arrange some kind of accidental meeting, when Italo Filippo Fallanca walked in, came directly to his table, and asked permission to sit with him.

I should have known you'd show up in your own sweet time.

They covered all the niceties . . .

. . . first, the weather—"I don't remember such a hot August. Do you, Don Salvatore?"

"No, I don't."

"Well, that means you'll have a good crop, thank God." He lifted his glass and toasted him.

Salvatore toasted him back. *Drop dead.*

. . . then, the local gossip—"I imagine you've heard that the old woman finally confessed to poisoning our food that night. She told the whole story on her death bed."

"Yes, I heard."

"Tch, tch, tch. And, your poor brother . . . he had to get the brunt of it. What a waste."

"Yes . . . Benedetto never had any luck."

. . . lastly, politics—"Did you read what Mussolini said today? He said, 'The crowd is like a woman.'"

"Yes, I read that."

"I hope he's right. Because if he is, he'll have to keep looking over his shoulder for the rest of his life."

He's killing you off one by one, isn't he?

. . . then, came the business at hand—Fallanca assumed the position. He bent forward, planted both elbows firmly on the table with his forearms resting on it and his palms straight down. He looked Salvatore squarely in the eyes and asked: "What does your cousin think he's doing? Our deal never included the Beckmann wines, or the LoGiudice wines, or the Pire wines either. What does he take me for? An idiot!"

What was the deal?

"He's taking advantage of my good nature."

Salvatore had moved closer because he'd known that these

341

words would be hushed. He knew, also, that the man was waiting for some kind of reply; but, now was not the time to give one.

Fallanca continued. "I get reports . . . reports that I don't like. My man, Pace . . . he tells me that he approaches the others and they all tell him the same thing. They tell him to talk to Tullio Barragatto. They say that Tullio Barragatto handles this part of their business for them." He slapped the table hard and people from the nearby tables all looked at him, but quickly looked away. "I's got to stop! That wasn't our deal!"

What was the deal? What was it? Come on, keep talking. What was it? Keep talking. What was the deal? I can't answer until you tell me. Keep talking, damn you!

"I made it very clear to Benedetto that night . . ."

. . . But he never got the chance to write us . . . What did you make clear to him?

"Barragatto . . . he saves my son's life . . . so, I owe him . . ."

Your son's life! What!

". . . but, that's where the debt ends. It doesn't include anybody else."

Is that what it was? Your son's life? A debt? Is that what it was, you scum? Is that what it was?

"So! So, what does he do? He takes advantage!"

Salvatore sat back, poured more wine, and said: "I'll tell my cousin of your dissatisfaction. There's a chance he might have misinterpreted Benedetto's letter."

Fallanca sat back also. "See that he gets the message straight this time," he said. Then, he said, "It's getting late. I have to go, now." He stood. "It's good that we had this little talk."

Salvatore stood also.

Fallanca added: "Oh, my congratulations. I heard you've just had a baby boy."

"Yes. Thank you."

Salvatore Crispino watched the man leave the cafe. He had two bodyguards with him. Another waited in his car with

342

the driver .

Il Duce . . . he's killing you off one by one . . . just like he said he would. You're afraid of your own shadow, Fallanca. You're scared to death. You all are. The whole lot of you.

He relaxed and breathed deeply. He could return to New York now. The vineyards were in good shape. There were enough cousins left in Orvietto to see to that; and, if they knew about nothing else, they knew the grape—the vineyards were in very good shape. Moreover, he had a son now; he wasn't the last Crispino anymore—and, since he and his wife had reconciled (really reconciled), who could tell?—there might even be more sons in the future! And, finally, he knew how North American Distributors stood with Carmine Pace. Finally! Now, he could go back. He wrote Tullio that same evening. He told him all he'd learned, and he added:

Fallanca means business. He's fuming. Don't press your luck. Let LoGiudice and Beckmann and Pire fend for themselves. They'd never walk a tightrope for us. The important thing is that *we're* going to have a free ride. *We* don't have to deal with Pace if *we* don't want to, but keep up your present stance, and the debt might be cancelled. I'll see you in about a month and we'll talk.

"I see you're all packed. Magdalena told me you'll be leaving tomorrow."

"Yes, early tomorrow morning. I thanked her for her hospitality. She's really been a very gracious hostess."

He sat atop one of the trunks. He asked, "What are you going to do if this annulment goes through? Where will you go?"

"If? There are no if's about it, Tullio. Gerhard promised me he would cooperate. He won't contest it. I trust him. He'll keep his word." She paused and looked at him. "Has he said anything contrary to you?"

He didn't answer. He asked again, "What will you do?

343

Where will you go?"

"I'll go home, back to Belgium."

"To Antwerp?"

"Yes."

"Living with your parents again?"

"Yes."

"Well . . . if that's what you really want. Is it, Nicole? Is that what you want to do?"

"What else, Tullio? What would you suggest?"

"I can't make any suggestions. It's up to you. It's your decision. It's all up to you."

It was now or never, she thought. She had to ask him now: "Do you love me, Tullio? Do you love me at all? Oh, I know you don't feel the same way that I do. But, is there any love there at all? Any, at all? I'd like to know that before I leave. I don't want to go away wondering."

"I'm married, Nicole."

She feigned a smile and said, "Nobody is more aware of that than I am. And, believe it or not, nobody's more reconciled to it, either. But, that's not what I asked you. I asked if you love me."

"Yes! All right? I do! All right?"

"And, your wife? Do you love her?"

"Yes," he answered, "a lot more. Much more than you think."

"Don't be angry," Nicole told him. "It was just something that I had to know. It's such a torture to have to guess about things like that. Don't be angry." She touched his face with the back of her hand. "Thank you for telling me the truth."

"There's nothing to thank me about."

"Yes, there is. At least, now, I know what to do."

"Which is?"

"To wait. To go home and wait."

"For what?"

"For things to change . . . and they will . . . and, I'll be there, right there, waiting for you."

"Don't."

"I will wait for you, Tullio."

"Don't wait for me, Nicole. I won't be leaving my wife. And, I don't want you to think, even for one moment, that that might ever happen. Now, I'm being as honest with you as I can possibly be. Be smart, and listen to what I'm saying. Don't waste any time waiting around for something that's not going to be. Get the annulment, if you have to. And, go back to Antwerp, if you have to. But, don't wait around for me. Make a new life for yourself. Meet somebody else and marry him and have children."

"If you let me wait too long, I just might do that. But, even then, all you'll have to do is say the word . . . and I'll leave them all . . . husband, children, everybody. So, don't let me wait too long, Tullio."

"Nicole! You're insane! This whole conversation is insane! I'm sorry I even came in to talk to you! I should have let you leave without a word!"

"But, you didn't, Tullio. You couldn't. You couldn't stay away from me today. Not on my last day here. Not any more than I could have stayed away from you. If you hadn't come to me, I would have come to you. I don't know how, but I would have managed. There were just too many things that had to be said. Too much that I had to know. Too much that I had to make sure that you know." She moved toward him then, and held both his hands. "So, make love to me, Tullio. Right here. Right now. Because it's going to be such a long, long time before we see each other again."

"We might never see each other again, Nicole."

"I'll take that chance." She kissed him. "I'll take that chance, Tullio. I'll take whatever chance I have to."

He dared not try to fool himself or her. This is why he'd come to the guest cottage. He wanted her. He'd lain awake all night, and he knew how much he wanted her and so did she; and he feared he might never see her again.

He held her closely and began to caress her. He almost hoped

345

they'd never meet again—because she was trouble; because she could be so much trouble—but, he definitely feared it, also.

Nicole and Gerhard left the next morning. Kostenov's chauffeur drove them to the dock. Their ship sailed in late afternoon.

The Wine-Runner

Chapter One

August dies unwillingly, with thunderclaps and lightning and summer storms and one last burst of hellish heat. The Labor Day weekend comes then, and people look at themselves, and recognize that they are one year older. Those most hit by this feeling are discontented lovers and parents of school-age children. Since Tullio Barragatto was both, he was especially melancholy during this September of 1926.

Tullio could not claim, in any way, to be a victim of unrequited love. He was not discontented, in that sense of the word. On the contrary, the women of his heart were enraptured by him. He admitted this matter-of-factly, but without conceit, because he didn't know what they saw in him. Since he was neither unintelligent nor blind, he was forced to realize that he was handsome, well-built, and had a certain amount of charm. Still, he could easily think of a number of men more striking than himself, so this offered no clue to the reason for his appeal. He probably had that special something that Bella had once mentioned, he decided; and only women understood it and recognized it. Whatever it was, he suspected that he would be better off without it. In that way, he would not have two women who loved him very much; and he, subsequently, might not want the both of them so much, in return. This, he admitted also—that he wanted them both: Magdalena and Nicole. If that be an illogical wish—to have them both; then, he was a fool. And, if that be unfair—to own both their hearts—then, he was selfish. There, in that realization, lay his discontent.

Aside from their physical beauty, neither woman was lacking in desirable qualities. Still, each had an extra touch that the other didn't. So, even though they were ideal when they were apart, if they could be fused, there was no doubt in his mind that they would make one perfect female. And, if there were such a thing—the perfect female—it was man's God given right to pursue her. It was the same as an artist's right to mix his paints for that one perfect hue; or a chef's to blend his herbs; or a poet's to form his rhyme. Therefore, Tullio Barragatto had the right to both Nicole and Magdalena. He had the right to mix them and blend them and join them at will so they would be made perfect. At least, this is how he reasoned; and this is what he told himself so many times that he began to believe it.

Yet, how could his desire for both women be realized if the annulment might not, in fact, go through? Surely, there was no valid reason for one, and if Gerhard wanted to block it, there was no way it could come about.

There was nothing to do but wait. One of them would be in touch with him soon, and there was no way he could find out about the annulment until then. It would be difficult, because he'd always been impatient, but he had no choice.

He was a businessman, though, and he had to be practical. Even if the annulment should come through, he could never chance Gerhard's discovering anything about Nicole and himself. If he did, that would be the end of everything—the prefabricated parts, the motels, everything! Gerhard wouldn't care how much money was involved; he'd chuck it all. Gerhard was not one to cross.

And, if Magdalena should find out? Magdalena? He could

never chance that loss. He would not want to live through that. Anything but that.

September—it would be a month of waiting . . . just waiting . . . a long month. He'd always liked September before.

When the long month ended, the Island exploded into the beauty that October brings, and Tullio's spirits were raised. He started looking forward to the weekends at home. He enjoyed taking Rebecca sailing, and Stefano horseback riding, and Carlo fishing. He liked early evening strolls with Magdalena, and chess games with Aleksey, and having the Asheleys for Sunday afternoon barbecues. And, he was certain that, any day now, he would be hearing from Nicole.

Then, November came. Other than the regular dispatches from Orvietto and Milan, the only mail he received from Europe was the letter from his cousin, and that news floored him.

Fallanca! Of all people! The father of Giulio Fallanca!

The revelation was bittersweet. He'd not played the leopard, after all. It had not been his finesse, or his courage, or his cunning that had kept Pace from his door. He'd merely been collecting a debt, one that he'd not even known about. The other wine barons didn't really owe him a thing. They'd soon realize this, because they'd all be approached again, in the very near future; and Pace would probably tell them to check, once more, with Tullio Barragatto.

Pace might even laugh. He wouldn't mention the debt. Such things weren't done. Still, he might say to them: Listen, you get in touch with Barragatto again. I think you'll find that he no longer gives a damn whether you sell us your wine or not.

They would. One by one, they would contact him.

What would he tell them? That they were on their own? That it was every man for himself? That he'd reached some private agreement with Pace, and that they should try doing the same? Surely, this is what Salvatore was advising. Or, would he tell them flatly that nothing had changed?

In either case, he still had time. Fallanca would give

Salvatore enough time to get back to New York and deliver the message in person. In the meanwhile, it was very nice to feel so safe. He wouldn't have to look over his shoulder, or suspect every stranger that came close, or skip a heartbeat with every loud noise. He was under Fallanca's protection. He was free—completely—for the first time in years. And, it would last until just before Christmas, because that was when Salvatore's ship would dock.

And, by then, he was positive he would have heard from Nicole.

But, he thought this point over. It was very possible, he reasoned, that Nicole could not take the chance to write. Of course, she would send the letter to the office, not to the estate; but, there was always the possibility of someone else's opening it. That would be improbable, because nobody would open an envelope marked Personal; still, she was intelligent enough not to risk it. She would wait, he decided. She would wait until the annulment was a fact. Then, with no way that Gerhard could interfere in her life, she would have nothing to fear.

She's smart. Too smart to be impatient.

Having come to that conclusion, Tullio would rather not hear anything at all now, not even from Gerhard. If Gerhard had not succeeded in changing Nicole's mind, as he'd said he would, he would be too disconcerted to mention it. He wouldn't want to talk about it, not for a while, anyway; so, silence was the best news Tullio could hope for.

Christmas was grand with Salvatore and his family back. Magdalena decorated the big house with garlands and lights, and, in every room, there was the hint of spruce. The children had helped her with the decorating, and they were especially proud when visitors would comment upon it.

There were lots of visitors to the estate lately. Tullio's birthday party had brought that about. There was no longer any sense in trying to hide. In that way, the party had changed this aspect of Magdalena's life.

Tullio liked the way Americans celebrated Christmas. It was especially festive within the *Walls of Jericho* because Magdalena, knowing how much he missed the old country, combined the traditions of his childhood with the new ways. There was a decorated tree in his living room; but, there was a Nativity scene there, also. The children looked forward to a visit from Santa Claus. The feasting on Christmas Day was sumptuous; but, on Christmas Eve, after midnight mass, every kind of seafood he could think of was on his table. There was nothing she'd overlooked. She knew this, and she knew that her husband was glad he'd married her.

Jimmy Walker was the mayor of New York. A sign of the times, he was flamboyant and loud, and he winked at the law of the land. There was as much bootlegged liquor in City Hall as there was in any speakeasy on the streets. His escapades made front-page news, and the people read of his antics on a daily basis, the same as they read about the great parties on the Gold Coast. On Christmas morning, as Tullio finished reading about another outlandish thing the mayor had done, Magdalena brought in the Christmas cards. She'd not opened any of them until now, having wanted to save them all for this day.

"Oh, here's one from Gerhard," she said, and handed it to Tullio. "I wonder how they're doing," she added, and she began looking through the other cards.

The greetings message was in German. Across the bottom, Tullio read: "Congratulate me. Nicole expects a baby at the end of May." He stared dumbly at the card for a few seconds. He left the table then. He said he was tired and that he wanted to get more sleep.

To reach the back stairs to the bedrooms, Tullio had to pass the study. Salvatore was waiting for him there.

"Tullio, what do you say we talk?"

From his tone of voice, Tullio knew that Salvatore wanted to discuss the Pace situation. "Right now?"

"Yes, right now. You know what I want to talk about and,

every time I bring up the subject, you change it. We can't avoid it anymore."

He knew his cousin was right. He couldn't put off his decision any longer. Any day now, the other wine men's attorneys would be coming to him. He had to make up his mind. He had to be ready with his answer. He listened to Salvatore talk, and everything the young lawyer said made sense. His logic was pure and concise and detached from everything but the facts.

Yet, Salvatore Crispino had picked the wrong moment to force a decision from his cousin. Tullio had just lost too much when he'd read Gerhard's card; and Tullio was not accustomed to losing, especially with women.

He said to Salvatore: "I made a pact with those men in Orvietto. I won't go back on it here."

"What in hell are you, suicidal?"

"No, I'm not suicidal. But, I'm not about to crawl, either. Anyway, it's just a matter of time before the Fascists get complete control over there. You just said that Mussolini is killing them off one by one, didn't you? Well, if that's true, then it's just a matter of time. All we have to do is hold off a little bit longer. Mussolini will do the rest. He'll get rid of the scum, once and for all."

Salvatore replied: "There are some strong indications, lately, that a lot of the New York families have been starting to operate independently. If that trend continues, whatever Mussolini does over there won't do us any good at all over here."

Tullio had also heard this rumor; but he said and believed, "They'll never be completely independent. Never *completely*. It's impossible. Anyway, we'll cross that bridge if and when we reach it."

His cousin said evenly: "They'll kill you, Tullio."

"I don't think so."

"I'm the one who sat across from Fallanca, not you. And, I know what I saw written all over his face. There won't be another warning."

"I'm going to sleep."

"To sleep? You're going to sleep? I tell you I think somebody's going to kill you, and you answer that you're going to sleep?"

"Don't get excited," he told Salvatore. "I have an idea, and, if it works—which it will—nobody's going to get hurt. Just let me formulate it in my mind, and I'll explain the whole thing to you. But, right now, I'm going to sleep."

Tullio did not sleep as soon as he returned to his room. Instead, he wrote a letter to Erich Veidt, in care of Gerhard Moeller. Then, he wrote another letter, this to Gerhard, himself. He marked them both: PERSONAL AND CONFIDENTIAL. At the end of Gerhard's letter, he postscripted, "Received your card. Congratulations!" He thought to write also, "Regards to Nicole," but he changed his mind. Then, he went to sleep, because there was nothing else he could do.

The next day, Tullio told Magdalena that he would be leaving for Europe in a week or so. He promised her that he would return by the end of March. Once again she pleaded with him to take her but he insisted that she not leave the children.

"If you can put off the trip until summer, we can all go with you," she said.

"That would be nice," he answered, "but the business I have to take care of can't hold that long." He was starting to miss her already. Even now, as he was checking his passport, he wished there were some way he could avoid leaving her.

"The last time you said you'd be gone only a short while, I didn't see you again for two years."

He'd not forgotten that. He kissed her and replied: "I tell you what: if I'm not back by the end of March, you can hop on the first ship leaving New York and come and get me."

"I will." She returned his kiss then, but hers was much more gentle than his had been, and her touch made him shiver.

He was very tempted to reconsider. He didn't want to be separated from her again, no matter for how short a time. The more he looked at her, the more he wanted to stay. And, the more she began to touch him in her own special way, the more he started to vacillate between calling the whole trip off and saying: Come with me, Magda . . . forget about the children . . . they'll be all right . . . just come with me, and forget about everything else . . . just come with me, Magda. . . .

But, he could do neither, and he refused even to think about it again. He had to leave, and he could not take her with him. Any other decision would be foolish, and dangerous; and, it was folly to dwell on it.

With Carlo in school, there was no one for Magdalena to fuss over during the day. For the first two weeks after Tullio left, she tried spending some time at the club, but she found nothing to do there that interested her. The place was almost desolate in daytime during the winter, and only a few matrons sat around, lunching and playing bridge. It was a relief when she heard from Bella, who said she'd be in New York for the rest of the month.

The two women shopped almost every day. It was a mild winter and it was easy for Guido to drive Magdalena back and forth from the city without much trouble. Sometimes, they met Aleksey for lunch, but usually, they lunched during a fashion show or charity function.

"How would you like to go to a speakeasy?" Bella asked her once.

"In the middle of the day?"

"Why not?"

"By ourselves?"

Bella shrugged and laughed. "The place I'm thinking about is really just a restaurant where they serve drinks. At nighttime, its whole character changes, though, and it becomes a regular nightclub."

"Just a restaurant? Really?"

"Cross my heart. And, believe it or not, they serve good food."

Magdalena answered immediately, "Yes, let's go."

It was unfortunate that, this day, and for the first time, the little restaurant was raided. Bella had just motioned to her waiter to bring the check when the police broke into the room. She and Magdalena panicked and ran into the kitchen, hoping to escape through a back door, but, when they stumbled out into the alley, more policemen were waiting there. The press was there, also, and flashbulbs burst in front of them. There were so many flashes that all they could see after the first few seconds were dozens of black and white spots in front of their eyes.

Guido had been parked across the street from the restaurant. He stared ahead, with almost stark disbelief, as his mistress and her friend were ushered into a patrol wagon along with waiters and cooks and other well-dressed patrons. One of the men was resisting, and was being physically pushed up the steps of the wagon, and some of the women were shouting. The photographers, all the while, were shooting as much film as they could, and passersby were gaping and laughing at the scene. When the wagon was driven away, he followed it to the station.

In such cases, the only people arrested were those who actually worked for the speakeasy. Once it was established that somebody was merely a patron, that person would be released, having suffered no more than the embarrassment and inconvenience of the raid. Guido, however, was not familiar with the law. He imagined Magdalena being finger-printed and put behind bars; and, by the time he reached the station, he was so frustrated and excited that he began telling everybody who she was, and that she was an honest woman who'd never broken the law before. He told them her husband's name, and how many children she had, and where she lived; and, he even swore that she went to mass every morning. He shouted everything he could possibly think of that might sway them in her favor. When, eventually, she and Bella did walk out into the lobby, he was sure it was his intercession that had saved them from disgrace. He was shocked, though, because they were laughing.

Magdalena's laughter subsided the very next morning, however, because pictures of the raid were spread across the centerfolds of a number of Tullio's competitors' publications. One had an especially large photograph of her trying to hide her face, and it was captioned: THE GOLD COAST COMES TO TOWN. A second tabloid mentioned the raid in its society column; it read: "What does Mrs. 'B' do while Mr. 'B' is away? Naughty . . . naughty . . . naughty!" A third, seizing the opportunity to recount Tullio's birthday party, asked, "Don't they ever stop celebrating?"

Magdalena refused to answer the telephone all day, even when she was told it was Salvatore Crispino calling; and, when Aleksey came home that evening, she sent word that she had a headache and would be eating upstairs, in her room. She had no intention of listening to either of them preach to her. She already had enough problems with Rebecca today. Rebecca had come home after lunch recess and would not return to school because the other girls were teasing her about the raid. Some had even brought the newspapers into the classroom with them.

It would all calm down in a few days, Magdalena told herself, and everybody would forget about it. In the meantime, she would stay within *The Walls*, and out of trouble. Still she could not help thinking of the fun she and Bella had had, and, every now and then, she would laugh very quietly to herself.

Chapter Two

When Giulio Fallanca had first been sent to Germany by Tullio, he'd been given a new identity: Erich Veidt. He'd lived there ever since, working for Gerhard Moeller. Quick to learn, he'd soon become a valuable asset to the company, as well as Gerhard's friend and most trusted employee.

On Christmas Day, Tullio Barragatto had written to Erich Veidt, offering him a key position with North American Distributors. It would require his relocating to New York, and, in addition to his other duties, he would be the chief liaison between the German and Stateside entity that had been set up for the motels venture. He would receive all other information concerning the position directly from Gerhard Moeller, who was aware of the offer. That particular information was of too personal and confidential a nature to be put in writing, Tullio had explained, but Gerhard had his complete confidence.

When Erich Veidt confronted Gerhard Moeller with Tullio's proposition, Gerhard explained the entire Pace situation. He also told him everything he had learned, starting with the wine men's meeting in Orvietto, and ending with Salvatore Crispino's recent meeting with Erich's father. He paused often, allowing the young man to ask as many questions as were necessary so the picture would be clear to him.

After deliberating for a while, Erich Veidt said: "I assume that my primary function would be acting as intermediary between Tullio and my father. Am I right?"

Gerhard nodded and said, "I know what a difficult thing this would be for you to do, since it would seriously strain your relationship with your father . . . but, I can't impress upon you strongly enough how important it would be to Tullio, and how important it is for you to decide, one way or the other, as quickly as possible. Tullio will be in Italy next month, so, whichever way you go, it will have to be a firm commitment by then. There'll be no turning back."

The tables had turned: now it was Tullio Barragatto who needed Giulio Fallanca's help; this was what Erich Veidt was thinking. And, even though he'd made a whole new and comfortable life for himself, he could not forget that he owed it all to the man who'd saved him from being returned to Guidonia—or, at best, from spending the rest of his days as a fugitive. All tables turn. He asked, "Are there any alternative solutions to this problem?"

"You and Tullio spent two years in a cell together. You must have gotten to know one another very well . . ."

"Yes, we did," Erich said, "and, I see what you mean. I know he would not be asking such a thing if there were any other way out for him." After a short silence, he added: "But, what if I decline?"

Gerhard replied, "In that case, we'll both understand. After all, your father is your father. You'll continue working here, in your present function, just as though the subject had never been brought up. You have our word on that."

Because of Gerhard's answer, Erich Veidt said: "I don't need a month to think about it. I'll do it."

Tullio arrived in Orvietto in mid-February. It felt very good to be home. He spent his first few days riding through his vineyards and visiting his pickers and other old friends. Having become accustomed to the neat vineyards of America, though, he was almost amused by his own. He wondered if "vineyard" was even the right word for them because the vines wandered everywhere. They jumped over roofs and crawled along walls, and sneaked into his neighbors' gardens, there mingling with the beans and the tomatoes and the squash. They were marvelous; they had their own mind and wouldn't be told where to grow. It was very, very good to be home. Within the week, however, Erich Veidt also arrived in Orvietto, and the time for such feelings was finished; his work would begin now—now that Erich was here; and, if he could complete it as scheduled, he would have just enough time to spend a week in his Milan office before returning to New York by the end of March.

God, why'd I promise her the end of March?

Giulio Fallanca visited his father within the first few hours after his arrival in town. He told the gate guard: "Please tell Don Italo that Erich Veidt is here to see him."

The man answered: "Does he know you? Does he expect you? Don Italo doesn't see anybody without an appointment."

"Just mention my name to him," he replied. "He'll see me."

The *patrono* had just been informed of Tullio Barragatto's return to Orvietto. He was thinking about it when his man announced that a German called Veidt was here to see him. He was, at once, both thrilled and shocked. He'd never expected to see his son again unless he, himself, might travel to Germany. There was still a price on Giulio Fallanca's head. He hurried downstairs and embraced him. When they were alone, he almost cried.

"You've taken a big risk crossing the border," Fallanca told his son, "a very big risk. You're still a wanted man, you know. No others know you're here, do they?"

"Only the man I work for, Papa. Only him."

"How long are you staying?"

"Just a few days."

"Well, even a few days is better than nothing," the elder

replied. "Now, you come in and tell me everything you've been up to. I realize that you couldn't tell me everything in your letters. I still have every one of your letters, you know. Every one of them."

Erich stared at his father. The man was a lot smaller than he remembered him to be, so the visit would be even more unpleasant than he had expected. He decided that he would avoid telling him its purpose for as long as possible. He would put it off until the night before leaving. There was no point in ruining the entire short time they would have together. He wished his father were as tall as he'd remembered.

The reunion was a good one. The Fallancas spent their first two days and nights laughing over old family stories and comparing memories. On the third day, however, Italo Filippo Fallanca said to his son: "You've told me everything you've been doing . . . all about your successes . . . all about your failures . . . but you haven't said a word about your future. What are your plans? Where do you go from here? Do you have anything special in mind?"

Erich became uneasy, and his father eyed him suspiciously.

"Ah, so you do," the elder said, "and you've been saving that part of your news for last. Right?"

He'd not wanted to talk about it yet. They still had two more days. He shrugged and answered, "It can wait." He thought he'd said it rather nonchalantly, but his father counterpointed:

"Giulio . . . when something is so important that it can wait . . . it's usually better to get it over with right away. No?"

Giulio Fallanca/Erich Veidt blurted out: "I'm changing the kind of work I've been doing. I'll still be working for Gerhard Moeller, but I'll be working directly under his partner from now on, his partner in New York."

"New York? You've moving to New York?"

"Yes."

"Moeller has a partner in New York?"

"Yes, as far as the prefabricated motels are concerned."

362

"Have you ever met him? Do you even know the man?"

"Yes."

"Who is he?"

"Tullio Barragatto."

"Who?"

"Tullio Barragatto."

"Who!"

"Barragatto. Tullio Barragatto. As of now, I am working for Tullio Barragatto. There. That's the news. His interests are mine. What's good for him is good for me . . . and vice versa. If he chooses to sell you his wine in the United States, I would negotiate the price. And, if he chooses to continue fighting the idea . . . and, if he chooses to continue speaking for the Pire wineries, and the Beckmann wineries, and the LoGiudice wineries, then, I might very well be doing a lot of the speaking for him . . . whether it be directly to you, or to Carmine Pace . . . and, if anyone at all should get hurt over that matter, it might very well be Tullio . . . but it would more likely be me . . . because Tullio and I, we'll be working side by side. That's the news, Papa."

He wondered if he should have given it to him in stages.

No, it's better this way. At least, I've gotten the whole thing off my chest. Oh, my God, just look at him.

He continued: "Besides my wanting to see you before I leave for America, I came here, also, to tell you about this: It was to let you know that the message you sent to Tullio Barragatto through his cousin Salvatore was received . . . and that it was understood very clearly . . . and that your patience, up to now, has been very much appreciated . . . but that the policy of not selling their wine illegally in the States or Canada remains. They will not do business with your people. I don't know whether they will ever change their minds, Papa . . . but, if they do, I will let you know."

To live under the same roof—even for two more days— would be as intolerable for him as it would be for his father. If the man had argued at all, it might be possible; but Italo Filippo

Fallanca had stared at his son with unbelievable and dead silence, and there was nothing for Giulio to do except to leave the room and pack.

Before he left the house, Giulio said: "I'm going now."

For a long moment, he waited for a reply. There was none.

It was planned that there would be no contact between Tullio Barragatto and Erich Veidt while in Orvietto. It was also prearranged that Erich Veidt would spend no more time in Orvietto than was necessary for his work. His work was completed now, so he went directly from his father's house to the railroad station, where he boarded a train for Milan. This was a safety measure, as he would be less likely recognized in Milan than in a small town like Orvietto. He would remain in Milan until Tullio could catch up with him. From there, they would motor to Genoa; and from there, they would sail.

An hour later, a youngster gave Tullio a note. "A German sent it to you," the boy said. "He gave me this,"—he showed Tullio a handful of lire—"but he said you would give me more when I delivered it." He held open his palm, and Tullio filled it and thanked him.

The note said:

> The gentleman has been informed of our policy. I am leaving on the 3:40 train and shall leave word at our office where you can find me.
>
> Veidt

Tullio was pleased that Erich had used the word "our" when referring to the policy and the office; he'd not expected this so quickly. He noticed, also, the tone of the note; it seemed to have been written by a man who was definitely no longer an Italian. He lit the paper with his cigarette ash and watched it go up in flames in his ashtray. Then, he visited the local chapter of Fascists.

Tullio had been one of the chapter's founders and was received very cordially. When he requested a closed-door meeting with their leaders, it was granted as soon as it could be arranged, which would be midnight that night. He'd already learned that its leaders were still all old-line Fascists like himself; he was grateful for that. He would not know how to approach the new element in the Party, but he could speak with confidence to his peers, who felt as removed and alienated from the new membership as he did.

After dinner, Tullio went to a cafe where he would wait until the time for the meeting. Several of the patrons were drinking what his own orchards had yielded. He could see his label on the bottles in front of them. It was a wonderful sight for him. He tried to lock the picture within his memory, and when he thought of America's unholy law that said such pleasure was a crime, he cursed softly and shook his head. He cursed again when he found that he had no more aspirins left.

"What are you doing, talking to yourself?"

Tullio looked up at the man who'd just asked him that, and he asked, in return, "Why? What's it to you?"

The stranger shrugged. "I don't care. I just came over to tell you that Don Italo wants to talk to you."

Tullio looked around. "Where is he? I don't see him."

"He just left. But, that doesn't matter. He doesn't want to talk to you now, anyway. He said tomorrow. He'll be here tomorrow afternoon." The man left then, just as quickly as he'd approached.

Tullio sat back in his chair. He was relieved. He'd not wanted to speak with Fallanca, not yet, anyway. This was why he'd arranged a meeting with the chapter leaders; it was to talk with them about Fallanca.

The next hour went slowly and, twice, Tullio checked the time with a man at the neighboring table because he thought his watch had stopped. At eleven forty-five, he went to the chapter clubroom. The others were already there and waiting for him.

The leaders were patriots, each devoted to the original purpose of the Party: to fight Communism and organized crime, and to foster education for the majority. Tullio knew each of the four personally. Two were merchants; one was a wine man; and the other was an educator. He knew, also, that they were fanatics and would stop at nothing to further the cause. They stuffed ballot boxes and bribed townspeople to vote Party members into key posts. They arranged most of the local "spontaneous" demonstrations. When Communists were murdered in the streets, they were nearby. And, when a crime chief's family was destroyed, no one had to ask who'd been responsible.

They each respected Tullio. His publications were famous as a rallying point for Fascism, and they needed a friend like him in the United States. They liked his person, too; and, they approved of the way he dressed and deported himself, which was important to them. They expected that he might be coming to them for a favor, but they didn't care and were willing to do whatever he was about to ask of them.

But Tullio Barragatto shocked them. They could never have imagined he would ask such a thing. He wanted that no harm should come to Italo Filippo Fallanca, the *patrono* on the hill.

"It's a personal matter," he told them, "and I can't tell you the reason for my request, but you would be doing me a personal favor that I would never forget. It's very important to me, and to my whole family, that Fallanca remains alive."

"Tullio, you come to us, asking us to protect one of *them?*"

He replied, "I'm not asking you to give him any kind of protection. I'm just telling you that it would be very harmful to my interests if he were killed."

Somberly, a merchant asked: "You're not dealing with them, are you?"

"No, I'm not," he answered.

"And Benedetto? On the night he died, he'd dined with Fallanca. Had your cousin Benedetto been doing business with Fallanca?"

"No. Nobody in my family has any dealings with them. Nobody at all. Not here, and not in the States, either."

The wine man asked him, "Tullio, does this have anything to do with the American Prohibition law?"

He answered, "Yes, it does."

When Tullio left, he had an uneasy feeling that a plan for Fallanca's assassination had already been under way. But, he suspected, also, that the wine man had understood more than he'd let the others realize, and that, because of him, Fallanca would not be killed, at least, not if these four men had any real control over the new members of this chapter.

In the morning, he visited his aunts. They scolded him because he hadn't come to them sooner. He brought them presents, though, and the two old ladies wept. They'd always been very good with tears, he mused. It was like old times again. They asked him to stay for lunch, but he declined, saying he had a meeting.

"Have you read today's paper?" one of them asked him.

"No, not yet," he said.

"Well, we're finished with it. Here, you can have it."

He left then, and because he would not be seeing them again before leaving for America, they started to cry again. He wished this wasn't the way he would have to remember them; but it would be asking too much of them to stay dry-eyed.

Tullio had a good lunch at the cafe with some of his younger cousins. After the meal, the young men left to return to the vineyards, and he began reading the tabloid his aunt had given him.

There it was! The local paper had not even bothered to confine it to the society section. After all, how often did one of the town's most prominent families have such a scandal to shout about? The wife of Tullio Barragatto . . . being dragged by New York policemen from a drunken brawl . . . being arrested . . . being pushed into a patrol wagon with other drunken patrons of an illegal establishment . . .

Magdalena's photograph was splattered all over the page. And, everyone in Orvietto could easily recognize the woman with her—who could forget Bella? Did Sra. Barragatto consort with whores now? It didn't exactly say that, but it was implied.

He could barely believe what he was seeing. He didn't know what to do. The whole town must have seen it by now. His cousins. His waiter. The chapter leaders. His pickers. His friends. Certainly, his aunts—that's why they'd given him the paper! Certainly, his aunts!

Jesus Christ, Magda! How could you do this! Jesus Christ!

In one of the photographs, she looked confused; in another, scared; but, in another, he was positive she was laughing.

What did you do, Magdalena! I could kill you!

His Magdalena . . . his own wife . . . in a speakeasy . . . in the middle of the day. The middle of the day! Since when did she do such things?

He glared at the picture in which she looked to be laughing. That was the worst of all. It showed her already in the patrol wagon, and a man being pushed up into it, stumbling almost into her arms.

Here was another picture . . . walking out of the police station, Bella at her side . . . and Guido . . . Guido looked very serious and Bella was trying to hide her own face . . . but Magdalena . . . *Damn it! she's laughing again! What the hell's wrong with her! Laughing! . . .* Magdalena wasn't trying to hide at all!

Aagh! I'll kill her!

"Don Barragatto?"

I swear to God! I'll murder her!

"Don Barragatto?"

"What? What? What do you want?"

"It's Don Italo . . . he wants to see you."

"What?"

"Don Italo! He's over there! He wants to see you!"

Tullio jumped up and the chair fell. Had Fallanca also read the papers? "Where is he? Oh, I see him. Tell him I'll be right there. I just have to pay this check first."

The waiter was fumbling over the bill. Good—a respite—an extra couple of minutes before he'd have to face Fallanca. But then, it was all straightened out. One cousin had ordered veal, but had changed it to chicken—that's what the confusion had been over—the price of chicken and veal was different, the waiter explained, and he was very sorry for the mistake.

"Are you sure it's all right now?" Tullio asked him. "Do you want to check it over again? I don't want you to cheat yourself."

There was no mistake this time. The man had double-checked. There were no more minutes to waste. He paid the bill, rolled up his newspaper like a long billy club, and walked toward Italo Filippo Fallanca's table, holding the paper, all the time, as though he were about to hit someone with it.

Fallanca dismissed his guards and asked Tullio to be seated.

When Tullio sat down, he realized the position his newspaper was in, so he let it unroll and then folded it neatly in front of him.

"Are you finished?" Fallanca asked.

"Finished?"

"Yes, with fixing that newspaper. Are you finished?"

"Yes," Tullio replied. "I'm sorry. I didn't mean to . . ."

Fallanca waved his wrist, as though to say: What's the difference? He said, "I've invited you to my table because I wanted to see what you look like."

Fallanca continued: "There are all kinds of people on this earth, and they do all kinds of things to get what they want. Some kill. Some steal. Some lie. Some start wars. But, very few of them would turn a son against his father. Your own must be turning over in his grave."

Of this—dishonoring his father—Tullio Barragatto had never been accused. Erect in his seat, it was he who, this time, asked, "Are you finished?"

"No," the elder replied. "I have one other thing to say. It's that you had better get down on your knees every day and pray that nothing happens to either my son or me, because on the day one of us comes to any harm, you're a dead man. Remember that, Barragatto. A dead man." In the deadly

369

silence of his oath, his pupils bull's-eyed Tullio's. Then, he said, "Now. Now, I'm finished."

Tullio left Fallanca's table and walked from the cafe, his newspaper folded under his arm. He could feel Fallanca's eyes still on him as he exited. He knew he'd won part of the war, no matter how temporarily. He was supposed to feel proud, the victor. He did feel safe—he would be safe, as long as both Fallancas lived—but, he was supposed to feel proud, too.

Chapter Three

Tullio Barragatto and Erich Veidt met in Milan, as arranged. After spending one week going over last-minute paperwork, they drove to Genoa, where they set sail on the Asheley ship leaving that afternoon. Not once did Tullio mention his encounter with the elder Fallanca, even though the man's threat hung over him, echoing so often that he awakened one night in a cold sweat, having dreamed of it. Likewise, Erich did not speak of his father, even though he kept seeing the disbelief in the man's eyes and hearing the silence that followed him from his father's house. Thus, both needing to avoid talking of their last meeting with Italo Filippo Fallanca, each avoided any conversation that might lead them to it.

Tullio was amazed because Erich Veidt was positively German. It wasn't so much his face or figure or coloring; these were unmistakably Mediterranean, as any student of race could easily recognize. It was, instead, the manner that he'd developed: the way he walked—now in cadence; the way he spoke to the waiters—directing, not requesting their service; even the way he nodded his head—a quick, single up-and-down thrust. It was astonishing how German he'd become! There wasn't a hint of his head-shaved cellmate nor of the bewildered fugitive he'd cut loose from the *scugnizzi's* trap. No matter how hard he searched, he could not find a trace of Giulio Fallanca. He recalled that Giulio had once confided that his mother was German. Perhaps Erich Veidt had always been hiding inside Giulio Fallanca.

Once, Erich said to Tullio, "Sometimes, I feel like a bug under a microscope when we're together. It's as though you're studying me. Is that true? Are you studying me?"

Tullio was about to reply when Erich continued: "Oh, forget that I even asked such a thing. It was stupid. I must have gotten a little paranoid while I was in hiding. That happens, you know. After a while, you suspect that everyone who looks your way is scrutinizing you, just waiting for you to make a mistake so they can trap you. It's a lousy life, going underground, denying your past, your tastes, your whole self . . . No matter how successful you become, you aren't *you*. You don't know what happened to you. You can actually see yourself, the way you would in a dream, from eyes outside of you, just as though they belonged to somebody else. It's the feeling that you get when you're floating in water with absolutely nobody else around. It is a complete detachment from everything except the matter of not sinking—or, in my case, the matter of not being discovered—when you know, damned well, that a wave is going to come along any minute and pull you under. Nobody can float forever, because the ocean won't permit it. In the same way, nobody can deny who he is forever, because his damned ego won't permit it. At least, that's the only logical thing I can blame it on: ego. It must be ego."

After a few brief moments of reflection, Tullio said, "It sounds to me as though you want people to find out who you really are. That would be insane, because if they did, you might wind up back in Guidonia. Can anybody's ego be that powerful? That others have to know him by his real identity, and, by that knowing, seal his fate?"

Erich had neither spoken nor heard that word—Guidonia—since he'd left Genoa. He'd thought of it. Certainly, he'd dreamed of it. But, he'd never said it. He said it now: "Guidonia. Guidonia. A leper colony would be better."

"You could have sent word to your father to meet you at the border, which I'm sure he would have done," Tullio said. "Why didn't you? What made you choose Orvietto? What made you take such a chance?"

Because Erich Veidt did not reply, and because he had a questioning look on his face, Tullio assumed that Erich, himself, did not know the answer. He wondered if it had been ego. Or daring. Or a bit of insanity. Maybe it was none of these, or all three. Who could know? Who could guess?

What did it matter, anyway? Tullio mused. All that was important to him, right now, was that this man remain a little paranoid: that he stay Erich Veidt, and not suddenly decide, once having reached haven in New York, to return to using his old name. For then, how could he explain away the chauffeur living within *The Walls?* Two men with the same name? Nobody would think it just a coincidence—certainly not the immigration authorities, should Pace want to make trouble— especially if both men were sponsored by the same Tullio Barragatto.

In the meantime, there was the long Atlantic crossing ahead of them; and, during this voyage, Tullio was determined to learn as much about this German as he'd known about his cellmate. It was a matter of life and death, he realized. It was vital that he understand how Erich Veidt, the son of Italo Filippo Fallanca, thought; how he would react to different situations; how deeply his loyalties ran; and the size of his ego.

Once, Tullio asked him, "How did you manage to convince the other people working for Gerhard that you were German? After all, no matter how fluently you spoke their language, you still have an Italian accent."

"That was simple," Erich replied. "I told them that my family moved around a lot when I was a child. I said that we lived in villages along the border, places where Italian was spoken just as much as German, and, because of that, I grew up speaking both languages."

"And your family? What did you tell them about your family?"

"I said that my family was killed during the war. Once you say that to people, they never ask another question about it. Everybody reacts exactly the same way, almost as if he'd started the war, himself, and was now ashamed that he'd brought up the subject."

So it went, night after night—the questioning, the prodding, the exacting of information, until Tullio said, "I hope you don't mind my asking all these questions. But, you see, since we'll be working very closely together, I think it better that we know as much about each other as possible."

"Yes, I see what you mean," Erich interrupted. "In case of an emergency, it's important that we each have an idea as to how the other would want the matter handled. Yes, that's very logical."

This was a German response, Tullio decided, a very German response. If something was logical, it made sense, and was acceptable. Yet, by Erich's reply, Tullio understood that he, too, would be questioned about many things, and that he must be ready to reply in truth.

They spoke about their politics. Tullio expounded upon the virtues of Fascism, and he was disturbed when Erich said:

"Unless you're thinking of becoming a politician, yourself, bothering about politics is playing the fool. Politics! Hah! Why, it's all a damned public relations game, and it has only one end: to turn little thieves into big thieves. Have you ever taken a good look at politicians? A really good, close look?" He laughed, then added: "God, they could never make a living in any other business. They would either go bankrupt or be shot for embezzlement."

"Not all of them," Tullio answered. "Maybe most of them, but not all of them. Once in a while, a politician comes along who's really interested in the people's welfare. When that happens, you've got to support him. All those who don't . . .

all those who say that they're not interested in politics . . . well, then, they can't complain about their country's fate. When everything turns sour, they're the first to cry, but they have no one to blame but themselves, all because they weren't interested in politics."

Erich asked, "Do you really believe that the common, working-man can shape history?"

"Yes, if enough people hear what he has to say."

Erich grinned. "You mean if he has a good public relations man. Right?"

"I mean exactly what I said. Nothing more, nothing less."

"Are you serious?"

"Yes."

The two expatriates glared at each other. They knew that, if they had to work together and depend upon one another, they'd best never approach this subject again. It was too frivolous for one, and too sacred to the other.

The Atlantic was choppy and they were both seasick more often than not. Tullio wondered why he always wound up making the crossing in mid-winter, rather than during a time of year when the water might be less violent. He promised himself, once again, that this would be the last winter voyage he'd take.

The ocean seemed to become less quarrelsome during the very early evening, just before dusk. At that hour, it didn't even look as ugly as usual, and they would, very often, stroll the deck before dressing for dinner. They had a lot to talk about, most of it being business matters with which Tullio had to acquaint Erich so he could get to work as quickly as possible after docking in New York. During one of their strolls, they agreed that Erich would move into the Manhattan apartment.

"It's a good bachelor's apartment," Tullio said. "I don't think a woman would like it so much. But, I have a feeling you're not contemplating marriage so soon, anyway."

"Marriage? Me? God, no! I'm not looking to start a dynasty, for heaven's sake. And, that's the only valid reason for

375

marriage, isn't it? Why else would you get yourself into something like that? It's so you can pass down your name."

"What would you do if you did get married?" Tullio asked him. "What would you do about the name? Would you go back to Fallanca, or would your children be called Veidt?"

"I must have asked myself that same question more than a hundred times, and I still don't know. I swear, I really don't know."

Tullio believed him, because he, himself, would not know what to do in such a case. "I don't envy you the decision," he said, "but, you'd better be ready with one, just in case."

"Just in case what?"

"In case some woman comes along. You can never tell. It can happen. I myself planned to be a priest—now look at me. You fall in love, and the next thing you know, you're making a decision on the spur of the moment. It's better to plan ahead, to know what you would do if such and such a thing should happen."

"If I should fall in love," Erich replied, "there's no reason why I can't take care of the woman for the rest of her life without marrying her. I'm still not looking to start a dynasty, remember."

"But, if the woman loves you . . ."

". . . if she loves me, I won't have to marry her. That's real love." He looked at Tullio then, and asked, "You don't disagree with me about that, do you?"

Tullio answered, "No." There was a time he would not have been so quick to reply this way, but all that had changed since he'd known Nicole. He would not have to marry Nicole. He repeated, "No. I don't disagree with you about that. But, I wouldn't say that what a wife gives you isn't real love . . . that's real love, too . . . it's just a different kind. I'll go one step further, and I'll say that the kind of love you get from a mistress is more complete, because it's the most unselfish kind of love a woman can give . . . that, I have to admit . . . a mistress has to love a man on a much grander scale than a wife does, just to put up with her role in his life . . ." He paused, only to make sure he had Erich's complete attention. He added, then, "But, don't make the mistake of thinking a wife's love isn't powerful, because it is."

In this way, the men passed most of their time—talking about any matter that presented itself. Insignificant things. Important things. Totally absurd things. And, it was in this way that they came to know one another, for many changes had taken place in both of them since their last days in Guidonia.

Tullio missed Magdalena and the children and he was glad that the voyage would end in a week. He thought of Nicole a lot, also, and he suspected he could get some information about her from Erich. It was during one of their strolls on deck that he asked about Nicole. He did it indirectly, not mentioning her name, but wondering out loud how Gerhard was faring, "now that he's married."

"Well," Erich said, "his wings aren't exactly clipped, especially since the separation."

Tullio had to make sure he'd heard right. "Separation? I thought his wife was having a baby."

"She is, but they're not living together anymore."

Did Gerhard move out of the house, or was she the one who'd left? Is she still in Germany, or had she gone back to Belgium? Are they getting a divorce? Definitely not an annulment—that would make the baby illegitimate—but a divorce is possible. Or, are they just going to remain married, but live separately? And, how could he find her? How could he know anything at all that was happening, unless Erich would keep talking? He certainly could not ask him these questions. He could not show that much interest in Gerhard and Nicole's private lives. He waited for Erich to continue, to make any kind of comment, no matter how trivial.

Say something! Tell me more! Say something!

Erich said nothing more about Gerhard and Nicole. By the time they docked in New York, he was resigned to not knowing anything further of Nicole, except for what he would make it his business to discover.

It was surprising how much more enchanting Magdalena was each time he returned to her. Because the ship docked on a Saturday, she'd brought the children to the pier with her, but he didn't look so much at them from his position at the rail as he did at her. What a vision to come home to, he thought. My Magdalena. My Magda. The sight of her thrilled him. His arms ached with the thought of what it would feel like to hold her again. From the look on her face, he guessed that she was reading his mind, and that excited him more and made his smile broader. But—damn it!—the children were here, and Erich, and Guido; so, he could not take her directly to the apartment where they could be alone. And, he was positive that Kostenov and the Asheleys would be waiting at *The Walls* to welcome him home. There would go the rest of the day!

How many hours would it be before he could touch her—really touch her? By the time they'd gather the trunks and get to Jericho, at least two hours would go by. Earl and Louise and Aleksey would take up another few hours. And, of course, the children: they wouldn't leave him alone for a minute in between. By then, it would be dinner time, and Salvatore and his wife and children would probably drop in to complete the circle.

His smile was growing weaker. He could have a heart attack by the time he'd get her in bed. He could be dead by then. With mute resignation, he flipped his cigarette butt into the murky water and stepped from the gangplank to America. He felt like a bridegroom waiting for the wedding feast to end, waiting for the last guests to leave. He could be very dead by then.

The children were boisterous and flung themselves into Tullio's arms, and Guido was as talkative as he'd always been; but Magdalena's public welcome was so restrained that it teased him with secret, quiet promises. She'd moistened her lips before kissing him, and she'd sucked in the tip of his tongue with such careful discretion that he was positive nobody, even those just inches away, could guess what she'd just done to him. Then, with a gracious nonchalance, she'd turned to welcome Erich Veidt to America.

Whether or not he was wearing his heart on his sleeve, Tullio could not care any less. He gaped at his Magdalena with open admiration.

What a temptress she'd become, this little girl from the wagons. What a *grande dame* this poor farmer's wife had turned into. How could she have changed so much? And, why did it feel like years since he'd last seen her, when it had only been a couple of months?

It was all in his imagination, he decided. It was all because he'd missed her so much. It was all because none of Orvietto's women, nor Milan's women, nor those aboard ship—all to whom he'd availed himself unsparingly—could ever match her beauty or take her place. That was why, he concluded. That was why she seemed so different each time he returned to her. It was really because she was never any different at all, but because she was always the same, just as perfect as one human female can possibly be. And, although this thought did not stop him from thinking of and yearning for Nicole, it did not lessen his appetite for the woman who now walked with him toward the waiting limousine.

Magdalena remarked about how much Erich and Guido resembled one another. Indeed, the two men noticed it also, but Tullio shrugged, saying that they didn't appear so much alike to him; then, he quickly changed the subject.

"There are seven of us," Tullio said. "I don't know how we're going to fit in the car, what with all the luggage we have."

Magdalena winked at Guido and said to Tullio, "Well, maybe, we won't have as much trouble as you think." When they reached the car, she kept walking past it, to another one directly in front of it. "It's for you, darling," she said, "a surprise . . . to replace the one you crashed in."

It was a new LaSalle, a convertible, pale blue with a white

interior, and Tullio was speechless.

"And, I have another surprise," she said. "Guess who drove it in! Me! Guido taught me how to drive. I followed him all the way into the city from Jericho! I was a little bit afraid to drive such a long way, but he's a great teacher, and he drove very slowly so I could keep up with him. Well? Say something!"

"It's beautiful!"

"Listen to how beautifully its radio plays." She turned it on and *Blue Skies* was being played . . . one of her favorite songs, she said.

"It's beautiful," Tullio repeated, "it's really a beauty."

As men will be with machines, he and Erich and Guido opened its trunk and its hood and examined its chrome and did all the things that are incidental to women; and while they were discussing its performance capabilities, they didn't even notice Magdalena slip into the driver's seat until she asked:

"Are we ready?"

"Yes," Tullio answered, "move over."

She would have pouted because she wanted to drive it again, but she smiled because she was so glad that Tullio was pleased with it. "You like the color?" she asked. "You don't think I made them put too much chrome on it, do you?"

"It's perfect," he said. He told the others to go ahead and that they would catch up with them. He grinned because he knew he wasn't going to have a heart attack, after all . . . he could very easily drive to the apartment, which should be empty and waiting. He wondered if she hadn't planned it that way, and he laughed. "We'll see you at *The Walls*," he shouted. As Guido and Erich drove away, he could hear the children still complaining because they'd wanted to accompany their parents. Whatever small twinge of guilt he felt about this vanished quickly enough, however, when Magdalena kissed him again.

When they reached the apartment they headed straight for the bedroom. Their moments together were so rare that they had to make the most of every second. They made love with renewed fervor, their passion kindled by a long separation and the unspoken fear that they would be separated soon again.

Later, as they lay together, she realized he was watching her. It was as though he were a university student who was studying the mementos of his youth. He asked her to lie still and he didn't touch her for a long time. He only wanted to look at her, but he could not explain why.

Tullio and Magdalena arrived at *The Walls of Jericho* shortly before dinner time. The children were very upset and kept asking what had taken them so long. "Did you get lost, Daddy? "Did you get a flat tire?" but no one else asked. As he'd expected, Salvatore and his family had also come to the house; and, also as he'd expected, the young attorney and his new associate had already covered several points of business by that hour. He'd known that Erich and Salvatore would get along very well. How could they not, when they both embraced logic with such passion? Aleksey was unchanged, and it seemed only yesterday since he'd last spoken to Louise and Earl. There wasn't a single thing he could find that was any different, other than the addition of Erich Veidt to the circle. It was as though he'd never gone away.

Erich had been made comfortable in one of the spare bedrooms of the main residence, and not in the guest house; since he'd be here only one or two days before settling into the Manhattan apartment, Magdalena had thought this the best arrangement.

"Why should he have to sleep in that house all by himself?" she asked them. "There's plenty of room here. Anyway, he doesn't have a wife or children with him, so he doesn't require so much privacy. Right, Erich? Or, would you prefer the guest cottage? It's all the same to me. Really, it is."

He agreed with her. He didn't need all the privacy of the guest cottage, he said, and preferred staying in the big house with the family. He added: "Frankly, Magdalena, I can't imagine anybody ever disagreeing with you about anything."

She looked at him with a smile and replied, "I don't know how to take that."

"As a compliment, I assure you. Most definitely, as a compliment."

"Well, thank you very much."

Tullio watched the two exchange pleasantries. He listened to them laugh at each other's jokes and tell one another stories of their childhoods. He didn't like it. He didn't like the way Erich looked at her; nor did he like it when any man paid his wife compliments. He didn't consider it jealousy; he just didn't like it. He was glad that Erich would be living in Manhattan.

Despite his annoyance with Erich, though, he was as amazed as Salvatore at how well their new associate made up tales. Along with the others, they listened to him speak of his youth in the German/Italian border towns. They realized that he must have told these same stories over and over, because there wasn't a person in the room who could ever guess that it was all a farce. They could easily understand why Giulio's transition to Erich had gone so smoothly: the man was a magnificent liar. Now, if he could out-maneuver Carmine Pace even half as well, their biggest problem would be over. In the Pace situation, however, it would not be a matter of lying, it would be more like a jousting match.

The company didn't leave *The Walls* until after midnight, and Aleksey and Erich had just begun to play chess when Tullio finally said goodnight to them. Magdalena had gone upstairs earlier, to help the nurse put the children to sleep. He was very grateful that they'd had the afternoon in the apartment because, by now, he was very, very tired.

"You were acting very strangely this afternoon," Magdalena told him, "as if you had a secret you didn't want to share with me."

He knew what she meant. It had been the way he'd been

382

looking at her. "I just wanted to look at you. After all, I haven't seen you in a long time. There's nothing strange about that, is there?"

"You weren't looking at me, Tullio, not just looking at me. It was something else. It was like the way a doctor looks at a child when he thinks it has the measles or something. It was like being examined. It wasn't just being looked at."

"You didn't seem to mind it then."

"Well, I didn't, not very much, not really . . . and I still don't. I just don't understand why you acted that way."

He wanted to say: I just wanted to look at you . . . the very same way I'd look at old toys and photographs and letters. But, he didn't say this to her, because he didn't think she would understand. He said, instead:

"I missed you, Magda. I can't tell you how much, but I did. I didn't even know how much, myself, until this afternoon. There are some things I just can't explain to you. Maybe, another man could, but I can't . . . I just can't find the right words. But, that's why I was looking at you . . . it was because I'd missed you so much. I know I was acting a little crazy. I know it must have been bothering you, just lying there for such a long time, not being allowed to move. I know it was a crazy thing, but I just wanted to look at you. That's all. Can you understand that? Can you try to?"

Because it was the truth, he didn't mind admitting it to her. He knew his explanation might have been awkward, but it was the best he could offer.

She moved closer to him and said, "Tullio, you're not going back to Italy without me again. From now on, I come with you. I know something's going on, and if you're in trouble I should be with you."

Perhaps, she did understand, he reasoned. Perhaps, the words that wouldn't come to him weren't necessary, after all. Perhaps, she understood a lot more than he could ever give her credit for. He wondered about this. He wondered how much she understood, and how much she knew, and how much she just didn't choose to mention. He didn't reply to what she'd just said. To tell her: No, you can't come with me—that might be the worst answer he could give her right now. Yet, to say: Yes, from now on, we'll travel together—that could be a promise he might very easily regret. It was better to say nothing at all.

Chapter Four

When Tullio unpacked his trunks the following day, he found the newspaper he'd carried home from Orvietto. Not once during the long afternoon of their love-making or the party that had followed had he remembered it. Now, it infuriated him, just as though he were seeing it for the first time, and he felt the shock, if not the surprise, once again. He'd had to suppress his anger throughout the long voyage. But silence was no longer necessary. He told a maid to tell Magdalena to come upstairs.

Magdalena took longer than he'd expected, and certainly longer than she used to. He was thinking that there was a time when she would have come to him immediately, especially when they'd still been living in Orvietto, when she walked into their bedroom.

"What's wrong?" she asked him. "Luisa said you wanted to see me right away."

"Well, why didn't you come up right away, then?"

"Because I was busy."

"Busy? With what? What could you be so busy about?"

"From that question, and from the tone of your voice, I can only guess that you're trying to start an argument. But, I don't know why."

"An argument?" he asked. "You think I'm looking for some kind of excuse to start an argument?"

"Yes, I do," she answered, "and I'd like to know why."

"Just because I asked you what you could possibly be so busy about? That's what you call trying to start an argument?" He sat down and looked at her. "Okay," he continued, "you don't have to answer me. I'll try to guess. Let's see . . . what could make you so busy? The children? No. We hire people to take care of them for you. Housekeeping? No, of course not. You have servants doing everything there is to do. Or, maybe, you were in the kitchen. No, that wouldn't be the reason, either. We have a cook."

"Tullio, I don't know what's wrong with you. I left you an hour ago and everything was just fine. I come back upstairs, and you're acting like this."

Rebecca was standing in the doorway. He told her to close the door and leave them alone. Once the girl left, he said to Magdalena, "From what I can see, you really have nothing to do around here, and you must be very bored."

"No, I'm not bored. I have lots of things to do."

"Like what?"

"Tullio, for God's sake, will you tell me what's on your mind? What are you so mad about?"

He threw the newspaper at her and, shocked by his suddenness, she stood very still and stared at him, letting the paper fall to the floor.

"Pick it up!" he shouted. "Pick it up and take a look at yourself!" And, because she did not do this—she was too frightened by his outburst to move—he picked it up, himself. "Are you going to look at it, yourself, or do I have to read it to you?"

Warily, she took the tabloid from him. When she saw the front page, she gasped. She'd never dreamed that such an incident could be newsworthy enough to be published in Europe. "I was going to tell you, Tullio. I can explain everything."

"Never, not once, has there ever been any breath of scandal in my family. Not even once."

She did not like the way he was talking—it was too low, barely audible, with each word said distinctly. She trusted him more when he was shouting. Now, he reminded her of the dogs that didn't bark. "I really was going to tell you," she said again. "That whole thing . . . it was just an accident . . . I can explain the whole thing."

"You were there, and you shouldn't have been there. You were with Bella Modesto, and you shouldn't have been with her. You were arrested, arm in arm with a prostitute, like a common whore, and you were laughing about it. And, when you were walking out of the police station, you were still laughing." He held her gaze until she looked away. "Have I said one incorrect thing so far? Have I? Well, have I?"

"No . . . not exactly incorrect . . . but, it's not all what it seems, either. There's an explanation."

"There's no need for an explanation, because it will never happen again. Also, because what's happened, happened. It can't be undone. Not the shame. Not the disgrace you've brought to my family's name. None of it can be undone."

"About Bella," Magdalena said, "nobody here knows she was a prostitute. They know about her in Orvietto, but no one knows anything about her over here."

"That's irrelevant. You're not going to see her again."

"Why?"

"Because I just said so."

She thought of answering: That's not a good enough reason. She didn't reply this way, though, because he was still speaking too softly to be provoked.

"There are a few things I have to say to you, Magdalena, and I want you to listen very carefully. Since the first concerns Guido, also, I want you to go get him so I can talk to the both of you at the same time."

She left the room without answering. She found Rebecca and Stefano outside, in the upstairs foyer, and directed them to fetch the young driver. She didn't return to the bedroom until Guido arrived.

"Guido," Tullio said, "I hired you to drive Signora Barragatto around, not to teach her how to drive, herself. She won't be driving anyplace on her own, again. Hereafter, no matter where she goes, you take her. Understood?"

Guido nodded.

"One other thing," Tullio told him. "You're never to take her anywhere without my permission. No matter where . . . even if she asks you to take her to the city to go shopping, you call me at the office first, and get my permission to do so. Is that clear?"

Magdalena was incensed, but silent. Guido was relieved, because these new orders would prevent any kind of trouble, should his mistress want to go to the wrong kinds of places. He was very glad to be excused. He left without making any comment. He suspected that Sr. Barragatto had found out about the speakeasy raid, and he was grateful to be getting off so easily. He'd expected to be fired; and, having altered papers, he'd be deported.

When they were again alone, Magdalena asked, "Do you realize that you've embarrassed me in front of a servant?"

Ignoring the question, Tullio continued: "The next thing I have to say to you is even more important, so don't interrupt."

"Tullio, stop this."

"Don't interrupt me, Magdalena. Let me finish."

She sat opposite him, but refused to look his way as he spoke.

"I happen to know that restaurant. I've gone there, myself, a few times, because I've had some business dealings there. There were thousands of others that you could have chosen to go to, but you had to go to that one. Why? Did Pace invite you and Bella there?"

"Pace? Pace? What does he have to do with this?"

"You're not going to say that you didn't know he owns it, are you?"

388

"No! I didn't! I had no idea!"

"Damn it, Magda! Don't make a bad situation worse by lying!"

"I'm not lying. How could I know he has anything to do with that place? How could I know?"

"Just as you didn't know the man who kissed you in the restaurant that day . . . the man who kissed your hand . . . just as you didn't know who he was, then. That's how! Just some old stranger—that's how you described him, wasn't it? Just some old stranger? If you lied then, why should you tell the truth now?"

With slow movement, she looked with amazement at her husband. "You knew it was Carmine Pace?"

He thought to answer truthfully, that he'd not found out until a few days later. He replied instead: "Yes, I did. I knew, all the while, that you were lying. I gave you the opportunity to tell the truth, but you wouldn't. Now, I'd like to know why."

"That was a very sneaky thing you did, Tullio. To make me lie and make a fool of myself."

"I didn't make you lie. I let you lie. There's a big difference. Now, I want you to tell me the reason. How did you meet Carmine Pace? What kind of relationship could there be between you and him? Why wouldn't you admit you knew him?"

"Okay," she said, "I lied to you that day. It was Carmine that I met at the restaurant. I'm sorry. But, I'm not lying now. I didn't know it was his speakeasy."

"Magdalena, it's very important that I know exactly what you've had to do with Carmine Pace, no matter how insignificant it might be. It's very important. I have business with this man. I don't, for one second, suspect any kind of infidelity on your part, so don't be afraid that anything like that is going through my mind. But, I have to know the truth."

They heard shuffling at the door then and Tullio opened it suddenly. Rebecca and Stefano had been leaning on it and fell in, toward the bedroom.

"Have you been listening at this door?" Tullio demanded.

Caught eavesdropping, the children began to stammer, offering ridiculous excuses for having been there. Their father looked like an angry giant to them.

"Get into your rooms! The both of you! And, you can't come out again until Monday morning to go to school! You hear me? Don't you dare take a step out of your rooms! Either of you!"

He slammed the door, not waiting for them to say anything. "Now," he said to Magdalena, "let's continue. Pace has gambling rooms. Have you ever lost money there while I was away? Do you owe him money? Is that it?"

"No."

"You haven't borrowed any money, have you? Maybe, from somebody who turned out to be one of Pace's shylocks? I can't imagine why you would ever need to borrow any money."

"No."

"Damn it, Magda! Tell me! I don't have any patience for guessing games!"

"Years ago, just before Carlo was born, that's when I met Carmine Pace. It was in Saratoga. Salvatore and Aleksey and Earl had taken us to Saratoga, but they'd had to return to the office. They left Louise and me and the children there, in Saratoga, and, that's when I met him. He said he was a friend of Salvatore's. He took Louise and me to dinner."

"Louise and you? He took the both of you to dinner?"

"Yes . . . but, one night, Louise wasn't feeling well . . . and I went with him alone."

"You had some nerve doing that."

"I wasn't going to. Louise insisted. She said that there was no reason why we should both stay home, just because she had a bad sunburn. Oh, I'm not blaming her . . . It was my own decision . . . I should have stayed home, too . . . but, I didn't. I went with him. I was sorry right away. I left Saratoga the very next day. And, I never told you, because I knew you wouldn't like it."

"You're damned right, I wouldn't like it. I don't know

what's come over you since you're in this country. Back home, you'd never do such a thing."

"I'm sorry. I thought it would be just a simple, harmless evening out . . . just to have dinner with someone . . . I know it was wrong, but . . ."

"But, you did it anyway. Okay, okay. What's done is done." After a short silence, he said, "Magda, I have to know if anything at all happened that night. I have business with Pace. I can't let him have anything hanging over my head. If there's anything that I should know about, you'd better tell me right now, no matter what it might be."

She answered: "He took me to dinner, and then he brought me home."

"That's all?"

"Yes."

"He didn't make a pass at you?"

"No."

"Not even once? That doesn't sound like Pace."

"It's just as I said. He took me to dinner, and then he took me home. He didn't even come in."

Tullio thought about this. He answered, "All right, that's possible. Since he knew you were my wife, it's possible. Now, what about that speakeasy?"

"I swear that I had no idea it belonged to him."

"How often had you gone there?"

"That was the only time. I'd never gone to any others, either, except with you."

"Have you ever had anything else to do with Pace?"

"Just when I met him in the restaurant on Rebecca's birthday. He just happened to be there. That's all."

"I hope you're telling me everything, Magdalena, because if you're not—if you're holding back anything at all—you could be causing me a lot of problems. More than you can possibly imagine."

She didn't answer.

"Okay," he said, "we'll leave it at that. Just remember what

I said."

Salvatore Crispino arrived in early afternoon to drive Erich Veidt into the city. Erich and Tullio were out riding and he decided not to join them, but to wait in the house. When he saw a maid bringing a tray upstairs, he asked if anyone was sick. She told him that it was for the children, that they were being punished—she couldn't imagine for what, she said—and that they were not permitted to come out of their rooms, even for their meals.

After the maid left, Salvatore went upstairs, into Rebecca's room. He asked her what she and Stefano had done to make their father so angry. She told him, and asked if he would speak to her father for her. "Ask him to let us come out, Uncle Salvatore. Ask him. He'll let us, if you ask him to."

"I'm sorry, Rebecca, but I can't do that. You and Stefano did a very bad thing. You should never spy on anyone, and that's just exactly what you were doing . . . spying." He tried not to sound too stern because she cried easily. He added, "Maybe, your mother will say something. Maybe, she'll ask him to let you come out."

"I don't want her to ask him anything," she answered. "I hate her. She has a boyfriend. I hate her. That's why they were fighting. Because she has a boyfriend. I even saw them together once. They were kissing in a restaurant."

"What! Rebecca, shame on you!"

"No, it's true, Uncle Salvatore! Honest! It's true! I saw them! It was on my birthday! That's what they were fighting about! Because she has a boyfriend! I hate her!"

The attorney could barely believe what he was hearing. He knew he should silence the girl, but he didn't. He listened to every word, watched every tear, and said nothing. He didn't know for whom he felt the most pity—the children, because they'd learned such a thing about their mother; or his cousin Tullio.

"Do you remember those terrible pictures of her in the

newspapers?" Rebecca asked him, sniffling all the while. "All the girls at school saw them. They all saw them! They were all teasing me about her!"

"You mean the raid at the restaurant where she'd gone for lunch?"

"Yes! Well, she had gone there to meet her boyfriend! He'd invited her and Aunt Bella there! That's what Daddy said! She'd been invited there! That's why I got so embarrassed in front of all my friends! Just because she wanted to go see her boyfriend! I hate her! And I hate him, too! If I ever find him, I'll kill him! I know his name! They said his name! It's Carmine Pace! That's what his name is! I hate him! I hope he dies!"

Anything but this! Magdalena unfaithful? Magdalena? And Carmine Pace? Carmine Pace? Magdalena and Pace? He stared at the child. She continued to rant about her mother and her boyfriend.

"We had the right to listen! He's my father! And she shouldn't have a boyfriend! I hate her!"

He had to quiet her. He had to put aside his anger, his shock. "Rebecca, you must never repeat this," he told her. "If I find out that you've ever told anyone about this, I'll be very angry with you. You must never, ever tell anyone. You hear me? Nobody at all. Now, I want you to promise me that." He comforted her then, and said, "Maybe, you misunderstood what you heard."

"No, Uncle Salvatore, I didn't misunderstand. Even Stefano heard it. You can ask Stefano, if you want. He heard everything, too. And, he heard the man's name, too."

Magdalena and Pace?

His head was swimming when he went downstairs again. The child had promised she would tell nobody else. He didn't know if she would keep her word. Perhaps, he should talk to Stefano. Perhaps, he should tell the boy to keep silent, also. No, maybe it was better to say nothing. They were children. They could forget about it very easily if the subject weren't impressed upon them. That might be the best course—don't say anything

393

further about it.

He tried to picture himself in Tullio's place. Tullio, who was always so proud. Tullio, whose honor meant so much to him. *Of all the men in the world! Pace!*

Should he console his cousin? No. To let Tullio know that others knew about his wife—that would only cause him more grief. No, he'd not say anything. If Tullio should ever want to speak of it, he would. Until then, he'd say nothing.

He wondered what he would have done in his place.

Pace? How the hell'd she ever meet Pace?

That bitch. She has everything a woman could ask for, and she turns around and does something like this.

He looked up, toward the bedrooms, and he felt very sorry for his niece and nephew. At least, Carlo was too young to understand if he'd heard anything at all.

"I'd like to speak with you, Erich. It's confidential."

"Very well, Magdalena."

She brought him into the greenhouse, where they were less likely to be overheard. "I'm sorry to have to drag you into this," she said, "but I don't know whom else I can approach. And, the only reason I'm saying anything at all is because my husband said it might cause him problems in the future. I don't know how it could, but Tullio tells me so little about what he's doing, that I just can't take any chances. Maybe, by your knowing about this, whatever problems he was talking about can be avoided."

Magdalena told Erich Veidt everything she could remember: all that had happened in Saratoga, omitting nothing; the explanation Pace had given to her in the coffee shop; their chance meeting at the restaurant; the raid in his speakeasy; and lastly, just how much of the truth she'd let Tullio know.

Through it all, he said nothing, but listened as though he were storing each word in an invisible bank.

She ended: "I don't know what Tullio means when he says he can't let Pace have anything hanging over him."

"I'm glad that you've told me about this, Magdalena. There's not much I can do about what's happened—the damage is done—but, it's good that I know about it, just in case something should come up in the future."

"In the future? But, what could possibly . . ."

He waved the question aside. "You said that Aleksey found no record of a shooting death in Saratoga that week?"

"Yes. That's what Carmine told me. Why would he lie about it?"

Erich answered, "Don't worry about it anymore. You've done the right thing by telling me. And, I understand why you couldn't tell Tullio everything, or even Salvatore."

"I had a feeling that you would," she said. "You know how they are. Their rules. Their ideas about women. Everything's all so black and white. There's nothing in between. Not if women are wives. No room for mistakes."

"I understand," he repeated. "Yes, I understand all too well."

Magdalena had an unexplainable confidence in Erich Veidt, even though she'd known him less than two days—if he told her not to worry, she had no need to. When he and Salvatore left *The Walls,* she felt as though some great burden had been lifted from her. Salvatore had not seemed as friendly as usual—he'd appeared almost to ignore her—but she dismissed this as just another one of his legal moods. As for herself, she felt wonderful, and she hummed *Blue Skies* for most of what was left of her Sunday.

Chapter Five

1927. What a magnificent time to be rich and living in
America! The thrills! The excitement! The fantastic decadence
of it all! 1927. It was like one grand Mad Hatter's Ball.
Everyone had the chance to (and most did) step through the
looking glass, and, from there, choose his special road to
craziness. No matter which path he followed, whether he
skipped around in maddening circles or flew as straight as a
crow, he didn't believe he could ever lose his way. It was 1927
and, as far as he was concerned, nothing could burst his
bubble.

He was a little old Harlem bag-lady, earning a quarter of a
million dollars a year. *He* was a young secretary on Thirty-
fourth Street, manipulating a small parcel into a real estate
fortune. *He* was a hopeful messenger boy, playing the market
as recklessly as any mogul. *He* was a neighborhood barber,
turning bathtub-gin into a booming business. *He* was a corner
rag peddler, but he suddenly owned a piece of Seventh Avenue.
He was everybody with a dream or a scheme, or even an ounce
of brain. And, he had become rich very easily.

Yet, if the average man was on top of the world; the
Barragattos lived in heaven. It was a strange heaven—devoid

396

of Grace, and not suffering for the lack of it.

Magdalena and Tullio were an unbeatable combination. They had good looks, and good health, and youth, and more money than they could spend. Add to that their wit, their charm, and their continental touch, and it was no wonder that they'd become one of the most sought after couples on the Gold Coast. They were invited everywhere, and they seldom declined an invitation. What was especially noticeable was that they were in love, and that they actually liked each other, and that they had so much fun.

Magdalena wondered about the change that had come over Tullio. So did Aleksey. Only Salvatore understood it. Tullio was like an eagle set free of a cage; that's what the presence of Giulio-turned-Erich had done for him—he was a whole schoolful of children at three o'clock. Aleksey and Magdalena marveled about him; Salvatore just grinned and felt good.

Salvatore had never dreamed that Tullio's plan would come even close to succeeding, let alone be so effective. Now, he was stymied. Because of Erich, their willing hostage, Pace hadn't been heard from in months; and, when Pace did come around, it was with a totally different attitude.

Once, seeing the frustration Pace was trying to hide, Tullio almost laughed in his face. Salvatore, forever cautious, would never have done this, and he chastised his cousin; but, Tullio was too elated with his suddenly found freedom to be concerned.

"Some day, the tables might turn," Salvatore said. "Don't make an enemy of the man!"

Tullio and Pace crossed each other's paths often. They met at racetracks and speakeasies. They patronized the same restaurants. They were even guests at the same parties. When this would happen, they would nod politely toward each other; and after that, each would try to pretend the other wasn't there. There were times, though, that ignoring one another was literally impossible. For instance, they once found themselves at the same poker table; they both played very well that night.

The parties in *The Walls of Jericho* fell in with the times. They were extravagant, each surpassing the last, and often lasting the entire weekend. After a while, Aleksey stopped grumbling about them, and the children came to accept them as the normal way of life.

Tullio's office hours were as fast-paced as his evenings because North American Distributors was busier than ever. The steamships were booked to capacity, and the New England ski lodges were set to open with the first snowfall. *Piccolo Villaggio* was seeing profits it had never imagined. The touring company in southern Italy was setting up its first round of seasonal tours, and the prefabricated motels were already built and waiting for the vacationers' onslaught. Veidt worked well with the men and was an asset to the company, a fact Kostenov and Asheley quickly accepted; and his role as buffer between the wine men and Pace's people was firmly cemented. This year, 1927, was one with which no one could find any fault.

Carlo, just seven years old, was unimpressed by what was going on around him. Stefano and Rebecca, however, twelve and eleven, liked what they saw. It was the way they would live when they were adults, they figured, and they liked it. Sometimes, they were permitted to be present at their parents' parties. Stefano cracked jokes, and Rebecca, pretending to be as grown up as she could, amused the guests with her impressions of famous actresses.

"I'm going to be on the stage some day," she'd announce. "A dancer, maybe, or a serious actress. I'm not sure which one, not yet. But, one of them for sure! Maybe, both if I feel like it."

Many of the onlookers eyed her suspiciously. She was much more flirtatious than other Gold Coast girls of her age, and far too dark and exotic-looking to be just another of tomorrow's debutantes. She appeared at least fifteen or sixteen, and there were already traces of sensuality in her movements, something Tullio had also noticed.

"You'd better keep a careful eye on her," Tullio warned

398

Magdalena. "Sometimes, she worries me."

"Why? What's wrong?"

"She acts too old sometimes. Too old for her age."

"All girls want to act grown up," she said. "Rebecca's not unique. She just plays better at it than most. She's talented."

"That's just what I'm afraid of," he answered.

They'd both thought Aleksey was snoozing in his armchair, but he surprised them and interrupted. "Well, how in the world do you two expect her to act? Do you want her to be prim and proper when you expose her to all kinds of goings on? The things that happen at these parties are enough to turn any young girl's head, and any boy's, too. Don't, even for one minute, think your Stefano's eyes aren't wide open, also. They're getting some education, those two."

"We've always sent the children upstairs at a respectable hour," Magdalena replied, "especially if we thought things might get a little raucous."

"Well, it just might interest you to know that that doesn't always help," Aleksey continued. "Last week, Stefano had to sleep in my room because he found some people in his own bed. So! What do you say to that? Some example! You never saw anything like that when you were their ages." He glared at them, then almost shouted: "Well, did you? Hmmph! I know Tullio didn't!"

Magdalena almost giggled, remembering lots of what she'd seen in the wagons. She became serious again very quickly, though, because Tullio was silent.

"It's not right," Aleksey said. "It's not right. Bootleggers coming and going, musicians, actresses, gamblers. They're being set a very bad example. Why, they think *everybody* lives this way." Facing Tullio, he asked. "What would they think of you back home?"

"*This* is our home, Aleksey," Magdalena said.

He waited for Tullio's answer.

"*This* is our home," she repeated.

Aleksey still waited for Tullio's reply.

"Well, say something," she demanded of her husband. "This is our home. Right here! Here! Right here!"

"Tullio," Aleksey went on, "think of who you are. Your name. Your family. Think about it." After saying this, he felt sorry for Magdalena; there was such a look of dismay about her. He thought it best to add: "There's nothing wrong with entertaining and going out to lots of places. I'm not suggesting you return to the old way—it was like a morgue around here. I'm only saying that moderation never hurts. You don't have to be what they call 'cafe society' to have fun. Think about it."

Tullio broke his silence. "Cafe society?" It sounded repugnant to him. "Cafe society?"

"How else would you describe the life you've fallen into lately?" Aleksey asked him. "You—a Barragatto."

"Cafe society?" Tullio repeated. "Is that what they call us?"

"Don't you remember how it was at home?" Aleksey persisted. "Don't you remember? Do you want to throw all that to the wind? The dignity? The tradition? When was the last time you attended a concert? And, tell me, when was the last time you sat at the head of your own table, eating dinner with your children?"

Magdalena felt a sort of life sentence being formulated between the men. A life like she'd led in Orvietto was all that could come of it, she feared. The longer her husband remained silent, the more positive she became of the danger. She saw thoughts taking shape in his mind. "It isn't possible for us to eat with the children," she said. "Tullio gets home from work so late. It would be unfair to them. They'd be starving by the time he gets home."

"True," Aleksey answered, "true. But, what of Saturdays and Sundays? Especially Sundays."

"Sundays," Magdalena said, "that's when they go to the movies. Once a week. Sunday afternoons." She wished Tullio would say something. But, no—he seemed to be having a private conversation with Aleksey, one where he didn't need words.

Tullio thought back to his Sundays in Orvietto. He'd taken them for granted. He'd never really appreciated them before. Now, he did, and he understood why Kostenov was mentioning them: because it was there, at the Sunday dinner table, where the strands of his and his cousins' lives had been woven; because it was there where they'd learned who they were and what was expected of them; because it was there where the generations had been bridged.

Every Sunday, whether at the Barragatto house or the Crispino house, the family ate together. Tullio's father sat at one end of the table and Salvatore's father, Zio Carlo, was at the opposite end. The men were flanked by the eldest boys. The women sat toward the center of the long table with the younger children. Whether or not he and his cousins had been consciously listening to their fathers' conversations, they'd heard them. Whether or not they'd been aware of the hierarchy of seating, they'd been a part of it. He realized this now, all within the moment. The solutions to his everyday business problems, the thousand and one ways in which he directed his operations—they were all a repetition of the lessons he'd not known he was studying and of the lectures he'd never known he was attending. And his cousins: they might disagree with him but, in the end, his word was final because it was he, Tullio, the eldest of the youths, who'd sat nearest the head of the table while his father was still the head of the family. The training had been as effective as it was subtle; and, by the time he'd left Orvietto to travel with his tutor, it was the Sundays, more than anything else, that had prepared him for life. He did not have to tell Aleksey any of this; Aleksey knew.

As though talking aloud to himself, Tullio said: "When my father died, I sat opposite Zio Carlo. And, when Zio Carlo died, Benedetto took his place because Salvatore was already in New York."

Magdalena frowned. "Why do you talk about a dining room table as though it were a succession to a crown? It's not. It's

401

just a table."

Tullio continued: "When my cousins have a problem in the vineyards, they know what to do. That's because they've heard those same problems being spoken about over and over again since their infancy, and because they've heard how to solve each one . . . over and over again . . . every Sunday afternoon."

"But we don't make wine here, Tullio. It's illegal, remember?"

He answered her: "When Zio Carlo and my father were both dead, and there was an especially difficult problem to solve, they all knew who would decide what to do. None of them took the initiative unless he first checked with me. That was because, by then, I was at the head of the table."

"No," she said. "It was because you were the oldest, the head of the family . . . not because you sat at the head of the table."

He looked at her with a most unusual, questioning expression. "It's the same thing," he said. "I can't believe that you don't understand that. It's the same thing. Tell her, Aleksey. It's the same thing. Magda, I really can't believe you don't understand."

She answered: "This is ridiculous. A table is a table. A seat is a seat. Just because one of the children decides he wants to sit at the head of the table, it doesn't mean that we're all going to suddenly start taking orders from him. Well, does it?"

"You're impossible," he exploded.

Aleksey Kostenov said, "I feel like some anisette. How about you two?"

Magdalena said, "Yes," and rang for the butler. They remained silent as he brought in a tray, poured three small glasses, and left. As soon as he was gone, Tullio resumed their discussion:

"Where are the children, anyway?"

"In the kitchen, having a snack."

"Why are they eating in the kitchen?"

402

"They always have their snacks in the kitchen," she answered.

"I didn't know that," he said.

She raised her eyebrows and shrugged.

"I've never eaten in the kitchen in my life," Tullio said.

Magdalena shrugged again, and Aleksey smiled.

When Magdalena and Aleksey began to talk about other things, Tullio left the room and went to the kitchen. He stood at the door for about a minute, just looking in. The three children were seated around a small square table in the center of the kitchen. Guido and the gardener were sitting with them. There was one empty chair left; it was for the cook, who was taking some cold cuts from the ice box. It was when she turned to join the others at the table that she saw him.

"Signor Barragatto, I didn't know you were there," the cook said. She smiled and asked, "Would you like me to make you a nice sandwich? Oh, maybe, a nice antipasto?"

"No, thank you," he said. "I was just looking for my sons." To the boys, he said, "When you're finished, come inside."

Rebecca said, "I have to go to my dancing lesson when I'm finished. Guido's taking me."

Tullio nodded. He said, "Take your elbows off the table. And you, Stefano, stop gobbling down your food as though you were starving. And, keep your mouth shut when you chew."

When Tullio left the kitchen, Guido grimaced. "You two did something bad, right?" he asked the boys.

"No," Stefano said, "not me. Did you?"

Carlo shook his head. "I didn't do anything."

The boys walked into the study apprehensively. Neither could think of any wrongdoing, so they'd decided that Rebecca must have done something wrong and that they were getting blamed for it. They were surprised to find that their father wasn't angry. He just wanted to talk with them for a while, he said; nothing was wrong; he only wanted to talk.

"What do you want to talk about?" Carlo asked him.

"Anything," he answered. "What do you talk about with

403

Guido, or with the gardener or the cook? What were you talking about in the kitchen?"

"The cat. The grey one, without the tail. She had more kittens yesterday. Two died. Mrs. Bianco's sister is having another baby. Her husband never leaves her alone. That's what Mrs. Bianco told Guido."

Stefano shook his head with impatience. "We talk about a lot of things."

"Yes, I'm sure of that," Tullio answered. "Now, I want you to tell me why you eat in the kitchen. We have a great, big dining room. We have a patio with tables and chairs. Why do you eat in the kitchen when there are much nicer places?"

They both shrugged, but Stefano asked, "Why? Don't you want us to eat in the kitchen?"

"No, I don't. The kitchen is where the servants eat. You shouldn't be eating with the servants."

"Don't you like them?"

"Yes, I like them, but that doesn't mean I'm going to eat with them," Tullio answered. "Do you eat with the sixth-graders?" he asked Stefano.

"No," Stefano said. "I'm in the seventh grade. I eat with my own class."

"Don't you like the sixth-graders?" Tullio asked him.

"They're okay," Stefano answered, "but I'm not going to eat with them. I eat with my own class."

"Well, that's the same thing as eating with your servants," Tullio told him. "You're different from your servants. That's just the same as though you were in a different class than they're in. You don't eat with them. You can like them, but you don't eat with them."

"We can't eat in the kitchen anymore?" Carlo asked.

"That's right."

"What about Rebecca? Can she eat in the kitchen?"

"No, not Rebecca either."

"But, it's fun eating in the kitchen," the child persisted.

"You can't eat there anymore," Tullio said.

"Why?"

"Because I said so!"

There was a glint of understanding in Stefano's eyes, but there was resentment in them also. The resentment was masked; but it was there, nonetheless, tempered by the respect he'd been taught to show. Tullio recognized the look; he'd seen it often enough in the eyes of the farmers speaking to their landlords. Stefano was a farmer's son. He had to break the silence quickly, before the boy's blood started talking to him.

"What do you say we go horseback riding?" he asked them.

Stefano was receptive, immediately forgetting the conversation. Carlo said okay, but he wasn't as happy as his brother, because he was still a little peeved over being barred from the kitchen. It usually took Carlo longer than Stefano to forget about things. When they reached the stables, the younger boy was still pouting a little.

Even as their horses broke from a trot to a slow gallop, Tullio wondered: Cafe society? Is that what they're calling us?

Besides the matter of the kitchen, other things began changing in *The Walls of Jericho*.

The Barragattos started giving parties less often, and their guest lists were narrowed down considerably. Magdalena didn't like this, but, grateful that they'd not been eliminated completely, she complained as little as possible about it. It was better than living in "a little Orvietto," she'd say to Aleksey, "but, we've been having mostly dinner parties, lately, rather than real parties . . . and you know how much I hate planning menus. And, oh, the people Tullio invites over! They're so boring!"

Without the many extravagant parties, the Barragatto name appeared less and less in the gossip columns. This pleased Tullio because he'd always looked upon publicity as plebeian. Besides that, the notoriety had caused him some embarrassment lately. He'd received a note from the leader of a local Fascist club. The man had written:

"How can a person like you, somebody whose publications champion our cause, possibly explain spending more money on one single party than many of our countrymen see in a lifetime? How can you forget that so many of our people are starving? What do you tell your conscience when you throw away so much food in one night? In your columns, you tell us what *Il Duce* asks of us, but I don't see you tightening your own belt."

Because the leader might be voicing this same opinion to others, Tullio mentioned the letter lightly during his next club meeting. He said, "Obviously, this man is confusing us with Communists. They're the only ones who go around saying that personal wealth is some kind of sin. How did he ever get to be a chapter leader? He can use some education, or maybe, a little investigating."

Tullio did not want anyone to realize how much the note had bothered him, so he said no more about it. Even though, his last remark had found its niche within his listeners' hearts; and he knew he couldn't be blamed if, thereafter, that club leader was suspected of fostering the enemy philosophy.

He grinned imperceptively and slid into the meeting agenda, mentioning that he was thinking of hosting a fund-raising party at *The Walls*. "You'd be surprised how many financiers believe in what we're trying to do," he said, "only, they call themselves 'reformers' instead of Fascists."

They agreed with him almost instinctively, as though each had fostered the thought he were only echoing. He was in the best position of them all, they decided, and told him so. His publications convinced the masses, and his social standing befriended the powerful. Nobody, they said, could do more for Fascism in America than he.

The following week, the children were sent to the movies on Saturday afternoon. On Sunday, they ate in the dining room with Tullio, Magdalena and Aleksey. The men sat at opposite heads of the table. To Tullio's right, was Stefano; to his left, was Carlo. Magdalena sat at Aleksey's right, next to Carlo; and

Rebecca sat at Aleksey's left, next to Stefano.

Rebecca didn't really care where she sat, but she was indignant at being told where to sit.

Magdalena was almost tempted to say: You aren't being told where to sit. You're being told where your place is. She kept quiet, though, because she was certain the girl would not understand. Silently furious, she took her own place at the center of the table.

She watched Tullio pour wine into her sons' glasses.

She watched Stefano sip it slowly and smile.

She watched Carlo raise his glass and heard him say to his father, "*Salùte!*"

She watched and said, "Oh, my God."

Tullio looked toward her. "What's wrong?" he asked.

"Nothing. Nothing's wrong," she answered. "It's only that I'd suddenly gotten the feeling that everything that's happening now, for the first time, had happened once before. The way you poured the wine . . . Stefano—the way he sipped it . . . and Carlo—he held up the glass exactly the same way, and he said the same thing . . . you were wearing the same clothes."

"*Déjà vu*," Aleksey said. "You've just experienced *déjà vu*. It's nothing to be concerned about. It's really quite common."

"Yes," Magdalena said, "I've heard of that. But that's not what happened just now. It wasn't that. It was different."

"We had that word in school last week," Stefano said. "I know what it means. It's French. It means when you remember everything about something that's happening for the first time."

Rebecca said, "That's impossible. You can't remember something if it's never happened before."

Magdalena shook her head. "No," she said, "it wasn't *déjà vu*. It was different."

After dinner, she said to Tullio: "It was very different. When I think of it, even now, it gives me the chills. What I felt was something quite extraordinary. I felt as though I were

407

looking at you and the boys through somebody else's eyes, not my own. I was watching the three of you, but I was somebody else."

"Well, try to forget about it," he told her.

They discussed Stefano's school then. Stefano would be leaving in September. Louise Asheley had managed to enroll him in the same school she'd sent her own son to. "It's the finest school in the East," she'd told them; and, from the price of tuition, Tullio could only guess that she must be right.

"I don't know how I'll stand having him away from home so long," she said. "I'll miss him so much. I wonder if he'll be homesick."

"Don't worry," he said. "It will do him a world of good. It will prepare him for college. He'll have to be away from home when he goes to college. Right?"

"But, he's still so young to be away from home," she answered.

"He'll be coming home for the holidays and the summers," he continued. "Come to think of it, he's a year older than I was when I first left home." He looked toward Aleksey and asked, "That's how old I was. Right, Aleksey?"

"Yes, you were twelve when we started our travels. You were twelve."

Aleksey was about to say something else, but Magdalena interrupted: "Tullio, how old were your brothers and sisters when they died? Oh, never mind about your sisters. How old were your brothers?"

"One died in infancy, and the other was about ten or eleven."

"You were the youngest. I remember your telling me that. You were the youngest."

"Yes, that's right. What made you think of that now?"

"Tullio, I know what happened at the table this afternoon. It wasn't *déjà vu*. It was what the gypsies call a *calling*. That's what it was—a *calling*. It's when somebody from the past, somebody who's dead, lets you see something they saw. They do that when they're trying to tell you something, or when they're trying to warn you about something. They let you take their place in a particular situation, or whatever."

He shook his head. "You don't really believe that, do you? Where'd you ever hear of such a thing? Oh, I know. I'll bet it was when you were still in the wagons, when you were still a little girl."

"Yes."

"I thought so. It's just some gypsy superstition."

"I don't care whether you and Aleksey believe me or not. I had a *calling* this afternoon."

"Okay," he answered, "call what happened whatever you want. But, what does it have to do with my brothers?"

"It was your mother," Magdalena replied. "She was the one who called me."

"What!"

"Yes, that's what happened. She was the one who called me. She called me to see something she had seen a long time ago. She'd been watching you and your brother and your father. Carlo—he was you. And Stefano—he was your brother, the one who died about ten or eleven. And you—you were your father. She let me see them. Rather, she let me see you three playing their parts. They were all at the table—they meaning you, your brother and your father."

Tullio almost, but did not, make the sign of the cross upon himself. He did close his eyes for a couple of seconds. Then, he said, "I don't want to hear you talking like this again. This is just some crazy gypsy superstition. Nobody from the dead comes back and shows anything to the living. There's no contact after death."

"Don't be so sure," she said.

"Magdalena, when I first met you, you were filled with all kinds of these superstitions. Almost everything you did was based on some kind of superstition. I'd thought you'd gotten over all of that. I'd thought you'd grown out of it."

She grimaced. "You still knock on wood."

Aleksey laughed and said: "She surely got you there, Tullio!"

Tullio smiled and nodded. "Okay," he said, "I plead guilty. I admit that I knock on wood and that I do a lot of dumb things. But, it's different with me. I do those things only out of habit. I don't do them because I think they really help anything. They're just superstitions; and I take them for just what they are." He sat forward and became serious. "But, Magdalena, this thing you're talking about . . . this *calling*. I know you. You really believe in it. You're going to dwell upon it. I don't want you to. There's no such thing."

Chapter Six

Kostenov frowned. "At first, I thought Tullio was just making a mountain out of a molehill. Now, I think differently. He certainly knows you well, Magdalena. You really are dwelling upon this. A whole month has gone by, and you're still concerned about it."

"I have to be, Aleksey. Don't you see? His mother is trying to tell me something. I'm afraid it's something I'd already known on my own . . . only, I had to have it confirmed by somebody else—in this case, Christina Barragatto. She's the only one who could have done it. Maybe, it's because she's the only one who really knows how I feel. And now, I know how she must have felt."

"Tch, tch, tch. Magdalena, the dead don't talk to the living. It's 1928. 1928. Nobody believes in such things anymore. The dead are dead. There's no communication between them and us." He did not say this harshly, but as paternally as possible, because he saw how deeply the *calling* was bothering her. "Anyway, why would a woman whom you've never met come back from the grave and talk to you? If she had some kind of message to give, wouldn't she be giving it to her own son, Tullio, instead of to you? You don't even know anything about the lady."

"Oh, but I do," Magdalena answered. "I know quite a lo
about her. Some from Tullio's father, and some from th
servants who'd tended to her. And, my maid in Orvietto wa
the daughter of Tullio's mother's maid . . . she told me lots o
things, also . . . things that Tullio might not even know about
You know what I mean . . . woman talk . . . the things men
never get to know about their wives or mothers."

"Tell me what you know about her," he said.

"Her name was Christina. She came from Siracusa. That's in
Sicily. She was Tullio's grandfather's goddaughter. When she
was about fifteen years old, her family was wiped out—
something to do with a *vendetta*, I think. Anyway, the old man
sent for her and raised her with his own children in Orvietto
Eventually, she married his son, Tullio's father.

"She'd never gotten along with Tullio's aunts when she was
a young girl. She was very Sicilian, you know . . . she had very
different ways than they did . . . and, after the marriage to
their brother, it became worse. I don't know if Tullio's father
ever realized what bad relations there were between his wife
and those sisters of his. He might have been too busy with his
vineyards to notice. But, take it from me: all the servants knew
what bad blood there was among those women! They all knew
about it! Christina hated everything about Orvietto! If she
could have, she would have spent her whole life back in
Siracusa! She hated Orvietto just as much as I did! All the
restrictions that were placed upon her—she felt like a
prisoner."

Aleksey Kostenov held up his hand. "I knew Tullio's father
very well," he said, "and he denied his wife nothing. Christina
Barragatto had the best of everything, the best money could
buy."

"You're missing my point, Aleksey," she said. "It's true,
that Christina might have had whatever she wanted, insofar as
material things are concerned, but it's also true that she had
nothing. She didn't have the right to say how her children

412

would be raised. She didn't have the right to ask her husband any questions about what he was doing, or where he was going at night. She didn't have the right to plan any vacations, or dinner parties, or anything at all, unless her husband and his sisters approved. She wasn't allowed to select her clothing or jewelry; that was all done for her, also. And, she wasn't even permitted to sit where she wanted at her own dinner table."

"Aha! So, that's what this is all about! You don't like sitting near the center of the table and, just because Christina probably had to sit near the center, also, you think she's coming back to share your complaints about it! For heaven's sake, Magdalena! You're the one who said that a seat is a seat is a seat! Right? Wasn't that what you said?"

She smiled lethargically. "I was putting on a brave show, Aleksey, because I knew what your talk with Tullio might be leading to. You see, in any other family, a seat is a seat is a seat. But not in this one. In this family, where you sit says who you are. Don't you remember the Sundays in Orvietto, Aleksey? Don't you remember when all the aunts and the uncles and the cousins got together? Somebody had to die or leave the country before one of the younger cousins got to sit closer to the head of the table. Of course, the women's seats were never changed—we always sat in dead center."

The man cupped his hands and asked her: "What's the harm in sitting near the center of the table?"

She replied: "The one who sits at the head of the table is like a king. He has the first and last word about everything. Those sitting closest to him are next in line. But, when you're at the center of the table—as far as you can possibly be from its head—you have no opinions about anything and, if you do have opinions, you might as well not voice them at all, because they'll be ignored. Sitting at the center of their table is just like being one of their thoroughbred horses. They'll give you the best care possible. They'll coddle you. They'll protect you. They'll show you off. But they'll never allow you the right to your own will."

413

Aleksey Kostenov reflected upon this. "I mentioned Sunday dinners," he said, "because I think families should eat together. I still do. Eating together helps keep a family close. As far as any special seating arrangement is concerned, well, I assure you, that was the furthest thing from my mind. As for myself, I don't care where I sit."

"I know you don't care, Aleksey, but Tullio does."

"I'm sorry I ever brought up the subject," Aleksey said. "If it's going to make you the least bit unhappy, I'll have a talk with Tullio. You tell me exactly where you want to sit, and I'll suggest it to him. All right?"

"Oh, my darling Aleksey, you might be trying to listen to me, but you don't hear a thing I'm saying. Don't you understand? If you tell him anything like that, it would be the same as telling him he should move his prize thoroughbred to a different stable. In the end, the decision would have been Tullio's, and not mine. He would simply have been placating me. In that case, I would be sitting in a different seat, but only physically because, no matter where that seat might be, I would still be in the center of the table. Don't you see?"

"No, Magdalena, I honestly don't."

"Aleksey, let me put it this way. I'm not afraid of my husband. He's really very good to me. And, considering his background, he's never been especially domineering. So, all in all, I don't need you to tell him that I want to change my seat. I can do that on my own. As a matter of fact, I know very well that I can sit wherever I feel like. If, this coming Sunday, I choose to sit next to him—or even at the opposite head of the table—he'll not say a word about it."

"So, what's the problem?"

"The problem is that deep down inside it will aggravate him. Then, so his pride won't be insulted, he'll decide that he's *allowing* me to sit there . . . *that he's giving me permission.* In other words, he would be treating me like a child who was having a temper tantrum in a sickbed: just giving in, very temporarily, until the fever is gone. Slowly but surely, he'd have me back at the center of the table before much time goes by. That's because he doesn't really believe I have the *right* to sit anywhere else except toward the center because, if I did, I'd also have the right to make decisions that he considers to be all his own."

Magdalena, do you expect Tullio to behave like an American husband? Like another Earl Asheley? Like the men at Capits Rock? Now, answer me truthfully, because I'm talking to you just as though you were my own daughter. Is that what you expect of Tullio?"

"No, Aleksey, I'm not looking to wear the pants in this family. All I want is not to be treated like a cherished pet. Tullio was brought up to treat women that way, and I guess that his aunts were brought up to accept it. But not me . . . and not his mother, either."

"I didn't realize you were so unhappy in Orvietto, Magdalena."

"Well, I was. I certainly was. If I'd known what it was going to be like, it's possible that I never would have accepted Tullio's marriage proposal. But then, once we were married, I didn't have much choice except to do as I was told. Everything that I was told. And, everybody told me what to do. But I've been away from there too long now, Aleksey, and I just can't go back to that way of life again. I just can't do it."

"It won't come to that, Magdalena."

"I think it might. I think it's the reason why Christina called me. She was trying to warn me about what might be coming. She doesn't want Tullio to do the same thing to me that his father did to her. Or, maybe, she doesn't want us to wind up the way they did."

"What do you mean by that?" Aleksey asked.

"Well, once she told her maid that she felt like she was nothing but an imported brood mare—a disappointing one, because all of her offspring kept dying so young. Another time, she told that same maid that she felt like her husband had turned her into a statue, and that he'd put her up on a pedestal;

415

and, there she would stand, just being admired, but never being able to say anything."

"That's a very sad commentary on a marriage," Aleksey said. "Either that, or Christina Barragatto was very dramatic. Whatever . . . I doubt that merely sitting around a dinner table is going to lead to all that. This is, after all, Jericho, Long Island, New York, and not Orvietto about thirty years ago."

Magdalena continued: "I thought that was the case, too. Living here, in this country, Tullio was starting to change. For a while, it seemed that he'd left the old ways behind. Then, whammo! the Sunday dinners! I'm sure that's what triggered it, Aleksey. I'm sure of it."

"Triggered what?"

"The way he's been acting lately. So formal. Even with the children. He reminds me very much of my father-in-law. And the children . . . it's having an effect on them. I can see that already. The other day, I overheard Carlo telling the cook to bring a sandwich out to him on the patio. How do you like that? My little Carlo . . . giving orders to the servants."

Aleksey laughed about this, but Magdalena didn't think it was funny.

"The next thing you know, he'll be giving me orders," she said.

In August, Tullio rented a house in Saratoga for the season. He was too busy at the office to take a real vacation, but he would arrange to spend the weekends in Saratoga, he told her. Magdalena wasn't looking forward to it.

"I don't know how I'll pass the time," she said. "I don't like horse racing, and there isn't anything else to do there during the day, except, of course, to go down to the Springs and take mud baths. It would be different if Louise were going to be with me. But, with her going on a cruise. Well, I would really rather stay here, at home."

"It's too late, now," Tullio said. "The house has been rented and all the arrangements have been made. Anyway, Saratoga is where you should be in August. Don't worry. You'll see, you'll find things to do. I'm sure the children will keep you busy."

"Still, I wish you had asked me before you made these plans. It's not that I don't appreciate it. I do. I just wish you would have talked to me about it first."

Sometimes, Tullio had a hurt-little-boy look about him. Magdalena saw that in him now, and she felt guilty for having complained about the vacation plans. She said: "On second thought, it might be a very good opportunity for Rebecca to start meeting people. You know how it is around the paddock. All those women parading their daughters back and forth. Now that I think of it, Rebecca's time is just about coming. Her circle of friends has been so small until now. So restricted. Why, she doesn't know anyone at all who doesn't live on Long Island. She can meet so many young girls in Saratoga. Girls from the wealthiest families on the Continent will be there. They all come there, you know. Yes, Tullio, I'm glad you got us that house. It will come in very handy. She can make some good connections there. And Stefano, too. I have a feeling that a lot of the boys he'll be meeting in that school come September will also be at Saratoga. It will give him a head start. He'll already have made friends with some of his new schoolmates."

Tullio nodded. He seemed to be satisfied.

The house in Saratoga had upstairs and downstairs porches that completely encircled it. They were edged with lacy parapets which were so low that anyone sitting in one of the numerous rockers or swings could easily see what was happening on the street below. Likewise, passersby could see the people sitting on the porch without much trouble. The porches had been especially designed for viewing, Magdalena decided, and certainly not for anyone who might want a little privacy.

"It's so public here, that we might as well be eating our lunch down by the track," she mumbled. Although she'd said it

417

only in passing, Stefano had heard her; and, seeing the gleam in his eyes, she added: "Okay, why don't we? Let's go. Call your brother and sister. We'll eat at the track. We can walk. We won't need Guido to take us."

"That's good," he replied, "because Guido isn't here. He didn't come home last night. I wonder where he slept."

"Hmmph! I'll have to have a little talk with him."

When they reached trackside, it seemed to Magdalena that the entire population of the Gold Coast had moved to the little town for the season. Familiar faces nodded greetings.

I don't see so many of my neighbors when I'm at home!

She wondered if anyone at all was lunching at the club today, besides its staff.

In the open dining area, they met several women from Capits Rock. To her relief, the tables were too small for any of them to join her and the children. "Thank goodness," she whispered to Rebecca. "At least, we can eat in peace."

After lunch, she decided to sit there for a while, because the sun felt so good. A man sat at the neighboring table. She hadn't noticed him at first; it was Rebecca's expression that made her turn to look toward him.

"Well, hello," he said.

"Mr. Pace!"

"It's nice to see you again," he told her. "Are you here with that same friend again?"

"Oh, Louise Asheley? No. She's gone on a cruise this summer. I'm here with my children only. My husband will be joining us on the weekends. This is my daughter, Rebecca. My boys just ran off toward the paddock."

Rebecca glared at Pace. "What is he doing here?" she asked, not taking her sights from him. "Did you know he was going to be here? Did Daddy know?"

"Rebecca! What kind of questions are those? What's come over you? Really, Mr. Pace, this is very unlike her. You apologize, young lady. Right now!"

"I remember him. He was the one in the restaurant. The

man you said you didn't know."

"Rebecca, stop this, this instant!"

Pace held up his hand. "Please," he said, "I don't know what's going on here, but, whatever it is, I seem to be the cause of it." To Rebecca, he asked, "Will you tell me what you're angry about?"

"That won't be necessary," Magdalena said. "Rebecca, go back to the house at once, and stay there. Don't come out again. I won't stand for this kind of behavior. You stay in that house until I get there. But, before you leave, you apologize to Mr. Pace."

"Did you know he was going to be here? Did Daddy know?"

"Rebecca!"

"He's the one who owns the speakeasy you were arrested in!"

"Rebecca!"

"Did Daddy know he was going to be here?"

"Rebecca!"

"I can answer that," Pace said.

"There's no need," Magdalena told him.

"But, I want to," he answered. "I don't know about your mother, but I'm sure your father knew I'd be here. I'm sure that he knows that I come to Saratoga every August. What's wrong with that?"

She stared from one to the other. Here they were: her mother and her boyfriend from the restaurant . . . the man she and Daddy had been arguing about. Here they were. Right out in the open. Where everybody could see them. "You have no right to make such a fool out of Daddy! You have no right to do that! Right here! Right out in the open! The least you can do is to bring him in the house, so nobody else can see you together."

Carmine Pace was visibly confused, but Magdalena was as furious as she was embarrassed.

Magdalena stood up. "Go get your brothers. We're leaving. All of us. Right now. Do what I'm saying, right now, Rebecca."

She turned to Pace and said, "I'm very sorry," and left before he could fathom what had just happened.

Rebecca walked ahead of Magdalena all the way back to the house, and, when she reached it, she went upstairs and locked her bedroom door behind her. The boys were complaining about having had to return so quickly. Magdalena was livid and quite speechless. Rebecca stayed in her room for the rest of the day. She was sent no dinner, and, even though the boys asked Magdalena what had happened, Magdalena remained almost completely silent. The only thing she did tell them was that they would be returning to Jericho the following morning.

"But, we just got here," Stefano moaned. "We just got here! It's not fair! Just because Rebecca did something, why should we all get punished? It's not fair!"

"Tell Guido that we'll be leaving in the morning. I want to leave as early as possible."

"He's not here," Carlo said.

"What!"

"He didn't get back," Stefano said. "His bed isn't even mussed."

"You mean he still isn't back from last night?"

"I guess not."

"But, it's been more than twenty-four hours!"

The boys looked at her blankly, and she felt foolish for saying such a thing to them. "Well, let's start packing," she said.

At ten-thirty, Magdalena had the butler lock the door. *He'll have to ring the doorbell to get in. He won't be able to sneak in. Then, I'll really give him a piece of my mind.*

The bell rang hours later. She'd fallen asleep and was confused when she awoke on the sofa. Within seconds, though, she remembered why she was there, and the anger came back. She rushed to the front door.

"I hear you. I hear you. Stop ringing the bell. You'll wake all the children."

It was too late. Stefano, Rebecca and Carlo were downstairs

before she could unlatch the locks.

Magdalena opened the door and looked out. Standing there in the darkness were two burly strangers. They each had Guido by an arm. His uniform—or what was left of it—was torn and filthy, and as he lifted his head Rebecca screamed.

"Oh my God! Guido!"

That was when Carmine Pace emerged from the shadows.

"Don't get excited," he said smoothly. "He'll be all right."

"What happened to Guido?" Rebecca screamed. "Look at his face." He had been badly beaten, his face was black and blue and covered with dried blood.

"Don't get excited," Pace said. "He'll be all right. He'll be all right."

"What happened to Guido?" Rebecca repeated.

"Go back to bed," Magdalena shouted back. "Oh, my God, what happened? Come in. Come in. What happened?"

She wished she were having a nightmare—just a bad dream—and that she'd wake up to find nobody there.

"We found him outside one of the clubs," Pace answered. "At first, I thought he was just some bum lying there, but then I recognized him, so I told my driver to find out what house you'd rented, and we brought him here. It's better than a hospital. You know the way hospitals are. They'd ask a lot of questions."

"Of course. Of course. It's good that you brought him here. Bring him inside. His bedroom is next to the kitchen."

She watched the men carry Guido through the rooms. Then, she rushed ahead of them to open the door and pull the covers from his bed. "Shouldn't he have a doctor?"

"I've already called for one. He'll be here any minute now. I know him. He's okay. There won't be any questions. No reports. Nothing."

"What happened? Look at his face! His eyes!"

"From what I could gather," Pace said, "he was in a crap game on the wrong side of town. That wasn't too smart of him . . . going there alone, I mean. Some kind of fight started,

I guess. Don't worry, he'll be okay. He just got himself a bad beating, that's all."

The doctor came and left. The butler prepared sandwiches and coffee. The children were wide awake and ate again before returning to their rooms. Through it all, Magdalena spoke very little. Most of the time, she was thinking of how much she hated Saratoga. Each time she came here, something terrible happened. Pace's driver left with the doctor, but Pace remained for a while. Magdalena and he had more coffee; and, before she knew it, it was almost dawn.

"I'd better be going," he said. "You must be exhausted."

"Thank you for everything. I don't know what I would have done without you tonight. I'll tell my husband what a help you were. I'm returning to Jericho today."

"No you're not," he replied. "There's no way at all that he's going to be able to drive."

"Yes," she agreed thoughtfully. "I'm afraid you're right."

"Anyway, why go home? The season is just starting."

At the door, Pace said: "At least, one good thing's come out of tonight. Your daughter doesn't hate me anymore. She thinks I'm some kind of guardian angel, now. She's really very attached to your driver, isn't she?"

"We're all very fond of Guido. He's like one of the family. I don't know how to thank you."

"I do. Have lunch with me tomorrow. And then, watch the races with me."

"Well . . ."

". . . and bring the children, if you'd like. Now, you get yourself some sleep."

After a few hours of sorely needed sleep, Magdalena said to Rebecca, "I'm having lunch with Mr. Pace. Would you like to come with us, or would you prefer staying home? If you come, I'll expect you to behave yourself."

"Are Stefano and Carlo going with you?"

"Yes."

"Who's going to stay here and take care of Guido?"

"Marcello and Giulia are here. Anyway, Guido doesn't need any taking care of. All he needs is some rest."

She asked: "Are you going to tell Daddy about yesterday?"

"I might, and I might not. That all depends upon how you act until he gets here. Now, do you want to come with us or don't you? After lunch, we'll be watching the races."

"No. I want to stay home."

Pace called for them promptly at one. Rebecca stayed in her room until after they left. It would be a long day for her, she realized, and she was sorry she'd not gone with them. When they returned, she was sitting on the downstairs porch. She picked up a magazine, and pretended to be reading.

"You missed a good time today," Pace said to her. "Your brothers had a good time. Too bad you didn't feel well."

She looked sharply at Magdalena and said, "I wasn't sick. I only stayed home to take care of Guido."

"You like him, huh?" he asked.

"Of course, I do. Everybody likes Guido. Thank you for helping him last night."

"You're welcome," he told her, "but you thanked me enough last night. Tell me, would you like to join us tomorrow?"

"Tomorrow?" she asked.

"Yes," he said, "there's a horse called 'Rebecca's Darling.' We can put a bet on her, if you'd like."

She asked Magdalena, "You're going tomorrow, too?"

"Yes."

"All right, I'll come."

Magdalena and the children ate at home that evening. The boys were noisy, but Rebecca spoke very little.

"When I looked in on Guido before, he was sleeping," Magdalena told her. "How was he feeling today? Did he have any lunch?"

"I don't know."

"I thought you stayed home just to take care of him," Stefano said.

"Well, he needed rest, so I didn't bother him. But, I looked at him through his bedroom window. He didn't see me." She broke off there, because she didn't feel like talking anymore. She was thinking of what she might wear the following day. After dinner, she tried on several dresses before she settled upon a new pink one. Then, she piled her hair high and stared into the mirror.

She picks these dresses out on purpose. She wants me to look like a baby.

"When is Daddy coming?" she asked.

"If he's not too tired, he'll come straight from work on Friday night. Otherwise, he'll come Saturday. Why?"

"I was just wondering if he would take us to the races too."

She looked at herself in the mirror again. She would give Mr. Pace two dollars to bet on 'Rebecca's Darling' for her. She had ten.

He's nice.

"How much can you win if you bet two dollars?"

"I don't know," Magdalena answered.

"What about if you bet ten dollars?"

"I don't know."

Tullio got to Saratoga late Friday night, after the children were asleep. Magdalena had waited up, hoping he'd come.

"I must have a little witch in me," she said, "because I knew those were your headlights. Even when you were two blocks away, I knew it was you."

She told him about Guido and that she'd gone to the races with Pace. "I know you don't like my being with him, but, after all, he really did help us. And it would have looked so ungrateful to have refused to meet him the next day."

"And, you didn't want to seem ungrateful, so you went with him. Well, I'm sure he showed you a very good time."

"Oh, he did. He's such a gentleman, you know. You're not angry are you, Tullio? We really did have a very good time. Especially the boys. They love it down at the paddock. Rebecca

424

gets a little bored with the actual racing—so do I, after the second or third race—but I think she likes the glamour. You know, the dressing up, the strutting about, well, you know how she is."

He grinned. "Yes, she'd like that part of it."

Magdalena continued talking about all they'd done, all the new people they'd met, all the Gold Coasters they'd run into, and almost everything she could remember about the past few days. Then, she realized that he wasn't listening. "Is anything wrong?" she asked. "Tullio?"

"What?"

"Haven't you heard a word I've been saying?"

He asked: "What has Guido told you since that night?"

"What do you mean?"

"Did Guido tell you how he got beat up?"

"No, Carmine did. I've already told you that. Guido's hardly spoken at all. Every time I look in on him, he's sleeping."

"And Guido hasn't said one word about it?" he asked her.

"No, why should he?"

"Look, why don't you go upstairs? I'll be up in a little while. I want to have a talk with Guido."

"But, he must be sleeping."

"So, I'll wake him up!"

Magdalena was relieved. She'd thought that Tullio might be angry over her having been in Pace's company. "I'll be upstairs," she said. "You won't be long, will you?"

He'd not heard her. He'd already gone to the kitchen and was knocking on Guido's bedroom door. He didn't wait for an answer, but walked in. He winced when he saw Guido's face. He walked closer to the bed and, in a whisper, asked:

"Who did this . . . Pace?"

Guido nodded.

Tullio mumbled, "I had a feeling—I had that feeling."

It was difficult for Guido to talk, but he said: "He told me, 'Tell your boss that I'm getting impatient.' That's all he said. Nothing else."

"Did he see your credentials? Your name? Did he go through your wallet at all?" He paused then, and answered himself. "No, he'd have no reason to."

Guido mouthed, "I don't know. Why?"

Tullio didn't reply, but in a few seconds, said, "Maybe, you would be better off in a hospital. That guy they brought in could have been a horse doctor, for all we know."

Guido said, "No. No hospital. No hospital."

"All right, all right. What if I were to drive you back to *The Walls* tomorrow, so our own doctor can take a look at you? You think you can take that ride?"

He nodded.

Chapter Seven

When Tullio left Guido's bedroom, he sat on the downstairs porch for a while. He had to think very clearly, he decided, and possibly restructure his whole treatment of the Pace situation. He reasoned:

—He can't force me to do business with him. He can force others, but not me, not as long as I'm under Fallanca's protection. And, with me fronting for LoGiudice and Pire and Beckmann, he can't get any of their business, either. So, he's hurting.

—Still, he has to keep trying to convince me to go in with him. But by now, he must know that there's no way he can do that. Not without force. And, that brings him back to where he started: nowhere.

—So, now what? Now, he sends me a message.

—No! Now he sends me two messages, one through Guido, and the other through Magdalena and the children.

—Through Guido, he tells me how he feels—that he's frustrated, that he's furious—maybe, even with Fallanca, himself, for having put him in this position. At the same time, though, he lets me know that he's still level-headed enough to negotiate . . . to do business . . . and he proves it by not

427

actually killing Guido, which he could have done very easily, but by only beating him, and then, making sure he gets home.

—And, through Magdalena. That message was very clear, too. He just wanted to show me how vulnerable they are, that he can get to them anytime he wants. Well, almost anytime. I can't be with them twenty-four hours a day . . . and, I can't keep them on the estate all the time, either. And, what about Stefano? He'll be off to school next month . . . he'll be by himself . . . and I can't call the school every day, just to see if he's okay!

He sat in one of the deep, low swings and propped his legs up on the lacy balcony in front of him. There was no moon, and he might as well have been in a closet, it was so dark. He stared ahead at the black, quiet street that would explode into life in the morning. Then, he went over the facts once more, and decided:

—I've been too cocksure . . . too careless since Erich's here. But, Erich's not the answer . . . he's only a temporary play for time. How can I be so stupid not to have realized that before? Pace won't stand for this indefinitely. Fallanca or no Fallanca, Pace is losing too much money without my business, and, any day now, he might go over Fallanca's head, if he hasn't, already.

He rested his elbows on the swing's arms and brought his hands together and steepled his fingers: perhaps, he could think better now.

—No. There's no other way to look at it. I can twist it and turn it, but it all comes out the same in the end.

—That's that. He hasn't left me any choice.

He walked back into the living room and telephoned Salvatore. After telling his cousin what had happened, he asked that he and Erich come, in one car, to Saratoga. "That way, we'll have an extra driver to get Guido's car back to Jericho," he ended. "There's no way Guido, himself, can do any driving. He's a mess."

"We'll leave the first thing in the morning," Salvatore said.

"No, leave tonight. I'd like you both here by morning."

"Tullio, that's a long, long drive, and we didn't get any sleep yet."

He answered, "Yes, I know. I just got here, myself. Drive carefully. I'll see you in the morning." He heard Salvatore grunt before hanging up.

"Who in the world are you calling at this hour?" Magdalena asked him.

"I thought you went upstairs."

"I did, but I just came down to see what was keeping you."

He said, "I want you to start packing. We're leaving in the morning."

"What! Why?"

"Magda, please! For once in your life, don't ask questions! And, don't give me any arguments. Just do what I'm saying. Pack as much as you can tonight, and then, get some sleep. I want as little as possible left to do in the morning. We'll be leaving very early."

"No. I will not do that. I will not move. I'm going to stand right here until you tell me what's going on."

He was about to say something, but the telephone rang. It was Salvatore again.

"Tullio, I don't trust you," he said. "You're up to something, aren't you? Something crazy . . ."

"Like what?" he asked, then turned toward Magdalena and said: "Will you please go upstairs?"

She didn't move.

Salvatore said, "You're going after Pace tonight, aren't you? I can feel it in my bones."

Tullio took a deep breath, then asked, "Well, what in hell else can I do? What would you do if you were in my place?" He wanted to say more, but Magdalena was there. He held his hand over the speaker part of the telephone and said to her: "I asked you to go upstairs."

She folded her arms in front of her and stood very still.

Tullio could hear Salvatore sigh; he could hear the click of his cigarette lighter; he could hear him exhale. Then:

"Okay, okay," Salvatore replied. "I'll agree that there might be no alternative. But, wait. Wait for us to get there. Will you do that? Will you wait? Will you wait, just until morning?"

"Hold on," Tullio said. "I'll be right back." He put down the telephone receiver and walked toward Magdalena. Then, without hesitation, he half-dragged and half-carried her up the steps.

Magdalena fought him all the while. She tried to pull loose. She tried to kick him away. She tried not to cry.

He pushed her into the bedroom and said: "I don't want you to come downstairs again," then closed the door behind him.

When Tullio returned to the telephone, Salvatore asked: "What's going on there?"

"Nothing," he answered, "nothing."

"So, what do you say? Will you wait in that house until morning?"

"What I was thinking," Tullio said, "was that I can get him tonight. Nobody even knows that I'm here in Saratoga, so I wouldn't even be suspect. By the time I find him and finish, it might be about dawn. I would come back to the house then, pick up Magdalena and the kids and probably be gone before anyone even finds him. You and Erich should be here by then, and you can get Guido and the luggage back to Jericho."

For a few moments, there was silence on the telephone, because they were both thinking. Tullio broke the silence. "It's best that you leave here early, too, just in case Pace's boys put two and two together. You never know—they might come nosing around—you never know. Anyway, there's no sense in anybody knowing that you and Erich came up here, either. That way, we're all in the clear."

"You can't push me around like that!" Magdalena cried out. Tullio jumped because she'd startled him.

"I'm not your mother, you know!"

He said, "I don't believe you're down here again. I don't

believe it."

Salvatore asked him what was wrong.

"Nothing. It's just Magdalena."

"All right. Listen, Tullio, be careful. Don't take any chances tonight. If you see it's going to be rough, well, then, put it off. We'll get him another time."

The cousins spoke for a few more seconds. When they were through, Tullio said to Magdalena: "I really can't believe that you walked out of that bedroom and actually came down those steps again. You're one for the books."

"You can't push me around," she said. "Not you. Not anybody."

He didn't want to argue. Not now. Not tonight. He put on his jacket.

She glared at him. "You're going out?"

He didn't answer. He counted the bills in his money clip.

"First, you push me around like a bag of potatoes? And then, you go out? . . . just like that?"

He thought he'd brought more money with him. He recounted it.

"Where are you going?"

He returned her glare and said, "I'm going out to kill somebody. All right?"

She had no words, or too many; she didn't know which.

He said, "I'm sorry, but I really do have to go out. It's something that just came up. I'll be back in a few hours, maybe less."

He expected some kind of answer. He waited for one. But, Magdalena had no intention of talking with anything but her eyes. He took a deep breath, mumbled, "Don't forget to lock the door behind me," and left.

Carmine Pace usually stayed in Hager House. Tullio drove there and parked directly across from its main entrance. He called the hotel from a telephone booth alongside his car.

"Mr. Pace? Yes, he's with us," the clerk answered. "Room 304. But, he's out just now. Would you care to leave a message?"

"No, thank you," Tullio said, "I'll call back tomorrow."

Tullio was glad that Pace hadn't returned yet, because, even though he would use the stairs to Pace's room instead of the elevator, he would still have to walk through the lobby, and someone might recognize him. It was safer waiting in the car.

He glanced at his watch. The clubs would be closing soon. He shouldn't have too long to wait. He hoped that Pace wouldn't bring a woman back to the hotel; that would ruin everything—he'd have to catch Pace alone. He checked the clip in his pistol, then switched on some soft music and tried to make himself comfortable.

He'd drive the estate car, rather than his own, to Hager House because nobody would notice a black limousine during racing season; everybody owned one, or, at least, rented one until September. He remembered the instructions he'd given Guido in Orvietto. He unlocked the glove compartment and found one of the three guns he'd had made; from this, he assumed that another was in the trunk. He winced and shook his head when he thought of Guido again. He'd have to ask him why he'd not had a chance to protect himself with the third gun, the one he was supposed to have been wearing under his uniform. He doubted very much that the driver would have gone out without it.

He checked his watch again and, realizing how tired he was, hoped he would not fall asleep. He was very surprised that he felt so calm. He should be nervous, he reasoned. He should be upset. He should, at the very least, be a little bit scared. It was murder, after all. He couldn't pretend it was anything else. That's what just sitting and waiting to kill someone was called. Murder. Cold-blooded murder. He didn't know why he didn't feel anything. He was amazed, not only with himself, but with Salvatore, too, because they'd discussed it so matter-of-factly over the telephone, as though they'd been planning just

432

another annoying, but necessary, business meeting.

No, he thought, Salvatore had had some feeling. He'd asked him to be careful, not to take any chances. That showed concern, and concern is some kind of feeling.

But, he, himself? He couldn't feel anything. He was so amazed that, were the matter not so serious, he would think it funny.

He wondered if he could have known all along—from the very moment he'd left Guido's room—that he would be doing this tonight. Had all the arguments he'd offered himself on the porch been only a means to excuse the action? Or, had he simply been trying to appease his conscience, since he'd already made up his mind?

Appease his conscience? That would imply some feeling of guilt. That would be fine, except that he didn't feel guilty. He didn't feel anything.

Maybe, this was normal. Maybe, this is what always happened when usually law-abiding men decided to commit murder. Maybe, a complete lack of emotion was absolutely necessary. Maybe, if there were emotions—fear, misgivings, second thoughts—they couldn't go through with it. He didn't know. Anything was possible.

He shrugged, almost grimaced, because he didn't care.

The music was very mellow. *Blue Skies* was being played, and this made him think of Magdalena. He wondered if she had started to pack. He was sorry he'd lost his temper with her. He'd come very close to striking her. Too close. He might have hurt her. He'd have to sit her down and have a long talk with her. He'd asked her, three times, to go upstairs; she should know better than to just stand there while he was trying to talk business. Business? Was he in the killing business now? No matter. They'd have to have a very long talk. What did his mother have to do with this? She'd mentioned his mother. She never even knew his mother.

A car pulled up in front of Hager House. He shut off the radio. He waited. In a few seconds, an elderly couple got out and walked into the hotel. Then their chauffeur drove away.

Tullio was annoyed. He'd thought that this might be the end of his vigil. Instead, his head was starting to ache again. He leaned back again and yawned. Within the minute, thinking that he would close his eyes for just a few seconds, he dozed off.

It was just a few moments after Tullio fell asleep that Carmine Pace arrived.

As Pace's yellow Rolls turned the corner, its headlights lit up the telephone booth and the car in front of it. He recognized the license plate number and directed his driver to ease up next to it. He leaned his head out the window and said:

"Well, well, well, Barragatto, I can't think of any other reason for you to be sitting here at such an hour, except to be waiting for me."

Tullio's eyes blinked wide awake when he heard Pace's voice. He cursed under his breath, furious with himself that he'd fallen asleep. He looked at the driver and at a third man who was seated next to Pace. He recognized them. He'd seen them with Pace in New York. He sat up straight. He wondered if he could get all three—no, it would be stupid even to try.

Pace smirked, as though he were reading his mind. Then, he asked: "Well? You want to talk?"

"I got your message," Tullio replied.

"I'd gathered that much, as soon as I saw you sitting here," he answered. "So? Do we talk or don't we?"

"Not with them. Alone."

Carmine Pace said something to his men, then smiled at Tullio and said, "Fine, we talk alone." He stepped out from his car and asked: "Upstairs? In my suite?"

"No, here," Tullio answered.

Pace nodded. He waited for Tullio to unlock the passenger door, then climbed in alongside of him. When Tullio looked at the other men, Pace said: "They're not leaving . . . but, they can't hear a word we say if you roll up your window." He paused and shrugged. "That's as alone as we'll be getting."

Tullio didn't know what to say. He hadn't planned on

434

talking. He said: "This thing with us . . . it's been going on too long and, it's got to stop."

"Well, it's good to see that there's something we agree on. It's about time."

"It's got to stop right now," Tullio continued, "because, if it doesn't . . ."

"If it doesn't . . . what?" Pace held open his palms.

Tullio gave him a quick, dirty look.

Pace repeated: "If it doesn't, what? What's going to happen? You're going to come and shoot me between the eyes? Something like that?" He paused. "Well, that's what you were up to tonight, wasn't it? Only, you didn't expect me to have any company with me, did you?"

"That's right," Tullio answered. "That's exactly right."

Pace smiled nastily. "Tch, tch, tch. What a pity. That would have caused such a waste. A beautiful young woman like that . . ."

"I have a feeling that you're going to tell me what you're talking about," Tullio said, "whether I want to hear about it or not."

Pace answered, "That's right. I am going to tell you. All these years, I've tried to avoid it. I thought that we could do business without my having to bring up such an unpleasant subject. But, we're at that point, right now, where you just don't leave me any choice. You see, not too many years ago, I saw a young woman kill a man. It wasn't a very pretty sight. She almost blew his head off. Of course, I wasn't the only one who saw it happen. There was somebody with me at the time. He would have gone to the police, and that sweet little lady would have been arrested for murder. But I sort of talked him out of it. Now, if something were to happen to me, I have a very strong feeling that he would tell all. As a matter of fact, I'm pretty sure that he would, since those are his orders."

"Get to the point, Pace."

"The point?" Carmine Pace grinned and said, "All in good time."

Tullio interrupted. "Who was it? Bella? She killed someone?"

"As I was saying," Pace continued, "it would be a real pity if that lovely young woman were to be arrested for murder. And, I'm sure you wouldn't like to see it happen, either. And, by the way . . . it wasn't Bella."

For the first time since Pace had sat in the car, Tullio faced him.

"Whoever the hell the woman was, what does it have to do with us . . . you and me . . . here and now?"

"It has a lot to do with us. As a matter of fact, it's what's going to make you decide to play ball. From now on, we're partners. Either that, or I blow the whistle on her."

A cloud of uneasiness fell over Tullio like a crumbling question mark. What some woman did years ago could not be totally unrelated to him, not if Pace were talking in such terms. He knew Pace better than that. He said: "All right, let's not play guessing games. Who was she, and what makes you think I'd sell you my wine just to protect her?"

"She was your wife."

Carmine Pace seized the silence to continue: "We—the other witness and I—we buried the man and the gun just outside the county line. Ask her about it. I don't think she'll be able to fill in all the details, since she was feeling no pain at the time . . . but, you have nothing to lose by asking." He opened the car door and said, "I don't think you're going to hear another word I say tonight. We'll talk again, back in the City."

Pace stepped out from Tullio's car. He walked around it and sent his men away. Then, he walked across the street and, just before entering Hager House, nodded his goodnight toward Tullio.

Tullio did not know how long he sat there, just gaping at the stained-glass doors through which Carmine Pace had disappeared. He could only guess that it was a long time, because he'd begun a fresh pack of cigarettes just before meeting Pace and now had only a few left.

He could, as Pace had suggested, ask her about it; but, why bother? Pace would never make up such a story.

When he drove back to the rented house, Salvatore's car was parked in front. He would have driven away again, because he didn't want to see them just yet, but Erich waved to him from the window.

Both men came out to the porch. There were questions all over their faces. Erich said, "We just got here, about ten minutes ago. Everything okay?" and Salvatore's eyes asked, "How did it go?"

Tullio squinted because the sunrise was teasing the streets and bouncing off the window panes. His head ached worse than ever. He didn't answer. He wished he didn't have to talk. He wasn't ready. He said, "Is there any coffee made?"

Salvatore asked him, "What happened, Tullio?"

"I met him. We talked for a while."

"That's all?" Erich asked. "Talked? Just talked?"

Salvatore said, "That's okay. We'll get him another time. It's better you didn't take any chances."

"We talked," Tullio repeated, "and I've decided to go in with him."

His response shocked them. He'd expected that it would. He gave them a moment to absorb it, then added, "We're losing too much money by not dealing with him. Anyway, if anything were to happen to Pace, he'd be replaced within the week. We all know that. There's no way of getting around it."

Erich said, "But, we've always known that. That's nothing new. Why the sudden concern about it?"

Tullio replied, "Pace is under your father's thumb. His replacement might not be."

Erich said, "So? We've always known that, too."

Tullio said, "Then, it's about time that we admitted it out loud. It's no use. There's no sense in continuing what we've been doing. They'll win in the end. Sooner or later, one way or another, they're going to have their way. They always do. So, we might as well cash in on it, while we still can."

437

"What do I tell Beckmann?" Veidt asked. "And LoGiudice? And Pire? What do I say to them? That all deals are off? That we've suddenly had a change of heart? That, now, it's every man for himself?"

Salvatore motioned for Erich Veidt not to get excited, but the young man refused to be quieted. He continued: "They all would have gone in with Pace a long time ago, but you talked them out of it. Their vineyards have been scorched. Their cellars have been flooded. A lot of their pickers have been scared away. But, still, they've agreed not to deal with Pace. And, all because of you. Because you shamed them into it. Because you made it sound like some kind of holy principle." He waited for Tullio to say something in his own defense; but, when no answer came, he said, "They'll all have to deal with Pace if Barragatto Wineries does. They'll have no choice. And, they'll think that you sold them out, that you made some kind of deal, that you'll be getting a higher percentage than they'd get."

"We didn't discuss numbers," Tullio said. "As a matter of fact, Pace doesn't even know yet what I've decided."

Magdalena walked out to the porch. She was carrying a coffee pot and a maid was following her with a tray filled with cups and saucers and buns. She didn't look at her husband. Nor did he look at her. She said, "The children are still asleep, and I thought we'd have some breakfast before they wake up. The packing is almost done. As soon as they wake up, I'll feed and dress them, and we can leave."

This wasn't the Magdalena whom Erich knew. She had no smile and her speech and movements were abrupt. "A little early for you, isn't it?" he said; but, since she only shrugged, he didn't say anymore. He expected that, at any moment, Tullio would ask her to excuse them, that he would tell her they were discussing business; he was certain that Salvatore was waiting for this, also. But, this didn't happen.

The two men gaped at one another from over their coffee cups. They couldn't ask her to leave. They couldn't say a word to her. It was up to her husband.

After a silent breakfast, Magdalena asked if there was anything else they would like. When they said no, that they'd had enough, and the maid began loading the dishes on the tray, Magdalena was about to leave when Tullio said: "Sit down, Magda, I want to talk to you."

Erich said, "Since there's no more reason for us to hurry anymore, I'm going to take a nap." He left them.

Tullio motioned for his cousin to remain.

Magdalena was still too angry with Tullio over what had happened the previous night and much too tired to be really interested in what he had to say, but she sat down again, as requested. She'd been surprised when Salvatore and Erich had arrived so early. She'd had no idea they were coming. This had upset her also; she felt that she should have been told to expect company. She waited for Tullio to begin. When he didn't right away, she asked, "Well, what is it?"

He replied, "I don't want to get into any long discussions, and I don't want any explanations. Not now, anyway. All I need, right now, are simple 'yes' or 'no' answers. Understood?"

Tullio's voice was almost in a whisper, and this made Salvatore's eyes narrow. He looked from Tullio to Magdalena, suspecting that something quite serious was about to unfold. He waited with the same blank silence as Magdalena until his cousin said:

"A few years back, you shot a man. Yes or no."

"Oh!" This was all she could say.

"I gather that means yes."

She stared at him with contempt.

". . . and, if so, who else, besides Pace was witness to it? Well? Was there somebody else there? Yes or no? Or, were you really so drunk that you didn't notice?" He didn't bother looking at either his wife or his cousin as he spoke. He could feel the thunderbolt that he'd hit them with. Why bother looking at it? "I've been told that there's another witness. Try to think clearly, if that's not asking the impossible. Was there somebody else there?"

"Who told you? Erich? Did Erich tell you?"

Salvatore asked, "How does Erich know about this?"

"Erich knows?" Tullio was as amazed as Salvatore.

"I told him about it," Magdalena said.

"Who else?" Salvatore asked her. "Who else knows?"

"Aleksey," she said. "Erich and Aleksey."

"You don't tell me, your own husband . . . or, Salvatore, who's at least part of the family . . . but you tell them . . ."

"The man was shot in the ear. That's all. In the ear."

There was a glint of hope in Tullio. He asked, "In the ear? You actually saw that it was only his ear? You saw him walk away?"

Salvatore interrupted. "Magdalena," he said, "it's very important that you tell us the truth. What's done is done. It can't be undone. But, we have to know exactly what happened."

"I don't know if he walked away or not. That's what Carmine told me happened. He said the man was shot in the ear. He took care of the man. He brought him to a doctor. That's what he told me."

"Then, you really don't know!" Tullio said.

"Was there somebody else there?" Salvatore asked. "Another witness?"

"I don't know."

"How can you not know such a thing?" he persisted.

"Because she was drunk," Tullio replied, "that's how. She was cockeyed drunk."

"It isn't very difficult to hate you, Tullio. It isn't very difficult at all," she said.

He answered, "Since the moment I got back to this house, I've been trying not to wipe the floor with you. It's getting harder and harder every second. So, I suggest you make yourself invisible—right now—since I can't hold out much longer."

She would have lunged at her husband, but Salvatore was

between them. The only things close enough for her to reach out for were the cups and saucers on the tray. She threw them to the floor with such violence that Salvatore cringed, holding his hands up in front of his eyes to protect them from the splattering china. Tullio didn't budge.

"You're very good at pushing around women," she said, "at threatening them and condemning them before you know all the facts."

"You'd better get out of my sight," he answered.

"But you're not any good at listening. If you were the type of husband who would listen once in a while, I wouldn't have to go telling my problems to others, like Aleksey and Erich. I'd be able to come straight to you. But, no. Even now, you don't want an explanation. I knew you'd react this way. That's why I couldn't tell you the whole truth!"

"I've never hit you," he said, "but, I will, if you don't get away from here right now. You'd better not say another word. And, you'd better get out of my sight."

"Come on! Magdalena! Tullio! Both of you!" Salvatore said. "You're both getting too excited! It's not going to do anybody any good!"

"She ruined me, that bitch! She ruined me!"

Tullio's voice had cracked as he'd shouted, and his eyes had watered. His cousin and wife stared at him with equal amazement and he flushed with anger and embarrassment. He stood up awkwardly and the chair fell back.

Salvatore said, "Magdalena, go inside. Go inside. Finish the packing."

She threw up her hands in despair and left the cousins alone. She passed Erich on the way in.

"What's going on?" he asked her. Because she didn't answer, he walked out to the porch. He saw the broken china scattered all over and looked from it to Salvatore and Tullio. "What happened? What's all the yelling about? As soon as I put my head on the pillow, it sounded like all hell was breaking loose."

Salvatore said, "You should have told us about her shooting

a man. She said that she told you. Whatever possessed you to keep such a thing from us?"

"Oh, she told you about that."

"No, Pace did."

"Why didn't you tell me?" Tullio asked him.

"Because she asked me not to," he answered. He added, "I checked into it . . . and I couldn't find any record of any shooting at the time it was supposed to have happened. So, whatever happened, there wasn't any harm done. The guy was patched up, and that was that."

Salvatore said to Tullio, "Pace could be lying."

Tullio asked him, "Do you think he'd say something he couldn't back up?"

Salvatore rubbed his hands over his face and said, "No, no, I don't think so."

Erich said, "So, that's what this is all about. Okay. I'll get rid of Pace myself."

Tullio replied, "He says there was another witness."

"So what!" Erich answered. "Big deal! Two men saw another one shot in the ear! Big deal!"

"Pace says the man was killed, that he's buried outside the county line. He wasn't just shot in the ear."

"He might be lying," Erich said.

Tullio said, "I don't think so."

Chapter Eight

Tullio had never forgiven Magdalena. She'd had the chance to tell him the whole truth, and, by not doing so, she'd left it to be used against him. She'd compromised him, as far as he was concerned, and that was unpardonable. He still desired her; that hadn't changed. He still protected her; he believed it was his duty. But, he did not think that any of this was enough reason to forgive her, or ever to trust her again.

Salvatore had met with each of the wine men individually. Tullio had not wanted to face them. He could imagine the unspoken accusations of betrayal in their eyes—his fall from honor. It was easier for Salvatore because the decision wasn't his own, but his cousin's; that was Salvatore's own reasoning when he'd volunteered to break the news to the wine men.

"I'm my cousin's attorney," Salvatore told them. "It's not my place to make excuses for his decisions." He elaborated, saying, "Anyway, I, personally, am in favor of it. We've held out long enough. We've accomplished a great deal. We've shown Pace that we can't be pushed around so easily. That gives us a stronger bargaining base. We can still deal with him as one unit, if you'll agree to come in with us. It's up to you."

The idea had unnerved LoGiudice. He was a Fascist. "There

was a good chance that I might become the captain of my district," he said, "a very good chance. But, it will never happen now. Not once they learn I'm running wine for the *malandrini*. They're sure to find out. You can't keep something like that a secret." He clasped his hands and said, "Up until now, I've been hiding only from the *malandrini*. Once my own people find out, I'll be looking over my shoulder for them, instead."

Salvatore had been surprised that LoGiudice gave in so easily. He'd expected that the man would come around in the end, but he'd never thought it would be with so little argument. The only reason he could fathom was that LoGiudice had no sons to help him fight Pace. A man who has only daughters needs partners when he grows old.

Pire had acquiesced without any resistance at all. "To tell you the truth," he said, "I was thinking of going in with Pace. I'm tired of trying to fight him off. I've got to admit, though, that I'm surprised that it was Barragatto who was the first to give in."

"He didn't give in," Salvatore had said, "he just changed his mind. That's all."

Pire had laughed softly at this and had answered, "Okay, okay, he just changed his mind."

Beckmann had refused to comply. "I don't bend to racketeers," he said, "and I'm disappointed in your cousin. I never thought he would be a turncoat. I expected better things from him. I've no doubt that my wife's son, Gerhard, disagrees with me, but it makes no difference, since mine is still the last word in my family . . . and I will not run wine! You tell this to Tullio, and you tell him that he's a very big disappointment."

Salvatore had reported to Tullio only: "Beckmann's going to stay on his own. Pire and LoGiudice will work with us."

"What did Beckmann say?"

"Just what I told you. That he'll work it out on his own."

"Pace won't stand for that. He wants the whole package, and that includes the Rhine white."

"That's not our problem any longer. It's Beckmann's."

"They'll kill him."

"That's not our problem, either."

"I don't believe Beckmann didn't say anything else."

"That's your problem."

Within the next few months, the operation had begun. The wine was brought into the States by the Asheley Steamships in crates marked "Prefabricated Parts." When, several weeks later, Herr Beckmann was in a fatal automobile accident, Gerhard Moeller joined the group. Now, the package was complete.

America was thirsty. She had beer runners and whisky runners; but Pace's organization was the only one that was supplying her with the fine wines, directly from the home cellars. The largest restaurants and private clubs flocked to him. He had no reason to try to force them to buy; the demand was more than he could handle. By the end of the first year, the group was the main source of supply for southeastern Canada, as well.

Tullio Barragatto charged Carmine Pace top dollar for the wines. Salvatore warned him against it each time he raised the price, but, to the attorney's surprise, Pace accepted each price increase without resistance.

"Why should Pace care what the price is?" Tullio asked. "He passes the increase on to his buyers, so he doesn't lose anything. Anyway, the more you charge certain people for something, the more they want it."

Tullio directed the sale of the wines just as well as he directed the legal facets of North American Distributors. He made all the decisions, Salvatore did the negotiating, and Erich oversaw the actual transfer of the goods. It was up to Pace to provide protection from the authorities, and he did this very well. The one most difficult aspect of the entire operation was hiding it from Earl Asheley and Aleksey Kostenov.

"I had lunch at Lacey's today," Earl once said to him. "They served me some *Barragatto*. The other day, I was served some

445

at the club."

"They have good taste," Tullio replied.

"Did you know that it was getting into the country?" the man asked.

"Everything gets into the country," he said, "one way or another."

"But, were you aware of it?"

"I've heard that it's around. I've heard that Gerhard's is around, too. Whoever's bringing it in, all the power to them."

"But, you must have some idea of who they are. You know your own customers. You know who's buying it packed for export."

"Earl, once the bottles leave Orvietto, I have no idea where they wind up. So, just get what you can, and enjoy it."

The answer didn't satisfy Asheley. He, himself, had been involved in too many of the wrong things during his youth. He didn't press the issue, though. He hoped only that whatever his young partner was into didn't involve North American Distributors.

Kostenov, however, was not so easily quieted. He said, "Earl will be retiring in a few months, and I'll be taking on a lot more work. If there's something I should know, tell me, now, so I don't get hit with it all at once."

Tullio was in the midst of opening his morning mail. "What do you mean, something you should know?"

"Tullio, Tullio, you're still trying to make a monkey out of me. Well, all right, rather than playing around with words . . . how come the manifests show so many pre-fabricated parts? The motels up in New England are finished. What are these parts for?"

"We're expanding the units up there. We're building in Vermont and Massachusetts."

Kostenov started tapping his fingers on the windowsill. "I went down to the docks yesterday, Tullio. One of the trucks that the crates were being loaded into was heading out to Illinois. I spoke to the driver."

Tullio took a long, deep breath, but he didn't comment.

"Well?" Kostenov asked. "Are you building motels in Illinois, also?"

Tullio put down the bulk of unopened envelopes. "Okay, Aleksey. So, you know."

"I'm quite amazed that Earl would go along with this."

"He doesn't know a thing about it."

"I see," Kostenov answered. "How long do you think you can get away with it?"

"As long as I have to," he said. "Well, Jesus Christ! It's a damned, stupid law, anyway! People are going to drink whether it's legal or not! They might as well drink my stuff!"

Aleksey sat across from him. "Tullio, are you doing this independently?"

He didn't answer his old tutor.

"So, as I was afraid . . . you've stepped right into quick-sand."

"Nobody's getting hurt in this, Aleksey. There's no strong-arm business. No one's getting pushed around. No one's being forced to buy the wine. All we're doing is supplying a demand, and the demand is very big right now."

"Quicksand," Aleksey said, "that's what you've gotten yourself into, quicksand. I've kept quiet all these years about that whorehouse you're running, but . . ."

There was a quick, furtive glance.

"Yes, yes, I've known about that for a long time. You're still not smart enough to fool me for too long."

"You knew?"

"Yes, I knew. It's harmless, so I let you and your cousin have your fun. But it's harmless only because you're running it independently. But this . . . this thing you've gotten yourselves into . . . this is different. There's nothing harm-less about this."

"Well, we're in it. So, that's that." He put down the letter he was trying to read and said, "Look, Aleksey, I don't expect you to get involved with it. As a matter of fact, I'd rather you'd

447

stay out."

"How thoughtful of you. Have you given as much thought to your sons? Once you do business with the vermin, you're in that business for the rest of your life. What happens when you're too old to run things for yourself? Who do you think is going to pick up where you leave off? Your sons! Stefano and Carlo!"

"That will never happen."

"Your grandfather did business with them, your father did, and now, you. It's a national disease with you people. Every single generation. You always find some reason to deal with them. What's yours? Do you owe them any favors? Are they threatening the family? Or, are you just simply afraid of them? What's your reason? You'd better have a good one, because, some day, your sons are going to ask what it was."

"I said that they'll never be involved, Aleksey. I meant it."

"Then, prevent it. Break the chain now."

"I can't."

"Yes, you can."

"I said I can't! It's too involved! I can't!"

Aleksey left Tullio's office. He mumbled something again about quicksand, and something that sounded like *It's in the blood,* but Tullio couldn't hear what he'd said. He'd wanted to ask Aleksey to repeat it, but he changed his mind because it might lead to another argument. He could feel another headache coming on, but he continued reading his morning mail. One of the letters was from Nicole. It was the first time he'd heard from her since he'd last seen her, three years before.

As soon as he'd seen the envelope, he'd known it was from Nicole. There wasn't a return address on it, but it was postmarked from Antwerp, and she was the only Belgian he knew. A flurry of excitement rushed through him, and he almost ripped the letter as he opened the envelope. He'd not wanted to open it until Aleksey was out of the office.

She wrote that she was living near her parents in "a small

apartment, but certainly large enough for my daughter and me." Because of the baby, an annulment had been impossible, so she'd asked Gerhard for a divorce. He'd agreed finally "and, I'm free now, my darling. It's taken so long, and it's been so painful in the process, but I'm free. That's all that's important. Naturally, my neighbors all think I'm a widow."

She explained that she'd not dared to write him until all the legalities were finalized because she'd feared any repercussions. Had he thought she'd forgotten him? Or, had he thought she'd found another? Hadn't he known that he was still in her heart? "Most important, the thought that you might no longer think of me frightens me every day and wakes me in the middle of the night. You do still want me, don't you? You do still feel the same way? I can understand why I haven't heard from you. After all, you didn't know where I was. But, you know now, and you know that I'm waiting, just as I said I would."

It was a long letter, filled with words of love and promises, and it made him uneasy. She wanted to know when he was coming to Antwerp, or if he would prefer that she come to New York.

He read the letter again, then burned it. He was tempted to answer immediately, and say: Remember? Don't you remember what I said? Don't you remember that I said you shouldn't wait for me? Don't you remember? Why are you speaking as though I'd made some kind of commitment, when I didn't?

But, he didn't write. Not only did he not want to hurt her by saying these things, but he was afraid to put anything at all in writing. He couldn't trust her, not anymore than he could trust Magdalena . . . they weren't that terribly different from one another . . . they could do such stupid things, these women. In one fleeting moment of fear or anger, they could wreak such havoc. A woman was capable of anything. No, he could not trust her. If Magdalena, whom he'd thought he'd known so well, could shoot a man, what could Nicole do?

Two months later, he received a second letter from Nicole. She said, among other things: ". . . and I can't delude myself into thinking that you might not have received my first letter. I know that you did. Why haven't I heard from you? I wait by my window every morning, just watching for the postman, and every morning it's the same disappointment."

This letter was longer than the previous one. Near the end, she wrote: "It seems that all the patience I've had these past three years has suddenly vanished, now that I know I am free to be with you. Of course, there could be a very good reason for your silence, and I fear even to guess what that might be."

She'd included a return address on the envelope this time. He jotted it into his pocket notebook; then, he burned this letter, also. He left the office a few minutes later. He had some last minute arrangements to make, because he was sailing to Italy the following day.

Since moving to America, the farthest from Jericho that Magdalena had travelled was Saratoga. She was thrilled when Tullio agreed to take her and the children abroad with him this year. For the past couple of months, she'd been preparing. Louise Asheley had been caught up in Magdalena's excitement, and Tullio, having noticed this, had invited her to come along, also, if Earl wouldn't mind.

"I won't have much time to give them once we dock," he'd told Earl, "because I'll be too busy, what with harvest and all. I'll have a couple of my cousins show them the country, though. They should enjoy that."

Because it was late summer, the sailing was almost a good one, as far as Tullio's stomach was concerned. He had almost no complaints this trip. He seldom saw Stefano and Carlo between meals because there was so much for the boys to do. He gambled a lot, when he wasn't escorting Magdalena and Louise in and out of dining rooms and lounges. Rebecca was pursued by a few teenage boys during the bulk of the voyage, and this seemed to flatter him more than it did her. When they docked in Genoa, he was a little sorry that the sailing had ended.

Home

Chapter One

The gates fronting the Barragatto compound, unlike those at *The Walls of Jericho,* were never locked, and the children were free to come and go at will, a liberty they'd never been allowed at home. Because they were already bilingual, they had no trouble mixing with their newly-found friends and relatives, and this made their stay in Orvietto even more enjoyable. It was obvious to Magdalena and Tullio, and even to Louise, that the children had never been so happy.

Stefano left the house the earliest every morning. He took to the vineyards as though he'd been born to them, and spent endless hours alongside the pickers' children. Then, when the farmboys would go home for dinner, he would return to the compound and go into the cellars; and there, he'd gaze up at the vats and kegs and breathe in the vapors all around him until he was light-headed and a little giddy. He'd nap before dinner, and then—the Barragattos never ate before nine—he'd pose dozens of questions to Tullio while they were at the table. He'd ask about vintage years, and native grapes, and hybrids, and dominants; and Tullio, forgetting himself, would relish the boy's curiosity and respond and explain in such detail that the two of them might as well have been alone because they had no conversation left for anyone else.

Carlo, who'd been used to receiving most of his father's attention, was a little jealous of Stefano at first, but the feeling soon gave way because he was the darling of Tullio's aunts. He beamed each time they commented about how much like his father he looked; and, because the old ladies smothered him with hugs and kisses and home-made candies, his self-importance zoomed. There was no question about it: Carlo was the new prince of the compound. Even the servants nodded slightly when he spoke to them.

Rebecca, without a doubt, was the most sophisticated thirteen-year-old in Orvietto. The other girls flocked around her like ladies-in-waiting and listened to her tales of Gold Coast parties and bootleggers and flappers and speakeasies. One of them, who'd heard about the racing season in Saratoga, was stymied because she'd finally met someone who'd actually been there. That girl's ooh's and aah's lent even more credence to Rebecca's stories, so the young New Yorker was quickly the most popular of her peers.

To Louise and Magdalena, though, Orvietto was something quite different.

The quiet little town was merely a stopover for Louise, a place to regain her landlegs after the long ocean voyage, a home base from which she would set out to tour the rest of the country. She saw it as a comfortable example of the Old World, something quaint that she'd heard about and read about, but had never been able to imagine; and she suddenly understood more about Tullio than she ever had; he'd always seemed a little unusual to her before, but now, he was just as natural as can be.

Magdalena found Orvietto the same as she'd left it. For a while—a very short while aboard ship—she'd thought that it might be pleasant to revisit the grand old house. She'd almost looked forward to seeing its high, frescoed ceilings again, and to gathering up her favorite lilac flowers that ran rampant near the fountains. When she'd docked in Genoa, she'd praised the old place to Louise, describing its paintings and furnishings in startling detail. It wasn't until she'd actually walked into the entrance foyer that her loathing for the place returned. It had been early evening, and it had just stopped raining. Everything had had a musky feeling about it. The first thing she'd seen when the huge entrance doors opened for her was the look in the eyes of Tullio's aunts. And, she'd wondered immediately how she could ever have forgotten that look.

"You know, Magdalena," Tullio said, "my aunts are very reserved. Just because they don't beam whenever they see you, it doesn't mean that they don't like you."

"I'm not asking that they like me," she answered. "As a matter of fact, I really don't care whether they like me or not. That's not the point."

"Then, what is it, for heaven's sake? You're constantly picking on them. There isn't a thing they do or say that you don't have something to complain over."

She said, "Tullio, the moment their eyes met mine, it started again. Without saying a single word, without uttering even a sound, they asked, 'You low-born creature, you. How did you get the nerve to marry one of us?'"

"That's ridiculous. You just have an inferiority complex when you're around them."

". . . and," she continued, "when they look at Rebecca . . . and when they look at Stefano, too . . . their eyes ask, 'What rights do you two have to our name?'"

"Stop this, Magda! I absolutely forbid you to keep talking like this!"

"The only times their witch-eyes don't hiss is when they're with you and Carlo."

"I said stop it!"

"And, as I said before, I really don't care whether they like me or not. Believe me, as God is my judge, I couldn't care less about that . . . just as I'm sure they don't care what I think about them. What I do care about, and what I expect you to put a halt to, is the total lack of respect they give me. You see,

455

whether they can accept it in their hearts or not, I am your wife. And, I swear to you, Tullio: if you should die before they do . . . which would leave the bulk of the Barragatto fortune in my hands until the children are of age, I swear that I will kick them both out in the street without a penny. I will kick them out, right out on their hypocritical asses."

While he was momentarily too shocked to respond, she put newspaper clippings in his lap. "As you can see," she said, "they're of Bella and me in the speakeasy raid. I found them in my dresser drawer this morning. Who do you think put them there, Tullio? Some disgruntled maid? Some servant who had nothing better to do than to save them all this time, just waiting for me to come back so she could throw them in my face? Or, maybe, it might have been some ex-mistress of yours . . . some poor woman whom you might have spurned for me . . . some sweet innocent who now wants to get even with you by hurting your wife. Now, who could possibly have been vicious enough to cut out little pieces of paper, and save them, and sneak into my bedroom, and place them where I'd be certain to find them? Who could it possibly have been, Tullio?"

He crumbled the clippings and said, "It wasn't either of my aunts. I don't know who put them there, but it wasn't my aunts."

"What did I marry?" she asked him. "A blind man, or a fool?"

He closed the book he'd been trying to read.

"I'm sorry," she said. "I'm sorry. I didn't mean that. I really didn't."

"I think you did."

"No. It's just this place. It gives me the creeps. It's so old. It's so against anything and anyone it thinks doesn't belong. It makes me say things I don't want to say. It's good that Louise and I will be starting our tour tomorrow."

"You've always hated Orvietto, haven't you?"

"I'm really very excited about touring the country. I never did see much of it, you know. It's funny. I had to wait to become an American tourist to come back and see Rome and Florence. It is a little funny, isn't it?"

"You didn't answer me."

"What was the question?"

"I asked if you've always hated Orvietto."

"It doesn't matter."

"It matters to me. This is my home. This is the place we'll be coming back to some day."

"What are you talking about?"

"What do you mean: what am I talking about? You know what I'm talking about."

"Tullio, if you think that, some day, we'll be moving back here for good, you're very mistaken. I'll never move back to Orvietto. We have a new home, you and I, and I like it very much. I'll never return to Orvietto. To come here for a visit is one thing. But, never to live here. Never to live here."

"Magda, what are you saying?"

They glared at one another.

Surely, they must have discussed this before. Or, had they? They both tried to remember.

How could he possibly think that she would return to this life? Even ten years from now! Never! It was out of the question!

How could she possibly prefer New York to Orvietto? Was she insane? It had always been understood. New York was just temporary!

"Tullio, we have a new home now. *The Walls*. That's our home. This place . . . it was your father's, your family's, never ours. *The Walls* . . . that's where we belong . . . that's ours."

"No, Magdalena."

Louise came into the room then and said, "I've been talking with Rebecca. I've been trying to convince her to come on tour with us, but to no avail. It's a shame. It's such a good opportunity for her, but she insists on staying here until we get back. I really don't know what she's going to do here for the next few weeks. What, with Tullio being so busy, and us away,

457

I just can't imagine how she'll spend her time."

"She'll spend her time the same way all the other girls in the village spend theirs," Tullio said. "What makes you think that the girls who live here are bored?"

"Well, I didn't mean it that way . . . Orvietto is really a very lovely place . . . it's just that, well . . ."

Magdalena interrupted: "I'm sure she'll manage. Anyway, even if she should get bored stiff, you can be sure that she'll never admit it to us. She's very stubborn."

"The people who live here don't get bored," Tullio insisted. "Only outsiders get bored. Outsiders, who don't know how to relax."

"I didn't mean to infer that it's a boring place," Louise said. She was visibly flushed.

"Don't apologize, Louise," Magdalena told her. "It's not necessary. After all, what you said is the simple truth. Rebecca is not going to know what to do with herself within a few days after we leave. Nobody should have to apologize for telling the truth."

The door opened suddenly. Stefano entered. His hair was tousled and there was a patch of red under one of his eyes. His upper lip was already starting to swell.

"Oh, my God, Stefano! What happened? Did you fall off a horse?" Magdalena ran toward him and pulled her arms around him.

"Wait a minute, Magda," Tullio said. "What happened, Stefano? Have you been in a fight?"

Magdalena looked at her son with surprise. "You weren't fighting, were you, Stefano? Were you? Of course, he wasn't. What happened, darling?"

The boy replied: "Why do they keep calling Rebecca 'la nera'? That means 'the black girl' and I don't understand why they say that. It's not the first time I heard that."

"Who said that?" Tullio asked him. "Who said that? Has Rebecca ever heard that?"

Magdalena glared at her husband and muttered: "Why did

458

we have to come back to this God-awful place? Why?"

"Why do they call her that?" Stefano asked again.
"Grandma Louise, if they won't tell me, will you? Why do they
call her that?"

Tullio brushed his fingers through Stefano's hair and asked
him: "Is that what happened? Someone called Rebecca 'la
nera' and you fought with him? If that's what happened, then,
you were right to fight. Is that what happened, Stefano?"

"Yes," he answered. "That's what happened. But, why?
Why do they call her that? I've heard it a few times already."

"Has she?" Magdalena asked. "Do you know if she has?"

"Yes, she has," the boy answered. "She gets mad when they
say it. Only she says that it means they're calling her 'the
brunette' because her hair is so black. That's stupid, isn't it?
They're not calling her 'the brunette.' They're calling her 'the
black girl,' aren't they? They're not talking about her hair, are
they? They're talking about *her*."

Tullio had often thought about the day when he would have
to tell Stefano and Rebecca of their backgrounds. He'd
expected that it would be at a later date, perhaps when they'd
reached their late teens; he'd even considered that it could be
put off until their early twenties. But, no—it should have been
done a long time ago, he now decided. "Where is Rebecca?" he
asked Stefano.

"No," Magdalena told him, knowing what he was thinking.
"Not now. It doesn't have to be done now."

Stefano replied, "She's right inside. Why?"

"Tullio, we should talk about this first," Magdalena said.

"Ask Rebecca to come in here," he told the boy. When
Stefano left to fetch his sister, Tullio said, "This shouldn't be
put off any longer, Magda. In a way, I'm glad that the time has
come. It's good that we can get it over with."

"But, it might hurt them. They're not ready."

"I'll leave you alone," Louise said.

"No," he told her. "Stay. I think it would be better if you
were here for this."

Magdalena sat close to Louise. She almost wanted to hold her hand. She said, "Be very gentle with them, Tullio. Oh, I didn't mean that. I know you'll be gentle. What I meant is be extra understanding if they get upset, or angry, or . . ."

"I will. Don't worry. I know what you mean."

Rebecca and Stefano came in and Rebecca asked, "Is something wrong, Papa?"

She'd always called him "Daddy" at *The Walls*, but, shortly after they'd arrived in Orvietto, she'd started to call him "Papa." He liked this. It had a better sound to it. He suspected that he liked it mostly because it had come about so naturally.

"No, nothing is wrong." He kissed his daughter; but he did this often, so the gesture gave her no reason to suspect anything unusual was forthcoming. "There's nothing wrong," he said again. "It's just that, now, that you're both old enough to understand, there's something we'd like you to know about."

"Does it have something to do with what we were just talking about?" Stefano asked.

"Please, Stefano, just sit down and listen," he replied. "Then, after I finish saying what I want to say, you can both ask all the questions you want, and we'll answer each one of them."

They sat opposite him. To the adults' surprise, neither fidgeted.

"To begin with," Tullio said, "let's consider your relationship with your Grandma Louise. You both know that you're not related to her. Right?"

They nodded.

"But, do you think she and you could love one another any more if she were your natural grandmother? Does it make any difference?"

"No, Papa," Rebecca answered. "Of course not."

Stefano shook his head.

Louise Asheley smiled and blew kisses toward them.

"But, suppose it was just the opposite," Tullio said.

"Suppose that, all this time, you had thought she was your real blood grandmother . . . and then, you'd suddenly found out that she wasn't. How would you feel about it, then?"

"I would feel just the same about Grandma Louise," his daughter answered. "After all, she'd still be the same person that we knew before we learned the truth about her. It wouldn't change anything about her."

"Do you feel the same way, Stefano?" Tullio asked.

"Yeah."

"That's good, that's good," Tullio said. "Well, remembering what we've just realized is true about Grandma Louise and you, I'd like you to listen carefully to something else."

The children's eyes were so wide open with expectation that he had to smile at them. He said, "Once, there was a young man who had led a very sheltered life. While he was still quite young and inexperienced, he met a woman . . ."

". . . and she became his first girlfriend?" Rebecca asked.

"Yes," he answered, "in a way, his first . . . girlfriend. But, after a very short time, the woman went away. In the meantime, he met another lady, a young farmer's widow. Her husband had just died, leaving her with an infant son. This young man fell in love with the widow, and he married her."

"What about her son?" Stefano asked.

"When the man made the widow his wife, he accepted her son, and he learned to love him just as though he were his own son." He paused, waiting for any questions, but they didn't come. After a short, quiet moment, he continued: "Then, one day, the young man's wife brought a little baby girl to him. She told him that the little girl was his own daughter, and that the little girl's mother was his first girlfriend."

"You mean he had a baby girl with his first girlfriend without getting married to her? That's terrible!" Rebecca said.

Tullio suddenly thought: She knows about the facts of life. Magdalena's already told her about sex . . . I never even thought to wonder about it before. He said, "Well, these things happen sometimes, Rebecca."

461

"Well, they aren't supposed to. That's a mortal sin."

He looked at his daughter, then at Stefano, and then at Magdalena. "Yes, I know," he answered, "but, nevertheless, that's what happened."

"Let your father finish," Magdalena told Rebecca.

Tullio continued: "The man's wife said that she would raise the little girl as her own. So, you see, just as the man was accepting the widow's child as his own son, the lady was, in turn, doing the same thing by wanting to be a mother to the little girl."

"You mean it was like they adopted each other's children?" Stefano asked.

"Yes, that's one way of putting it. Shortly after that, they moved far away and they had one more child. But, just because this third child was born from the two of them together, it didn't make any difference so far as the first two children were concerned. They loved all three children alike."

Rebecca asked, "What is this story all about? What does it have to do with us?"

Because the young girl's voice was so icy, Tullio realized that she'd not really had to ask the question. She'd understood; only, she'd been hoping that she hadn't.

He answerd her, anyway: "I was that young man." Then, to Stefano, he said: "Your mother was the widow."

There is a split-moment silence that occurs when the last word of a very long novel is finished being read. It is unique— no other silence compares to it; and, no matter how brief it is, there is a special, unmistakable finality to it. It was almost that kind of silence which fell into the room. It was as quick-hitting as The End, and each of them was caught in it until Stefano quipped an annoyed: "What do you mean?"

Rebecca said to him: "He means that he's not your father and that she's not my mother. And that we're not even brother and sister. But that Carlo is a half-brother to you and a half-brother to me."

"What?" the boy asked.

"Rebecca, you don't refer to your parents as he or she. It's disrespectful. You know better than that," Tullio said.

"Who's not my father?" Stefano asked. "Who's not my father?"

Magdalena wanted to go to her son—to cradle him in her arms as she had when he was an infant—but she sat frozen, holding on to Louise's hand. She said, "One of the things that we're trying to tell you is that I was married to another man once. He was a farmer. We lived on his farm. It was in the Province of Lombardy, here, in Italy. He was your father. He died. They took him into the army and he died." She took a long, deep breath when she finished.

Stefano gaped at her. "You were married before? You had another husband?"

"Yes," she replied.

"You're not my real father? My father was somebody else? A farmer?"

"That's right, Stefano," Tullio answered. "Your natural father was a farmer. But, he never got to see you. He died just before you were born. When I met your mother, you were still an infant, though, and I feel the same way about you—having known you since you were so young—as I would feel if I were your natural father."

He gave a soft muttering: "You're not my real father."

"Only an accident of birth makes me not your natural father. But, since I'm your father by choice, that should be enough for you to consider me your real father. At least, I feel as though you're my real son. A real son has a real father, doesn't he?"

Stefano shrugged. "Yeah." He looked squarely at Tullio, who knew that he was being studied. "Yeah," he repeated, then added, "No wonder we don't look alike."

Tullio brushed his fingertips through Stefano's hair. "No, we don't look at all alike."

To Magdalena, he asked, "Do I look like my . . . you know . . . my first . . . father?"

"Yes, you do. A lot of the Lombardians are of German stock. Your father was tall and handsome and blonde. You look very much like him."

"What was his name?"

"Tomaso. Tomaso Stefano Disanti."

"That used to be my name? Disanti?"

"Yes, it was Disanti."

"What was my mother's name?" Rebecca asked.

"Her name was Tea."

"Tea? What kind of a name is that? Did she have a farm, too? Was she a Lombardian, too?"

"No," Tullio answered, "she wasn't from Lombardy. That's where we met, but she wasn't from there originally."

"But, she was an Italian, wasn't she? Where was she from? What was her last name? Why didn't you marry her? How could you make her have your baby and not marry her? Why wouldn't you marry her?"

"Rebecca, please. Please don't cry. I realize that this must be hard to understand, but . . . ."

". . . but, you should have married her. You had no right not to marry her. Why didn't you?" She left the room without waiting for an answer.

"Let me speak with her," Magdalena told him.

"No, she's my daughter and I owe her an explanation. That's the least I can do. I can explain. At least, I can try."

"No, Tullio. I'll talk with her, first. There are some things that only women should talk about to young girls. Of course, she might have some questions that only you could answer. But, let me talk with her first. This way, she'll, at least, not too embarrassed to ask what she has to know." She didn't wait to hear whether or not Tullio agreed with her. She left the room in search of Rebecca.

Stefano, still studying this suddenly strange man, asked, "Does this have something to do with why they call Rebecca *la nera?*"

"Yes, it does."

Louise said, "I know that I'm interfering, but you were right, Tullio. You, yourself, should be explaining this to Rebecca. Not Magdalena, but you. Not only that: It shouldn't be behind closed doors. This is a family matter. Especially this *la nera* thing. The special, personal questions—if there are any left over—can come later. Whether they're between you and Rebecca, or between Magdalena and Stefano. They can come later. First, you should clear the air and get as much out in the open as possible. The four of you should talk together now. You're a family. And, in a few years, Carlo will be ready to be told." She smiled, and there was a hint of nervousness to it because she wasn't sure if her host had wanted to hear this. "Well," she continued, "enough interference from me. I've said my piece. Now, I'll go finish my packing for tomorrow."

"You're not interfering, Louise. If I'd thought of you as an outsider, I wouldn't have spoken to them in front of you. I consider you their grandmother, and I always will."

"Thank you," she replied. She clasped her hands in her lap. "Thank you, Tullio."

He nodded.

"Well," she said, "enough of this, before I start blubbering. I do foolish things like that, you know. I confuse poor Earl so terribly. I have a habit of dropping tears when they're least expected."

"There's nothing wrong with sensitivity," he replied. "Sensitive people, as far as I'm concerned, are probably the only ones who can give complete love."

When Louise left, he said to Stefano, "Go tell your mother and sister to come back. Tell them that we're going to talk about this together, as Grandma Louise says, like a family. Tell them that I want them back right now."

"Suppose they say 'no'?" But the boy already knew that his mother would not do this.

"Just go call them," Tullio replied.

Tullio's head had been throbbing since morning and he was wondering if he'd developed a resistance to aspirin. To make matters worse, he'd received a telephone call from Sr. Pavetto, who'd said that a letter had arrived . . . "from an N. Moeller, and it's marked 'Personal,' Signor Barragatto." He was anxious to read it, but he wouldn't get to Milan for another week. When his secretary had asked if he should forward it to Orvietto with the rest of the mail, he'd told him not to.

How did she know I'm in Europe? Only two possible ways: she wrote to New York, and Salvatore told her . . . or Gerhard mentioned it to her.

Do she and Gerhard keep in touch? Maybe. Why not? He'd want to know how his child is doing. Nothing wrong with that. It's only natural.

"Stefano said you wanted us." Magdalena stood in front of him, erect and visibly incensed. "He said you wanted us *right now.*"

He cleared his throat. He'd not heard them enter. "Yes," he answered. "I think we should speak about this matter together, not separately. Sit down, Magda." He motioned to his daughter and, patting the cushion next to him on the divan, added, "Come here, Rebecca. Sit here."

The young girl didn't sit where he'd directed. Instead, she chose a seat at the opposite side of the room. "I can hear you from here, Papa."

"What have you told her so far?" he asked his wife.

"Only that Tea was different than the women she's met until now. That she was different because she'd come from a different culture. I told her that she mustn't be upset with you for not having married Tea, and that you'd not even known Tea was pregnant. Also, I asked her to understand that, to somebody like Tea—somebody so different than all the people she's ever met—that . . ."

Rebecca interrupted: ". . . that it wasn't such a terrible thing for her to have abandoned me when I was still an infant."

Tullio said, "You say that as though you can't accept it."

"It's not very easy, Papa. After all, she was my mother. Just because somebody is a gypsy, it shouldn't make any difference

466

as far as her own baby is concerned."

"Don't be so ready to condemn her," Tullio said. "The times were hard. There was a war going on, and . . ."

"Is that why they call her *la nera?* Because her mother was a gypsy?" Stefano looked directly at Tullio, determined to have an answer.

"Mama was a gypsy too! *Your mother!* My mother was married to one of Mama's cousins! They were both gypsies!"

"Stop this!" Tullio said. "Both of you! I'm surprised at the both of you!"

"Why do they call me that, Papa? Is it because my hair is so black?"

"Rebecca," he replied, "when you were just a small baby, there were certain characteristics of your mother's that were very visible in you. Your features. Your coloring. The way your hair curled. As you grew older, those traits became less and less prominent. Naturally, the people here, in Orvietto . . . the staff, the pickers . . . they remember you as you looked when you were a baby, when you looked like your mother's parents."

"So?" she asked. "Everybody looks like somebody. My goodness! What's wrong with that? If I didn't look like her, I would have looked like you. And, if I didn't look like either of you, I could have looked like my grandparents. Maybe, even, like some aunt or uncle. Everybody looks like somebody. So? Big deal! I looked like her parents!"

Tullio said, "Rebecca, Tea's mother was from Africa. She was a Moor."

"A Moor? From Africa?"

"Yes," he replied, "a Moor. The Moors are Moslems. They're descended from the Arabs and the Berbers. Tea was half-Moor."

"From Africa?"

"Yes."

Stefano asked: "Was she colored?"

"Was she colored?" Rebecca echoed.

"Half."

467

"She was half-colored? My grandmother was colored? From Africa?"

"Yes."

The boy asked, "Does that mean that Rebecca's colored, too?"

"All it means," Tullio replied, "is that Rebecca's natural grandmother was a Moor."

Rebecca said, not to anyone in particular, "It means that I'm part colored. All the servants know. All the pickers. And, they probably told their children. So, that's why they call me *la nera*. All the girls . . . they must know, too." Her voice broke—not into a sobbing or a gradual softening, but suddenly, as though a radio had been turned off. "*La nera*— that's what it means."

She didn't like the way Stefano was looking at her. She returned his glare and thrust out her chin.

Magdalena muttered, "We shouldn't have come back to Orvietto," but, since she'd spoken in a whisper, more to herself than to anyone else, Tullio had heard only one word: Orvietto.

"Don't go blaming Orvietto for everything," he said. "People are the same all over the world. What's important is that Rebecca understands that she'll always be a Barragatto. That's a name that's respected."

"Would you mind if I left the room now?" the girl asked.

"If you'd like," her father replied. "If you feel that you'd like to be alone."

Rebecca stared at her reflection. She could swear that she looked different. She decided that she'd probably never really looked at herself before. *I would have realized I wasn't the same as them. I should have looked better.*

That's why those women used to say I look exotic. All those women at those parties. "Oh, your daughter is so exotic-looking! Oh, she's such an odd beauty, your daughter!" I'm not even her daughter. She was probably laughing at them under her breath all the time. I'll bet she was.

She remained in her room for most of the day. At dinner, she told Louise and Magdalena that she would like to tour the country with them, and that she would start packing as soon as she finished eating.

"On second thought," she said, "I'll tell the maid what I want packed. I might as well let her do it for me. That's what we have maids for." When no one answered, she asked, "Well, isn't that what we have them for?"

"Yes, darling," Magdalena said. "That's why we have them. To help us."

Chapter Two

They lingered over lunch longer, but, other than that, Tullio
was convinced that the Milanese aren't any different than New
Yorkers. Their pace is just as frenzied, their conversations are
as excitable and varied, and they take their politics just as
seriously. Entering his office in Milan felt the same as walking
into the lobby of North American Distributors. Only the
language was different.

Besides Nicole's letter, there were very few pieces of
correspondence on Tullio's desk. Sr. Pavetto, as efficient as
ever, had managed to answer most of the mail himself, and the
cousin that Tullio had left in charge of the office could easily
have attended to everything else. In one way, this pleased
Tullio because he realized that the Milan operation was in good
hands; in another way, though, the fact that he wasn't vitally
needed hurt his ego.

He wondered about the New York office. About Kostenov.
About Asheley. About his cousin, Salvatore. He secretly hoped
that at least one of them was saying: We'll have to ask Tullio
about this when he gets back. He's the one who knows the most
about this type of thing. He'd know how to handle it . . .
Surely, there must be *something* that no one could tackle as

well as he! Then, he wondered about Pace. Then, about Italo Filippo Fallanca—he'd not run into him even once while in Orvietto.

He slit open the envelope and immediately recognized Nicole's perfume. Too bad that he'd not thought to ask her its name. He would have asked Magdalena to buy some.

A photograph of Nicole and her daughter slipped out. Nicole looked as beautiful as ever. The child resembled her, but there was a lot of Gerhard in her, also.

He was surprised that the letter was only one short page. After not having heard from her for such a long time, he'd expected that she would have much more to say—unless, of course, she no longer wanted him; or was going to tell him that she'd found a new love; or was saying that she was going back with Gerhard. None of these things would require more than one page; and, he resented the brevity of the tissue-thin pale blue note paper. Deciding that its purpose was definitely one of the three, he handled it carelessly, almost ripping it along the fold. He read:

My dearest Tullio,

What makes a woman want one man above all others? What makes her walk around as though blindfolded until she can see him again? Weeks pass, then months and years, and, instead of the yearning for him beginning to lessen, it increases. Why? Shouldn't it be the opposite? I ask these questions endlessly, but I get no answers.

I am lonely. Even in a room filled with people, it's the same. I don't know what else to say except that I love you and that I need you. When can we see one another again? I don't want to wait any longer. If you can't come to me, I'll come to you.

No—she still wanted him. No—she'd found no new love. No—she'd not gone back to Gerhard.

It was a Nicole letter, all right! Direct. To the point. No

unnecessary words.

Magdalena, Louise and Rebecca were on tour. Stefano and Carlo were at his aunts' house while he was in Milan.

Why not?

"Signor Pavetto."

"Yes, Signor Barragatto?"

"I have some business to attend to. I'll be away for a while. A week. Maybe, two. Definitely no longer."

"Can you be reached?"

"No, not after tomorrow morning. Until then, I'll be in my apartment. Send one of the boys at eight. I'll give him some editorials I want delivered to Party headquarters."

"Eight, tonight?"

"No, Signor Pavetto. Eight, tomorrow morning. And, please make sure he's prompt, because I'll be waiting for him. I won't be able to leave until he gets there."

He looked from his secretary back to the letter, and he wondered why Nicole hadn't signed it. Then, he put it into his ashtray and burned it.

Tullio wondered about the absence of any signature even while he was writing his editorials back in his apartment.

Even if she didn't want to write "love, Nicole," she should have at least signed, "Nicole!" I have to remember to ask her about that.

Oh, for heaven's sake! What the heck is the difference? Signature. No signature. What's the difference?

He'd been asked to write a column for one of the Party newsletters. His subject was Benedetto Croce, who, formerly with the Party, had turned against it. Croce's magazine, *La Critica*, and other voluminous works had made him the strongest anti-Fascist voice in Italy, and thousands of Fascist-schooled young men were suddenly switching to Croce liberalism.

Croce had been one of the country's most eminent thinkers for more than half a century, and he'd first looked to Fascism as a reform movement. Tullio had always regarded him as a great philosopher, a man whom history would remember,

472

someone worthy of his respect. Now, however, Croce was just another enemy—an enemy of Fascism, and so, also, of Tullio Barragatto. Croce was being expelled from one academy and society after another, but the Party believed—and so did Tullio—that this wasn't enough. Benedetto Croce had to be silenced.

Tullio revised the cólumn four times. He didn't want it to be too strong or irate. He wanted to incense the rank membership against Croce, but not so much that the old philosopher might be physically harmed. That would turn him into a martyr and make matters worse.

It was almost dawn when the final draft was completed. He was satisfied with it, proud of it, and fell asleep at the desk.

The return address read *Frankrijklei 92*. He'd shown the envelope to a taxi driver at the train station, and he was hoping that the man wasn't like those back home when they know they have a tourist at their mercy. Twenty minutes later, having passed the same landmark twice, he realized that his hopes were in vain. Eventually, he saw the street name, *Frankrijklei*, and the cab driver smiled at him through the rear view mirror, saying something he couldn't understand. In a short while, the man pointed to the left, and he saw the sign, *92*, but they went right past it.

"Hey! Hey! Stop!"

Again, the driver said something that Tullio couldn't understand, and Tullio realized that he was speaking Flemish. He wished he could remember the curse words Nicole had taught him.

The driver stopped in front of a low, grey building. Two young boys came to the car. One opened the door for Tullio, and the other, who had a key to the car trunk, removed his baggage from it. The younger of the boys (the one who'd opened the door) smiled and bowed slightly. Then, the taxi cab driver smiled and—since he knew his passenger couldn't understand Flemish—wrote down the amount he was owed.

After Tullio paid him, he motioned for Tullio to follow the boys.

"But, why in hell didn't you just leave me off in front of Number 92? Why'd we have to come three blocks past it?"

What an ass I am. He doesn't speak Italian.

He continued speaking in Italian, anyway. "I see what your game is. You bring all of us suckers to these kids and then divide the tips I give them. They're probably your own sons, right?"

The boys were already twenty or thirty feet away from him, their heavy burdens on their shoulders, heading back to *Frankrijklei 92*. When he looked from them back to the driver (whom he was now positive was their father), it suddenly struck him funny—he hadn't been made a fool of in a very long time.

This time, he spoke in French. Everyone in Antwerp speaks French, and he wondered why he'd not thought to speak it earlier: "Okay, buddy, okay. No harm done. Congratulations. You're one up on me. I owe you."

The driver nodded, grinned and shrugged innocently. He made Tullio feel very much at home (not at home in Orvietto; but at home in Milan or in New York) so Tullio returned the nod, the grin, and the shrug, and he followed the man's sons back to *Frankrijklei 92;* and he laughed part of the way.

I have to tell Salvatore about this. Me, of all people. Me, a sucker tourist.

He found the name, Moeller, on the mailbox. There were only four apartments in the building. Hers was on the second floor. The boys carried up his baggage, and he paid them more generously than they'd expected; he realized this by the size of their smiles. They even tipped their hats.

No one answered his tapping, and the door was locked, so he sat on his suitcase, wondering how long a wait he would have.

But, the boys had just reached the front door when he heard Nicole's voice. She was asking them what they wanted in the building, and they were telling her that they'd brought an talian upstairs.

Then, he heard her running up toward him, and a little girl sking, "What's the matter? Who's upstairs? What's an talian?"

"Tullio? Tullio?"

"Yes, yes, it's me."

"Oh, Tullio." She stopped short when she reached the anding. A wide smile covered her face. "This is my daughter, Sylvia," is all she said. She unlocked the door and stepped aside so that he could go in first.

The apartment was larger than he'd expected. There were wo bedrooms, and both had balconies. The living room was spacious, also, and the kitchen was more than adequate.

"What's his name?" Sylvia asked. "You told him mine, but you didn't tell me his."

"This is Tullio Barragatto, Sylvia. Signor Barragatto is a very old friend of mine. We know each other a long time."

"How long?"

"Since before you were even born."

"Oh." The answer satisifed her and she did not resist when her nurse suggested that they go out to a nearby park. As soon as they were gone, Tullio took Nicole in his arms.

"They won't be back for hours," she announced, then kissed him eagerly as his hands sought her ripe full breasts. She led him to her bedroom, strewing clothes as they went; by the time they reached her bed they were both naked. He lay back on the blue satin coverlet and she moved on top of him, teasing him with her mouth and when he could wait no longer she moved on top of him, moving together with him until they climaxed and, both spent, lay together in each other's arms.

"Your daughter is a lot like you," he finally said.

"Yes, I know." Then: "Why do I feel so suddenly awkward? I've been waiting for you. I've been dreaming about the time when I could see you again. And, here we are."

"I know what you mean," he said. Then, he took her hands in his and kissed them. He asked, "Does Gerhard keep in touch with you?"

"No. He never comes here. I receive money from hi
attorney once a month. That's the only contact we have. He'
not at all interested in Sylvia. At least, he's seen her only once
just a few months after she was born. He's never asked to se
her again. He's getting married again. Did you know?"

"No."

"I'm surprised he hasn't mentioned it."

"So am I," Tullio replied. "I'm really surprised."

"Well, as you can see from the apartment, he's been ver
generous. I never asked him for this much, but his attorne
said that it was part of the settlement. I'd not even know
about the settlement. I still don't know what it is. I've neve
seen the papers."

Tullio said, "Gerhard can afford it. Anyway, it wouldn't d
for a Moeller child not to have the best its father can provide
Don't feel any guilt, Nicole. It's not all generosity."

"I know," she answered, "I know Gerhard very well."

"Anyway," he said, "so much for Gerhard."

"That's right," she agreed. "We have too many other thing
to talk about. Too much catching up to do. How long will you
be here?"

"One or two weeks."

"Oh, no. That's not long enough. Not after all this time. You
can't come back into my life and then run out again after two
weeks. If you try to do that, I'll follow you, even all the way
back to America, if I have to."

"By the way, how did you know I was back in Italy?"

"I saw a newspaper picture of you and your family docking
in Genoa." She kissed him softly, and added, "I'm serious,
Tullio. I'll follow you."

"I've been doing a lot of thinking," he said, "a lot of
thinking. And, I'm going to tell you what my thoughts are, but
not now. Not now. Now, I just want you."

Then, he made love to her once more. It wasn't only passion.
It was affection, too. And, through it all, she still had a special

476

quality about her. He'd never been able to pinpoint that nature of hers, that specialness that made her a girl and a woman and a friend all at once; but he could never deny that it was there.

They left for the seashore that evening. They couldn't stay in her apartment, she explained, because she had to watch her reputation. He understood this. He'd not expected to be able to remain there with her. She was, after all, as all of her neighbors knew, a very respectable young widow.

One afternoon, just before lunch, he said, "Nicole, I want to talk about us. I've avoided the subject, I realize, and I appreciate the fact that you haven't brought it up, either . . ."

"I know, Tullio. I've been waiting for you to say something. When will our holiday be over? When will you be leaving? Tomorrow? The day after? It's almost two weeks."

"I know how unfair this is to you, Nicole. But, I don't want to lie to you. I love my wife. She's been a part of my life for so long, now. I don't think I would be the same without her."

"And me? What of me?"

"I love you, too. Not in the same way, but I love you, too. Oh, I know that it sounds ridiculous. I'll go even one step further, and sound even more ridiculous: I wish this were the Middle East, one of those countries where a man can have two wives, because, then, everything would be very simple."

"Well, it's not the Middle East, and I love you very much, Tullio. And, you say you love me, too. But, where does that leave me? Alone, with only your words for company? Is that what memories are made of? Words? Is that how you love me?"

As Nicole had spoken, she'd been keeping an eye on Sylvia, who was near the water's edge. Tullio was grateful for this, because he didn't want to face her just now. It was difficult just talking about this, but it would have made it a lot more difficult if he'd had to look at her and say:

"I want you to have an apartment in New York. And, perhaps, one in Orvietto. I want you to be on the ship whenever I sail between two places. I want you to be wherever

477

I can come to you . . . but, only when I can come to you . . . and you would have to understand that you could never expect me until I'd come walking through the door . . . and you would have to spend most of your time alone. This is what I want. I know how selfish it is of me."

He stopped, because she'd finally turned around and was now looking at him. Then, he continued: "No matter where you choose to live, Gerhard's attorney would see that you get the settlement money. But, even if he didn't, it wouldn't matter, because it would be over and above what I would give you. I would take care of everything for you, so, whatever you would receive from Gerhard would be extra. You wouldn't want for anything. You'd have more than enough, a lot more than most women ever see."

After a brief silence, he added, "That's all I can offer you, Nicole. Financial security. And the promise that I'll see you as often as I can break away."

"Nicole Grynszpan Moeller. Mistress." She didn't know or care whether she'd thought or spoken it.

"That's the size of it," he said. "It's mostly one-sided, and, maybe you'd be a fool to accept it. You're young enough to get almost any other man you want, on a whole lot better terms. But, it's the best I can do. It's how it would have to be if you and I are to continue."

"And, most of the time, I would be as I am now: alone."

"Yes, that's true." He bent toward her and squeezed her hand gently. "Don't give me your answer now, Nicole. Think about it."

"Tullio, is there any chance at all that you might leave your wife?"

"No, there isn't. And, I wouldn't expect you ever to ask me to. Or ever to ask me questions about how she and I are getting along. Or to ask me any questions of any kind regarding my home life."

"You certainly are making sure we know who's carrying the ball. I can see why your business deals come off so well

478

for you."

"Nicole, everything we do in life is a business deal. Even marriage. Isn't it better to talk about these things up front, and avoid some future problems? Isn't it fairer all around, to be completely honest from the beginning, so we'll know where we both stand?"

She shot him a feline look. "And, where would I stand if, a few months from now, or a few years from now, you got tired of me?"

He answered, "I'll deposit a lump sum of money into a bank for you, right at the start. No one would be able to touch it except you. It would have nothing to do with anything else I'd give you after that. It would just stay in that bank and grow— call it your security if you'd like—and we'd both forget it was even there. Does that make you feel better? This way, either of us can call it quits whenever we want. And, you'd have no fear for the future."

Her face softened. "I'm being bought, aren't I? Here I am, with the only man I've ever loved, and he's buying . . . and I'm selling. It's very different from how I'd always pictured it would be for us."

"Nicole, sweetheart, listen . . . be logical. Even when a couple marries, they're buying and selling. This is no different. I can't give you my name, or be with you on holidays, but I can compensate a little—and gifts, and money, and some kind of financial security for you and Sylvia is the only way that I can think of doing that." He smiled slightly and kissed her. "Please understand, Nicole. I love you. I really do. If I sound cold when I tell you the way things would have to be, I can't help it."

"It's not a question, so much, of sounding cold, my darling. It's something else," she replied.

"What's that?"

"It's the way we're both talking. As if we were already preparing to break up. As if we both had some kind of feeling that we won't last together. It almost puts a hex on us."

479

"I don't look at it that way, Nicole. All I'm doing is trying to put your mind at ease. After all, I'm not asking you to put anything in writing. I'm not asking for any kind of contract that says you won't make any claims on me in the future, am I?"

"That's true, Tullio. That's very true."

"So, you see," he said, "everything that will be done will be done for your protection and well-being."

She broke into a wide smile. "Okay, master. Behold your mistress."

"Don't talk like that, Nicole."

"When do we start furnishing my apartment, and where will it be? I sort of like that modern stuff I've been seeing lately. You know—the sofas and chairs with those big, fat arms? It will be so exciting, setting up our new place. What's your favorite color? Of course, I'll want the best decorator around to help me."

"Oh, my God, I can see you're going to cost me a fortune."

"Two fortunes, my darling. Two fortunes." She stood up and said, "Look at that kid. She won't stay out of the water. I have to go get her. I'll be right back."

She'd had to leave the table. She'd had to be away from his close scrutiny. She'd not been able to keep up the pretense. She'd needed a few moments to herself.

Nicole Grynszpan Moeller. Mistress. Is that what I've come to? Is this all it will ever be?

No! I won't share him with her forever! I might never have his name . . . but, by all that's holy, I'll have HIM! One way or another . . . I'll have HIM!

"Sylvia, come away from the water. It's time for lunch. And, after lunch, Tullio and I are going to take you on a long ride through the mountains. We're going to see how pretty the countryside is."

"We are?"

"Yes, and you know what else?"

"What else?"

"We're going to have a new house. Maybe, two new houses. Would you like that?"

"Will one of them be near a beach?"

"We'll see. We'll see." She was smiling when she returned to the table. "Let's order, now, Tullio. I'm starving."

"I want it near a beach," the child said, "I want a house near the beach."

And Tullio shook his head, grinned, and said, "Three fortunes. That's what you're going to cost me. Three fortunes."

"That's all right," Nicole answered, "I'm worth it."

The tour came to an end. Three weeks had been all they'd planned on because it would bring them up to September, and she would have to get back to America and put the children back in school. Also, this would be Stefano's first year in his school away from home, and she wanted to spend more time with him. She was upset to find that Tullio was still in Milan, and especially incensed when told that the boys had been living in the aunts' house since she'd left.

"How dare he abandon my sons to those two old witches!"

"Calm yourself," Louise told her. "We'll simply go get them. There's been no harm done."

"We will not go get them. We will send for them. Rebecca, please ask the gatekeeper to go fetch Carlo and Stefano."

When the girl left, Magdalena said, "Louise, can you believe my husband? Can you believe he would do such a thing? Not only did he not bother to be here, in Orvietto, when I return, but he had the audacity to send the boys to his aunts! What a nerve!"

"Magdalena, I realize that there's bad blood between you and his aunts, but, put yourself in Tullio's place for a moment."

"How do you mean?"

"Well, his wife goes off on tour, leaving him with two children to take care of. In the meantime, he has to go to Milan

481

on business. What else could he have done? Brought them with him to Milan? Of course not. He'd be too busy to look after them. And, would it have been better to leave them here, with only the servants to look after them? Of course not. The servants aren't going to take as good care of them as their aunts. Tch, tch, tch. Be sensible, Magdalena. Stop condemning the man. He did the best he could do under the circumstances."

"But, he should have at least been back here to welcome us home, Louise. There was a time when Tullio would have . . ."

". . . and, I'll bet there was a time when you never would have gone off and left him."

Magdalena sat down and smiled a sad smile. "I guess you're right, Louise, as usual. I shouldn't have left him here, all alone. I feel so guilty now."

Chapter Three

Magdalena had known, even before leaving America, that Tullio would remain in Orvietto until after the harvest; but that was no comfort on the day she had to sail.

"If you're so unhappy about going back without him, why do it?" Louise asked her.

"Because there's no way I can stay," she answered. "The children's school, you know."

"I can watch them very well aboard ship," Louise continued, "and I can very easily see that they start school in time."

"I know you can, Louise, but it's my responsibility."

"Well, have it your own way. You knew, all along, that you'd be leaving him behind, so I just can't understand this sudden concern."

Magdalena considered explaining her feelings to Louise, but she decided against it. No, she thought, it's too personal.

There had been a difference in Tullio lately—she'd noticed it when he'd returned from Milan—enough of a difference for Aleksey's words to return to her. *Remember, Magdalena: Man is a hunter.* She'd scoffed at the thought at first. Tullio wasn't a cheat. He wasn't another Salvatore.

But, if there's a countryside between us? Or a whole ocean? He's not a monk. Oh, Aleksey, you know him so well. And, you were trying to tell me . . .

When he kissed the children and her goodbye, she said, "I love you very much, Tullio. Don't forget that."

"I feel the very same way, Magda. The very same way. I'll see you soon. I'll be home as soon as possible."

He waved to her from the pier. Then he returned to the car and drove to the small cottage on the outskirts of Orvietto, where Nicole and Sylvia, having been moved in by Sr. Pavetto, would be waiting. He had no qualms about this. He'd told his wife the truth: he did love her, and he would be home as soon as possible.

Stefano had begun calling himself Carter during his first week at school. All it had taken for him to decide that, hereafter, he'd be Carter, was the first meeting with his roommate. The boy, whether or not he'd realized it, had winced slightly when Stefano was introduced to him.

"Stefano!" Stefano had said jokingly. "My God, nobody's called me that since I was an infant, but, I guess I'm stuck with it legally. It's on my papers!" He'd held out his hand and said, "The name's Carter. That's what I go by. Carter."

The young stranger had answered, "Oh, boy, thank God! I thought I was getting stuck with somebody just off the boat!"

So it went. Even when he wrote home, he was signing his letters with that name. Magdalena became resigned to it rather quickly, but she was glad that Tullio didn't know. She expected that Tullio would be returning late October; she'd have to remind Stefano not to resort to Carter in front of him.

The most notable difference—noticeable to everyone—was in Rebecca. Even Guido questioned the girl.

"What's wrong with the princess?" he asked Magdalena.

"Nothing. Why?"

"There's a change," he said, "a big change."

"She's growing up," Magdalena replied.

But Guido wasn't satisfied. One morning, while driving Rebecca to school, he asked: "Something's on your mind. Something serious. What's wrong? Aren't we still friends? Remember when you used to say that you trusted me more than anybody else in the world? Remember, Princess? Don't you trust me anymore? Don't you want to tell me your secret?"

Her eyes filled. "Nobody's ever going to marry me, Guido."

"How old are you now?"

"Thirteen."

"So, you're thirteen . . . and you think you're smart enough to say whether or not anybody's going to marry you. Well, you're not smart . . . you're stupid . . . that's what you are . . . stupid."

"Oh, Guido, stop fooling around."

"Fooling around? Already, you're as beautiful as an actress! And, you're only thirteen! Pssh! Why, if I weren't just a chauffeur, I'd marry you, myself!"

"No, you wouldn't."

"Yes, I would. Not now, of course. You're too young now. I'd have to wait a few years. But, I'd wait. And then, I'd ask your father if I could marry you. That's what I'd do, if I wasn't just his driver."

"What does being a driver have to do with anything?"

"Beautiful young girls, if they're very, very rich, don't marry drivers. They marry very, very rich young men." He winked at her through the rear view mirror. "No, Princess," he said, "you would never marry your father's driver. Your father would kill me first."

"I don't know why. There's nothing wrong with me marrying a driver. After all, my father married a farmer's wife, and she used to be a gypsy."

"That's not nice, Rebecca."

"It's true."

"It's not nice. Don't talk like that."

"It's true."

"I know, but it's not nice that you talk like that."

"Then, you knew the truth, didn't you? That she was a gypsy once?"

"Don't call your mother 'she.' That's not nice, either."

"And, you know that she's not my real mother, don't you? You know just about everything about my family, don't you? That's right, you came with them from Italy. You know all about us. Everything there is to know. And, about me. You know everything about me, don't you?"

"Like what?" he asked.

"Like . . . what I am."

"I don't know what you mean, Princess. All I know is that you're thirteen, and you're beautiful, and your name is Rebecca Barragatto, and that your mother's name is Magdalena and your father's name is Tullio."

"Oh, Guido! Stop this!"

". . . and that you have two brothers, Stefano and Carlo."

"I said stop!"

". . . and that you live in *The Walls of Jericho* . . . so, that makes you very, very rich . . . and that, some day, you'll grow up and marry one of those rich men who'll buy you diamonds and emeralds and furs, and make you very happy. That's all I know. Anyway, that's all I can think of right now."

"I hate you, Guido! I hate you, because you know the truth, and you won't admit it. I hate you and someday, I'll get even with you for this! You're just sitting there and laughing at me, and I'll get even with you for this! I swear I will! Nobody's going to laugh at me! Nobody!"

When the young girl left the car, he sat there, just watching her rush toward the main gate of the schoolyard. Once or twice before, he'd wondered if she'd ever discover the truth; now, he wondered how she had. He'd have to tell the signora about this. Perhaps, somebody in Orvietto had told the girl— that was all he could imagine, because, certainly, nobody in the family would say such a thing to her. Mixed race: that was not something to be admitted; and it would certainly not be spoken about openly by the Barragattos. Poor little girl. She was right. Who, if he knew, would ever marry her? Poor little girl. She knew what she was talking about.

When he returned home, he looked for Magdalena.

"Whatever you have to talk about will have to wait, Guido," she replied. "Right now, I have my hands full with Signor Kostenov. He's beside himself because of something that happened in the stock market. I don't understand. The one day he decides to stay home and nurse that cold of his everything has to go wrong. He's ranting and raving. He won't stay in bed as the doctor said he should."

Guido could hear Aleksey Kostenov. He was shouting orders into the telephone.

"Listen to the way that man is coughing! He can hardly stand up, and he's still doing business! We'll talk about your matter tomorrow, Guido. I'm sorry, but come back with it tomorrow." Then, she stopped short: "Guido, it's no emergency, is it? You're not in some kind of trouble, are you?"

"No, signora, I'm in no trouble."

"Oh, that's good. Then, tomorrow. I'll see you about it tomorrow."

"Damn you, man!" Aleksey shouted. "Send a cable to the ship! Signor Barragatto must be notified at once! At once! And, get right back to me! You hear? Right back to me! No! Don't hang up, you fool! Go to another phone! Put Crispino on this one! Well, go find him!"

"Aleksey, please! Calm yourself! You're just making your cough worse! Wall Street will still be there tomorrow! Right now, you should be in bed!"

But, the old man wouldn't listen to Magdalena. He slammed the door and locked her out. He came out of the room only once, and that was to say: "I want no one using any of the telephones today. No one!"

Exasperated and out of breath, Aleksey sat in the plump, soft chair and stared at the telephone. He'd been disconnected. He whistled into the air. Salvatore would be calling him back. He had better!

He'd warned them: Don't play with the market. Don't trust it. It's just another way of gambling.

Salvatore should be calling back any moment now.

He lost his patience. He redialed, but all lines to North American Distributors were busy. Were they trying to get through to the ship? Were they trying to get him? He'd better hang up.

Tullio and Nicole had just finished a late breakfast. It still amazed him when he'd watch Americans eating their breakfasts. How could they possibly eat so much in the morning? He grinned. He'd found himself doing exactly the same thing lately. It had been a good sailing so far. He hadn't been seasick so much. Nicole was taking the credit for this.

"It's because I'm with you. I've kept you too busy to be sick."

"You've kept me busy, all right," he answered, "and, that's an understatement."

They were relaxing in their deck chairs when he first noticed the scurrying back and forth.

"You'd think a war's just broken out, the way everybody's running around this morning," he commented. "Say, what's going on?" he asked one of the passengers.

"The market," one replied, "the market."

He smirked and he felt sorry for all those who'd made some kind of foolish investment. "They must all have the same crazy broker."

"What kind of apartment has Salvatore gotten me?" she asked.

"Something on Sutton Place."

"Is that good?"

"Yes. It's private. Nice. A duplex."

"Is it very far from your office?"

"No, I can reach it very easily." He was watching his fellow passengers. He was starting to feel uneasy. "Something's wrong. I'll be right back."

"But, it's only something about the market. It can hold."

"I'll be right back."

He speeded up his step because of the looks on the faces of the men hurrying by. It had to be something big. Something big. They all looked so frightened. He reached the lounge and found thirty or forty of them huddled together.

It was a hodgepodge of chatter; desperate sounds, some almost inarticulate, some resembling moans or curses or prayers; jerky movements; some arms widespread; some hands clasped together.

"What's wrong? What's happened?"

Some stared at him. Nobody answered. He hurried away, toward the radio room. When he reached the corridor, he found it packed with shouting passengers, all pushing in toward the little room. A crew member was trying to hold them back.

"What's happened?" he shouted. "What's going on?"

"God, man! Where have you been all morning? It's the market! The market! It's gone berserk!"

"What happened?"

The first mate was requesting that the corridor be cleared, but no one was moving.

"Tell the captain I want this corridor cleared," Tullio told him. "You know who I am, don't you?"

"Yes, Signor Barragatto, I'm doing my best."

"Get it cleared now. I want to get into the radio room."

"If I push you through before the others, I'll have a riot on my hands, sir."

"If you don't, you won't have a job."

"Yes, sir. Stay right behind me, Mr. Barragatto. I'll clear the way."

It took almost five minutes for Tullio to get into the little radio room. The wireless operator said, "Mister Barragatto, the office has been calling you all morning, but I haven't been able to get any messages out. They're going crazy out that door, so

489

I couldn't get anyone to pick up the messages."

"Put me through to them," he replied, and wrote down: EXPLAIN IN DETAIL WHAT IS HAPPENING WITH THE MARKET. I AM STANDING NEXT TO THE OPERATOR SO CAN RESPOND IMMEDIATELY. TULLIO.

Passengers were pounding on the door. He could hear the first mate pleading with them to be patient. Presently, the little machine began its ticking; the operator started recording the letters feverishly; the ticking wouldn't stop; the return message seemed endless. The young man handed it to him.

"That's the whole of it, sir," he said. "They've ended."

Tullio could hear his heart beating more quickly. The message seemed unbelievable. How could this have happened? How could everybody in New York suddenly want to sell so much? What did he have on margin? He couldn't remember. It was all so cloudy. But, Salvatore was insisting upon instructions. What could he salvage from his margin account? What was worth trying to salvage? He'd have to do it with cash. Where could he get so much cash on such short notice?

The Sicilian operation . . . LoGiudice had been hinting that he'd consider buying him out. But, could he cable LoGiudice? Make the deal from ship to shore? Over a cable? Ridiculous! That wouldn't give him the cash immediately. No, LoGiudice would want terms, anyway.

There was a lot of cash in the safe at *Piccolo Villaggio*. Was it enough? No, it couldn't be enough, not for all the margin he had to cover. What was in his margin account?

"Send this out," he told the wireless operator: WHAT DO I HAVE IN MARGIN AND WHAT IS BEING CALLED IN? NEED COMPLETE BREAKDOWN.

He paced the small room, awaiting the answer.

Salvatore stared at Tullio's message. Aleksey was on the telephone; he was shouting, and Salvatore wasn't even listening to what he was saying anymore. He, himself, could barely breathe.

Earl Asheley stared ahead, out of the window. "I'm wiped out," he said, "wiped out."

The line was being kept open to Tullio's broker. As the man gave the information, the secretary recorded it.

"Wiped out. Wiped out."

"It's not as bad as it looks, Earl."

"Here's what the broker gave me," the young secretary said.

"Cable it to Mister Barragatto," Salvatore said.

"The whole thing?"

"Yes, everything," he replied. Then, he joined Earl Asheley, who was still staring out the window. Neither of them could believe what had just happened. By eleven o'clock, the market had degenerated into a mad scramble of sales; and by eleven-thirty, panic had set in. And, no one seemed to know what had started the whole thing.

When Tullio's ship docked, two days later, Salvatore stared at him with the same blank expression that he'd given the little ticker-tape machine. He had no answers, no explanations. He said, only: "I still don't have any idea how much we've lost. Magdalena Tours was the first to go. And, the ski lodges. I had no choice. I had to sell a piece of them. We needed quick cash."

"Jesus, Salvatore! In just a couple of days! All that, in just a couple of days!"

Salvatore looked straight down at their feet, and Tullio felt guilty for having lost his patience with him. "There was nothing else we could do," the lawyer said. "Pace had the money, and we didn't, and that was . . ."

"Pace?"

"Yes. We needed cash, right away, to cover the margin . . . and it seemed the most logical thing. It was the best deal I could get under the circumstances, and . . ."

"How much did we give him?"

"He owns fifty percent of the lodges."

Tullio smirked. "So, now we go partners with scum. Very nice. Not only do we sell him our wine, but we split the lodges. Very nice. What other good news do you have for me? Who got

Magdalena Tours? Oh, never mind. What the hell's the difference?"

They drove quietly to Sutton Place. Salvatore had told Magdalena that the ship would be docking the following day, this per Tullio's instructions, so that they could get Nicole settled into her apartment with the least fuss possible. He planned to remain with her a few hours, then go home to *The Walls*.

All went as scheduled, and, when Tullio drove home, Magdalena was as surprised as he'd expected.

"How does this stock market crash affect us?" she asked him. "Have we lost very much money? Aleksey is beside himself. He won't even talk to me, so you'll have to tell me about it."

"Yes, we've lost a great deal, probably more than you even knew we had."

"How much?"

"You mean, the exact amount?" He shook his head. "Honestly, Magda, I don't even know yet. And, now, if you don't mind, I don't feel like talking about it."

He'd not speak anymore of this subject. She knew his mood, she recognized the look. It wasn't obstinate or stubborn in any way, just final.

These first few weeks after the crash were chaotic. Tullio and Salvatore were seldom home, and Aleksey and Earl spent inordinate amounts of time in the office also. When the men did get home, they did nothing but talk business. They had little to say to Magdalena or Rebecca or Louise; and, when they did respond to a question, it was usually a quick "yes" or "no."

"But, everything is so crazy, lately," Magdalena said. "Why, look at that Jimmy Walker! Re-elected! And, Aleksey says he's just a big crook."

"It's a symbol of the times," Louise said. "That's what Earl says about Walker's being re-elected."

"Well, whatever the times are . . . market crash or not . . .

492

Jimmy Walker or not . . . I can't see what it all has to do with us. I don't know what the big fuss is all about."

It was difficult for Magdalena Barragatto and Louise Asheley to understand the impact of the stock market crash upon the population, just as difficult as it was for any of the other women living along the Gold Coast, for their lives were little affected. So many of their husbands had hidden assets—hidden from the government, from their partners, and even from their families. Most assets were cold, hard cash. Tullio's was in a safe in *Piccolo Villaggio,* and not even Bella Modesto knew of the existence of the safe. If he'd been in New York at the time of the crash, he would have used the money to save Magdalena Tours, and he would have safeguarded the Sicilian operation, and Carmine Pace would not now own a part of the ski lodges. Yet, he could not mention any of this, for to say something would let the others know that he'd kept these funds secret from them. Even though he realized that they, too, had hidden assets, he thought it best for each of them—at least, on the surface—to be able to say: "We have no secrets from one another. That's how much we trust each other. We each know exactly what the other is worth, and we can rely upon one another completely." They didn't really mistrust one another. It is only that each had been given the same advice by their parents, or had learned it somewhere along the way: No one should know everything about anyone. A little secrecy is the greatest safeguard, perhaps the only safeguard.

Almost immediately, America, the land of abundance, had changed her face. She'd stopped laughing. She'd forgotten how to smile, or tap her foot, or sing. Long-established firms went bankrupt, and their employees, who'd never before been without work, didn't know where their next meals were coming from.

The working man was the hardest hit because he'd painstakingly, within the last couple of decades, pulled himself up out of poverty, only now to be thrown back into its muck with a force that appeared unbeatable. He found himself poorer than his immigrant ancestors. Those early immigrants had been aided by philanthropic organizations—mostly of their own ethnic backgrounds—that had helped them settle into their new lives; but, there were no helping hands for these suddenly destitute. These workers had invested every penny they had in everything from elastic girdles to wax whistles, and few had bothered to save any money. Nobody had imagined such times could ever visit them. Secretaries had invested heavily in the market. So had barbers, chauffeurs, truck drivers, and salesgirls.

The only people not shaken by the depression that set in were the black of Harlem, the poor whites of the South, and the elite.

In Harlem, where one was born into, lived with, and died in poverty, the word "Depression" meant only a few less tips when society visited its nightclubs. The suffering and squalor were no greater than the blacks had always encountered.

On the Gold Coast, one of the biggest problems was difficulty in acquiring the proper size avocado for a luncheon plate. And, since everything is relative, it could easily be said that the elite felt the Depression: it was, at least, an inconvenience.

"The whole world is starving," Tullio complained, "and our daughter is complaining because we haven't bought her a new fur this season."

"But, she should have a new one," Magdalena argued. "Do you want her to wear the same coat she wore last year? She'd be too embarrassed to go to school."

Rebecca received her fur.

Carter—who, by now, refused to call himself anything else, even in front of Tullio—had his allowance increased, in keeping with his classmates.

Carlo's teacher once brought him and his class to Manhattan. There, they took a walking tour; and they saw the soup kitchens and the bread lines; and afterwards, they dined in the park; and, the next day, they handed in reports describing their outing. Carlo received a good mark.

"Sometimes, I think my family is in a world that is looking at another world," Tullio said to Aleksey, "but I don't know what to do about it, and I don't know if they really see that other world."

"Just be grateful," Aleksey told him. "Maybe, you should even be grateful if they don't really see that other world."

"But suppose—just suppose—that, someday, theirs should come crumbling down? If they're not aware that any other kind of life exists, how will they come through?"

"Like we all do. Like I did during the revolution, like the other . . ." Aleksey cut off in the middle of his sentence. He did this often lately, and Tullio was beginning to get used to it.

"Erich finally admitted, the other day, that he lost just about everything," Tullio said. "I'd had no idea he'd played the market."

"Pssh," Aleksey responded, "you all played. All but me. I always told you not to. Always."

"I guess you were right," Tullio said.

"The revolution, it was just a little revolution."

"The revolution?" He stared up at Aleksey. "Oh, yes," he said. "The revolution. Well, try to forget about it for a while, Aleksey."

Salvatore said to Tullio: "He doesn't hear a word you're saying. If you ask me, he should retire. He's been wandering too much lately. It might cause some big problems."

"I know, but I don't know how to get him to stay home."

"That's when my Anna died, you know. That's when it happened. She was pregnant, you know."

"Yes, we know."

"I wonder what she would have had . . ."

"Well, we'll never know, Aleksey, and you shouldn't keep thinking about it."

"I would be the happiest man in the world if I could know what she would have had. But, she died, you know."

"Yes, we know."

"It's a good thing I didn't play the market. That's why North American Distributors is safe," Aleksey continued, "because I—if you'll remember, I was the one—who insisted we keep it a closed corporation."

"Yes, I remember," Salvatore told him. "We all remember."

The parties at the Gold Coast mansions continued. Invariably, one guest would blurt out, "But, d-a-r-l-i-n-g, there's a Depression going on . . . or had you forgotten?" And, equally without variance, someone would reply: "A what? A Depression, did you say? Nasty. Nasty. Nasty."

Nicole became disgusted with the streets of Manhattan. Everything was so depressing, she would say; so Tullio bought her a house in the country. She kept the city apartment, though, for those evenings when she and Tullio would visit Harlem.

Chapter Four

In March, Tullio heard about what happened to Benedetto Croce—his home had almost been wrecked by Fascist thugs. This had occurred immediately after Tullio had written his scathing editorial.

"I don't understand why I never heard about it until now," Tullio said. "Why, I wrote that article . . . let's see . . . it was about five months ago! Certainly, somebody in Orvietto would have told me about it! At least, somebody at the club!"

"Maybe, none of them wanted to say anything to you about it, Tullio," Salvatore said. "You know, Croce has a lot of sympathizers."

"So? So, he has sympathizers. Why would that stop people from telling me about the attack on his house?"

"Those sympathizers might have been afraid to mention it to you."

"Why should they be afraid of me?" He waited for an answer. When it didn't come, he became incensed. "Are you suggesting that they might think I'd write something about them, too?"

Salvatore shrugged.

"Are you hinting that my editorial caused the problem at

Croce's house?"

Salvatore shrugged again. "What's the difference? It's all over. It can't be undone."

"The pen is a very powerful weapon," Aleksey offered.

They'd both thought he was sleeping. They were surprised when he spoke.

He continued, "Yes, a very powerful weapon. A gun is powerful, too. But a gun, once it's shot off, it's shot off; and, a lot of times, the bullet misses its mark."

Tullio didn't try to hide his impatience with the man.

Aleksey added, "A good speech, is effective too . . . but, people forget about it. Not the pen! The pen is something else. The words stay there. And people mull over them."

"It wasn't my doing that they attacked his house!"

Salvatore held his hands up. "Calm down," he said. "What are you getting so excited about?"

"It was Croce's own goddamned fault."

"Perhaps," Aleksey said, "perhaps."

"Well," Tullio said, "I don't like the insinuation."

"Okay," Aleksey replied, "okay. By the way, do you remember a certain Senator Richard Jaysen you wrote about once?"

"Jaysen?" Tullio squinted. "Oh, yes, I remember. Why?"

Aleksey handed Tullio a competitor's newspaper. "Well, the good senator is out to get you, my dear young friend. You were pretty rough on him once. Now, he's out to get you."

Tullio read the article. It did everything but name him outright. It said that a certain newspaper publisher was pushing Fascism on the American public; that that publisher was also tied in with the illegal wine-running business; that that publisher owned a brothel in New York State, one fronting as a gentleman's spa; that that publisher had the audacity to pass himself and his family off to the rest of society as one of its own. It ended: *Isn't it time for we Americans to send him and his kind back where they came from?*

Tullio sat back and stared at the tabloid. After almost a

minute passed, he asked Salvatore, "Did you know about this?"

"Yes. It's not the first attack Jaysen's made on you."

Tullio glared at his cousin, then at Aleksey. "Why didn't you ever tell me about it?"

"What good would it do?"

"I'm going to get him for this. I'll sue the bastard for libel!" His head was throbbing with pain.

"Don't be ridiculous. That would stir up a hornet's nest. That's just what he wants," Salvatore replied. "He's looking for notoriety right now. He's trying to set up some kind of commission, and you'd be giving him the meat to get it rolling."

"So?"

"Once that happens," Salvatore continued, "it would just be the beginning. There would be no end to it."

"Listen to your cousin, Tullio. Ignore Jaysen. Just this once: listen."

Tullio crumbled the newspaper and threw it on the floor. After taking some aspirin, he left the office.

"Where are you off to?" Salvatore asked him.

"Union Square."

"For the Communist demonstration?"

"Yes."

"But, we have reporters assigned to that. And two photographers."

"I know," Tullio said, "but I want to cover it for the Party."

This day saw the biggest Communist demonstration in the history of New York. And, by provoking the police, all too eager to crack skulls, the Reds incited the riot they'd sought. The police beat them mercilessly, and the photographers didn't have enough film to capture the chaos.

Tullio, outstanding in his pale blue melton, watched with concern. He nodded approvingly to one of the policemen, who smiled at him within seconds of landing his billyclub into one of the demonstrators' heads.

499

"I'm with the press," Tullio said. "Will you stand for a picture, officer?"

The man complied. The demonstrator was lying at his feet. "What newspaper are you with?" he asked Tullio.

Tullio gave him two cards.

"Oh, I know that magazine," the policeman said, "but, this other one . . . what is it? Some kind of foreign thing?"

"It's published in Italy," Tullio answered. "We want to show Italians how you American police handle these Reds. Who knows? They might learn a thing or two."

"They just might, at that," the office said.

When Tullio left Union Square, he was elated. He had enough material to fill four pages in the Party paper. And the photographs—if they could only be in color!—might warrant a special section. Once, Mussolini himself had applauded him for his work; he was sure to get the leader's attention again.

He'd work on it immediately, he decided, then dispatch it to Milan with instructions that they make certain a copy was sent to Orvietto.

"Mrs. Barragatto is here, sir. She's sitting in your office."

"My wife? Here?"

"Yes, sir. She arrived about twenty minutes ago."

When he entered his private office, Magdalena was standing at the window. "Magda, what are you doing here? I didn't expect you. Are you shopping?" He looked at his watch. "I'm running late, I have to send some work out to Milan. I just came from Union Square. A couple of thousand Reds just got their heads bashed in."

"No, I'm not shopping."

He kissed her hurriedly. "How are the kids?"

"Tullio, I haven't come here to shop. As a matter of fact, I won't be staying long. Didn't you see Guido downstairs?"

"No, I didn't."

"Well, he must have taken a ride around the block, or something like that."

"What did you come into the city for, if not to shop?"

"To show you something. I would have shown it to you the day before yesterday, when it arrived, but you weren't home. And, I would have shown it to you last night, but you never got home last night, either."

"Okay, Magdalena. What's bothering you?"

She handed him some pages of writing.

"This is your handwriting," he said. "What is this all about? You writing me letters now?"

"Yes, I know it's my handwriting," she replied. "And, no, I'm not writing you letters. Somebody wrote me a letter. All I did was copy it. I've saved the original. But, I assure you, I didn't leave a single comma or period out, let alone any words. It's exactly as it was written."

He looked at her with a strange expression on his face.

"Well? Are you going to read it or aren't you? Aren't you curious?"

He shrugged. He was busy, too busy for this nonsense. He lit a cigarette and said, "All right, all right." He picked up the letter, said, "You want to read it for me?"

"Just read it, Tullio."

He smirked, then read:

Dear. Mrs. Barragatto,

There is something that you should know about your husband. It is that he keeps a mistress. She lives in Manhattan and he is a constant visitor to her apartment. She is a foreigner, blonde, and in her early thirties, and she has a small child.

I'm not writing this to be vicious, but when I see a respectable, God-fearing woman like you being made such a fool of, I have to speak up. After all, why should you be the only one not to know about her?

I would strongly advise you to tend to your mate.

You may not think that I am, but I really am,

A friend

"Is the child yours?" she asked.

"You don't believe this, do you?"

"I asked if the child is yours?"

He almost shouted: No! But, he caught himself, instead, and said, "I don't know anything about a blonde foreigner with a child. And, frankly, I'm very disappointed in you, Magda, for even wasting your time showing me such a letter. How can you even begin to believe such a thing? My God, be sensible. How could I find the time to keep a mistress?"

She replied: "Get rid of her, Tullio."

He slammed his palm on his desk. "This is ridiculous!"

"Just get rid of her," she said. "Don't come home until you do." She left the office.

Tullio sat there, mulling over the letter. It could have been one of the Capits Rock women, he thought. They all seemed bored enough to do such a thing. Maybe, one of their husbands who'd met Nicole had spoken about it. But, no—men stick together in these matters . . . it's an unwritten law. No, it wasn't from a woman who'd learned anything from her husband.

So, who?

He reread the letter. Maybe, he could recognize a familiar phrasing, a certain manner of speech, anything. It didn't help. There was no clue.

Why was she saving the original letter? What was she planning to do with it? *If I ask her to show it to me, she might. Maybe, I could find out who it was by the handwriting.*

No, I won't ask her to see it. It's better to drop the whole matter.

Boris Pachenker smiled at Magdalena. She was still a puzzle to him. He escorted her to the car and opened the door for her before Guido could do it. He liked this pretty stranger. She had a nice face, a kind face, but it was troubled today—obviously, Barragatto was taking advantage of her again.

"Thank you, Boris," she said.

He nodded. He didn't know how she knew his name.

"Let's go home now," she told Guido. "No, on second thought, take me to *Swansgarten*," she added, then rolled up the window between the driver and passenger portions of the car. She didn't feel like talking right now.

Tullio stayed in his office for a while longer, working on the article for the Milan papers. When it was finished, he realized that it wasn't as good as he'd hoped; he blamed this on his state of mind, not having been able to concentrate on it completely. His headache was worse than ever. Afterwards, he went directly to Nicole's apartment.

He gave her the letter. "What do you know about this?"

"Let's see."

When she finished reading it, she asked: "How could I possibly know anything about it?" She waited.

He didn't answer.

"You're not insinuating that I'm behind it, are you?"

"It's crossed my mind," he replied.

"In that case, Tullio, why don't you go back out and not come in all over again?"

"So help me God, Nicole . . . if you had anything to do with this, we're through."

"Listen to me, Tullio, and listen well. If and when I want your wife to know about me, I'll tell her to her face. You understand? To her face! Now, do us both a favor and get out of here. You disgust me! You and your suspicions! You think everybody's as devious as you! You judge everybody else by what you, yourself, are! A sneak! Get out!"

He left without another word. He didn't know when he'd begun to suspect Nicole. Perhaps, it had been in his mind when he'd been reading the letter; perhaps, not until he'd walked through the door. He didn't know. Or, perhaps, he'd just made a fool of himself by accusing her . . . he didn't know about that, either. He spent the night in the company apartment. He'd not been there for a long time, and had almost forgotten how sumptuous it was. He was glad to be alone, though. It felt good to be alone for a change.

Magdalena had spent the rest of the day at *Swansgarten*. Louise had been waiting for her at the pond.

"Well?" Louise had asked her. "I've been waiting to hear how everything turned out."

"Exactly as I knew it would," Magdalena said.

"And, you don't have any idea who could have sent you that letter? No idea at all?" the woman asked.

"Well, now, I'll tell you the whole truth," Magdalena replied.

"The whole truth? There's more to it than you've told me?"

"Yes, Louise. There's more to it."

"Then, you do know who sent it?"

"Nobody sent it. I wrote it myself."

Louise stared at her young companion. "Now, I've heard of everything."

"You see, Louise, I know there's another woman. And, I know he's keeping her."

"Do you know who she is?"

"Yes, I know that, too. I've known for a while, now."

"How?"

"I followed him once."

"Oh, Magdalena! How could you!"

"And, this is the only way to handle Tullio. If I were to come right out and tell him what I know, that is, once he knows that I know the truth, it would make it too hard for him. This way, I'm giving him the opportunity to get rid of her as easily as possible."

"How do you mean?"

"Well, Louise, my husband is the type who always has to save face. As long as he can deny the truth, as long as he's not positive that I know the truth, he can drop her without further problems. And, frankly, if I push just a little bit more, I'm pretty certain that he'll drop her immediately. Then, he'll come back to me completely . . . and . . . of course, he'll never admit to having had her around in the first place."

"I hope you know what you're doing, Magdalena."

504

"I do, Louise, I do. You see, I know him very well. Before I'm finished with him, he might even hate her."

"Hate her? How?"

"I'll have him suspecting her of everything. By the time I'm finished with her, he won't trust her to give him the right time of day."

"Be careful, Magdalena. That's all I have to say. It can backfire on you."

"No, it won't, Louise. Not if I don't deviate one iota from my plan."

"What are you going to say to him when he comes home tonight?"

"Oh, he won't be home tonight. He wouldn't give me the satisfaction to do that. Maybe, in another day or two, but not tonight. You see, if he were to come home now, it might look like I'd frightened him into it. He wouldn't want me to think I'd frightened him. No, he won't be home tonight. He'll play out his little game. He'll continue to try to make me think that the letter doesn't mean a thing to him, and that he's ignoring it, and that I should ignore it, too. Yes, that's what he'll do. He'll play his little game."

Tullio came home a few days later, as Magdalena had predicted; and, also as she'd said, he didn't mention a thing about the letter. She kissed him when he entered the house, enjoyed pleasant conversation with him and Aleksey and the children during dinner, and allowed him to make love to her that evening; and neither did she say anything about the letter. He came home every night thereafter for a week. On the seventh evening, she said to him:

"I received four telephone calls today. Each time, the party stayed on the phone, but didn't say anything. Do you think somebody's trying to tell me something, Tullio?"

"What do you mean?"

"What I mean is: Do you think somebody's trying to let me know that she's still around?"

He glared at her.

"I thought that, once you'd come home, you'd gotten rid of her, but, I see you haven't."

"There's nobody to get rid of."

"First the letter. Now, the telephone calls. Do you think that I was born yesterday?"

Carlo came into the room then, and Tullio didn't reply, but Magdalena continued: "She's going too far, now. I'm warning you . . . I won't put up with it."

He didn't reply. He left the room, went upstairs to his bedroom, and pretended to be sleeping when she came in, not too much later. She knew he was pretending; she enjoyed this. She felt quite good about it. She decided that she would wait another week or two before complaining about any other telephone calls. She mustn't overdo, as Louise had warned her, or it might backfire on her; and, above all, she mustn't deviate one iota from her plan.

Nicole was in her bathrobe when Tullio let himself in. He was glad that the nurse had already taken Sylvia to the park. He didn't want anyone else there.

"This is a beautiful surprise on a beautiful morning," Nicole told him. But, when she moved closer to kiss him, she read his face. "I know something's happened. It's written all over you."

Tullio eased her away from him. He found it difficult not to push her away. "We're finished, Nicole. It's all over."

He didn't expect that she would be so quiet or so still. Nor did he expect the sudden gush of tears from eyes that looked like they weren't even blinking. They had to be blinking, he told himself.

He waited for some kind of outburst. Some questions. Some protests. Anything. But, nothing came except more tears. He added: "And, when I say it's all over, I mean completely over. No letters. No phone calls. No contact whatsoever. Not with me. And, not with my family. Understood?"

She was still not visibly blinking, and, since it didn't appear that she was going to say anything, he left.

Nicole returned to the chair upon which she'd been sitting when Tullio had entered. From there, she stared at the door.

Why am I crying? Why did I cry like that in front of him? Why did I let him see me like that? God, what happened? WHY is it over? He loves me. I know he does. I know it. Oh, why in hell did I let him see me like that? Why'd I act like such an ass?

It was a busy day in the office. Fridays were always busy at North American Distributors, and Tullio's secretary was surprised that he'd come in so late. The manifests had already been placed on his desk and the mail had been opened. Some correspondence he'd dictated the night before was awaiting his signature.

He sat behind the mounds of paper. He felt uneasy. He didn't know if he was because he'd just broken with Nicole or because there had been no scene. He'd expected a scene, an ugly one, when he'd entered her apartment.

He signed all of his letters without reading them over. He tried to remember if he'd ever done this before. No, he hadn't; he'd always been especially careful to check for errors. Then, he began reading the manifests. He was quite sure he'd not have time for lunch today. He asked his secretary to hold all telephone calls, and he worked without respite until two in the afternoon, at which time he put down his pen and began resting his eyes. This is when Nicole walked into his office.

"I'm sorry, Mister Barragatto, but . . ."

He nodded toward his secretary and said, "It's all right."

When she left him and Nicole alone, he said, "I don't want any scenes here, Nicole."

"Neither do I. But, I do want some answers. You owe me that much."

"What kind of questions could you possibly have?" he asked. "I've warned you, more than once, that if you ever tried anything, we would be finished. And, you have. So, we are."

"I have *what?*"

"Damn it, Nicole, don't play innocent. You made those

calls, and you know it."

"Calls? What calls?"

She looked quite beautiful today, so he looked away. He replied, "First, you sent that letter to my wife—or, you put somebody up to doing it, which is more likely."

"I didn't!"

"Then, not satisfied with the letter—and, I was even starting to believe that you might not have had anything to do with it—you started calling my home and hanging up."

"Calling your home and hanging up? I didn't!"

"You did!"

"I did not!"

"Don't raise your voice."

"I didn't make any calls!"

"Nicole, let's just get it over with, once and for all. Our situation—it's all been a mistake from the very beginning. Now, you've proven that. So, get out of my life."

"Just like that?" She snapped her fingers. "Nicole, get out of my life? Just like that?"

"That's right," he answered.

She stood and faced him. "Tullio, I had nothing to do with that letter. And I haven't been making any calls to your house. I won't tell you that again. If you believe me, you believe me. If you don't, you don't. Right now, I don't really care. All I want to do is just what you said: get out of your life. And, please make sure you stay out of mine. You're not quite good enough for me, you know. Goodbye, Tullio."

Chapter Five

In a way, Tullio was relieved that Nicole had left his office so abruptly. He was thankful that there'd been no scene. It wouldn't do for his employees to know anything more about his personal life than was necessary.

But, there had been no scene. As though she didn't even care that he didn't want to see her again.

She's putting on a big front. I'll give her a week, maybe two. Then, I'll hear from her again. But, I'll stand pat. We're through.

Kostenov was surprised when, at four-thirty, Tullio suggested they go home. "Whatever's left can wait for Monday morning," Tullio said.

"Don't you feel well?"

"Yes, of course I do. But, I think that, for a change, we should go home early, while it's still daylight. What's wrong with that?"

Aleksey Kostenov shrugged. "Okay, so we leave early. Nothing wrong with that."

In the weeks that followed, the men were home almost every night. Magdalena never mentioned the calls to Tullio. The one time when he brought up the letter, she said, "I've thrown it away. There isn't any sense in keeping it, is there?"

"No, I guess not. But, I would like to have seen it."

"Why?"

"No special reason. Just curiosity. It's not important."

He began taking Magdalena out again, mostly to nightclubs, usually in Salvatore's company, and very often to the same places to which he'd brought Nicole. The music was the same, the faces the same, and the entertainment never changed. And the parties within *The Walls of Jericho* resumed; but as though to spite the Depression, they were louder and lasted longer, and were more lavish than ever before.

Aleksey said once, "I think that we entertain the way we do to ease our consciences. When we go to the city, we pass bread lines and soup kitchens. And, we see whole families sitting around on sidewalks with their scant possessions because they've been evicted for non-payment of rent. We turn away from pitiful creatures. We don't want to look at them because we find ourselves wondering why we've been so blessed. These parties of ours . . . they help us forget for a little while."

"I have nothing to ease my conscience about," Tullio replied. "I work very hard for every dollar I have. I earn my money. I feel sorry for those less fortunate than me, but no, I feel no guilt. My conscience is clear."

"Still," Kostenov said, "it seems to me that there should be some kind of equalizer."

"Aleksey, you're starting to sound like a communist."

"And you, like Marie Antoinette!"

Tullio didn't know why Aleksey had sounded so angry. Surely, he'd not meant to insult his old tutor. *Marie Antoinette? Me?* He grinned because he found it funny. "What's wrong with you, Aleksey? You're getting so grumpy lately."

Aleksey mumbled something that Tullio couldn't hear, then left.

Erich Veidt was spending this weekend with them; and Erich grinned also, but not until after Kostenov was out of the room. "I understand there's some more building going on a couple of miles from here," he said.

"Yes. So, I hear. And, I don't like it."

"Aren't your zoning laws supposed to prevent that kind of thing?"

"Yes, but, obviously, somebody's decided to make himself some money."

"Well, there's been a hell of a lot of money lost lately. They have to make it up from somewhere," Erich answered. "As a matter of fact, I wouldn't be surprised if it were some of the men from your own club. Some of them really got hit hard in the crash."

"Yes, I know. I've thought of that."

Lately, there had been a flurry of building along the southern and western sections of the Gold Coast, too much to be ignored any longer. It was a threat to a way of life, maybe even a portent. The elite tried not to discuss it, but they were very much aware of it. Estate servants' children. Blue collar workers. Civil servants. God knows who else. They were moving in. They were coming from out of nowhere. Wood-frame houses with shingle siding. Little grocery stores. A tavern here and there. A public school. There were traces of them almost everywhere. Yet, everyone was supposed to be so poor! Where were they getting the money to buy land? Land? Not real land. One acre. A half-acre or a quarter. A tiny piece of the island. Enough to satisfy that element. There'd certainly been some monkeying with the zoning laws.

"Nothing like this could happen at home," Tullio said.

"At home?"

"Yes, at home. Italy."

"Oh, Italy," Erich said. "Italy."

"Don't you consider that home?" Tullio asked him.

"No. Come to think of it, no, I don't any longer. I guess I haven't for a long time."

Tullio shook his head and looked at the man. "You sound like my wife."

Erich laughed. "Aleksey sounds like a Communist. You sound like Marie Antoinette. And, I sound like your wife. Perhaps, we should all re-evaluate ourselves . . . or have a costume party . . . one or the other."

Tullio had a headache again. He'd woken with it and had taken several aspirin already. He swallowed two more.

"Can't anything be done about that?" Erich asked him. "Try some new doctors."

Tullio waved his hand in disgust. "I've tried them all. They don't have any answers." He closed his eyes then, and laid his head back, and Erich knew to leave him alone for a while.

Nicole had been uncertain as to what to do when she'd left Tullio's office. She'd known only that she'd been accused wrongly, but that she could not prove it.

Still, she'd been insulted and angered enough by the accusation not to want to disprove it. He'd had no right to judge her guilty. He'd had the right to be angry, the right to ask if she'd made the calls—but not the right to prejudge her.

Hell, no! He didn't even have the right to suspect me!

She decided to leave Manhattan for a while—to leave it to its soup kitchens and bread lines—and to stay in the country house. She could think more clearly in the country. There were no newsboys yelling out their headlines, no peddlers and their loud, creaking wagons passing under her windows, no honking horns; and mostly, there was much less temptation to go walking into Tullio's office again, since it was so very inconvenient to take the train in from the Island.

I love you, Tullio. And, I would like, very much, to say to that woman: "Magdalena Barragatto, I love your husband and he loves me."

And, maybe, I would like, very much, to have made those telephone calls. Or, to have written that letter. But, I didn't. I'd be too scared to do those things.

The timing is wrong for me. It's not the time to force you into making a decision. Not yet. I know what the outcome would be. I'd lose you, maybe forever. No, it would be the wrong time. I could never hope to gain anything but your contempt.

But, who could possibly gain by doing such things? Who?

Oh, God! Who else? How could I have been so blind? Her!

She thought of confronting Tullio with this. She thought of

saying: It was your wife! Your wife! She framed me!

But, she reconsidered because she had no proof. He might not believe her, and, without proof of any kind, accusing Magdalena could only make matters worse: he might defend Magdalena, and she couldn't stand hearing him defend Magdalena.

There was something else: whether or not Magdalena knew that Nicole was the other woman; and this question, above all others, plagued Nicole in the weeks that followed. It was one thing for Magdalena to have framed a stranger, but quite another matter if she'd known the woman was Nicole. If the second case were true, Nicole could pursue any road she wished. She wouldn't have to worry about not hurting Magdalena too much. She could be as vicious as she pleased, with no misgivings—but, only if Magdalena had known whom she was framing.

Tullio was surprised when, after a few months passed, he'd not heard a word from Nicole. Surely, she should have made some attempt to see him by now. A telephone call. A note. Something. An excuse of some kind . . . maybe, a question about the lease on the apartment, or about the certificates in her vault, or even about the contract with the gardener at the country house. Any kind of excuse, no matter how feeble, would suffice. It would start them talking. At least, talking. But, no . . . she was a stubborn bitch . . . she'd cut off her nose to spite her face . . . no matter how much she wanted him, she didn't want to give in . . . but, she would, sooner or later, she would—and this last thought satisfied him to some degree.

He shared his thoughts about this with one person, Bella Modesto. She came to Manhattan once and they had lunch together.

"I still can't figure out why you're easier to talk to than anyone else," he told her. "Maybe, it's because we never have to pretend when we're together."

"That might be it, Tullio," she answered. "As far as what we were talking about before—the letter, I mean, and the

513

telephone calls—have you ever considered that Nicole might be completely innocent?"

"Who else would have done that?" he asked her.

"Somebody who would be happy to see you and Nicole break up. Another man, perhaps, who might want Nicole for himself. Do you know of anyone who's been trying to gain her affections?"

"No, she would have mentioned him to me."

"Are you positive of that?"

"Yes, Bella. I know this sounds conceited, but there's one thing I'm positive of. It's that Nicole loved me, and that she was loyal to me. She'd never even think of looking at another man."

"Oh, I see. Well, if that's the case, then, maybe, it's a woman who wants you to herself. Whom have you been playing around with, Tullio? Somebody you haven't told me about?"

"No."

"Nobody?"

"No, Bella. There haven't been any others. God, where would I find the time?"

Bella Modesto grinned. She'd known her share of wives in her prime, and she knew all the wives' tricks. Yet, liking all three—Tullio, Nicole and Magdalena—she thought it best to say no more about the subject, for to do so would surely alienate at least one of them.

"Well, Tullio," she said, "I'm sure that, in time, this will all blow over, and you'll again have the best of two worlds."

"That didn't sound very nice, Bella."

She shrugged and laughed. "Well, that's what you had, wasn't it, Tullio? The best of two worlds? Nicole and Magdalena?"

He didn't like the sound of her words. But, neither did he feel like having to defend himself and his past. He was glad it was only a lunch date, and that it was Salvatore who would be spending the rest of the afternoon going over the books with her. He was getting a little tired of women, anyway. Tired of their double-talking, unclear messages. Tired of their secretive smiles. Tired of always having to guess what they were really saying behind their words. He should stick to politics, and business, and publishing; these matters were so much less complicated than women, more easily understood, so much more honest. He was certain of this, and he could appreciate why Aleksey had never remarried.

He expected Pace this afternoon. Pace came to the office on the first Monday of each month. He wasn't looking forward to the meeting. Pace would give him an envelope filled with cash—Tullio's share of the profits from their arrangement. He wouldn't bother to count it. That wouldn't be necessary. Then, Pace would say: "See you in a few weeks," and leave. There was a rumbling, lately, to repeal the Prohibition law. He was sure that Pace was aware of it; but, this glint of hope didn't help, not so long as it was so indefinite, so Tullio quietly cursed the rest of the day that lay ahead.

This Monday was different, though, because Pace handed him a second envelope. "They're IOUs," Pace told him. "I bought them from a couple of not so gentle characters. It seems that your son, Stefano—they know him as Carter Barragatto—is quite the gambler."

"He's only a kid! He's only seventeen!"

Carmine Pace smiled and lifted his shoulders in a shrug. "Kids like him, rich, spoiled, they grow up fast, especially when they don't live at home. That must be some fancy school you're sending him to."

Tullio examined the notes. Two hundred dollars. One thousand dollars. Eight hundred dollars. Some were signed *Carter Barragatto*; some, *S. Barragatto*; one said *Carter Asheley*. He added up the amounts and matched the total with some of the cash from the first envelope Pace had given him.

Pace shook his head. "No. Keep it. Consider it a little token of our partnership." He turned then, and walked toward the door. But, before leaving the office, he said, "I'd watch out for my son, though, if I were you. From the looks of it, he's getting into pretty deep waters."

"What kind of crumbs gamble with kids?"

Pace replied: "Your son he doesn't look his age. He looks older, maybe twenty. Anyway, when they find out who his old man is, they know they're not going to get stuck. Right?"

That night, Tullio asked Magdalena, "Have you been sending any extra money to Stefano?"

"Yes," she answered, "now and then. Everything is so expensive nowadays."

"How much do you send him?"

"Oh, it depends upon what he needs it for. New clothes. A special weekend outing. It all depends."

He nodded. "Yes, I'm sure. It all depends . . ."

"Why?"

"I was just wondering. That's all. He'll be coming home for Rebecca's party next week, won't he?"

"Of course," she replied. "Rebecca would never forgive him if he didn't come home for her party. It's so important to her. Imagine, our Rebecca, sixteen years old . . . and, two princesses on her guest list . . ."

"And, how do you think she'll introduce her brother to them? As Stefano Barragatto or as Carter Asheley?"

"Oh, Tullio, he doesn't go around calling himself Carter Asheley . . . unless, of course, it's when Louise is having one of her spells, and then, only in front of her. He does it sometimes, then, just out of kindness, just to placate her, that's all."

"We both know that that isn't true, Magda. Oh, I realize that it may have been so when he was very young. He was always very attached to Louise. But, it's not true any longer."

"Yes, Tullio, he . . ."

"No. Stefano is ashamed of his name. It's not American enough. Not the kind of name those fancy friends of his in that fancy school have. A boy like Stefano has to be like everybody else. Even his name has to sound the same. That's the truth. You know it. I know it." He paused, then added, "Don't you remember how Stefano acted in Orvietto? Half the time, like the owner of the whole winery. And, half the time, like a grape

516

picker's son. He had to be like everybody else. That was the only time in his whole life that he enjoyed being called Stefano Barragatto. That's because it was where someone called Stefano Barragatto belonged."

"Maybe—I don't know—I'm not sure. Maybe, you're right. But, I'm sure he'll grow out of it." She was looking over the guest list again, and Tullio wondered if she cared at all about what he was saying.

"Well, perhaps Stefano might consider spending his college years in Italy."

"I doubt it."

"It's just a thought," he said.

The hesitation of Americans to abandon their virtuous prohibitions appeared in the shrewd reluctance of the Democratic presidential candidate, Franklin Delano Roosevelt, to take a firm stand for repeal during his campaign. Yet the Depression, unemployment, and the need for jobs in a legalized liquor industry were making temperance a costly luxury. This subject dominated the discussions of the adults present at Rebecca's party.

"How do you feel about repeal of Prohibition, Stefano?"

The boy was surprised that Tullio would ask his opinion. "It wouldn't make much difference to me," Stefano replied. "After all, don't we have all we want to drink, legal or not? Just look at everyone in our group. There's nobody without a drink in his hand." He shrugged. "No, it doesn't matter to me, not one way or the other."

Tullio grinned. "Sometimes, I think you're too old for your age. Especially when you say things like that." Then, turning to the others in their company, he asked, "Don't you agree with me, gentlemen?"

There was a polite murmur, and few noticed the antagonism in their host's voice. It didn't escape Stefano, however; he knew that his father was upset about something, something other than the answer he'd just given. He couldn't imagine what it might be. He'd received excellent grades, hadn't been

517

cutting any classes, and had written home regularly. "I didn't mean to sound like some kind of smart alec," he said. "Did I come across that way?"

Tullio shook his head. "Of course not. You're entitled to your honest opinion, just like anybody else. Anyway, if I didn't want you to answer honestly, I wouldn't have asked you."

The other men, returning to their discussion of Roosevelt, slowly began drifting away, but Tullio motioned for Stefano to remain. He pointed to the chair alongside his, and Stefano sat down, realizing that he would be learning, very shortly, what was bothering Tullio. It was evident, though, that Tullio had no intention of uttering a word until they were alone, and it seemed like ages to Stefano before the room was finally emptied of guests. When that happened, and before the youth could ask what was wrong, Tullio handed him a thousand dollar IOU. Stefano's astonishment could not be hidden.

"You think you're a bigshot, don't you?"

"How'd you get that?"

"I paid for it. That's how. Don't you want to know how many others I've bought, Mr. Bigshot? Who the hell do you think you are? You don't even have a decent beard yet, and you're going around gambling like this. Tell me how you were planning on paying these debts. What were you going to do? Ask your mother for more money? What reason were you going to give her for the money? A new wardrobe, maybe? Or would it be some other cockeyed reason that only a mother would believe?"

Stefano didn't answer. He had an arrogant look about him, though, and this angered Tullio.

"You listen to me, Stefano. When you start gambling, mixing with this sort of men, the men who held these IOUs, you're treading in some very dangerous waters. They're bad people, very bad people. They'll suck you in, let you get in way over your head. They'll let you win now and then, just to keep you coming back for more. After a while, they'll have you owing them so much money that you'll be willing to do anything to pay them off. Anything! Now, are you stupid enough to want to put yourself in such a position? Well, are you?"

He shook his head. "I didn't really mean to start gambling so much. It was just something to do. You know, there's not much to do where I go to school. On a weekend, there's just nothing to do . . . so, we go to the speaks, and, before you know it, we're in the back rooms, and . . ."

Tullio held up his hand. "I know, I know." He leaned forward and asked, "Do you know exactly how much you owe out and to whom? *Exactly*. That's important."

"Yes, I've kept a careful record."

"Okay. Tomorrow morning, you give me all the details and I'll have Erich go buy the notes back. By the way, about how much do you owe out?" He waited. "Approximately how much?"

Stefano hesitated for a moment, then said, "About eleven thousand."

Tullio glared at him. He didn't know if he were more angry than shocked, and he rasped a low, slow, "Son-of-a-bitch." He repeated, "Eleven thousand. Eleven thousand dollars. I have a good mind to . . ."

"Why are you getting so excited? This party's probably costing that much, if not more."

"God damn it! You're only seventeen years old, and you've already gambled away eleven thousand dollars! I never got that much in debt in my life! And, nobody in my family ever has, either! And no punk kid like you is going to come along and dirty up my name running up gambling notes! You hear me?"

"Nobody's dirtying up anybody's name," Stefano said.

"And, while we're on the subject of names, yours isn't Carter Asheley! Remember that! It's Barragatto! And, as long as it's Barragatto, I don't want to see it sprawled across any IOUs until you can make good for them! Nobody in this family welshes! I'm buying the notes this time, but only this time! From now on, you stay away from all gambling rooms! You hear me? I'm warning you! No gambling until you can pay off your own debts!"

"I didn't ask you to pay them for me, did I?"

He struck Stefano. He'd never done that before. He'd never even spanked any of the children; but now, he'd actually struck one the way he would strike out at another adult, and he wasn't sorry. "Don't you ever talk to me like that again," he said.

Aleksey opened the door and asked, "Why don't you two come and join the party? Some of the guests have been asking for you."

Ignoring Aleksey completely, Stefano said to Tullio, "You're so afraid of the Barragatto name getting blemished. Well, it's not me who's blackening it. It's you. Everybody knows all about you. You and your whorehouse and your wine smuggling and your racketeer friends and your Fascist newspapers. They even write about you in the papers. And, everybody at school knows about you, too."

"Enough!" Aleksey said. He held his finger up. "Enough," he repeated, looking from one to the other. "Whatever I've just come upon in here can wait until tomorrow. There are strangers in this house today."

Stefano turned away and left the room.

Aleksey said, "I've never seen him act disrespectfully before. What in the world brought that about?"

Tullio said, "He's ashamed of me . . . and he's under the impression that he has the right to be my judge."

"No, no, no. He's just a boy. Just a boy. He didn't mean it. He was just being vicious. He was trying to get back at you for something. That's all. What'd you do? Insult him? His eyes were filled with tears."

"No," Tullio answered, "I didn't insult him. I socked him."

"You socked him? You hit him? My God! Why?"

"Because he deserved it."

Aleksey shook his head. There was no talking with Tullio when he was in this mood. "Tomorrow. Leave it all for tomorrow. Come. Join the party. Rebecca's been asking where you are."

"I'll be out in a minute," Tullio said. And, when it did not appear that Aleksey was leaving, he reassured him, "Really, I'll be out in a minute."

Once alone, he rang for a servant. "Ask my son Stefano to come in here, please," he said.

When Stefano appeared, Tullio said, "Sit down." He waited. "I said, 'Sit down.'"

He began: "Yes, I'm a Fascist. It's obvious that you don't approve of my choice of politics, but that's your problem, and not mine. I'm proud to have been one of the original members of my party, and I'll always be one.

"As for your remark about my running a whorehouse . . . I merely helped an old friend set up the business she knew best. It's not some cheap brothel. It's a spa, and they come by reservation only. Actually, some of the fathers of your fancy friends are my most loyal clients.

"And, I don't have any racketeer friends. I don't know where you ever got that idea, and it's so absurd that I won't say anything else about it.

"Now, the last thing you mentioned. About the wine. My family has made wine for over a hundred years. Nevertheless, when it became illegal, we stopped all shipments into the States, and we stopped its production upstate, also. Unfortunately, circumstances evolved later on that forced us—yes, I said *forced* us—to enter into certain negotiations. What those circumstances were are none of your business. If Prohibition is repealed—and, nobody wants that more than I do—we can go back to making and selling our wine legally. In the meantime, that's the way it's got to be. And, it's not for somebody of your age and lack of experience to judge us."

Stefano fidgeted. He didn't know if Tullio was finished. He wondered if he should take the chance to stand up, then decided against it. It was safer to wait.

Tullio's fingers were steepled in front of his face, but he kept looking directly at Stefano, whose eyes tried to dart away toward different parts of the room; they kept returning to Tullio's, though, and Stefano finally asked, "Is that all? Can I go now?"

"No. There's something else. Something I've been thinking

about since we were in Orvietto. And now, I'm starting to believe that it's the right thing to do, as far as you're concerned."

"What's that?"

"You'll be starting college next September. Have you any plans as far as which one you want to go to?"

"No, I haven't given it much thought."

"Well, I have. Salvatore will be going to Orvietto for a while. Would you want to go there with him and, when September comes, enter the University of Milan?"

"Where would I live, in Uncle Sal's house?"

"If you wanted to, during vacation time that is. While in school, you would live at the university. During vacation, you can either live with your uncle, or at the Barragatto compound. In either case, you would be learning the business from both ends."

Stefano was silent for a while. Tullio could imagine what might be going through his mind.

"It would be a big move on your part," Tullio said. "And, if you should decide to, you might even want to remain there after college. Running the winery. Or the Milan office."

Stefano could picture himself. The newest Barragatto. All the servants, all the pickers, all the employees under him. He, at the head of the table. "I don't know."

"Think about it. If you don't want to go, fine. But, if you do . . . you'll have a lot of responsibilities . . . not much time left over for playing."

He could see himself in the Milan apartment, too. And in the office. Behind that intimidating oak desk. "Yes, I'll think about it."

The old cook . . . she would probably call him Don Stefano . . . but everybody else, they would address him as Sr. Barragatto . . . "It might not be a bad idea," he mumbled.

"No snap decisions," Tullio said. "Think about it. When you come home for Easter vacation, you tell me what you've decided." With that last word, Tullio left.

Chapter Six

Rebecca knew how many society writers had attended her party. She knew they had noted her dress, and her hairdo, and her titled guests. She knew they had scampered through the house and grounds like just so many ants, and that the servants—having had them pointed out to them—had given them preferential treatment. She was positive that her own name would appear in every major society column in the Sunday papers. She could barely wait for Guido to return from town, the bulging tabloids heavy under his arms. She was almost as excited as Magdalena when he finally did arrive, placing his burden on the table in front of them, and she didn't even try to stop from squealing when he said, "As of today, everybody in the world knows who Rebecca Barragatto is! At least, everybody who's anybody! Look for yourself, Princess. I already did. I cheated. I read the columns before I got home."

"Oh, Guido! Let me see! Let me see!"

The two women reminded him of children looking for toys under a Christmas tree. Then, he looked from them toward Tullio, who, seated at the same table, was almost totally detached. He wondered if anything at all excited Tullio anymore.

Tullio said, "I have to meet someone at the club today. I won't be gone long. A few hours, maybe."

"The club, sir?"

"That's all right, Guido. I'll drive, myself."

"Will you be home for dinner?" Magdalena asked.

"I just said that I'd be home in a few hours."

"Oh, yes, that's right." She didn't know why he'd snapped at her, or if he, indeed, had; but, determined not to let anything spoil her day, she said, "Well, drive carefully. I'll see you later."

When he passed Capits Rock, Tullio wondered if he should continue. Perhaps, he should just go into the club, as he'd said. Perhaps, he should forget the whole silly idea—for that's what he was considering it might be by now: a silly idea. But, no. He kept travelling east. And, within the half-hour, he started seeing familiar signposts. Soon, he turned onto a private, winding road and, at the top of the hill, he proceeded into a small driveway. Before he could get out of his car, Nicole had opened her front door to see who her visitor was. He felt awkward just standing there in the gravel, and the only thing that made the situation a lot less cumbersome was Sylvia, because she ran to him and threw her arms around him.

"How's my girl?" he asked the child.

She kissed him and yelled out something about what she and her friends and her new puppy were doing, then ran away.

"I just thought I'd drop by to see how you're doing, see what's new, you know."

"It's good to see you," Nicole answered. "It's been a long time. Come in."

Her smile made him feel unsure of himself. It was the kind of smile that was saying too many things. Only women could master it.

Her maid served them coffee, and they spoke of trivial matters. Both felt the strain of their very polite conversation. When it drifted to the weather, each knew it was time to say

524

what was on their minds or to say goodbye.

Nicole said, "Usually, I don't come out here until later in the season. Usually, I'd still be in the city. What made you think I'd be here? You've been to the apartment, haven't you? That's how you knew I'd be here." She smiled again. "Well? Isn't it?"

"Yes," he answered, "I was at the apartment about a month ago. Your doorman said that you'd closed it up a few months back."

"It was more than just a few months back," she said. "Didn't he say anything else?"

"Like what?"

"I'm selling it. All the furniture. Everything. I have no taste for the city anymore. And, Sylvia likes it so much out here that I've decided to live here the year round."

"It's hard to picture you as a country girl."

The awkwardness was reentering their conversation and, after a short lull, Tullio said, "Okay, Nicole, you've won. I've come to you. I'll admit that I'm surprised. I thought that I would have heard from you by now, but you held out, and I've come to you. Is that what you've been waiting to hear?"

She grinned. "I've missed you, Tullio, and I've thought about you constantly. And yes, that's what I was waiting to hear. Anyway, it was one of the things."

"So, what now?"

She echoed him: "So, what now?" Pensively, she added, "First, why don't you tell me what you have in mind." She smiled and said, "After all, you were the one who came to me. . . ."

He didn't answer immediately. After a short while, though, he said, "There isn't anything earthshaking that I have in mind, Nicole. Only that we pick up where we left off. It doesn't make any sense for us to not see each other. We had some good times. We can have them again."

"And, everything would be the same as before?"

"Yes. Maybe better," he answered. "Now, that we both

know how much we'd miss each other if we were to part again. I'm sure it would be better."

"That's not good enough, Tullio."

"What?"

She said, "I still love you, very much, maybe even more than the last time we were together. When we first broke up, I didn't know what to do. I was lost. I couldn't concentrate on anything. I couldn't even hold a decent conversation with anyone because my mind would keep wandering back to you. It was rough, Tullio. Really rough. And, believe me, that's putting it very mildly. I think I even began resenting Sylvia, because she was someone I had to keep on living for, and I didn't really want to. I used to cry myself to sleep at night. And, when I'd wake up, you'd be on my mind. So, I guess I must have been dreaming about you, also."

"Well, all that's over now," Tullio said.

She shook her head and continued. "For a time there, I began to feel like a very old woman. I found myself sighing, just the way old women do. And, I was starting to look old, too. And people were saying, 'What's the matter? Don't you feel well? Haven't you been sleeping well lately?' That was really crazy, because all I was doing was sleeping. Maybe, that was the only way I could escape the truth. I would sleep. I'd wake up in the morning, and then an hour later, go back to sleep. And I'd fall asleep for a few hours in the afternoon, or early evening. And then, I'd go to bed very early at night and sleep right through. And, of course, the thought of not seeing you anymore would greet me each time I awoke. I guess that's what it was . . . the thought of you . . . that's what was making me so tired . . . just the thought of you. You see, I used to think, and think, and think. In the morning, I'd think: *He just woke up. His wife woke up a few minutes ago. In a little while they'll be having breakfast together.* And then, a little while later, I would think: *Maybe, he just left for the office. Does he kiss her goodbye?* Afterwards, I would think that you might be calling your wife from the office for some reason or other, or that you might be taking her out to dinner in the evening. And the evenings . . . naturally, those were the worst times. I'm sure you know what I would be thinking about then . . . and that's when I needed to sleep the most . . . I tried so hard not to think about that . . . I tried so hard not to see you together.

"And then, it happened—whether it was my mind, or my body, I don't know . . . but one of the parts deep inside of me reached a saturation point . . . and the terrible hurting eased up. I actually became all right for a while. Whenever I thought of you—and that was still most of the time—I thought only of your bad points, and not of any of the good things about you . . . only of the times you'd left me alone, and not of the times you'd stayed with me . . . only of the arguments we'd had, and not of the laughs. And then, Tullio, I realized that you had lost a lot more than I had, because you had lost me."

She stopped. "Do you know what I'm saying, Tullio? Oh, I realize that you hear the words. But, do you really know what I'm saying?"

"Of course, I do," he answered. "But, that's all in the past. We'll start all over again, and it will be just like before, only better."

"But *like it was before* isn't good enough! I will not be your mistress again! I will not be your once-in-a-while woman again! I will not sit alone on the holidays again! I will not stay in the background again! That role I'd have to play for the pleasure of your company is not good enough! Not anymore! It never was, but I was too blind to see that! Oh, my God . . . did I just say *the pleasure of your company*? What pleasure? The pleasure of knowing that you'd be leaving my bed and going home to your wife again? The pleasure of never knowing when you'd be returning again? Pleasure?"

"Are you finished?"

"No, I'm not finished," she said. "I have one more thing to tell you. It's that if you and I are ever going to get together again it's going to be on my terms, and not on yours."

"I don't know why I bothered coming here today," he said.

"I have a good mind to get up and go."

"Good. Go."

That, he'd not expected. He sat quietly for about a half-minute, then left Nicole's house. He drove away without saying anything else. He didn't return directly to *The Walls*. Instead, he went to Capits Rock, sure that one of the women members would mention to Magdalena that he'd been there on Sunday. He was home by dinnertime.

"Grandma Louise—she tried to commit suicide!" Carlo said.

"What!"

"She took some pills! One of the maids found her! Grandpa Earl called us! He said that the doctor was there and that she's going to be all right!"

"What! Where's your mother?"

"She went to *Swansgarten*. Grandpa Aleksey and Rebecca went with her, too."

Tullio was about to telephone Magdalena when Carlo handed him a Sunday tabloid. "It all happened because of this," he said, "what they wrote in the papers here." He pointed to a society column headline that read, in large, bold print: OUR VISITING ARISTOCRACY—THE FAMOUS, THE IN-FAMOUS, AND THE FRAUDS.

A list of almost every European who had visited the Gold Coast during the twenties had been collected. Among the visitors' names was Bella Modesto's. The columnist had exposed Bella as a madame and was suggesting that her hostess, Mrs. Earl Asheley, had known all along that her guest hadn't been what she claimed. The writer was also suggesting that Mrs. Asheley had purposely fostered the fraud to further her own standing in society.

Tullio found humor in the article, especially the part where Bella was referred to as Lady X. He could understand why Louise would be embarrassed—he'd always considered the sham to be ridiculous, and had wondered if and when it would ever come to light—but he couldn't imagine why it should affect her seriously enough to attempt suicide.

"It's been quite a day, hasn't it?"

Tullio was startled. He'd not heard Stefano enter. "Yes," he replied, "it's been quite a day."

"I remember her," Stefano said. "They had me calling her 'Aunt Bella.' I liked her. Is it true that she's a whore?"

Tullio grinned and nodded.

"And, Mom knew, all the time, what she was?"

"Yes, but Grandma Louise never knew. She thought that Bella was an actress." He shook his head and grinned again. "I can't figure why she would try to kill herself over this."

"So, Rebecca was right after all. She said that Mom had probably known the truth." He shrugged. "Listen, can you drive me to the station? Nobody else is around with a car, and if I don't get there soon, I'll miss the train back to school."

Tullio agreed. He asked Carlo if he'd like to go along for the ride, but the youth refused because he had already returned to building a model airplane.

"He must have at least a hundred planes in his room," Stefano said.

"Yes, I know."

"He says he wants to be a pilot some day."

"He'll change his mind," Tullio replied.

Stefano said, "About going to school in Milan . . ."

"Give it some serious thought."

"I already have. I think I'd like that."

Tullio was glad to hear this, but he said, "Well, think about it some more. Wait until Easter vacation before you decide. That will still give us plenty of time to make arrangements for the fall semester." He paused. "And, whatever you do, remember, in the meantime, watch those gambling rooms."

"I will. I mean I won't gamble. No more."

"Stefano, there's nothing wrong with gambling, just as long as you don't lose anything more than you have in your pockets. I can't tell you not to gamble, because I do it myself. Just do it in moderation. That's the key word. Moderation. And, you'll never get hurt by it. Don't overdo. Okay?"

Stefano smiled at Tullio. "Okay."

Tullio watched Stefano board the train. He marveled at how handsome the boy was. He remembered that Magdalena had often mentioned the strong resemblance between Stefano and his real father. He didn't like to think that his wife's first husband had been so attractive. When he reached the *Swansgarten* driveway, he was still wondering what the Lombardian farmer had really looked like.

Earl Asheley greeted Tullio when he entered the house. He said that Louise was feeling better, and that Magdalena was upstairs in her room with her, and that Guido had already taken Aleksey and Rebecca back home. "I still find it hard to believe that she could ever attempt such a thing," Earl said. "You live with a woman so many years, and you think you know her. But you don't really." He held up his hands, his palms to the ceiling, and added, "And, all because of that newspaper article! I don't understand!"

Earl kept talking; and Tullio continued to nod or shake his head as each statement required. It was less than a half-hour later when Magdalena joined them, but it seemed a lot longer time to Tullio.

"Let's get out of here," Tullio whispered, "I can't take much more of this."

"You have no patience for anything, lately," she said. "Anyway, I can't go. I told Louise I'd stay here tonight."

"You mean sleep here?"

"Yes. Suppose she wakes up in the middle of the night and wants to talk to somebody?"

"Her husband is here. She can talk to him."

"No. He doesn't understand. She needs someone she can talk to. Someone who understands."

"Damnit, Magda! What's there to understand? That woman's a neurotic! When she's not drinking herself under the table, she's walking around calling you by her dead daughter-in-law's name, or Stefano by her son's name! Now, just because some farce she pulled off has finally been exposed, she goes and tries suicide! What's there to understand?"

"Tullio, you're like two different people. There are times

530

when you can be so tender, so understanding. But, there are other times, like now, for instance, when you're as cold as ice."

"I want my wife at home, in my bed, instead of having her sit up all night long with some spoiled woman, and that makes me as cold as ice?" He looked away from her. "Okay," he said, "have it your own way. Stay here."

A servant knocked and said, "Mrs. Barragatto, Mrs. Asheley is asking for you."

"I'm coming," Magdalena told her. "I'll be right there." Then, she said to Tullio, "Please, don't act like this."

"Then, come home with me."

"I can't, Tullio. She needs me."

"Magdalena . . . I need you, too."

She cocked her head slightly. Was this her husband talking? It sounded as though he were pleading. Her face wrinkled. She said, "Please, Tullio, I can't, please understand . . ."

"I understand all right," he said, then stormed out of the room.

Tullio left the door wide open and Magdalena could see his car speeding away from the grounds. She wasn't angry over what he'd just said. She was surprised, because it had been so out of character for him. She was sad also, because he'd seemed so unhappy.

It's been such a bad day. First Louise. Then Rebecca. Then him. It's such a rotten day.

She tried to remember the last time that Tullio had said he needed her. She couldn't.

I'll call him later.

She wondered what kind of need he'd meant, and she began to feel a little guilty. But, this wasn't the time to think of that because Louise was waiting for her. She wondered, also, if she might not be mixing her priorities; in the meantime, though, Louise was waiting.

When Tullio reached *The Walls of Jericho*, Aleksey said that he'd just spoken to Earl. "He told me that you just left ten minutes ago. You made good time."

531

"Yes."

"Did Magdalena tell you about Rebecca?"

"No," Tullio replied. "What happened with Rebecca?"

"Well, you should know . . ."

"What?"

"The only reason I'm telling you is because you should really do something about it. The way she spoke to Magdalena is unforgivable. She showed absolutely no respect."

"Aleksey, excuse me, but are you going to tell me what happened or aren't you? I can see that you're very upset about it."

"If she were just a little bit younger, I would have spanked her," Aleksey continued.

"Rebecca, come down here!" Tullio shouted. "Is she upstairs?"

Rebecca came in from the garden. Seeing her father's anger, she said, "Well, it was all her fault! It was! She knew, all the while, that that woman was a whore! She knew! She should never have let Grandma Louise go through with it! It was her fault! Grandma Louise might have died because of her!"

"You watch your mouth!" Tullio said.

"Well, it was her fault! I hate her!"

"Rebecca!"

"Well, it's true! She's always doing things she shouldn't! First, she lets a whore into our house! Then, she plays around with that gangster! Then, she gets arrested, and gets her face splashed all over the papers! She's always doing things to embarrass us! She's still a gypsy!"

Tullio slapped her. "Get upstairs," he said. "Don't come out of your room."

After a short silence, Aleksey said, "I'm sorry that it's come to this, but, ever since she found out that Magdalena isn't her mother, she's been wretched to her. She resents her terribly."

"I had no idea," Tullio said. "I had no idea."

"I'm not surprised. You don't take much notice of what goes on around here," Aleksey said. He shook his head. "As I said before, I'm sorry that it's come to this." He lit his pipe. "I certainly didn't expect you to strike the child. I wanted you just to talk to her."

Tullio said, "Yesterday, I hit my son. And now, this. I've never done any of these things before. I don't know, Aleksey . . . I just don't know what's happening."

Sorry that he'd mentioned anything at all, Aleksey said, "We all go through bad phases."

"Not this kind. Not when you've spent a lifetime training yourself to avoid such actions. Losing your temper—that's a sign of ignorance, of bad breeding. There's no excuse."

Aleksey, himself, had instilled this philosophy within his pupil, so he agreed. "That's true. There is no excuse. But, rather than lamenting, why not try to figure out the reason for the way you've been acting? Then, you can do something about it."

It was so quiet in the house. Aleksey was napping. Rebecca was in her room. Carlo was down at the stables. Tullio was deep in thought—the thought that two women who profess to love him would both refuse to be with him, and both on the same day.

He swallowed some aspirin. He'd learned that if he took aspirin at the moment when he felt one of his headaches beginning and then closed his eyes for a while, he could avoid blacking out. He felt better again soon, and left *The Walls*. He drove back to Nicole's house.

Sylvia had seen him through the window and opened the door before he could knock.

Nicole didn't say hello. She asked, "Have you eaten yet?"

"No," he said.

She asked the maid to bring a third plate to the table.

"Mommy was crying today," Sylvia said.

"Drink your milk," Nicole told her.

Tullio said, "I'm sorry."

Chapter Seven

Tullio filled Sylvia's dish and cut her meat. Later, he explained how important brushing her teeth after dinner was. Afterwards, he told her a fairy tale; and then, helped her into her pajamas; and lastly, kissed her goodnight and tucked her in. He managed to do all of this without really locking eyes with the child's mother; and Nicole sucked in the sides of her cheeks and was tempted to applaud.

"You've hardly said a word all evening," he told her.

"Well, I didn't want to upstage you."

"What is that supposed to mean?"

"What I mean is that I was too interested in your performance to interrupt."

"I'm glad you still find me enjoyable."

"I didn't say that I enjoyed what I saw. All I said is that it interested me—the performance, that is."

"You know very well that I've always been very fond of Sylvia," he said. "Why are you saying that it's suddenly all an act?"

"Tullio, please, let's not pretend. We're all alone now, so the show is over. Anyway, it should be. Do you want some coffee?"

"I wasn't pretending anything," he protested.

She lit a cigarette. He didn't approve of women smoking, and he suspected that she was doing this in front of him to spite him.

"Tullio," she said, "you haven't seen my daughter in about a year. You never so much as sent her a birthday card."

"Nicole, please, you know how bad I am with dates. I don't remember birthdays."

"All right," she replied, "I'll admit that men have a way of forgetting birthdays, but, what about Christmas? How fond could you be of Sylvia if you didn't even bother to buy her one lousy little toy for Christmas? And you, of all people! The closest thing to a father that she's ever known!"

He watched her light another cigarette. He noticed that her fingers had a nicotine stain. This surprised him. "How much do you smoke?" he asked.

Nicole didn't answer. She ignored the question. "She asked for you," she said. "She asked if you would be coming to her birthday party. But, I told her that you were far away on a ship, and that it wouldn't be possible for you to get back in time. Then she asked if you would be helping us decorate the Christmas tree. I made another excuse for you. I told her that you were up in the North Pole helping Santa make toys, and that, because of that, you would be too busy to come to our house. It satisfied her. I didn't think it would, but it did."

He watched her pour coffee only for herself.

"Oh, I don't know why I'm going on about this," she said. "After all, you aren't her father. You don't owe her a thing. Anyway, if Gerhard doesn't remember she's alive, why should you?"

Tullio poured some coffee for himself. He was trying to think of something to say about this.

Nicole shook her head. "You gave her so much attention tonight . . . so now, she's going to start asking for you all over again. Oh, Tullio, why did you come here?"

"You know better than to ask such a question. I came here because I love you, Nicole."

"I know that. That's what upsets me so much. It would be a lot easier if it were just a case of unrequited love. But, knowing that you do love me, and that you still choose to be with me, but, only as another woman's husband, this is what I can not accept. Not any longer. Can't you understand that, for my own peace of mind, I've got to have you completely or not at all?"

"You're being very unrealistic."

"No, I'm not. It's a matter of survival."

"Nicole, there's no reason for us to be apart."

"All right, Tullio, tell me something. Do you love me enough to leave your wife? If not, do you love me enough to leave me alone?"

"Nicole, I told you, right at the beginning, how it had to be. I've never led you on."

"What you said at the beginning doesn't hold water anymore. As time goes by, things change, and people have to keep up with those changes. I'm not saying that it's the people, themselves, who change. It's things . . . situations . . . problems . . . and the way we look at them, and at ourselves. We're—neither of us—getting any younger, you know."

"Is that what's on your mind, Nicole? Getting old? My God, we have so many years ahead of us! Why worry so much about what might happen twenty-five years from now? What's going to happen will happen! Why can't we just enjoy today?"

"Enjoy today?"

"Yes. You love me. I love you. Let's spend as much time together as we possibly can, and leave the future to the future. Let's just enjoy today."

"But, Tullio, I can't enjoy today. Today hurts me too much."

"Nicole, you're telling me that if I don't leave my wife, you don't want to see me at all?"

"Yes."

"God! Why do you have to have the whole pie? Why can't you be satisfied with just a piece of it?"

"Because just a piece of it isn't enough. That piece of pie

costs too much."

"Nicole, I won't start lying to you at this stage of the game by saying that I don't care for my wife; but, at the same time, I know that I'm not happy without you. And, I'm certain that you feel the same way. You can't look me straight in the eye and say that you haven't missed me, or that you've been happier without me. I'm sure of that."

"It's not a question of being happier, Tullio. It's a question of being less unhappy."

"Sometimes, you talk like a schoolgirl, like someone who doesn't know the score. My God, we can't, not any of us, have everything exactly the way we want it to be. Sometimes, we have to compromise."

"I don't want to know you anymore, Tullio, unless it's the way I say. Call it schoolgirl talk—call it anything you like—but that's the way it's got to be. I'm sorry. I love you very much, but that's the way it's got to be. I have to protect myself."

"How? By finding yourself another man?" He grimaced. "Come on, Nicole, I know you better than that."

"Somebody might come walking into my life tomorrow, Tullio. Nothing's impossible."

"That is."

"Why?"

"Because you wouldn't let anybody else in."

Nicole could feel tears in her throat. She knew, though, that Tullio could not detect them, and that gave her some satisfaction. He was right, she decided. She couldn't picture herself with another man. She couldn't even remember how it was with Gerhard. She asked him: "Are you as sure of your own wife as you are of me?"

"Yes, I am. In some ways, you two are very much alike. Why are you looking at me with murder in your eyes? I'm not being conceited. You're a one-man woman. So is she. There's nothing wrong with that. That's the way you are. And, you know it." He took her hand. "And, that's another reason why this whole conversation is so damned ridiculous. We both know that, sooner or later, we're going to wind up together again, so why go through all this nonsense?"

His hand was warm. It felt good. It was the first time he'd touched her. But, it felt too good, so she eased hers away. "It isn't nonsense."

"Nicole, we're wasting so much time."

She continued: "What we're talking about are things that have had to be said for a long time. That's not nonsense. They're important things. Anyway, they're important to me."

"Okay, Nicole. Get it all off your chest." He slumped in his chair and stretched his legs out in front of him. She must have been preparing this speech for a year—or ever since she'd walked out of his office—and there was no way he could avoid hearing it.

"I can read your mind, Tullio. Not all the time. But, right now, I can." She sighed. "So, let's just forget everything, and call it a day. I won't bore you anymore. You don't have to listen to another word." She glanced up at the kitchen clock. "It's getting late."

"Is that a hint?" he asked.

"Well, your wife is waiting for you, isn't she?"

"You couldn't resist that, could you?" he replied. "You know, Nicole, it took a lot for me to drive up here this morning. And, after all that you said, I came back this afternoon. That's twice in one day that I swallowed my pride."

"Tullio, your wife is waiting for you."

"Do you really want me to leave?"

She nodded.

"I hadn't planned to," he said.

"Weren't you afraid that, if you stayed here, your wife might get a few telephone calls during the night?"

"Why do you have to be so sarcastic?" he asked her. "Why do you say such things?"

"Because I know what I'm talking about."

"All right, all right, let's not go into that again. You really want me to leave?"

"Yes."

"If I leave now, I won't ever be coming back."

"I want you to come back, Tullio. But, I want you to come back with all of your clothes. And, that's the only way. It's that or nothing."

He glared at her. Tullio Barragatto being put out? "You're acting like a bigshot now," he said, "but, you'll be sorry for this."

As he walked out, he swore to her and to himself that he would never be back again.

It was a miserable evening for driving. There was an electrical storm. He hadn't been aware of the rain while he'd been in Nicole's house and guessed that it had begun just as she'd closed the door behind him. Already, the Island seemed a mass of mud.

He was glad that the garage door was open when he reached *The Walls;* it saved his having to get out of the car and get soaked, and he decided that this was the only thing that had gone right that day. He went into the house through the kitchen entrance from the garage. He could hear a female voice coming from Guido's room. He'd have to talk to Guido about this; the driver knew that visitors were forbidden. Then, he went directly upstairs to his dressing room. There was a light in his bedroom. He asked, "Who's there?"

"Me," Magdalena said.

"What are you doing home?" he asked her.

"I decided that I'd much rather be here, with you, than with Louise. I left there just a little while after you did. I was surprised that you weren't home yet."

"I went back to the club. Got into a game. Then, when it started to rain, I thought I could wait it out. Only, it fooled me. It got worse."

She was wearing a new nightgown the color of seafoam and her red hair was loose and fell to her shoulders. He could smell her perfume.

She said, "I called the club, Tullio."

539

He stepped into a shower. He didn't want to talk. Not just then. When he got out, he asked, "Why the sudden change of heart? What made you pick me over Louise?"

"It wasn't a question of picking you over Louise. It's not a contest, you know." She added: "Did you hear what I said? I said that I called the club."

"Nobody told me that you called. I didn't get any message," he replied. He put on his robe.

"Where are you going?"

"I have some work to do." He went into his small, private study beyond the bedroom.

Magdalena remained in the bedroom for a while, staring at the door that separated them. But, she hadn't left *Swansgarten* to be alone, so she, too, went into the study. Tullio didn't hear her enter. He was resting his head back and his eyes were closed. He looked to be sleeping, but she knew better. "They're getting worse, aren't they?" she said; and she began gently massaging his temples. "The headache will pass soon," she said. "Just relax a minute, and you'll feel better. And, forget about that work. You're not doing any paperwork tonight."

This time, the pain had been more intense, and had lasted longer, than usual. It had frightened Tullio because he'd felt so powerless against it. When it was gone, he was so relieved that he was drained of any other thought except to sleep. Magdalena led him back into their bedroom, helped him off with his robe and into bed, and tucked blankets over him. He wanted to thank her and to kiss her, but he did neither; he felt too uneasy to say or do anything to her because he might have been with Nicole at the moment. He wondered why he didn't feel guilty, because it was a strange uneasiness, and not any guilt that enveloped him; but, again, he was too spent to linger upon the thought.

Magdalena hardly slept at all. She realized that he'd lied about returning to Capits Rock, and having to wonder why aggravated her. Her investigations had shown her that Nicole Moeller had definitely moved. She'd spoken to the doorman.

540

She'd presumed that Nicole had returned to Europe, since the doorman had been given no forwarding address. Was there another woman? she wondered. If there was, it must be someone very new, since he'd been home every night—even tonight, when he thought that she, herself, wouldn't be.

She kept dozing and reawakening; each time, she knew that a dream had been interrupted. The dreams had no story to them. Nor did they connect with one another. She dreamed of hearing footsteps in the corridors; of somebody tip-toeing past her bedroom door; of speaking pig latin; of car engines starting; of people whispering so she couldn't hear what they were saying; and she dreamed of running barefoot through a meadow, trying to catch up with some gypsies' wagons; and, lastly, she dreamed that Aleksey Kostenov was calling her a *bella donna*.

In the morning, Magdalena was exhausted. Her eyes were red and burning. Tullio was long gone, but she was used to this, because he always left for the city very early on Mondays. She rolled over to his side of the bed and wished that it was Saturday again. She was tempted to have her breakfast sent up to her, but she never did this during the week. She always had breakfast with the children before sending them to school. She wished that Stefano were here. She missed him already, and she wished that Easter vacation would come quickly so she could see him again.

Carlo was already eating when Magdalena came down to the dining room.

"Will you please call my daughter?" she asked one of the maids.

The maid motioned to her. She could not imagine what the young woman wanted to say that she didn't want Carlo to hear, but she went to her and asked, "Yes? What's wrong?"

"I've just come from Miss Rebecca's room, Madam. She's not there. Her bed isn't mussed, either. She didn't sleep there last night. At least, that's what it looks like to me."

Magdalena asked, "How can that be?" and went upstairs,

herself. "What's going on here?" she asked herself aloud. "Where is that girl?"

She didn't know that the maid had followed her, and she was startled when the woman replied, "I don't know where she is, Madam. But, look here. A lot of her clothing is gone. It looks like she's packed and left."

"Packed? Left?"

The maid opened the closet door wider so that Magdalena could see. "It's almost empty," she said. "She must have taken quite a few suitcases."

Magdalena began pulling open drawer after drawer. She inspected Rebecca's dressing room, also. "There's so much missing," she said. "How could she have taken so much without anyone seeing or hearing anything?" She gaped at the maid. "Somebody had to be here . . . right outside the house . . . with a car. She couldn't carry all those clothes herself. Somebody helped her." She stopped short. "Oh, my God, I heard something last night! I wasn't dreaming! Oh, I have to call my husband!"

When she told Tullio what had happened, he could barely believe what he was hearing. He didn't want to believe it. Theirs was a good, respectable family, and Rebecca was a good, respectable girl. Such things didn't happen. "It can't be," he insisted.

"Should I call the police?" Magdalena asked him. "Should I question her teachers? Or her friends?"

"No! Are you insane? Do you want everybody to know?"

"But, everybody's going to know that she's gone when they don't see her in school!"

"We'll tell them that she's gone to visit her aunt."

"What aunt!"

"Magda! Why are you asking such a stupid question? Don't say anything to anyone! I'll be right home. In the meantime, get hold of Guido and find out if he knows if she has any boyfriends . . . or one boyfriend, in particular."

"I've already asked Carlo. He said no."

"She might have said something to Guido. She's always talking to him. I'll be right home."

Magdalena heard the click, then the dial tone. "Yes, that's true," she said. "They're always talking. I think they must have a lot of secrets, those two."

"Who?" Carlo asked.

"Oh, I almost forgot you were still here," she said. "You'd better get yourself off to school. And, whatever you do, don't say a thing to anybody about Rebecca."

"What if somebody asks for her?"

"Tell them that she went to see your aunt."

"What aunt?"

"Please, Carlo, just tell them that. They won't ask what aunt. If one of her teachers should ask you anything, tell them that you don't know anything at all, except that she went to see your aunt, and that I'll probably be sending them a note about it."

"I bet they'll all think that she's been kidnapped, and that we can't say anything about it yet. Everybody gets kidnapped nowadays."

"Oh, God forbid!"

He shrugged. "I was only kidding."

Magdalena hurried to the kitchen and up the steps of the small alcove that led to Guido's room. Tullio was right, she realized—Rebecca and Guido were always off talking to each other. If she'd confide in anyone at all, it would be Guido.

Guido wasn't in his room, so Magdalena looked in the garage. He wasn't there, either. She returned to the kitchen. Suddenly, she became afraid, and she whispered, "Oh, God, don't let it be. Please, don't let it be what I think." She unlocked the door to Guido's room and searched it. All of Guido's belongings were gone. She said, "Oh, God, I was right. Oh, my God, how could he be so stupid? They'll kill him."

She was afraid to tell Tullio. When he got home, Erich Veidt was with him. She stared at the both of them for a moment.

"Did you talk to Guido?" Tullio asked her. "What did he

say? Never mind. I want to talk to him, myself. Where is he?"

She answered, "He's gone. Guido is gone. All of his clothes are gone, too."

For a short while, Tullio stood there, as stiff and as quiet as a stone. Then, he said, "I thought it might be a young boy. Somebody close to her own age. Some kid like Stefano."

Tullio didn't say anything else about Guido and Rebecca. He went into both of their rooms for a while. He didn't say what he'd hoped to find in them. His thoughts were as private as his fury was visible. He didn't say anything at all.

A few days later, Salvatore Crispino died. He'd been in the hospital for more than a week. His lungs had collapsed. The death certificate said that it was pneumonia. When the funeral was over, Tullio said to Erich Veidt:

"I want you to find my daughter. I don't care how long it takes, or what it costs. It might be easier to track down Guido, himself. I have a hunch he would try to get connected with some racetracks. Check out all the big racing car outfits. All the tracks. Yes, I think that that's the first thing he'd try."

He gave Erich all the directions he could think of, no matter how far-fetched they seemed. He even suggested trying all the rifle clubs and skeet shooting clubs, because Guido might try to work for one of them as an instructor.

"Check out anyplace that has to do with car racing or guns," he said. "Find them."

That night, Tullio cried.

He cried for his cousin. He couldn't remember ever not having Salvatore right there when he'd needed him. His own cousin. His own blood. Somebody he'd played with. Grown up with. Someone who'd known him as well as he knew himself. Somebody closer than a wife or a lover.

He cried for his daughter. He'd never suspected a thing. She was still just a baby. Why hadn't she called yet? Just a telephone call to say that she was all right! That's all he wanted! No, not just a call. He wouldn't kid himself. He wanted to know why. Why a chauffeur? Why someone so much older than

544

herself? Why was she punishing him like this?

He cried because he was still doing business with Carmine Pace. Because he was accepting Pace's monthly envelopes. Because Italo Filippo Fallanca had won. Because he was ashamed.

He cried because he didn't like New York. Because he had to commute to work every morning. Because he couldn't relax in a sidewalk cafe. Because he had to rush through his lunches. Because the waiters weren't friendly.

He cried because Magdalena seemed so much stronger than him. Because she could adapt to all the little changes that he, himself, could not accept. Because nothing stopped her when she wanted to do something. Because it looked like she never had to compromise.

He cried because Nicole had refused to weaken. Because she had shown him how well she could live without him. Because she, more than anyone else, had pointed out how expendable he was.

He cried because Aleksey and Earl were getting too old to work a full day. Because more and more responsibilities were being left entirely to him. Because he didn't have enough hours in the day to tackle what had to be done.

He cried about almost everything that was bothering him. He cried as he hadn't cried since he was a child.

In the morning, he said to Aleksey: "I've been thinking of going home again."

Kostenov knew what Tullio meant when he said home.

"For how long?"

"For good, Aleksey. I just don't belong here. I never did."

"I wish that I could disagree with you, but I can't. I know you too well. No, you won't ever be satisfied to live anywhere but where you were born. There are some people like that."

"If only Magdalena could understand that."

"But," Aleksey said, "you can't go home yet." He threw his hands up in the air. "Who would take care of things around here? Earl and I? I don't kid myself. Especially now, with

Salvatore gone. No, Tullio, you can't leave yet. Not until your sons are old enough to run the business."

"I don't want to wait that long."

The man replied, "You don't have any choice."

"Stefano has to finish college. And, when he gets out, he still won't be ready to take over the office."

"Now, you're talking sense," Aleksey said.

"I'm sending him to school in Milan," Tullio said. "He wants to go. Who knows? He might even want to remain there—take over the Milan office."

"Does Magdalena know about this?"

"Not yet. We'll tell her when he gets home, at Easter."

"She's not going to like it."

"In a way, it might work out for the better, because, if Stefano is in Italy, Magdalena might want to live there, too."

"And, what about Carlo? He was born here. This is his country. He's no Italian, that boy."

"He's my son. He can live wherever he wants to when he grows up, but he's still my son, so he'll live in Orvietto, and he'll adapt to it."

"Just like you've adapted to this place?" Aleksey asked. He paused and said: "We are forgetting something, aren't we?"

"What?"

"Who will take care of the New York office?"

"Oh," Tullio said, "I forgot about that."

Aleksey patted him on the shoulder. "You're upset about Rebecca, about Salvatore, about a lot of things that aren't going right. Everything will work out."

Chapter Eight

"I want to go back to Orvietto, Magda. Not this year, and not next, either. That wouldn't be possible. But, some time in the future, we'll be going back. I want you to get used to the idea."

"I can't live there anymore, Tullio. I have a new life now, and it's here."

She protested every time he said that they would someday be returning to Italy; but this did not stop him from repeating his intentions. There were moments when she didn't even take him seriously, when she was positive that in time he would change his mind. Yet, there were other instances when she would become very aggravated about this; and, when this happened, she would say: "If you go, you go alone! I swear! You'll go alone!"

But, her threats did not dissuade him. He practically ignored them.

Months passed, and it seemed that the earth had swallowed up Rebecca and Guido. Every lead that Erich followed led him nowhere, and each time that he would return and report his bad news, Tullio would become more and more silently furious. Tullio wouldn't mention Rebecca's name at home, and no one else did while he was present. Sometimes, some of them wondered if he loved her or hated her.

The only one who did hear from Rebecca was Louise Asheley.

"You'll always be my Grandma Louise," the girl wrote, "and I want you to know that I'll always love you very much, but I can never come home because I know what my father would do to Guido."

Louise told Magdalena about the letter. "Rebecca said that they were in Indianapolis, and that they were leaving that day. She mentioned something about Mexico. Darn it! I should have brought the letter with me so you could read it yourself."

"Destroy it," Magdalena said, "and, whatever you do, never mention it to anyone, not even to Earl, because he might tell my husband. You haven't told Earl about it, have you?"

"No, I haven't. Magdalena, Tullio wouldn't really harm Guido, would he?"

"Yes," she answered. "He would."

"Then, I might never see Rebecca again."

"Oh, I'm sure she'll come back, but not for a long time."

"I miss her," Louise said.

"I miss them all," Magdalena said. "All of them—Rebecca, Guido, Stefano. I won't see my Stefano for at least a year. Tullio had no right to talk him into going to Milan. Not without asking me about it, first."

Tullio had known that sending Stefano away would bother Magdalena, but he'd not foreseen how deeply she would resent him for not consulting with her before discussing it with the boy. He still could not understand why she'd been so offended by this. Whether or not he'd spoken to her before or after his decision didn't make any difference, not so far as he could see. The decision, after all, had not been his own, but Stefano's.

But, everything bothered Magdalena lately! And, he didn't know what to do to please her! And he told her so over and over again!

"What's wrong with you two lately?" Aleksey asked Tullio. "When we sit down to dinner, you don't even speak. You stare

548

at the chair where Rebecca used to sit, and Magdalena stares at the chair where Stefano used to sit. In a couple of months, Carlo will be going off to school. What will you do then, with none of the children here?"

Tullio smirked and said, "That's a good question,"—he was annoyed that Kostenov had mentioned Rebecca—"and, since I don't have an answer for it, I'd appreciate your changing the subject."

Aleksey said, "You know, my Anna and I . . . we were always talking. Always enjoying each other. We didn't need any children, or the bond of any terrible problems, or to be making any special plans. We could talk all the time, even during the humdrum of everyday. That's the secret, you know. It's easy to be close during exciting times. Even easier when there's some kind of turmoil or tragedy, because people tend to cling to one another then. But, when a couple can be happy during the humdrum! That's the test! The humdrum days!"

Tullio expected that, at any moment, Aleksey would start talking about the revolution, about Anna's disappearance, and about the child she'd been carrying. He was in no mood to listen to that again. He had to prevent it. He saw the newspaper on the table. That offered a way out. "Look at that headline," he said. "You never know what's going to happen next."

Aleksey put on his reading glasses and said, "Let me see." Then, as Tullio expected, the man began reading the news, forgetting that they'd been having a conversation.

There were lots of headlines lately. Roosevelt was that kind of president. Tullio didn't like him very much. He didn't trust the man. "He's too much of a socialist," he said. "That's only one step away from being a communist."

The one thing that did please Tullio about the advent of the Roosevelt administration was the repeal of Prohibition, but he didn't credit Roosevelt for that.

He was sorry that Salvatore hadn't lived to see Carmine Pace's expression on the day he came to turn over his final envelope.

"I guess this is the end of our arrangement," Pace said.

"That's right," Tullio replied. "Now, I'll start growing grapes. That's one of the reasons I originally came to New York."

Pace's bushy eyebrows almost came together. "You mean you're going to turn *Piccolo Villaggio* into a vineyard again?"

"Yes. Exactly. I'll make the best white wine in the country."

"It'll take you years to develop a halfway decent wine, let alone a good one."

Tullio didn't comment. He knew what Pace was thinking.

Pace asked, "You're going to chuck it all? The main house? The cottages? Just to grow grapes?"

Tullio nodded. It was best to say nothing else at this moment, he decided. Let the thought sink into Pace's head. Let it develop and blossom. He was positive that it had already taken root. "If you'll excuse me now," he said, "I have a meeting in a few minutes."

When Carmine Pace left, Tullio smiled. There was no meeting scheduled. He'd wanted Pace to be alone with his thoughts; this way, Pace would believe it was his own idea to offer to buy the property.

Bella Modesto had just told Tullio she wanted to retire. Without her there, he would have to devote too much time to the spa to maintain it as he wanted; and, he could never trust an outsider to manage it, because he would always wonder about the true receipts. He'd considered sending Erich Veidt there—Erich had been willing—but Erich was too valuable in the New York office. He'd already discussed this with Erich. Several months earlier, he'd said: "I don't have any intention of keeping that place open, not knowing whether or not I'm being robbed from the inside. When Bella retires—she's been hinting that she's thinking of it, lately—I'll sell the place."

"But, you said that you think Prohibition will be repealed soon. Aren't you going to turn it into vineyards again, if that should happen?"

"No. If I were going to remain here, I would. But, I'm going home. Back to Orvietto."

"You're serious about going back?"

He nodded. "I'd like you to take over the New York office for me," he said. "You'd have the same authority that Salvatore had . . . and the same deal."

They shook hands, and the bond was made; and they each knew that North American Distributors—both its European and its American counterparts—would continue to flourish.

"Let's see," Erich said, "knowing you the way I do, you won't put the property up for sale. You'll wait for somebody to talk you into selling it, instead."

Tullio grinned. He was certain he'd selected the right person to leave in charge of the Stateside operation.

"Do you have any special buyer in mind?" Erich asked.

Tullio replied: "Who do you think would get hurt the most when Prohibition is repealed?"

Erich laughed. "Pace is going to have his hands full. He doesn't know the first thing about running a good house. Especially something like *Piccolo Villaggio!* It's a whole damned world of its own!"

Fiorello LaGuardia had just been sworn in as mayor of New York. Tullio's last bit of work for the day was to decide which of the inaugural photographs to use for the front page of his publication. When he finally locked his desk, he looked at his watch. Nine o'clock. It had been a very long day, and the thought of the long trip home bothered him. After debating for a while, he called Magdalena and told her he'd decided to spend the evening at the apartment.

"Make sure you get yourself something to eat," she said.

He promised her that he would, but he didn't. He was too tired to eat. He hailed a taxi, went directly to the apartment, and fell asleep on the sofa. He awoke at twelve and he wished that Magdalena were with him. He'd been dreaming about her. Then, he remembered that he'd also dreamed of Nicole.

He'd received a Christmas card from Nicole. She hadn't

signed the card, but it had been a lover's card, and he'd recognized her handwriting on the envelope. She'd not been trying to hide her identity from him. She'd known that signing her name wasn't necessary, and it could only cause trouble if the card should be found by someone else. She'd mailed it to the apartment. Nicole had never stopped being careful.

Tullio remembered now where he'd saved the card. He took it out and reread it. Then, he telephoned her. When she answered the phone, he knew he'd woken her. Unable to think of a good excuse for such a late call, especially after so much time had elapsed since they'd last spoken, he hung up.

When he got to his office the next morning, the first thing he thought of was to call Nicole again. He dialed. There was no answer. He was about to redial when his secretary announced that Carmine Pace was calling on another extension.

Pace wanted to see him. Could he come up this morning?

He'd waited almost a year for this. He was glad his patience had paid off. "Certainly," he replied. "Is Mister Pace still on the phone? I'll talk to him, myself."

That afternoon, Carmine Pace offered to buy *Piccolo Villaggio*. Tullio refused politely.

"I haven't begun the necessary renovations yet, but that's only because I haven't had the time. But, I still have every intention of turning it into vineyards again."

Pace returned the next week, and again, the following month. Each time, Tullio repeated his intentions, and he listened as Pace's offer became more lucrative with every refusal.

In 1935, two years after Tullio had planted the seed in Carmine Pace's mind, the sale was consummated. Tullio was satisfied that he could not have gotten a higher price anywhere. Erich was amazed by the staggering amount, and his admiration for the way Tullio had negotiated was beyond words. Aleksey and Earl didn't comment on the sale. Neither had ever been very interested in the upstate property.

To Tullio, the sale meant much more than big profits. It had brought him one step closer to Orvietto.

Tullio had known that he could never go home unless his house was in order. Now, everything was falling into place. He'd washed his hands of the vineyards which would have commanded his full and constant attention. As far as the New York office was concerned: Veidt could run it very nicely. Stefano would complete his schooling in one more year; and, with his youth and vitality, Stefano could very easily make the necessary trips between Milan and New York, as Tullio, himself, had once had to do. All was going well, and Tullio was satisfied. The only loose string was Rebecca.

Tullio thought of Rebecca often. At times, he would go into her bedroom and just sit there for a while. He'd told the maid to leave everything as the girl had left it. Even the page on her desk calendar had remained the same: March, 1932. It saddened Magdalena every time she knew that her husband was in that room. She couldn't console him over the loss of his daughter, except to say:

"Rebecca must be very happy, or she would have come back by now. Don't you think so, Tullio? I'm sure of it."

He shook his head. "I can't understand how they're living," he said. "Erich traced them to Mexico. Guido was part of the racing car circuit. When Erich got there, they'd just left, as though they'd known he was coming. And, it's happened each time. Whenever Erich gets a lead, he goes there, only to find that they'd just left. It's uncanny. They seem to know every move Erich makes. They always move on just before he reaches them."

"Where do you think they are now?" Magdalena asked.

"We have no idea. We've come to a complete dead end."

She said, "Tullio, I think it's time you stopped chasing them all over the place. Why don't you give them a while to settle down? Once they see that nobody is following them, they might not be so afraid of you. They might even come back on their own."

"The minute I see that bastard, I'll kill him."

"You'd have no right. Rebecca is nineteen now, and she's of legal age."

"But, she wasn't nineteen when he took her away! She was sixteen! Sixteen!"

"All right, that's true. He was wrong. But, she's not sixteen any longer. And, I'm sure he doesn't have her handcuffed to him. If she didn't want to be with him, she'd be here. Nobody forces Rebecca to do what she doesn't want to do, or to be where she doesn't want to be. We both know that. She has a mind of her own."

"He must have had her up in his apartment, night after night, right over our own kitchen." He shook his head again. "I never suspected a thing . . ."

Tullio thought about Nicole, too—not so often as he thought of Rebecca, but enough.

There were the Christmas cards, and the birthday cards. Nicole had always sent him cards. Never signed. Never with any kind of note on them. Three years worth of cards. All to the Manhattan apartment. All saved in the same place.

He'd never telephoned her again after that last midnight call, and she never called him. He wondered if she had met someone else. Three years. Anything could have happened in three years. He was sure that she still loved him. She wouldn't still be sending him the cards if she didn't. But, that didn't mean she couldn't have remarried. Anything was possible.

One Saturday morning, he got tired of wondering. Magdalena was attending one of Louise's charity bazaars. Aleksey was at the club. There was no one at home who could pick up an extension and hear what he was saying. He dialed Nicole's number. It had been disconnected. The operator had no new listing. He glanced at his watch. Magdalena and Aleksey wouldn't be home again for hours. He might as well take a ride. He had nothing to lose.

When Tullio reached the driveway of the little house, he saw a man standing in front of the kitchen door. He was instantly annoyed. The man looked very much at home. He was sure that he had moved in with her. Moved right in! Right into the house that he, Tullio Barragatto, had paid for!

"Can I help you?" the usurper asked.

"No, I'm here to see Mrs. Moeller."

"Moeller? She doesn't live here anymore. I bought this place from her about six months ago."

"She moved?"

"Yes. She moved to Belgium. I think that's where she said she was going."

He drove away without saying anything else to the stranger. He could hardly believe that Nicole had gone back home. She'd probably returned to Antwerp, to her family; and she'd left without a word.

In 1935, Communism in New York was on the upswing. Red rallies were commonplace, and Tullio's publications were filled with photographs of riots; but, he devoted equal, if not more, coverage, to the latest Fascist doings. Mussolini's domestic reforms had mostly been failures, and, during the early 1930s, the little dictator had started looking beyond Italy's borders. He'd been planning, for years, to invade Ethiopia, and although English and French diplomats had secretly offered to give him part of the country, he'd insisted on conquering it militarily. Proclaiming Italy the victim "of unprovoked aggression by Ethiopia," Mussolini attacked Ethiopia in October. The League of Nations imposed token sanctions, and most Americans didn't pay much attention. However, to Tullio Barragatto, Benito Mussolini could do no wrong, so Tullio praised *Il Duce's* actions and wrote editorial after editorial, condemning all who spoke against him.

There was word that Mussolini's reforms were troubling a lot of Italians, especially businessmen. Sr. Pavetto, in one of his letters to Tullio, had mentioned this. Tullio wasn't sure what his office manager was referring to, but he was sure that Pavetto was exaggerating. He'd make up his own mind, once he'd get home again.

Tullio could imagine what his life might have been like if he'd never left Italy. He was certain that he might have become one of the leaders of the Party, not only in this area, but nationwide. He mentioned this to Aleksey.

Kostenov agreed with Tullio, but grudgingly. "I don't know what you see in Mussolini," the man said. "Oh, I'll admit that he started out as a well-meaning soul, but, he's not the same person you listened to when you were a student. He's changed his whole outlook, his whole way of doing things. Frankly, I think he's getting a little . . ." Aleksey touched his forefinger to his temple.

"Italy would have turned communist a long time ago if it weren't for him," Tullio replied. "And Palermo . . . the Fascists are the only ones that Palermo is afraid of."

Again, Kostenov grudgingly agreed. Still, he didn't like this man, Mussolini, and he wanted Tullio to know that in no uncertain terms! "What about this friendship he's been cultivating with that Hitler? That one in Germany! What about that?" the old man shouted.

Tullio passed over this. "It's just politics," he answered.

"Don't be so sure," Aleksey replied. "There are some bad things going on in Germany. Your own friend—Gerhard— even he says so. And your precious Benito is playing politics with that German! It's not just politics. It's dangerous."

The decline of the Gold Coast was happening all around her, but Magdalena didn't know. She did know that things weren't the same as they used to be; that estate building had come to a halt; and that more and more middle income housing was going up. The Island just didn't seem the same anymore, but she didn't know why. The great parties were fewer and far between. Even worse, some of the families, especially those who had never recovered from the crash of 1929, were abandoning their estates, finding them too expensive to run. She would drive past once manicured grounds that were now overrun with weeds, and she would sadly reminisce, thinking of the lovely times she'd spent within them less than a decade before. Even the local newspapers had discontinued their society columns, because there was so little worth writing about any more. The elite—if there were truly any left—had retreated to their run-down country clubs where, in their private world, they could pretend to recapture what would never return.

"There's nothing in the news except politics, lately," she said. "No fashion. No gossip. Just politics. And Europe." She sighed. "Politics and Europe. It's so boring." She closed the tabloid.

Tullio replied: "We have a socialist in the White House and a clown in City Hall. That makes for interesting politics. Other than that, the only other things of interest are happening in Europe."

"Everything is changing," she said.

"Yes, I know," he answered. "We're getting out of here just in time."

"Getting out of here? Where are we supposed to be going?" She was opening a letter from Stefano as she was talking. "Oh," she said, "isn't that wonderful? Stefano's first in his class! Imagine that! In a university that size! To be first in his class!"

Tullio was very pleased. Stefano would be excellent in the Milan office. He'd always known the boy was intelligent, but first in such a large graduating class! He should have no trouble at all fitting into the business.

"You didn't answer me," Magdalena said. "Where are we getting out of? And, where are we supposed to be going?"

Tullio took a deep breath. "Magda, have I been talking to myself all these years? Don't you ever hear what I say?"

Her expression was a blank, and Tullio knew that she wasn't pretending. She really had no idea to what he was referring.

"Magdalena, put down the letter. Please."

She did so.

"This coming spring, we're going back to Orvietto," he said.

"Not just for a visit. For good. We don't belong here. We never have."

"No!"

"I've already started making the arrangements. For the business. For Carlo's schooling."

"No!"

"Don't act as though we've never discussed this, because we have. A hundred times."

"No! I won't! I won't go back. I won't be another Christina."

"What are you talking about?"

"I won't be like your mother! I won't live like that!"

"I want you to know that my mother was a very happy woman."

"I won't live there, Tullio," she said. "I won't talk about this anymore."

Chapter Nine

He'd been unconscious for several seconds, but what disturbed Tullio more than the blackout was the fact that he'd not been aware of it; and, what frightened him more than anything else was that Erich Veidt was insisting that this was not the first time it had happened.

"You were getting a headache. You swallowed some aspirin. The next thing I knew, I was talking to you, and you didn't hear a word I was saying. You weren't just resting your head back, either. You were out."

"Are you sure?" This was so hard for him to believe. "Are you positive?"

"The first time it happened, we'd had a few drinks . . . so, I thought that, maybe, it was the drinks. But there's no such excuse now."

"But I'd have to know it. I'd have to feel something if I'd passed out," he persisted. "It can't be possible."

"Tullio, you were unconscious. Believe me. You were. And, if it's happened in front of me two times already, it might be happening a lot." He stopped. He didn't like the look in Tullio's eyes. He wasn't used to seeing Tullio Barragatto so lost. He said: "But, who knows? It might have just happened only these two times. So what harm can it do if you put yourself into a hospital—get it checked out. It might be nothing."

Erich was motioning and grimacing like a bad actor, and Tullio was touched by all the concern that the man was trying to hide. He was glad that Gerhard walked into the room, because it gave them a reason to change the subject.

Gerhard Moeller had arrived in New York the previous day. He'd given no notice that he would be coming, and now, he was saying that it was possible that he could never return home again. He'd brought his new wife and child with him. "If I were alone, I might have tried to stick it out, but I had to get them out of there," he said. "Germany's not the best place for Jews any longer."

Tullio had heard rumblings of this nature, but, because they'd been in communications from Sr. Pavetto in the Milan office, he'd discounted them as exaggerations. "Even for someone like you?" he asked. "Someone with your money?"

"Especially for someone with my money," Gerhard replied.

Tullio knew that Gerhard never exaggerated. If anything, he understated. He realized that Gerhard's emigration must have been long deliberated and—also in the Moeller fashion—planned so that every last detail had been attended to. "Did you get all of your funds transferred out of the country?" he asked.

Gerhard nodded. "As much as I could without arousing suspicion."

"Do you mean that nobody knew you were leaving?" Erich asked.

"That's right. Even the family servants didn't know we were leaving Germany. They packed only our summer clothing for us, because we told them we were going to Rothenburg for a couple of months." He grinned and added: "I wonder if they still think we're on vacation."

Erich Veidt was astounded, but no more so than Tullio, who asked: "You actually had to sneak out of the country?"

"Yes." Then, almost as an afterthought, Gerhard said,

"Maybe, it wasn't absolutely necessary. To sneak out, I mean. But, I could not take the chance of being detained. So, I got us into Switzerland. From there, it was no problem at all."

Tullio was trying to imagine all of the intrigue and manipulations that must have preceded Gerhard's flight: the transferring of funds, the changing of banks, the signing and co-signing of countless pieces of paper, the secrecy, the bribes, the lies! But, he could not fathom, and nor could Erich, what could possibly have gone so wrong in Germany. They both knew that if a powerful and influential family like the Moellers felt uneasy, the problem had to be extraordinary. But they knew, also, that they would not learn the whole story until Gerhard was ready to tell it; and it was obvious that he didn't want to talk of it right now. They'd give him a week or so to settle in. That should do it. Then, they'd know what was wrong in Germany.

A couple of days later, Tullio met with a doctor friend of his. The man's practice was in Milan; he was here on a combination business trip and holiday. Tullio told him about the headaches and what Erich had said, after which the man sent him to an American colleague who could perform some tests. They put him into a hospital for two days. Nobody knew except Erich; everyone else was told that Tullio had to go upstate to finalize some of the details concerning the property sale. When he was released from the hospital, he revisited his physician friend to discuss the test results.

"You look like somebody with bad news," Tullio said.

"Tullio, at this point, all we can give you is an educated guess." He opened his hands and gestured with his palms facing upwards. "You see, the only way we can be sure about these things is to cut open a patient's head and look into it. In the meantime, all we do is guess."

"It's that bad, is it?" He wanted to run away.

The man let out a short, stifled sigh. He hated it when his patients were his personal friends. He always tried to avoid it.

"I asked you a question."

"Well, as I've just said, we can't be sure . . ."

Tullio interrupted. "And, if you were to operate and discover that what you suspect is true, could you do anything about it?"

"No. I'm sorry. No. Nothing."

There was silence for a few moments. They both needed it.

Tullio looked past the doctor, toward a painting on a far wall. He hadn't noticed it before.

"I can give you something to alleviate the pain, though. You won't be able to get in on your own, so use it sparingly. Here. I've prepared some for you. Never more than one packet at a time. Understand? Never more than one. And, not more than once a day."

Tullio looked away from the painting toward a generous supply of small, neatly folded envelopes. "What's in them?" he asked.

"Morphine sulphate," the doctor said. "You may not even need any of it for a long time. But, just in case. It can't do any harm to have it handy. In the meantime, just keep taking aspirin, as you've been doing. Then, if it should come to the point where the aspirin don't help anymore . . . then, you start taking this."

Tullio stared at the little white envelopes.

"You did say that, lately, the aspirin doesn't always work, didn't you?"

Tullio nodded.

"You told me that you're sailing back home this coming spring. I'm returning next week. So, don't worry. I'll be there, in Milan. And, when you run out of it, I'll keep you supplied."

"First, you said that you don't think I'll need any of this for a long time. Now, it sounds as though you suspect that I'll be needing it right away, and lots of it. Well, which is it?"

"I don't know. That's the truth. That's something I can't even guess about. Nobody can."

Tullio scrutinized the feathery white crystals inside one of

562

the envelopes. "This is what kept my father going during his last year or so. I had a feeling that you were the one he was getting it from, but, I wasn't sure."

"Your father was a very good friend of mine. I owed him a lot." He waited for Tullio to say something. When he didn't, he spoke again: "Don't think that you're going to be the way your father was. It will be different for you. That, I'm sure of. You'll be able to function, right up until the end."

He did not like the way Tullio was acting. He could not see any panic or fear in his eyes. Nor was there a tremor in his voice, or any visible stiffening of his muscles. This would not do. He preferred that his patients feel the full impact of such bad news while they were still with him. It was better than letting them go home and having the bad news sink in while they were alone, or worse, while they were with relatives who would choke up and cause them more grief.

"What are you thinking?" he asked Tullio.

"Nothing."

"That's impossible. Nobody could be that calm."

"All right. So, I am thinking of something. Actually, I'm thinking of a lot of things."

"Yes?"

"I'm thinking of my cousins. Benedetto . . . Ernesto . . . with them it was sudden. But, with Salvatore . . . it was different with him. He knew he was dying and, the only thing he wanted was to have a son to carry on his name. That's all he wanted, just a son . . ."

"And, what about you? Is there anything special that you want?" He leaned forward, waiting.

Tullio said, "You think I'll blow my brains out some day, the way my father did. It's written all over your face."

The physician grimaced. "No! Of course not!"

Tullio grinned. "Well, I won't." He kept fingering one of the envelopes. "Anyway, I've known about myself for quite some time, now. All you've done this morning is confirm it."

"Is that the truth?"

"Yes. Salvatore knew, too. He knew more than a year before his doctors told him." He paused, then added: "You know, we patients aren't so naive as you professionals—with your educated guesses—would like to think we are."

The doctor smiled slightly for the first time that morning. "Yes, I believe that you really did know." He breathed deeply. He said, "And, you came to me only for morphine. Isn't that right?"

Tullio hesitated. "I'm sorry, but I didn't know how to ask you outright. And, I had to be positive that you were the one supplying my father."

"Are the headaches so bad that you need it now, and couldn't wait until we got back home?"

"I think . . . maybe . . . I can use some now. Now and then."

His friend said that he would prepare more packets. He assured him: "You'll have more than you'll need to see you through the spring, and the same when you get home."

Tullio said, "I hope you don't die before I do."

The doctor smiled broadly this time. "It's remarkable how you can be so calm."

He replied, "I'm not so calm."

Erich was waiting downstairs. They were going to *Swansgarten* because it was Earl Asheley's birthday. Louise had planned a small dinner ". . . something intimate," she'd said, "because that's what my Earl likes the best. Something just for the family."

Erich's eyes were filled with questions, so Tullio said, "The tests didn't show a thing. I told you it would be a waste of time. It's good that we didn't tell anybody that I was going in. They would have worried for nothing."

Later that evening, when the small party was relaxing in the Asheleys' den, Tullio said: "I'm glad that we're all here together, because there's something I'd like to say. It's about Rebecca." He was a little surprised at how the sound of her name had hushed them. His eyes darted quickly from face to face. He continued: "I was forced to realize that there are some things about my daughter that I didn't know. For instance, I didn't know that she was growing up so fast. Well, that doesn't matter anymore. But, what does matter are the things that I do know about her. I do know that, until the day she left my house, she'd never changed a bed, or washed a dish, or swept a floor. She'd never had to, because she'd always had a maid. I know that she'd never brewed a pot of coffee, or toasted bread, or even boiled water. There had never been a need for any of that either, because she'd always had a cook. She'd never gone anywhere unescorted—let alone, had to locate a place on her own—because she'd always had a . . . a chauffeur. She'd never hemmed a dress, or even shopped for one, because a seamstress and a *couturier* had always come right here, to her. I could go on, and on, and on. But, I don't think there's any need to, is there? Because, the fact is, that Rebecca was prepared for nothing except the kind of life she'd led in *The Walls*. And, somebody like Guido . . . he can't give her that life. So . . . either she's very unhappy . . . miserably unhappy . . . and knows that she's made a very big mistake, or"—he looked up, toward his audience—"or she's getting help. Financial help. More than enough to keep her from running back home."

He allowed some moments for reflection. He discreetly searched their faces for any signs of embarrassment—he preferred that word over guilt; or for any hint of apology, or denial, or resentment. He even looked for indignation, since each knew that he was accusing them, either individually or jointly, of doing something behind his back, a betrayal he'd never forgive.

He said, "I don't want to know who in this room has been keeping Rebecca comfortable enough to stay away. I'm sure it's the same person who's warned her to run every time Erich's picked up their trail. All I want is for you . . . whoever you are . . . to get in touch with her. Tell her that I'm leaving America. You all know when I'm sailing. The thirtieth of March. Tell her that I want to see her just once before I go."

Nobody said anything. Nobody fidgeted. Nobody took a sip of his drink. Nobody looked at Tullio, or at another.

"Tell her," he continued, "that, if she comes to me on her own between now and when I sail . . . that I won't have her followed . . . that I won't try to find them . . . that she'll have nothing to be afraid of. And, tell her that, if she wants to come back and live here, she doesn't have to wait until we're dead, when she'll inherit the place . . . because she can move back in any day she wants . . . even tomorrow."

He knew that they were wondering if he would permit her to return with Guido. He knew, also, that none of them would dare to ask; he was grateful for this, because he didn't know what to say about it. If he were to reply: "Tell Guido that all's forgiven," they'd know he was lying. Yet, if he were to tell them otherwise, that might frighten her away even more.

"Just tell Rebecca that I want to see her again. Even if it's just one more time."

Then, as abruptly as Tullio had started talking, he stopped. He said to Magdalena and Aleksey that it was getting late, and that they should leave.

Magdalena cried when they got home. "You had no right to announce the date you were leaving. You announced it just like that!" She snapped her fingers. "Just as though it's all been settled already. I told you that I don't want to go back."

"Magda, I've had a very bad day. A day that, I'm sure, you wouldn't want to know about. And I don't want to argue about anything tonight."

"I don't want to argue, either, Tullio. But, I've told you the same thing so many times, and somehow, you just don't believe me. That's the part that's driving me crazy: the fact that you really don't believe that I won't go back with you. You really think that I'll argue and argue and argue, but that, in the end, I'll pack and sail." She shook her head. "But, I won't Tullio. Believe me. I don't know what to say to convince you."

He said, "Magda, you're my wife."

"I've never forgotten that."

"And, you would let me sail without you? You would let me

566

to back alone?" Until now, he couldn't believe that she would.

She answered, almost inaudibly, "Yes."

"Is that what a wife does?" he asked her.

He stared at her. And, for the very first time, he believed that she really might not go with him.

The next couple of months were chaotic, not only for Tullio, but for Erich, and Gerhard, and Stefano, as well. There were endless details to straighten out before Tullio could leave New York; and Earl and Aleksey weren't much help in this vein because, lately, they'd been doing less and less.

Gerhard had agreed to join the New York operation of North American Distributors. Until then, Tullio had not known what to do about the prefabricated motel parts. Gerhard would fit into that aspect of the business very nicely, so Tullio was devoting many hours to acquainting him with the day-to-day doings. Often, though, Gerhard would seize the advantage that their long, close workday resulted in by trying to dissuade Tullio from returning to Orvietto.

"It's not the time to be going back to Europe," Gerhard would say. "There's a big, black storm brewing over there. I'd hate to see you get caught in it."

Tullio replied once: "If you really think that there's going to be such trouble all over Europe, why don't you get your daughter out of there? Nicole brought her back to Belgium, you know. Why don't you tell them to leave? I'm sure that Nicole would take your advice."

"That's a very good idea," Gerhard answered. "Yes, I'll write Nicole tonight. By the way, how did you know she'd gone back?"

Tullio said, "She's always sent us a Christmas card. It had an Antwerp postmark on it." He wanted to change the subject quickly, so he said to Stefano, "Come. I want to show you the new manifests."

This had been Stefano's first Atlantic crossing on behalf of the company. He'd surprised Magdalena by arriving on New Year's Eve. It had been a tearful reunion; especially because he'd returned to her, not as the boy who'd left for the university, but as someone quite grown up. He seemed to have Tullio's ravenous appetite for business, and he certainly had the same commanding air when he addressed other men. By the cut of clothes, she knew that he was using Tullio's tailor. And by his body language, she realized that, as young as he was, he must be very good with women. What affected her adversely, though, was that he'd developed an unmistakably keen love for Orvietto: when he spoke about it, his voice mellowed, and his eyes softened, and the whole of his countenance became more pleasant.

"I've lost my son," she said to Aleksey. "I've lost him to sidewalk cafes, and cobblestones, and wine cellars, and old family retainers."

"But, Magdalena, you've always known that, when Stefano and Carlo grew up, they'd join the business. They'd have to travel back and forth between Italy and America, just the way Tullio used to."

"Yes, that's true, Aleksey. But, I didn't expect that, while Stefano is here, his heart would still be there." She paused for a moment, then arched one brow and sighed. "I can just picture it. The way he lives over there. In Orvietto, I mean. I'll bet he conducts his meetings in a white linen suit. And, he eats anisette toast for breakfast . . . it's always served to him on a little silver tray. And the townspeople . . . they nod their heads when he passes. And, everybody calls him Don Stefano. Yes, I've lost him, Aleksey. Just as I've lost my husband."

Kostenov said: "There will always be men who prefer the grape vine over the rose bush. You must either join that world which they choose, or you must accept living outside of it."

"It's not fair," she answered, "it's just not fair."

He took both of her hands in his and told her, "Magdalena, what you've said about losing your husband, well, I've practically raised you and Tullio, and, what's about to happen—he, moving to Orvietto! you, staying in New York!—it's wrong. Give in. Don't be as stubborn as he is."

"Why must it be me who swallows my pride? He's the one

who's leaving, Aleksey."

"I don't know if it's merely pride. Oh, I know that that has a lot to do with it. But there's something else. Something that I can't put my finger on. It's no secret that he's never liked New York, but lately . . . lately, it's as though he's afraid that if he doesn't go back home right away, he might never get back."

Magdalena looked puzzled. "You get that feeling, too?"

"Whatever! You're going to be unhappy if you let him go. And, he'll certainly feel the same way, having to leave without you. I know, because he's told me so."

Tullio saw Magdalena and Aleksey huddled together often, and he knew what they were talking about. Because of this, a slight glimmer of hope that she might change her mind, and return with him to Orvietto, eased some of the pressures that were building up during these, his last few weeks in *The Walls of Jericho*. Perhaps, she might even let him go, and then come sailing to him a month or so later! Anything was possible with Magdalena, especially if Kostenov were to keep talking to her.

But, what about Aleksey Kostenov? He'd tutored Tullio; and he'd guided him through those difficult teen years until he'd entered the university. Then, he'd become his father's manager and confidant. After that, he'd taken care of Magdalena and Stefano and Rebecca until Tullio had been released from Guidonia. And through all the years, his honesty and his loyalty and his devotion had remained above reproach. All of this, Tullio knew; and, while he still could cling to a tiny bit of hope that Magdalena would return with him, he realized that, once he'd sail, he would never see Aleksey Kostenov again.

Tullio did not know how to repay the man—not at first. Then, he began to think more and more about the emerald brooch that Magdalena had soldered to the silver cup on her dressing table; and, the more he thought about it, the more he became convinced that she really might be Kostenov's daughter, the child Aleksey's Anna had been carrying when she'd disappeared.

Everything points to it. The place. The time. The revolution.

Mikel wasn't her real father. And, her mother was high-born . . . not a gypsy, but a gentle woman who had wandered into their camp. Mikel told her that the brooch was her mother's. The czarina's cousin had had those brooches designed—one for Aleksey and one for Anna—and they were the only two of their kind . . . that's what Aleksey told me.

It's got to be.

He considered, though, that, if he were to convince Magdalena that she was Aleksey's daughter—*now! of all times!*—she'd surely not leave Jericho. She'd not want to leave Aleksey, if only because he was now so old.

Still, he could not tell her, *I'm dying, too, Magda, and I don't want to be alone.* He could not tell anybody this.

The week before his sailing, Tullio decided: he would give this present to Aleksey. Nothing could make Aleksey Kostenov happier than to know that he had Anna's child under his own roof. This was the least he could do for such a man. In the evening, he said:

"You told me that, when Magdalena docked in New York—the very first time you saw her—she reminded you of someone. A few times during the years, you've mentioned the same thing . . . that she reminds you of someone. Who is it that she makes you think of, Aleksey? Is it of Anna? Does Magdalena look like your wife, Anna?"

Aleksey Kostenov replied, very sadly, "Yes. It's really uncanny how much she resembles her. But, why do you ask such a question now? What made you think of that?"

"Aleksey," Tullio said, "this might sound a little crazy at first, but . . ." He stopped. "I'll be right back," he said. He went upstairs, to Magdalena's dressing room, and returned with the silver cup.

When Aleksey saw it, he gasped and stared at the emerald brooch.

Once Tullio knew he had Aleksey's full attention, he began to unravel his suspicions.

Aleksey Kostenov listened very quietly, his keen mind grabbing on to every word, his heartbeat quickening, and his eyes darting back and forth between the emerald brooch and Tullio. When the story was finished, he sent one of his servants to fetch the small velvet pouch that housed the emerald's mate. Then, he examined the brooches, side by side. He cried out: "My God! After all these years! Oh, dear God!"

There was no question in his mind. Now, he was as certain as was Tullio. Magdalena was Anna's. Magdalena was his. His very own. And that would make Stefano and Carlo his own grandsons. He told Tullio that all of his prayers had been answered; and he cried when he told Magdalena. He'd insisted upon telling her, himself.

Magdalena was speechless and was caught up in Aleksey's joy. But, Stefano, Carlo and Erich were stymied, and didn't say much of anything. Still, Tullio and Aleksey were positive; they didn't have a single doubt.

That night, Magdalena said, "That was a beautiful thing you did for Aleksey."

"Then, you don't believe that it's true?"

She smiled and replied, "I don't know, Tullio. It's so incredible. It might be true. It might be." She shook her head. "I don't know. The whole idea has me dizzy. But, I'll call Aleksey 'father.' He'd like that."

Tullio gave her a furtive glance and asked, "Have you given any more thought to coming with me?"

She said, "You should know that I think of nothing else, day after day. How could I stop thinking of that?"

He said, "Magda, I can't tie you up and carry you aboard that ship. But, I love you. You know that. And, I want you to come with me." He waited, then added: "I won't try to talk you into it anymore. It's all up to you."

"My children are here! My friends are here! My whole life is here now! I'm an American! How can you expect me to throw everything away? How can you ask me to return to that other life? That place! I hate it!"

"Don't start crying again," he said. "I'm sorry that I brought it up again."

* * *

On March 30, 1937, Tullio entered the owner's suite aboard the *Asheley Princess*. His family and his closest friends came to see him off. Magdalena had worn a smart navy blue suit and a wide-brimmed straw hat, but her eyes were red and puffy. Everyone knew that she had been crying.

As well-wishers crowded into the suite, Tullio spent most of his time with his sons.

"I hope you'll convince your mother to travel with you when you come to Italy this summer," he said.

Carlo looked as though he were about to speak, then thought better of it.

Stefano smiled and told his father, "I'm sure that, once Mama gets there, she won't be leaving you to come back to New York. How come you never lose a battle?"

"I've lost a few," Tullio answered, "a few big ones."

"Nobody would ever know it. Not from the looks of you."

Tullio patted Stefano on the shoulder. "Take care of your brother," he said, "and, remember what I told you. Within the next few months, start buying land. Buy all the land on the Island, if you can. Use the money from *Piccolo Villaggio*. That's what it's for. The Island is changing. Anyone can see that. Estates are going to die out, and the workers will be moving in. They'll need housing. Buy old, rundown estates. Buy lots at auctions. Buy any piece of property you can get your hands on, no matter how useless it might look to you."

"Papa, we've been over this at least a hundred times, and, I swear, I'll buy all the land that I can. And, I'll keep buying more every time I return to New York."

The whistle was blowing, the signal for visitors to disembark.

Erich came to him. "Tullio, what can I say?" They embraced, and he asked, "Will you check my father out: Will you see what you can do for him? I know that the Fascists must be giving him a hard time. Maybe, with a word from you, they might leave him alone. He's an old man."

Stefano said, "There's nobody named Veidt in Orvietto."

"That's a long story," Erich answered. "Some cold, rainy

day, I might tell you about it."

Tullio said to Erich, "I'll try to keep them away from him."

Louise and Earl Asheley said goodbye. They left after Erich. Gerhard Moeller followed.

Aleksey Kostenov blew his nose and said, "We've had some good years, you and I, but . . . just like everything else . . . things change."

"Goodbye, Aleksey," Tullio said. "Thank you for everything."

"I guess I'll see you in about six or seven months," Stefano said.

Tullio nodded. He embraced both his sons. "Be good," he said.

When the final whistle blew, and the last visitors were off the ship, and the gangplank was being pulled up, Tullio stood, with the thousands of other passengers, and looked down toward the pier. He leaned on the rail and studied the faces of the small circle of people who meant so much to him. He was searching the crowd for Magdalena when Louise Asheley began to wave frantically.

She was trying to tell him something, but he couldn't hear her. Then, she started pointing toward her left. He looked in that direction. It was Rebecca. He thought that his heart would stop.

When the young woman's eyes met her father's, she began to smile. There was a hesitation to the smile, but that was fleeting; it turned, very quickly, into the full-blown smile that Tullio had known. A few feet behind her, Guido held a child which appeared to be about a year old. Then, Rebecca shouted up: "I love you, Papa!"

So he was a grandfather now. He thought about that as the ship slowly slipped out of its berth and the faces in the crowd grew smaller. He was leaving behind an American grandchild. He stared at the skyline as the ship made its way down river. The buildings were a symbol of a country where he had never felt truly at home. He felt no regret at leaving it. The only sadness he felt was leaving Magdalena behind. After all they'd been through, he hadn't even been able to say a proper goodbye.

The *Asheley Princess* was passing the Statue of Liberty now. In a few minutes they would be on the open sea. He decided to go below deck. Perhaps there was some champagne left. That would help his seasickness. But could it do anything for the enormous sadness that had overwhelmed him?

The maid had not yet reached the suite and there were still empty glasses and a thick haze of cigarette smoke in the drawing room. But he found an unopened bottle of champagne in a bucket of half-melted ice and he took it with him as he walked toward the bedroom. He would drink until he passed out and if God had any mercy at all he would not dream.

He opened the bedroom door and that was when he saw her. She was sitting up on the bed. The hat and the suit were gone and the red hair was pulled back loosely with a green velvet ribbon. She laughed when she saw the champagne.

"What took you so long?" she asked.

"I wanted to get a good look at the harbor. I might not see it again."

"For one awful minute I was afraid that you'd changed your mind. Or that you'd gone after Guido and I'd be sailing to Italy alone."

"So you knew?"

She nodded. "Louise told me this morning. They call the baby Tullio."

"That's nice." He was still trying to convince himself that he hadn't blacked out, that this was not some dream. "Won't they be worried about you?"

"The boys and Aleksey know. They'll tell the others. So you see you're stuck with me."

He finally allowed himself to smile. He poured two glasses of champagne and handed her one. They raised them in a toast.

"You know, Magdalena," he confided as he sat beside her. "For the first time in my life, I'm looking forward to an ocean cruise."

574

TEMPESTUOUS, PASSIONATE
HISTORICAL ROMANCES!

PASSION'S RAPTURE   (912, $3.50)
by Penelope Neri
Ravishing Amanda Sommers becomes the captive of the very man who had ruined her life: scowling, handsome Miguel de Villarin. By day, she rages against her imprisonment—but by night, she succumbs to passion's thrall!

AMBER FIRE   (848, $3.50)
by Elaine Barbieri
Auburn-haired, amber-eyed Melanie Morganfield loves distinguished Asa Parker, the older man who can give her everything. But when she sees dark, young Stephen Hull, Melanie knows she will yield to Stephen's charms—and then beg him for more!

EUGENIA'S EMBRACE   (952, $3.25)
by Cassie Edwards
Eugenia Marie Scott looks like an experienced, sensual woman even though she is only sixteen. When she meets dark, adventurous Drew Jamieson, Eugenia knows she's not too young to love—and falls under Drew's spell for the rest of her life!

PASSION'S PARADISE   (765, $3.25)
by Sonya T. Pelton
When green-eyed Angel Sherwood sails from England to the New World, her heart is full of song and her thoughts are full of promise. But a pirate raids her ship—and changes her life, taking her to his hideaway in the Louisiana bayou, and teaching her his sweet, savage love!

Available wherever paperbacks are sold, or order direct from the Publisher. Send cover price plus 50¢ per copy for mailing and handling to Zebra Books, 475 Park Avenue South, New York, N.Y. 10016. DO NOT SEND CASH.